All He Wants for Christmas

KELLY HUNTER
NATALIE ANDERSON
TORI CARRINGTON

MILLS

Published in Great Britain 2015
by Mills & Boon, an imprint of Harlequin (UK) Limited,
Eton House, 18-24 Paradise Road, Richmond, Surrey, TW9 1SR

ALL HE WANTS FOR CHRISTMAS © 2015 Harlequin Books S. A.

Flirting With Intent, Blame it on the Bikini, Restless were first published in Great Britain by Harlequin (UK) Limited.

Flirting With Intent © 2011 Kelly Hunter
Blame it on the Bikini © 2012 Natalie Anderson
Restless © 2008 Lori and Tony Karayianni

ISBN: 978-0-263-25237-8

05-1115

Harlequin (UK) Limited's policy is to use papers that are natural, renewable and recyclable products and made from wood grown in sustainable forests. The logging and manufacturing processes conform to the legal environmental regulations of the country of origin.

Printed and bound in Spain
by CPI, Barcelona

Accidentally educated in the sciences, **Kelly Hunter** has always had a weakness for fairytales, fantasy worlds and losing herself in a good book. Husband. . .yes. Children. . . two boys. Cooking and cleaning. . .sigh. Sports. . . no, not really—in spite of the best efforts of her family. Gardening. . .yes. Roses, of course. Kelly was born in Australia and has travelled extensively. Although she enjoys living and working in different parts of the world, she still calls Australia home.

Kelly's novels SLEEPING PARTNER and REVEALED: A PRINCE AND A PREGNANCY were both finalists for the Romance Writers of America RITA® Award, in the Best Contemporary Series Romance category!

Visit Kelly online at www.kellyhunter.net.

CHAPTER ONE

CHRISTMAS was commerce and retail excess. Christmas was family and sometimes it was farce.

Add to the day a wide-open wallet and a city bathed in neon and the memory of a Hong Kong Christmas burned brightly for ever. Ruby Maguire—born to riches and living in Hong Kong for over six years now—knew this from experience. Which meant that she should have been able to organise a perfectly splendid Christmas for the children of one of Hong Kong's foremost investment bankers in her sleep.

A trip to Hong Kong Disney or Ocean Park. A holographic Christmas tree or three. More presents than they knew what to do with, a mad mix of Christmas lanterns and fake winter wonderlands and, if Santa was *really* on the ball, maybe their charming, handsome, super-important father would put in an appearance and make their day.

Except that the West children were all grown up these days, and, from the snippets of information Russell West's executive PA had let slip, Russell's eldest son was unlikely to be in attendance, his firstborn daughter was recovering from serious injury, his other daughter was a reclusive genius, and his fourth-born—

another son—was either a crime lord, a charming wastrel or James Bond.

So much for taking them to Disneyland.

Instead, Ruby had decked the halls of Russell West's pristine marble penthouse with as much high-class folly as she could find. White orchids; real ones. Poinsettias; silk ones. Tapered white candles just waiting to be lit and more fat goldfish for the glass-covered pond. The pond ran beneath the base of the stairs and along the atrium wall until it reached the tiny rooftop terrace where the songbirds reigned supreme. The only thing missing from the scene was a pet cricket in a bamboo cage. For Australian-born Russell West, owning a pet cricket was taking cultural assimilation one chirrup too far.

December twenty-second already, with the three younger West siblings due to arrive tomorrow. Upon arrival they would find immaculately prepared rooms, festive touches in the strangest places, and reservations for one of Hong Kong's premier restaurants, should they wish to dine out.

Ruby wasn't a housekeeper or a cook, though her current job strayed into such territory at times. She far preferred to think of herself as Russell West's social accountant—a position created just for her, out of pity most likely, but she'd tried to make herself useful, and the hefty bonus Russell had just presented her with gave credence to the notion that he thought her service of value.

She wrote Russell's charity dinner speeches, briefed him on the changes in status of Hong Kong's elite, and basically made his social engagements as stress-free and fruitful as possible.

Ruby's latest challenge had been the buying of Christmas gifts for the children of Russell's employees—an endeavour she had seen to with pleasure. Furthermore, Russell now had an up-to-date database citing the names, birthdates and interests of his employees' spouses and children. She'd even done one for the wives and children of his major business contacts. Whether Russell would *use* the information remained to be seen.

Trust a financial wizard to pay absolutely no attention whatsoever to the little things that went such a long way towards the cultivation of solid business relationships in Hong Kong.

As for the choosing of gifts for his *own* children; be they genius, wounded, idle, or missing…that was Ruby's job too and she had approximately twenty-four hours to do it in. Russell hadn't even given her a price range, let alone a guide as to what type of gifts they might enjoy.

'Not even a hint,' she muttered to herself as she dumped the box of sparkling mineral water on the kitchen counter and opened the French doors leading out to the terrace. 'It's not right.' She plucked a pair of thin plastic gloves from the terrace cupboard and headed for the songbird enclosure.

No tiny bamboo cages for these little oriental white-eyes but a large bamboo aviary that ran the length of the courtyard wall and incorporated branches and greenery, nesting and feeding areas, and a newspaper lined roll-out litter tray that Ruby refreshed every day. Western, very Western, and a source of no little amusement to many of Russell's acquaintances, but the birds sang their pleasure, and both Ruby and her employer took pride in the freedom of movement the little birds enjoyed.

'There should be a rule that says a father should damn well buy Christmas gifts for his children *himself*,' she told the flitty little birds who clung to the side of the cage in greeting. 'Why is that such a stretch?'

'Beats me,' said an amused male voice from the direction of the kitchen, and Ruby glanced around, eyes widening at the splendid vision that had just presented for her perusal. A raven-haired blue-eyed stranger stood just inside the terrace doors, wearing nothing but a snowy-white towel that rode low on his hips and clung lovingly to well-packed thighs. His chest was bare, his shoulders impressive. *Not* an everyday sight in penthouse sixty-one.

'Who are you?' she said as she straightened from her crouching position, the roll of bird-dropping stained newspaper still firmly in hand.

'My thoughts exactly,' he murmured with a grin that put Ruby in mind of mischief and at least one other thing she really shouldn't be thinking about if this was indeed one of Russell's sons.

'I'm Russell West's social organiser,' she said, ignoring that lazy smile as best she could. 'And you must be one of his sons. Trouble is, which one?' She let her gaze drift once more over his very fine form. 'One of you I wasn't expecting until tomorrow. The other one I wasn't expecting at all.'

'I could be the pool boy.'

'Yes, and I have absolutely no doubt that you'd make an excellent one, but alas there is no pool.' Ruby continued to study him. 'You'd think I'd be able to tell the difference between a mission-fatigued special intelligence officer and a feckless rogue by now, but you know what?' Ruby shook her head. 'You could be either.'

'I've never had an insult wrapped so skilfully inside a compliment before,' he murmured, that devilish gaze of his not leaving her face. 'You must practise.'

'And you must be Damon,' she guessed. 'Russell's youngest.'

Ruby dumped the soiled newspaper into the mulching bin, peeled off her gloves and brought forth her manners and her hand. 'I'm Ruby Maguire. I'm looking after Christmas for your father.'

'I see.' Damon West had a nice touch. Firm but not bone crunching. A man fully aware of his own strength. 'How's that working out for you?'

'So-so,' she said and took back her hand. 'Your sisters are due in on flights tomorrow afternoon. I'm afraid there's no word from your brother.'

Ruby watched a shadow steal across Damon West's well-cut face. She was an only child with a raft of stepsiblings she tended to avoid. Family politics was not her forte and she had no intention of getting involved in the West family's woes. 'I gather you've made yourself at home?' There were half a dozen bedrooms in the marble delight, each with en-suite. 'You've been here before, right? You don't need the grand tour?'

'Right.'

'Coffee?' Ruby headed for the wondrous stainless-steel-and-glass kitchen and set to washing her hands in the sink there. 'Tea? Cold drink? I'm hoping it's too early for gin but you never know in the tropics.'

'It's too early for gin,' Damon said and padded over to the other side of the counter. 'Coffee would be good. Espresso if it's an option.'

'It's an option.'

'So…Ruby. You live here?' he asked just a little too casually as she set up the coffee machine and took a cup from the cupboard.

'Hardly. No one lives here, unless you count your father sleeping here on occasion and entertaining here every so often. I feed the fish and the birds, water the plants, pick up your father's dry-cleaning, stock the fridge, organise housekeeping and gardening and pre-pare for house guests.'

'Has this always been your lot in life?'

'No. In another life I was a law graduate working my way through the corporate law system but that all fell through when my father the investment banker de-cided to go to the Caymans rather than to prison. It was a good call on his part. The prisons here aren't very nice.' Ruby opened the fridge and reached for the sugar bowl. 'Sweetener?'

'You're Harry Maguire's daughter?'

'Guilty.' She set the sugar down in front of him and leaned forward, elbows on the counter, wondering just what it was about this man that made her want to poke at him. 'I'd never have taken you for someone who reads the finance pages?'

'Sweetheart, your daddy skimming eight hundred and seventy-two million dollars in point-one-cent in-crements and then disappearing into the ether didn't

only make the finance pages. He's quite the crime star.'
Damon crooked his head in what Ruby decided was reluctant admiration. 'So, where is he now?'

'That's the eight-hundred-and-seventy-two-million-dollar question, Damon. And truthfully, I have no idea.'

'You weren't close?'

'We were very close.' Ruby dropped her gaze to the glossy countertop and gave him the truth. 'I grew up in a family of two. Me and my father and a never-ending raft of nannies, butlers, cooks and tutors. I worshipped the ground he walked on. Now I don't.'

'Because he broke the law? Or because he left you behind?' asked Damon West gently and Ruby looked at him, really looked at him, and she didn't see a charming wastrel any more. She saw a man who knew his way around the dark places of a person's psyche. One who seemed entirely comfortable dealing in shades of grey.

'The law's a slippery thing, Damon.'

'So it is.' Damon leaned across the counter as if to meet her halfway.

Hard not to let her gaze linger on his mouth but she managed. Hard not to enjoy the potent mix of lazy intensity in his eyes and wonder whether or not it would carry through into the bedroom. A betting woman would have to go with yes.

'Do you have any plans for the day?' she asked, for it was definitely time to change the subject.

'What are you suggesting?'

'Oh, I don't know. You. Me.' She had his absolute attention. 'Christmas gift shopping for your sisters.'

He drew back abruptly and Ruby smiled, wide and warm. 'Gotcha,' she whispered, rocking forward ever so slightly before turning back to the coffee maker to retrieve his espresso and set the machine up for a long black for herself. 'Do you really think I can afford to proposition the adored son of the only man in Hong Kong who'll employ me? Trust me, I'm not that reckless.'

'I'm not that adored.'

'Yes, you are, Damon. You'd only have to listen to the way your father talks about you to realise that. He speaks of you with a mixture of love, frustration, pride and respect, and I have to confess: the first couple are what I'd expect of most fathers, but that last one...the fact that one of the most influential money movers in the world respects *you*... Makes me wonder what you've done to earn it.'

'Keep wondering,' he murmured. 'I'm all in favour of keeping a fine mind exercised. As for going Christmas shopping with you, the answer is a reluctant yes. Give me five minutes to put some clothes on.'

'Good idea. Take your time. I'll need about fifteen to finish up here anyway.' Ruby pushed the tiny cup of super-strong coffee across the counter towards him and Damon West's fingers brushed hers as he took it. This time his touch sent desire skittering along her skin, and Ruby frowned as she whipped her fingers away from his. What the *hell* was that?

Apart from a rhetorical question for she knew desire when she felt it, knew the bite of it and the chaos it could bring. The question now became how could she have let this happen? Between one touch of hands and the next?

To *her* of all people. Ruby Maguire, who'd been out-playing players her entire life.

'What's wrong?' Lazy smile on a dangerous man. 'Coffee too hot?'

'That's one interpretation.' Ruby sighed. 'Regretfully, I'm going to have to ban the touching from now on in. And the teasing. Probably the question time as well. Sorry, Damon. I can't afford to play with you.'

'Because you work for my father? Would he really have to know?'

'Damon, please. I'm insulted that you even *tried* that line on me. Your father may not keep up with the social lives of all his business acquaintances—that's my job—but when it comes to the romantic liaisons of his children? Men like your father?' Ruby slanted him a quelling glance as she topped up her long black with cold water before lifting it to her lips. 'They always know.'

Ruby Maguire was a babe, decided Damon as he took his coffee back to his bedroom. A high-maintenance glossily gift-wrapped bundle of temptation and contradiction, and what was more she knew it.

Damon couldn't have asked for a better distraction.

Something to take his mind off a missing brother and a wounded sister and a Christmas that was shaping up to be anything but festive.

He slung his towel on the bed and rummaged through the meagre collection of clothes he kept at his father's house. A collared cotton shirt in white and a charcoal pinstriped suit. Bespoke, not made to measure. The expensive sports watch that his sisters had given him last Christmas. Clothes to suit his father's house and reflect his father's status—a Christmas tradition whereby Damon would look to be the type of son his father expected to see and in return his father would ask no questions as to what Damon had been up to the rest of the year.

What kind of man had Ruby Maguire's father been before his fall from grace? wondered Damon as he tossed the suit on the bed. Already a wealthy one, if he remembered correctly. Manhattan banking family. Influential. Chances were that Harry Maguire hadn't stolen the money because he'd needed it.

Maybe he'd been bored.

And colour Damon perceptive but the delectable Ruby Maguire also seemed somewhat overqualified for her current gofer position.

Ruby Maguire was used to dealing with the corporate lions of the world and holding her own. Ruby had severely underestimated her usefulness if she thought that no one but his father would employ her.

Which made Damon feel infinitely better about the seduction campaign he intended to wage on her.

She'd banned touching, teasing and question time but she hadn't banned looking and she hadn't banned scent.

Her bad.

The cologne collection in the en-suite cupboard gave him a wide and varied selection to choose from. Eeeny meeny miney mo. Catcha… That was the aim. To catch Ruby Maguire and play a while.

Gucci it was.

Run his fingers through his hair, find some shoes, put them on. Plastic in wallet, wallet in pocket.

Damon West was ready to shop.

He found her in the atrium, positioning a delicate porcelain Santa amongst the fern fronds that banked the goldfish pond. 'There,' she said as he approached. 'The perfect spot for Santa to enjoy a little R and R.'

Ruby Maguire stood and turned his way, no comment on the suit. She probably hadn't expected anything else.

She breathed in deeply though and closed her eyes and smiled. She had the freest smile he'd ever seen.

'I love that scent on a man,' she murmured approvingly. 'Brings back fond memories.'

'Old boyfriend?'

'Grandfather,' she corrected sweetly.

This woman was so *bad* for a man's ego. Damon smiled and meant it. Nothing like a challenge.

'Ready to go?' she said next, and he nodded and watched in silence as she headed for her oversized satchel, her ballet-style slippers making no sound on the marble floor. Odd choice of shoes to be wearing with crisply tailored grey trousers and a vivid fuchsia sleeveless silk top with an embroidered panel down the front that screamed couture, but all became clear when she opened the coat cupboard beside the front door and swapped her soft slippers for strappy black sandals with a stiletto heel.

'I can't stand high heels on marble floors,' she explained. 'It's the clickety-clack. Where's the elegance? Not to mention the ability to retreat without being seen or heard. That's a very useful skill on occasion. Not, I hasten to add, that I've ever had to use that ability here. Your father doesn't womanise.' She reset the alarm before closing the cupboard door. 'It's a refreshing change.'

'Yours did?' he asked as he ushered her out of the door and closed it behind them.

'Oh, yes. It was just a game, you see. Everything from stealing another man's woman to the removal of vast sums of other people's money—it was all just a game.'

'Where was your mother in all of this?'

'Living happily in Texas with oil baron husband number three. He doesn't womanise either, come to think of it. That's *two* I know.'

'Wouldn't *he* give you a job if you asked for one?'

'Probably, but I don't work for family, Damon. Never have, never will.'

'Another rule?'

'That one's more of a survival trait. Work for family and before you know it they're trying to control your life.' They stepped into the elevator and Ruby pressed the button to the foyer. 'How loaded is your daddy's credit card when it comes to buying Christmas gifts for his children?' she asked. 'Because I happen to have it with me.'

'He bought us a plane once,' said Damon. 'We had to share it though.'

'Poor baby,' she murmured with another one of those carefree smiles that put him in mind of a kid in a sweets shop. 'Not sure I can swing another aircraft or two at such short notice, but I've absolutely no objection to shopping with the sheiks and the sugar daddies if that's the norm. The Landmark it is.'

The Landmark shopping mall butted onto the Landmark Oriental Hotel, which meant valet parking and rampant indulgence. Ruby's mode of transport, an Audi R5 in panther-black with a pearl finish, would fit right in.

'Yours?' he murmured.

'Was that a question?' asked Ruby. 'I thought we'd banned personal questions.'

'You just asked me one.'

'I asked about the cost of Christmas gifts for your family. That was business.'

'No, that's about as personal as it gets. I, on the other hand, merely questioned whether this car was yours. It could be a company car. It could be my father's, though I doubt it. His taste runs to saloons.'

'It's mine. I chose it and paid for it myself. Happy now?'

'Yes. And I heartily approve of your choice of wheels. It almost makes up for your choice of hair accessory. What *is* that thing on your head anyway?' She'd slipped it on in the car. He'd been staring at it ever since.

'It's a headband. It keeps my hair out of my face and what's more, I guarantee it'll get us taken seriously when it comes to shopping where we're shopping. You'll see.'

'Ruby, it's a frothy pink bow on a leopard-skin band.'

'No, it's high-end couture. This is serious frou-frou.'

'I have another question,' he said.

'You're wondering where the money comes from,' she said. Which he was.

'Am I really that easy to read?'

'No, it's just that it's the first question everyone asks. Feds, lawyers, strangers... Everyone wants to know if I'm spending my father's ill-gotten gains. I'm not. The money's clean. I'm a trust-fund baby, courtesy of my late grandmother.'

'So you don't actually *need* to work for my father. I could, in effect, attempt to engage your affections with a clear conscience.'

'No, you'd still be stricken with guilt—that is, if you *do* guilt. My grandmother was not one to encourage idleness. The trust is set up so that for every dollar I earn it releases two. More if I throw in a good deed or two for charity, which, as luck would have it, I do.'

'And what would your grandmother have thought of the car?'

'She'd have *loved* the car,' said Ruby, and swung out of the car park and into the Hong Kong traffic with a confidence born of insanity. 'There's a massage option built into the seat if you feel the need to relax,' she murmured as she expertly cut her way across three lanes of traffic in order to take the next right.

'I'm fine,' he squeaked, but by the time they reached the shopping mall he had renewed his acquaintance with prayer and discovered that Ruby Maguire was either totally fearless, bent on annihilation by way of traffic incident or stark-raving mad.

The shopping centre did nothing to soothe Damon's already fragile peace of mind. 'You know what you're looking for, right?' he asked a touch desperately as he glanced up at the waterfall of retail stores rimming the central atrium.

'No,' said Ruby cheerfully. 'I have no idea. That's why you're here. You can start by telling me whether your sisters are girly girls when it comes to gifts or more practically inclined? Should I be thinking handbags for Poppy or season tickets to the Royal Ballet? She lives in London, right?'

'Right. And definitely the tickets. Buying tickets online would mean we wouldn't necessarily have to go into *any* of these shops. Problem solved.'

'Or we could put the tickets *in* the handbag,' murmured Ruby. 'Or in the pocket of a black velvet evening coat. Do you have her measurements?' Damon shook his head. Ruby sighed her impatience. 'C'mon, Damon. Work with me here. Surely a rake of your stature can hazard a decent guess as to dress size? We're not going to swing tailor-made at this time of year anyway. It'll have to be ready-to-wear.'

'In that case, Poppy's five seven and too slender for her own good. Size ten, Australian.'

'Thank you. I knew you could do it. What about Lena?'

'Lena is a little taller and has spent six of the last eight months in a wheelchair. She's even skinnier than Poppy these days. I hope it doesn't last.'

'So...dress size eight? Or ten?'

'Yes,' he said and earned himself an eye roll. 'Ten would be better. Give her something to aspire to.'

'And what size am I?'

Nice of Ruby to give him permission to study her delectable form. 'Arms above your head and turn around,' he directed smoothly.

'Funny man.' Ruby's honey-coloured eyes narrowed

and her hands went to her hips. Damon's gaze followed. Her waist was tiny but she did have hips. Not to mention a fine rear and full breasts. Her chestnut curls stayed clear of her face, courtesy of the ridiculous headband, and the black leather tote completed her general air of plenty.

Plenty of curves, plenty of attitude and plenty of challenge to be going on with. Damon smiled his appreciation.

'Somewhere between a size ten and a twelve, Ruby, though I'm guessing most of your clothes are custom fit. You've got that look. How am I doing so far?'

'You're a true expert on the female form. Lucky me. Now tell me what kind of clothes your sisters prefer to wear.'

Damon looked warily upwards once again, towards the retail floors filled with shops. They seemed like very spacious shops. Probably not *that* many per floor. 'Poppy likes layers. Lena hates dresses. Neither of them are into colour.'

'That's just sad,' she murmured. 'Do they like jewellery?'

'They have jewellery.'

'I'm working on the general assumption that they have everything,' said Ruby dryly. 'In here, Damon,' she said, gesturing to the nearest shopfront. 'No one does neutrals better than the French.'

Bracing himself, Damon followed her inside.

It wasn't Ruby's headband that got them exemplary service, decided Damon a few minutes later. It was her attitude. The way she knew not to browse the racks herself but describe what she wanted and then let the assistants fetch the stuff. The way she efficiently sorted the offerings into discards and items she wanted to consider. There was seating, and Damon availed himself of it. Refreshments, which he declined.

Three saleswomen and one curvaceous general. Two presents to purchase. Five minutes, tops.

He was so wrong.

What kind of maniac put a beige trench coat over what looked like a corseted black baby-doll nightie? Or covered a perfectly serviceable strapless black mini dress with a sheer purple overgown that rippled to the floor?

The purple gauzy thing and the mini beneath it were discarded on account of Lena not being one for colour or dresses. In the end, Ruby settled on a pewter-coloured miniskirt for Lena. It had ruffles and looked softly feminine and would not emphasise his sister's frailty. Damon approved. The ivory-coloured waist-length jacket Ruby chose to go with it had some sort of sculpted band around the hem but it went with the skirt better than expected. The beige trench coat and the baby-doll nightwear combo that she'd set aside was apparently for Poppy.

'Do I get a say?' he murmured and four perfectly styled women turned to regard him with varying degrees of pity. 'You said *handbags*,' he said to Ruby mildly. 'To put the tickets in?'

'Dammit, you're right,' she said, and turned to the attendants. 'We'll need to look at handbags too. Satchels, I think.'

'In the black?' asked an attendant.

'Of course.'

Half an hour later they left the shop, goodies in hand, and with Ruby sporting the kind of glow that only came from hitting a credit card hard. 'Now you,' she said. 'Would you like a new suit?'

'Why? What's wrong with my suit?'

'Nothing.'

'Then I don't want another one.'

'How about a watch?'

'I got this one from Poppy and Lena last Christmas. I've worn it once.'

'Well, that's hardly the watch's fault,' she said with a glance at his wrist. 'It's a very nice watch. What about gadgetry? New phone? Camera? Computer? What is it that you do?'

'I troubleshoot computer systems.'

'For who?' She looked intrigued.

'For those who ask.'

'Where are you based?'

'I don't have a base. The job's portable.'

'But surely life *isn't*? Or are you one of those people who just can't seem to settle anywhere?'

'Something wrong with variety?'

'I guess not.' She didn't sound impressed. 'All right. What about a new set of travel bags for Christmas? We're in the neighbourhood.'

'There's some new computer tech I'm interested in. Why don't you leave it with me?'

'That's not what I'm paid to do, and, frankly, I hate leaving jobs undone. It's a little quirk of mine.'

'Another one.'

'Exactly.' There was that disarming smile again. Feminine weaponry at its finest. 'If I don't have a gift for you by the end of the day I won't sleep. If I don't sleep I get cranky. It's not a good look.'

'How so? Do you abandon the fuchsia headband for a schoolmarm's bun and a riding crop?' It was possible. Judging by the shop they'd just raided, anything was possible. Ruby's golden eyes narrowed. Damon offered up his own disarming smile. 'I can see that working for you.'

'I'm glad we went shopping together,' she murmured. 'You've saved me from fantasising about you later.'

'Because I'm hard to buy for? Or because I'm homeless.'

'Neither. There's something else about you that makes you a dismal relationship choice, and once again I can credit my recently departed father for giving me a heads up.'

'Sounds ominous.'

'It is. It's about deception and disguise and people who deliberately portray themselves as something they're not. You make a charming wastrel, by the way. I'm very impressed. But that's not what you are.'

'So what am I?' he asked quietly.

'Far smarter than you're letting on, for starters,' she offered bluntly. 'Beautifully evasive when it comes to talking about your work, your needs and your lifestyle choices. An old hand, I surmise, at keeping whatever passes for the real you completely hidden from view. You're not feckless, Damon. You're a liar.'

CHAPTER TWO

IT REALLY wasn't supposed to work like this, thought Damon grimly. Finally he'd encountered a woman who saw more of him than most—and granted, she had the benefit of working for his father and therefore knowing more of his family background than most women did at first glance—but still…

Wasn't she supposed to *like* what she saw of the real Damon West? Admire his complexity and want to know more, not label him a liar and a bad relationship bet along with it.

'Everybody lies, Ruby,' he protested carefully, and watched her lips twist into a bitter smile.

'Not everybody, Damon. Not to the extent that you do. Few people misrepresent themselves the way you do. Only those with something to hide. Con men, thieves, spooks. Shadow people. The ones you can never know because they never let you, and the only thing you can count on is that you'll wake up one day and they'll be gone. Who are you really, Damon? What is it that you do? Are you a money tracker? Is that why your father respects you? Are you here looking for a lead on *my* father? Because I've already told you, I don't know where he is.'

'I'm not a money tracker.'

'Then what are you? Special intelligence service like your brother and sister? What? I'm being as forthright as I know how to be. Just tell me why you're here and what you need from me. If I have it, it's yours. No seduction required. No more pretty lies. I am so *sick* of lies.'

Her eyes were like bruises and they got to him more than he cared to admit.

'I'm not SIS, and I swear—on my father's honour— that I'm not hunting your father, or the money he stole, or anything else related to him or to you. Look at me,' he commanded softly and waited until she did. 'I'm here for Christmas with my family, that's all. No hidden agenda, Ruby. None.'

'Oh, hell,' she murmured, and looked around the shopping centre, blinking fast as if holding back tears. 'I'm sorry. I thought… It felt…'

'Like you were being played. You were, but not with nefarious intent.' She'd wanted the truth from him and he gave her what he could. 'I thought you could handle yourself. I thought you could handle me. Maybe I'm not all I seem to be, I'll give you that. Maybe I'm not the kind of man Ruby Maguire needs to have around her right now. I'll give you that too. I didn't know that earlier. Now I do. No more playing with Ruby, see?' He took a careful step back to emphasise his words. 'No harm done.'

'I'm sorry, I… You must think I'm a paranoid nutter,' she muttered, setting her shopping bags down so she could slide her headband off, shake her curls free and put it back on again. Busywork for her hands while she looked anywhere but at him.

'It's not wrong to be careful of other people, Ruby. I would be too, were I in your position.' He let her collect her composure. He looked at the nearest retail store, seeking distraction and finding it. 'I'm thinking I might need some casual wear,' he offered. 'As a Christmas gift from my father to me. They sell that kind of menswear around here, right?'

'Right,' she said and took a deep breath.

'Can we bypass the polo shirts though?'

'Good call,' she murmured. 'I'm betting upscale grunge is far more you. I'm thinking jeans to start with and we'll improvise from there. How are you off for underclothes?' She rallied fast, did Ruby Maguire, and Damon's admiration for her rose a notch.

'Do they have a brand name plastered all over them?'

'Only on the band.'

'In that case, I don't want any. I prefer my underwear anonymous.'

'Of course you do,' she murmured soothingly. 'I should have guessed. Would you like any help with your clothing selection, or shall I just wait?'

'I want your help. Whatever it was you did in the other store, do that,' he added. 'Only faster.'

Half an hour later Ruby had Damon outfitted in clothes that might even find their way into his travel bag, and relative amicability had been restored. Ruby had more shopping to do but none that required Damon's assistance. Damon had more shopping to do too, and he definitely didn't need assistance. Ruby had agreed to drop him off at the Golden Computer Shopping Centre in Kowloon. Damon would find his own way back to the apartment. Too easy.

'Mind the scams,' she said as they loaded up her car with his father's purchases.

'I shall enjoy them immensely,' he murmured and she shot him a perplexed glance. 'I'm only browsing, Ruby. Seeing what's new and improved or old and abused. I do it every time I come to Hong Kong.'

'So…you really do work with computers?'

Damon nodded. Not a lie, even if it wasn't the whole truth. Ruby headed for the driver's seat. Damon to the passenger side.

'Is there any particular type of food or beverage you'd like me to stock the apartment with?' she asked as they filled the car with shopping bags and then themselves. 'Your favourites? Your sisters' favourites?'

'Lena likes a good Sauvignon Blanc, Poppy loves lychees and I'm a sucker for crispy duck in pancake pockets with all the trimmings. No one's all that keen on a-thousand-year-old eggs, shark-fin soup, turtle jelly, or chicken-feet anything.'

'Not a problem. I'll steer clear of the swallow's nest tonics and imported Japanese blowfish too. And, Damon?'

The seriousness was back in her voice.

'I'm really sorry about our earlier misunderstanding.'

'Don't be,' he said gently. 'I've forgotten it already.'

Ruby hit the grocery stores after that. White wine, fresh fruit—including lychees—and crispy duck with all the trimmings. Snack food for Russell's fridge that she took back to the apartment immediately in the hope that Damon would still be out.

He wasn't.

'You shop too fast,' she said as she downed her numerous shopping bags, opened the coat cupboard and slipped out of her high heels and into her flats. He'd taken his jacket off and rolled up his shirtsleeves.

If a sexier version of manhood existed, Ruby hadn't seen it.

'Dare I suggest that you shop too much?' he countered as he closed the door behind her and picked up the shopping bags.

Now she'd seen it.

'I smell food,' he said.

'It's crispy duck. I was going to put it in the fridge for later.'

'Ruby, you spoil me.' Damon's grin became boyishly delighted.

'It's Christmas.'

'It's great.'

Ruby watched as Damon set the bags down next to the bench and found the one with his favourite food in it. Man and his stomach. Always the same, no matter what his pay grade. 'It's still hot,' he said.

'The restaurant's only a block away. If you like the food I'll give you their number.' Ruby started on the unpacking. The sooner she did her job, the sooner she could leave. Leaving was preferable to being around Damon. Damon called forth feelings she didn't want any part of. Starting with desire for a man who kept far too many secrets. 'Pretend I'm not here,' she told him.

'But you *are* here.'

'Then think of me as the hired help.'

'Of course.' He gestured towards the takeaway containers he'd lined up on the counter. 'Want some?'

Ruby rolled her eyes and kept right on unpacking. Fruit for the fruit bowl by way of a water rinse. She found the colander and started washing grapes. A grape escaped her and rolled across the counter towards him. He stopped it, ate it, and Ruby's gaze slid helplessly to his lips.

Not good.

'Does my father treat you like an employee?' he murmured.

'Why wouldn't he?'

'Just curious.'

'Whatever you're thinking just say it,' she said darkly

'I was thinking that I can see now why plenty of people *wouldn't* want to employ you. If there were women around you'd outclass them. Husbands around and you'd captivate them. Furthermore, I'm willing to bet that my father treats you more like a daughter than an employee.'

'I think it's because he met me a couple of times as a child. I'm trying to break him of the habit.'

'There it is,' he said softly. 'The reason you'll never make a good underling. You're too regal. Taking charge comes as automatically to you as breathing.'

'So?' For some reason his words wounded her.

'It's not a criticism, Ruby. I'm just saying that asking me to treat you like the hired help is all well and good but it's never going to happen. You're Ruby Maguire;

part princess, part seasoned survivor when it comes to the whims of the wealthy, and you know it. What's more, I know it. We're just going to have to come up with some other way of dealing with each other.'

'Are we having another serious conversation?' she demanded suspiciously. 'Because, I still remember how well the last one worked out for us.'

'You think we should stick to banter? Flirting without intent?'

'Yes,' she said firmly. 'It's the perfect solution. Easy as breathing, for both of us—no character assassination intended.'

'None taken,' he said dryly. 'Flirting is comfortable.'

'Exactly.'

'Predictable.' He seemed to be looking for a catch.

'I'm sure we can make it so.'

'Safe,' he said, watching her closely.

'Possibly a new experience for the mysterious Damon West, but yes,' she said airily. 'Flirting with me is comfortable, predictable, easy and safe.'

'Right.' Damon's enthusiasm for flirting—with or without intent—appeared to be on the wane. 'What if I fall asleep?'

'It's all right, Damon.' Hard not to smile at Damon West's thorough comprehension of self. 'I'll wake you before I leave.'

Ruby did leave Damon's company eventually, and she took with her plenty of food for thought. She'd never thought of herself in the terms that Damon West had described her. Part princess, part seasoned survivor.

Yes, she knew her way around the upper echelons of

society; with its games of one-upmanship and the ultimate scorecard that was money. Yes, she could relate to being a survivor. Always had been. Another lesson from her father. But she'd never thought of herself as authoritative, or a princess for that matter. She'd never considered herself a difficult woman to deal with.

Recent bouts of rampant paranoia aside.

She'd left Damon enjoying his meal and showing no signs of resentment towards her whatsoever, in the aftermath of her accusations and suspicions. Social disaster alleviated. Good for her. For her and Damon both, given that she'd be seeing a fair bit of him over the next few days.

The rest of Ruby's afternoon consisted of a charity meeting on Russell's behalf, and once she'd clocked off for the day, getting her nails done, and doing a spot of Christmas gift shopping, this time for herself. Her modest optic fibre Christmas tree had no gifts beneath it. Now it would.

Ruby let herself into her own apartment shortly after 7:30 p.m. Shoes off at the door—an old habit, drummed into her by a long-ago nanny—and a smile for the tiny half-grown cat who peered at her suspiciously from beneath the lounge chair. The kitten had been haunting the residents' underground car park, half starved, not tough enough for the streets, and Ruby had been lonely. They'd agreed on a one-week trial. Today was the start of week three and the ribbed look had faded somewhat but the little cat's wariness remained. 'Evening, C.'

Such a pity cats didn't talk back.

'I met a man today. A man who saw straight through me, and I through him.'

The little cat regarded her gravely.

'That's what I thought,' murmured Ruby as she knelt, stretched out her hand and managed to touch the little cat's shoulder with her fingertips before he retreated. 'Scary stuff, but we managed a respectable distance, of sorts. Eventually. Hey, I got you a present.' Ruby dug in her grocery bag and drew out a fluffy toy mouse and set it on the floor. The cat disappeared back beneath the lounge. So much for progress.

'All righty then. How about some food?'

Ruby headed for the galley kitchen, switching on lights with her elbow as she went. She fed the cat, set soothing music to playing and put a plate of leftover stir-fried vegetables in the microwave. She poured a glass of white wine and sipped it as she crossed to the window and stared out over the vast and bustling Victoria harbour.

This job for Russell West had only ever been a stop-gap while she recovered from the blow of her father's deception. She'd made of her duties what she could, and she would *always* be grateful to Russell for giving her safe haven when others had cast her aside, but it was time to move on and Damon's observations had merely confirmed it. Domestic servitude wasn't for her. She needed to find something else to do. Start her own business. Study a different type of law. One not associated with big business and big money. Something humanitarian.

'What do you think, cat? Would I make a good human rights advocate?' Sighing, Ruby pulled her headband from her hair and tossed it on the nearby table.

'No? How about family law? Prenups. Divorce.' Given her family history she knew plenty about both.

Damon West had thought her headband ridiculous.

Damon West had thought a lot of things about her, most of them accurate. Ruby in turn just couldn't seem to stop thinking about *him*.

Whether those thoughts were accurate was anyone's guess.

'What do you reckon he is, C? A thief?'

No answer from the little cat.

'But then, Russell would hardly be proud of a thief. Maybe Damon's a legitimate thief—moral ambiguity aside. Maybe he works for one of those government agencies no one's ever heard of. Either way, we don't want any part of him, right, Cat? We don't like people who keep secrets. Secrets bite. You'd know all about bites, right?'

Ruby took another sip of wine, and breathed a lonely sigh. 'You think I should have encouraged him, don't you? Used him to get through the Christmas lonelies, and yes, he'd have been perfect for that. Then I could have handed in my notice come New Year and we'd have never had to see each other again. It could've worked beautifully.'

She turned to look at the little cat and the little cat looked back.

'I disagree,' she said solemnly and hoped like hell that her decision would stick. 'I'm lonely; Damon's solitary. There's a difference.'

The little cat miaowed and Ruby nodded her agreement. 'I know,' she said. 'It's a big difference.'

* * *

For once in his life, Damon couldn't keep his mind on the job. He'd found his way to an internet café in Kowloon and logged on to an unsecured network somewhere in the vicinity. He had his laptop with him, the hardware he'd purchased earlier that day in place, he had need of information and he had the skill required to get it without anyone noticing. The clock said 1:00 a.m. Hong Kong time but he was wide-awake. He knew the codes, most of them anyway. All he had to do was bring up the page and start the run.

Why then, instead of doing just that, was he sitting there at the shabby, semi-private computer station obsessing over his recent encounters with one Ruby Maguire? Rewriting them in his head so that they played out the way he wanted them to play out. With him the hero and Ruby suitably awed by his air of mystery and rapier wit.

Not *now*, Damon. C'mon. *Concentrate.*

Lena had asked him to look into Jared's whereabouts. She'd wanted to know if ASIS had Jared listed as active, which would mean he was on a job rather than off doing heaven only knew what on his own. Didn't mean Lena suspected anything untoward. Didn't mean Jared was neck-deep in trouble. This was just an insurance run, nothing more. To set their minds at ease.

He pulled up the website he needed, started the run and sat back and put an online gaming map up on the screen while he waited. Two minutes, he estimated. Tops.

And then the laptop beeped and Damon switched screens, noting with a frown the distinct *lack* of anything remotely resembling his brother's employment file. Not good. Time to dig deeper and hope to hell he didn't find Jared's file down in the pit with all the other dark ponies. Swiftly, Damon cut his way further into the system, cursing inwardly as what should have been a two-minute milk-run turned into a five-minute nightmare.

Six minutes, seven minutes and way past time for Damon to be getting the hell out of the files he was sifting through and still he hadn't found any information concerning his brother.

Nine minutes into the run and he found a file strung full of encrypted numbers. Heading the string was Jared's employee number. It'd have to do.

Backing out of the system without a trace took Damon past the ten-minute mark—too long for comfort, with his safety margin well and truly shot.

Pack up, get out. Take the long way home. With the adrenalin blowing through his skull and every sense he owned on hyper-alert.

Minutes later, as he stepped onto the first underground train that came along, Damon West, IT engineer and specialist systems hacker ever since he'd found his way into his high school's assessment database at the tender age of twelve, grinned.

CHAPTER THREE

DECEMBER twenty-third came hot and humid. By midafternoon there'd be a deluge, Ruby predicted. A blast from the sky to wash away the stench of the day. A deluge to avoid if at all possible, she decided as she set about ensuring that she'd stocked Russell's apartment with everything the West family could possibly want or need over the Christmas break, including provisions for unexpected guests, should any drop in.

The rainclouds were still a long way off when Ruby phoned through to Russell's apartment at midday to say she was on her way up but no one picked up, and Ruby breathed a mingled sigh of disappointment and relief.

No Damon, no temptation. This was a good thing.

Dry-cleaning over one arm, shopping bag full of sushi dangling from her fingertips and a gingerbread house balanced precariously on top of the dry-cleaning, Ruby elbowed her way through the doorway to the apartment and slipped off her shoes. No time to put her flats on because if she didn't get rid of the gingerbread house soon she'd drop it and that really wouldn't do.

'Are you ever not carting things from one place to the

next?' asked a voice from behind her and Ruby jumped and the gingerbread house started to slide.

Damon caught it well before it hit the floor and Ruby's thanks came thin and grudging, seeing as he was the one who'd startled her into dropping it in the first place. She turned to look at him, taking in his choice of clothing for the day—a white linen shirt that she hadn't seen before, and well-fitting jeans that looked decidedly familiar. The clothes looked crisp and fresh. The body beneath them seemed a little rumpled. 'I thought you were out.'

'That was you on the phone five minutes ago?'

'Yes.'

'Sorry. I was asleep. By the time I'd found the phone and picked up, you'd put down.'

'Jet lag?'

'Possibly.'

'There are tonics for that.'

'It's Hong Kong. There are tonics for everything.'

'Just a suggestion,' she murmured and started towards Russell's rooms where his suits lived. When she returned and slid the sushi into the fridge, she found the gingerbread house on the kitchen bench and a tousle-haired Damon cracking open a fizzy drink that hadn't entered the apartment by way of Ruby.

'You've been shopping,' she accused.

'Guilty.'

'If you want anything like that, let me know. That's my department.'

'Ruby, I'm quite capable of stepping out for half a dozen cans of cola. Consider it exercise and a change of scenery on my part.'

'That's really not how it works.'

'No, that's usually exactly how it works,' he murmured with a crooked smile. 'Want one?'

'Just water, please. It's slick out. Hopefully the icing hasn't slid off the roof of the house.' Ruby gave the confectionary a careful once-over but all looked well with Santa's gingerbread cottage. 'Are we flirting yet?'

'Just working my way up to it,' he said with a smiling glance in her direction. 'It's all in the timing.' He looked back at the cellophane wrapped gingerbread house. 'Anyone ever tell you that you shop too much?'

'You're the first. Speaking of shopping, are those the jeans we bought for you yesterday?'

Damon nodded. 'Useful, aren't they?'

'There goes the Christmas present,' she murmured. 'Perhaps I forgot to mention the part where I wrap them up and put them under the tree?'

'That can still be arranged,' he said dryly.

'It's not the same. You're meant to wait. Take possession on Christmas *Day.*'

'It's just another day, Ruby.'

'Well, it is *now.* Take them off.'

Grinning, Damon set his drink down and reached for his fly. Ruby raised a delicate eyebrow but made no move to stop him. Eventually he stopped of his own accord.

'You're supposed to say "not here",' he said. 'And then you blush.'

'Not sure we're living in the same universe, my friend.'

'I'll say. Good thing I'm adaptable.' The trousers came off. He handed them to Ruby, who stripped his belt from the trousers and handed it back to him with considerable expertise.

'And the rest of the clothes from yesterday,' she said airily. 'When you're ready.'

'Good thing we didn't buy underwear,' he murmured and set off up the hall, not an ounce of self-consciousness anywhere in sight. Just strong, athletic legs, broad, shirt-covered shoulders, and a hint of mighty fine buttock. Put today's picture together with yesterday's man-and-his-towel image, and a woman could be excused for losing her breath.

'I know you're looking,' he said from halfway down the hall.

'No, I'm not.' But she said it with a smile, and she leaned over the counter the better to catch the show.

Only once he'd reached his room did Ruby drag her attention away from Damon West's very fine form to study his can of cola and note the label. She'd add it to the drinks order and make sure a case of it arrived later this evening with the last of the Christmas Day fare.

When Damon returned he had the rest of the clothes they'd purchased yesterday in hand and a pair of vivid Hawaiian board shorts on person.

'A leftover from your last stint as a pool boy?' she queried delicately.

'What? You don't like them? They're my favourite.'

'Oh, Damon. That's just...' Words failed her. 'Sad.' She handed the new trousers back to him with a sigh. 'Put them back on before your father sees you. He has a reputation to maintain.'

'Ruby, you confuse me,' he murmured, but he took

hold of the trousers deftly enough and the edges of his lips signalled his satisfaction.

'Player,' she accused.

'Despot.'

'Yes, but I'm a benevolent one. How many of these clothes we bought you yesterday are you going to need to wear tomorrow?'

'Only the shirt. And the jeans again. Maybe the jacket.'

Ruby sighed, temporarily defeated. Maybe she could shop with him in mind on the way home. Something with a V-neck and tiny little sleeves. Flared pants with spangles. 'Would it have killed you to get *two* sets of clothes when we were shopping earlier?'

'I wasn't sure that shop was me.'

'There *were* other shops.'

'Yes, I know,' he said with a shudder. 'They were everywhere. But two clothes shops a year is my limit and we did them both yesterday.'

'We need to build your stamina.'

'I have stamina,' he murmured. 'It's selective.'

'Ah,' she murmured. 'Now we're flirting.'

'Correct.'

Ruby's gaze cut to Damon's mouth. Flirting was meant to be light. Fun. Not deeply, emotionally satisfying.

Moments later those tempting lips got a great deal closer as Damon leaned towards her in much the same way as she had done the first time they'd met. Bench in between them but personal space still well and truly invaded. Her eyes moved up to meet Damon's gaze and there was a promise there waiting for her, and a challenge if she dared to accept it.

'Something you want from me, Ruby?' he asked silkily.

'Nope. Definitely not. Can't think of anything. At all.'

'Liar,' he whispered softly.

'Are you sure this is flirting without intent?' she whispered back.

'Now that you mention it, I may have acquired intent,' he murmured.

'That's really not part of the plan.'

'I know.' He rocked forward until his lips brushed hers. 'The plan was flawed. No pep.'

'Don't you have cola for that?'

'It's not enough.'

'Is that a favourite saying of yours?'

'It is of late.' He touched his lips to hers again and his big body grew very still. Warm lips against her own and a bench in between them as he waited for her response.

Time seemed to stop as Ruby battled for control of her wayward reaction to Damon West. Not flirty and easy but complex and needy. So much need in her to taste the essence of this man.

Tentatively, she set the tip of her tongue to one corner of his lips and tested the seam. In. He let her in, and he tasted of sweetness and his tongue knew how to tease, drawing her deeper into passionate play, and he led and she followed, and then she led and he let her.

Lightness of touch and an homage to languor and beneath it all a deep well of scorching heat. Ruby backed out of the kiss reluctantly, before it consumed her, and Damon moaned his protest and took one last fast taste before letting her pull back.

'God, we'd be good in bed together,' he rumbled and turned away and headed for the fridge.

Ruby closed her eyes and offered up a silent prayer. Dear God, not this one. *Please*, not this one, for his capacity to enchant was too high, and the likelihood of him giving much of himself seemed alarmingly low.

When Damon returned from his foray in the fridge, he had a bowl of ice cubes and a tin of caviar. The icebowl went between them on the counter and the caviar got upended on top of it. Next, he opened a packet of breadsticks and set it next to the rest.

'Eat,' he said. 'And remind me again why you're not going to sleep with me, apart from the fact that you work for my father, need to keep your job and consider me a habitual liar. I don't know about you, but it doesn't seem enough.'

Rather than answer, Ruby sampled the food on offer. A pause where pause was needed. An ice cube topped with caviar, and a cool and salty slide. She crunched down on the ice and let the textures mingle. 'Mmm.' Good manners prevented speech, so another *mmm* would have to be enough.

'Good, isn't it? Much like we'd be.' Sighing, Damon picked up a breadstick, loaded it with eggs and held it to her lips. 'The caviar usually runs out before the ice does. Say *aah*.'

'Ahumm.' The breadstick went in loaded and came out clean. A husky oath filled the air.

Damon's.

'Give me a reason not to, Ruby,' and his voice came low and guttural and slid down her spine like a lover's hand. 'Give me a reason to back off, or I swear I'll be inside of you before the day is through.'

Ruby swallowed hard and attempted to marshal her thoughts. 'I work for your father,' she said weakly.

'Not good enough.'

'I'll lose my job.'

'Says who?'

'I don't know you.'

'Would you like to?'

'Would you let me?' Finally an objection she could follow through on. 'Can you answer even the most casual of questions honestly?'

'I can try.'

'All right. Where were you this time last week? What were you doing? Just the briefest details of your day that's all I'm asking for.'

She saw him shut down. Watched his eyes as he sifted back through time, closing compartments as he went. Not that. Not that. Can't tell her that; and his reasons for not telling her were his own. He didn't even offer up an excuse.

'Okay, different question,' she said. 'Where will you be in a week's time? Snapshot that day.'

But he couldn't seem to do that either.

'Most people would be able to answer those questions, Damon,' she said quietly. 'But then, you're not most people, are you? I may have been wrong about you being after my father, but I wasn't wrong about the rest of it. About the way you keep the details of your life to yourself. About there being so much of you that you cannot, or will not, share. Not with strangers. Not with anyone.'

Finally he swore. One word.

Not something they'd be doing anytime soon.

'Glad we cleared that up,' she said carefully, no flirting in her now, just a pitiful and aching need for something that had never been on offer. 'I need honesty from a lover, Damon. I need to taste the truth in you, even if all we'd be doing is having mindless, no-strings-attached sex. It's a requirement of mine.' She dredged up a smile from somewhere.

'Make an exception,' he cajoled gruffly. 'For me.' Nothing like the penetrating gaze of a powerfully persuasive man to make a woman's mind waver. 'I hear what you're saying, Ruby. I swear I will not lie to you. Ever. I'll just…'

'Not answer,' she finished for him softly. 'I know how it works, Damon. And for what it's worth you tempt me. So much. But what you're offering…it's not enough.'

Damon stayed broodingly silent.

'I should go,' she said awkwardly, and then as reality intruded, 'I need to do the birds first.'

'I'll do them.'

'Thank you.' Ruby made it to the door and into her shoes before job necessities made her turn to Damon once more. 'I've arranged to collect Poppy from the airport at three and bring her here.'

'I'll get her.'

'Lena gets in at six.'

'I'll get her too.'

This time Ruby managed to make it through the

doorway, shutting the apartment door behind her with a quiet click. She drew a shuddering breath and closed her eyes briefly, before putting one foot determinedly in front of the other as she headed for the lift.

He wanted too much from her. Too much for too little.

There was nothing left to say.

CHAPTER FOUR

HEATSTROKE and insanity. That was what Ruby attributed those scorching kisses to. It was hot. She was insane. Simple.

Exactly what Damon West was, apart from obsessively secretive, was still open to interpretation.

Nothing but a memory, she told herself sternly. That was what she needed him to be. A vivid and beautiful memory that a woman could look to every so often. A memory to accompany a wistful sigh, a tiny half-smile and a harmless game of what-if.

What if he had been that little bit more open with her?

What if she'd made an exception for him?

Ruby had the feeling that, in the years to come, quite a nice little fantasy would follow on from those particular thoughts. Some of the pleasure and none of the pain. Bargain.

But there was no bargain to be had in her encounter with him today. Just heaviness and no small measure of regret.

With the day split wide-open and no work to fill it with, Ruby headed back to the office. To the desk she didn't deserve and the job that took her two hours a day to do, when she was being paid for eight.

'Is Russell in?' she asked Bea, Russell's proper PA—the one with her finger on the pulse of his business commitments, not his social ones.

Bea nodded, and briefly lifted her gaze from the computer screen to favour Ruby with a laserlike stare. Bea was—without a doubt—ten times more imposing than Russell could ever hope to be. Not that anyone mentioned it.

'Is he free?'

Another nod and a half-smile this time. 'Go on in.'

Russell West did not cut a particularly fatherly figure, never mind that his hair was grey and the creases on his face had been there a while. He did cut an authoritative figure. 'Russell, may I have a moment?'

'What can I do for you, Ruby?'

'You can accept my resignation.' One didn't beat around the bush with Russell West. Time was money. A great deal of money. 'I'd like to finish up in the New Year, once we get your major social commitments out of the way.'

'You mean the Chinese New Year?'

'Nice try. I mean mid-January.'

'Why?' Russell leaned back in his chair, trusting his imposing office surroundings to work to his advantage, which they probably would have had she not been in and out of offices just as grand as this one all her life.

'Bottom line? The job's not big enough. I feel like I'm taking money for nothing.'

'The company's profit margin has gone up thirty-six per cent since you signed on, Ruby. That's hardly nothing.'

'Your social networking strategy needed some work, that's all. But that was always going to be more of a consultant's gig than an ongoing role. My work here is done. Nowadays, I'm just filling in time.'

'You're welcome to stay on, Ruby. You know that.'

'I do know that.' She smiled fondly at the older man. 'And I can't thank you enough for giving me work when I needed it. When no one else would. But I want to see if there's still room for me in the world of law. Even if I have to work gratis for a while until I get the necessary accreditation and experience to go into a particular field. There's family law. International law. Defence law. Fields where my father's supposed transgressions won't—or shouldn't—reflect back on me. After that, I'll look towards establishing my own business. It's a solid plan, don't you think?'

'Well, it's a solid thought,' he said dryly. 'I wouldn't exactly call it a plan. Generally a plan requires details.'

'I'm working on it,' she said simply.

'Do you need start-up capital?'

'Are you offering it?'

Russell steepled his hands, and regarded her thoughtfully. 'Yes.'

'Just like that?'

'Yes.'

'Because of your former friendship with my father?'

'Because I have every confidence in Ruby Maguire's ability to succeed.'

'Oh.' Suddenly Ruby's big-girl voice deserted her. 'You're very kind.'

'I prefer to use the word *astute*. Okay, Ruby, resignation accepted. Let Bea know when you want to finish up. And, Ruby, I realise it's late notice but I do hope you'll join me and my family for a meal over this Christmas break. Say, tomorrow night or even Christmas Day if you prefer?'

'Russell, thank you, but—'

'Christmas is a time for family, I agree,' he interrupted gruffly. 'But when family isn't around you make do. You've already met Damon, and I've no doubt the girls will enjoy your company. Try making do with us.'

'I—'

'Make it Christmas Eve? That way you can join us at the restaurant. You booked for five people, didn't you?'

'Yes, but—'

'We'll swing by your apartment and pick you up at quarter to seven.'

'No, I—'

But Russell and steamroller tactics were old friends. 'Excellent,' he said and offered up a small smile. 'Join us, Ruby. There's plenty of room at our table. We have family missing this year too.'

Damon met Poppy at the arrival gate and together they hit an airport bar and settled down to wait for Lena. No point dropping Poppy off at the apartment, according to Poppy, and, seeing as it was Poppy's jet lag they were juggling, Damon went with whatever made his sister happy. A bottle of mineral water and an order of mini spring rolls would hold them. A chance to talk to Poppy alone wouldn't hurt either.

'Have you heard from Jared?' she wanted to know

as they settled into the comfiest seats they could find, and Damon watched a little bit of the light go out of his sister's eyes when he answered no.

'Do you know where he is?' she said next. Different question altogether.

'Not yet, but I think Lena was right and that Jared's working a job for someone in ASIS. I found a three-month-old file that has Jared's employee number embedded in it but other than that it's fully encrypted. It needs translating. Or decoding. Possibly both. Want to give it a shot?'

'Of course.'

'It's probably not a piece of paper you want to go waving around the corridors of Academia.'

'I gathered that,' she said lightly.

'It's probably not something you'd want to trust *anyone* with.'

Poppy propped her elbow on the table and her chin in her hand. 'You really don't want to give it to me, do you?'

'I really don't.' It went against every instinct Damon possessed to drag Poppy into his world of subterfuge and secrets. 'And don't trust computers. Even yours.'

'Are you always this paranoid?'

'I'm entitled.' Damon sipped his wine and considered his words. 'This one's playing out a little too close to home for comfort, Poppy. We don't want to draw attention to ourselves. We don't know what Jared's got himself into, or who's running him. Time to be careful.'

'I'll be careful,' said Poppy quietly.

By the time Lena's plane touched down humour had

been restored and Damon and Poppy had vacated the bar in favour of waiting for Lena at the arrival gates.

When Lena did finally emerge, she did it from a customs side door, meaning that customs had processed her separately, and she walked with the aid of a stick and the speed of a ninety-year-old. Her once gamine face now looked gaunt and the glaze in her eyes told him that pain ruled her these days. An airport employee walked beside her, towing a suitcase, and the relief on his face as Lena spotted them and waved was palpable.

So much for the full recovery Lena had been spouting about over the phone for the past two weeks.

'Miss West preferred not to avail herself of our wheelchair services,' said the airport employee, and with an almost-salute and a harried smile he handed the luggage off to Damon and disappeared back the way he'd come.

'Told you I could walk,' said Lena into the silence that followed, and Damon drew her silently into his arms for a hug, horrified anew by his sister's frailty and the quiet terror he saw in Poppy's eyes as she stared at her sister.

'You look wonderful,' said Lena as Damon released her. 'Both of you. It's so good to see you.'

More 'you look wonderfuls' and none of them true, followed by 'how was your flight?' and then came the question Damon really didn't want to answer. 'Have you heard from Jared?'

'No,' he murmured. 'Nothing.'

'Did you look into finding him?'

'Yeah,' he said gruffly, and with a warning glance at Poppy. 'Nothing yet.'

Poppy picked up on his silent cue and didn't add to the conversation, but he could tell by her frown that they'd be discussing what to tell Lena and what not to tell her later. *Nothing* being Damon's preference by far.

'I'll bring the car around,' he said and nodded towards the nearest door and fled with the luggage before either of his sisters could stop him. He didn't cope well with the battering Lena had taken. He couldn't look at her without remembering just how close they'd come to losing her, and if he knew his response was childish and unhelpful, well…Jared's had been worse.

Jared had damn near lost his mind when the doctor had told them that if Lena lived, chances were she wouldn't be able to walk.

Lena had been under Jared's command when she'd been injured—a simple recon of a suspected biological weapons lab in East Timor had gone badly wrong. The last thing Lena remembered was heavy crossfire, sticky blood, and lying in the dirt and looking up at the sky. God only knew what Jared remembered about the way things had gone down, or what he held himself responsible for.

Jared had haunted the hospital until Lena had regained consciousness. He'd told Lena that the mission had been compromised from the start and that he had some business to attend to. He'd told her he'd be back as soon as he could.

That had been six months ago.

Damn right 'Have you heard from Jared?' was the first question everyone in this family asked.

* * *

Supper that evening had a festive note to it, thanks in no small measure to Ruby Maguire's pampering.

A tree had appeared in the atrium. A fibre-optic plastic fantastic, with a scattering of perfectly wrapped presents beneath—including one for him from his father that Damon knew full well meant that Ruby had shopped again for him on his father's behalf.

The tree should have looked gaudy but dim the regular lights and set it to shining and it looked magical instead. Fine wine filled the wine chiller and the light supper fare Russell pulled from the fridge found immediate favour with the girls.

'Dad, is there something you're not telling us?' asked Lena from her perch on the sofa as Poppy beat an unhurried path to the bar, poured two glasses of wine and took one over to Lena with low-key grace and unobtrusiveness. 'Supper is perfect, Poppy's just handed me a glass of my favourite white, there are fresh flowers everywhere, and are those *fairy* lights out on the terrace? They are, aren't they? I'm sensing a woman's touch. And not just a housekeeper.'

'Ruby's been in,' said Russell, offhand, and Damon smothered a grin as Lena tried to digest that little snippet without giving in to rampant curiosity.

'Ruby's Dad's social planner,' Damon murmured helpfully.

'His what?'

'She's doing Christmas for him,' he added, unable to resist winding his sister up just that little bit more.

'Ruby's the daughter of an old colleague of mine,' said Russell evenly. 'She needed a job. I gave her one.

You'll meet her tomorrow. I've invited her to dine with us.'

'As your…companion?' asked Poppy delicately as she handed their father a G and T and dangled a beer in front of Damon. A beer Damon ignored, so intent was he on hearing his father's reply.

'Ruby's younger than you are, Poppet. Credit an old man with some sense.'

Poppy wiggled the beer in front of Damon's face. Damon took it and remembered how to breathe.

'So why is she joining us for dinner?' asked Lena.

'Ruby's on her own this Christmas due to…unforeseen circumstances,' said Russell. 'I thought you'd enjoy her company and she yours. Damon's met her.'

Yes, he had. And he hadn't exactly come away unscathed.

His sisters were eyeing him speculatively. 'What?' he asked warily.

'What's she like?' asked Lena.

'Organised.' And because he knew his sisters well enough to know that they'd be wanting more, he added, 'Confident.'

'Attractive?' asked Poppy.

'I guess,' he muttered and watched in dismay as Poppy and Lena exchanged glances.

'What?'

'He likes her,' said Lena.

'Yeah, I'm getting that too,' murmured Poppy.

'How?' he wanted to know. 'How could you possibly get that from this conversation?'

'Instinct,' said Lena sagely.

'Not exactly an accurate science,' he countered.

Poppy just smiled.

'So what was Ruby before she became a Christmas elf?' asked Lena. 'A stranded socialite?'

'A corporate lawyer,' said his father. 'She'll go back to practising some form of law soon, I believe. Just not corporate.'

'Why not corporate?' asked Lena.

'Why not ask her yourself?' Damon murmured and earned another set of curious glances for his efforts. So much easier to dissect someone else's life as opposed to examining one's own. 'Alternatively, don't be nosy.'

'He knows,' Lena said to her sister.

'Yep,' agreed Poppy.

'All I'm saying is that everyone's entitled to their secrets,' offered Damon. 'Why not let Ruby keep hers?'

'He *really* likes her,' said Lena, staring at him in amazement.

Poppy just looked at him and smiled her gentle smile.

Ruby prepared for dinner with Russell West and his family on Christmas Eve with a great many misgivings, most of them centred around seeing Damon again. She toyed with the idea of phoning Russell and pleading ill for the evening. Lies were useful, at times. Everybody lied.

Except she'd made honesty her platform when it came to dealing with Damon West, and how could she demand something from him that she wasn't prepared to give?

Opening up her wardrobe at 5:00 p.m. with almost two hours to go until pick-up gave some indication of her state of apprehension. The restaurant encouraged formal evening wear. Suits for the gentlemen, couture for the ladies. What would Poppy and Lena be wearing? Not colours, if Damon could be believed, and in this he probably could.

'What'll I wear, C?' she asked the little tortoiseshell beast who hovered in the doorway behind her, hedging his bets as to whether he would come into the room or stay out. 'Little black dress?' She pulled two from her cupboard, one strapless and fitted, the other one more modest but still fitted. Not really one for hiding her curves, Ruby. Curves were assets and assets worked best when seen.

'Too bleak for a Christmas dinner? I agree. What about the purple? Gorgeous cut, not too daring *and* there's a matching headband. Damon's going to love that. It'll give him something external to focus on, as opposed to worming his way inside my head and digging around. Excellent idea.'

Showering and dressing for dinner didn't take Ruby long. Six o'clock arrived, bringing with it yet another bundle of nerves for her to carry to the dinner table. Six-fifteen arrived and Ruby's patience with waiting and stewing, and stewing and waiting, ran out.

She rang Russell and told him she had a few errands to see to and that she would meet them at the restaurant at seven, no need for anyone to pick her up. Russell agreed and Ruby breathed a sigh of relief because arriving separately gave her mobility and options when it came to ending the evening on her terms.

'Win for Ruby,' she told the little cat when she got off the phone. 'Russell must have been distracted.'

At exactly 7:00 p.m., Ruby walked into the restaurant

to find the Wests taking possession of narrow flutes of champagne in the pre-dinner area. They made a pretty picture, all of them together, although the family resemblance was not that strong. Damon had black hair and so did Lena. Poppy's hair was a honey-blonde colour, and Russell's had salted to grey.

Poppy had cornflower-blue eyes and a touch of fairy in her, thought Ruby fancifully. Lena's eye colour tended more towards greyscale than blue and conjured up a touch of the devil. Different souls altogether, these two, but their smiles had a similar shape to them, and their voices—as they greeted Ruby politely—had a velvet musical quality to them that delighted the ear.

Lena wore slimline black trousers and a cream-coloured camisole that served only to emphasise her pallor and her fragility. Poppy fared better in a midnight-blue and silver A-line dress and a pretty pair of strappy silver sandals. Heaven only knew what they thought of Ruby's choice of apparel for the evening, but she could probably hazard a guess. Too theatrical, way too bright...

Wonder what else they didn't have in common?

And then Ruby turned to Damon and shouldered the impact of him dressed in crisp evening wear with as much panache as she could. A wry smile for him alone, and a promise to herself not to make this evening any more difficult than it already was. Be polite. Don't get personal. Keep her fascination for this man to herself. 'Damon.'

'Ruby.' How would he play this, for they hadn't exactly parted on the best of terms? Cool and distant? Politely dismissive? What? All he had to do was give her a clue and she would follow his lead. 'Nice head-band.'

Was he...*teasing* her?

'Thank you.' This one had a chiffon butterfly perched above her left ear. 'Not too plain?'

'Not at all.' A twitch of his lips. 'It's very festive.'

'Well, I try.' A swift glance down at his elegant charcoal tie, white shirt and charcoal suit, followed by the arch of her eyebrow told him exactly what she thought of his attempts at brightening up a person's day.

Damon's smile widened and Ruby felt herself relax, just a little. She turned back to Lena to find the other woman getting rid of a grin but leaning rather heavily on her cane. 'I'm sorry to have kept you all waiting,' she said. 'I hear the dining experience here is superb. Shall we take the champagne in and be seated?'

That took time, and ordering the meals took more. Conversation flowed around food likes and dislikes, and how long Ruby had been living in Hong Kong, and what she liked best about the expat lifestyle. From there it moved on to people's favourite places around the globe, a conversation even Poppy joined in, albeit shyly.

Social lubrication—Ruby was good at it, she'd been tutored by the best. But she'd been tutored in leading a conversation, not letting it ebb and flow at will. Get so-and-so to talk about this, her father would say, and sometimes he'd simply been training her and sometimes he'd been after information. Not a skill she wanted to employ at this table.

Don't lead. It was her second motto for the evening, right up there behind don't drool on Damon.

She managed to avoid both for quite some time. Right up until Russell mentioned that she'd soon be leaving his employ and Damon speared her with a glittering sapphire gaze.

'Why?' he wanted to know curtly, all pretence of social distance shattered.

'I want to get back to practising some kind of law,' Ruby offered carefully. Nothing to do with Damon, or what had transpired between them; she needed him to know that. 'I've been thinking about it for a while now. And then a remark someone made to me recently about my particular skill set cemented the notion that maybe I shouldn't have given up on a law career quite so quickly. You know how it is.' She smiled a quick smile. 'Sometimes it takes a stranger with a fresh eye to point out the obvious.'

'Will you stay in Hong Kong?' Another Damon question.

'There's no pressing need to stay here, no,' murmured Ruby. An answer Damon would probably find hypocritical given her fully voiced views on his inability to settle in any one place. 'I might try Geneva.'

'Are you interested in humanitarian law?' asked Poppy tentatively.

'Maybe. It's worth exploring as an option, at any rate. I'd need to retrain. Not that that's a problem.'

Ruby glanced at Damon and found him staring at her as if perplexed, and then his gaze cut to her choice of hair accessory as if that perplexed him even more. 'It's just a headband, Damon. A festive touch for a festive occasion. It doesn't define me.'

'I noticed that,' he countered quietly and held her

gaze, and Ruby cursed herself for her oversensitivity when it came to what this man thought of her, and for revealing that sensitivity to him and everyone else at this table.

Time to reach for her wine and shut her mouth and hope that someone else's manners would prevail when clearly hers had not.

'Geneva's a pleasant city,' said Damon as a waiter appeared from nowhere to top up everyone's wineglasses. 'I was there this time last week, on my way through from a job in Brussels. Catching up with an old employer.'

Damon didn't look at her as he delivered his words. He didn't look at anyone, just locked his gaze on the entreé another waiter placed in front of him and kept it there. 'He took me on a backdoor tour through the Palace of Nations. I recommend it.'

Ruby wasn't the only one who stared at him in astonishment. Both Lena and Poppy were gaping at him too.

Where to begin? What to pick up on? What to leave the hell alone?

'Huh,' said Lena, amazement running deeply through that one incautious sound.

Ruby couldn't even manage that.

'You didn't tell me you were in Brussels?' said Poppy, and her voice held disappointment and sorrow rather than amazement. 'We could have met up somewhere. Oxford's not *that* far away.'

'Sorry, Poppy.' Damon shot Poppy a guarded glance. 'You know I don't do family when I'm working.'

What the hell did Damon West *do* for a living that he had to eschew his family while he was doing it?

But Damon didn't say and Ruby sure as hell didn't ask. She just looked at him and Damon looked back, his bleak gaze meeting hers, and there was no smile in them, no invitation, just a man who knew he'd said too much already and had to shut it down before he came unstuck completely.

'Pretty place, Brussels,' she said, in a weak attempt to halt the growing silence. 'It's probably my favourite city centre of all the European cities. Not too big or overwhelming.' Unlike, say, Damon's attempt at openness and transparency. 'And then there's the chocolate.'

'And the waffles,' said Lena, joining the rescue party. 'And the beer.'

'Cherry beer,' said Ruby.

'Trappist beer,' said Lena, and with a gamine grin, 'Warm beer. Something for everyone.'

'Indeed.' Ruby could come to like Lena. A lot. 'Damon, what did you like best about Brussels?' Keeping it casual, forcing a direction, and to hell with letting the conversation find its own ebb and flow. Ruby had the helm now, and she was keeping it.

'The history,' he said, and talk turned to the fields of Flanders and the hallmarks of war.

Wine flowed and the food was indeed superb. Conversation flowed too, and turned to future endeavours. To Lena hoping to build her strength and get back to work, and Poppy, who couldn't decide whether to learn Korean or study Mayan script, and to Russell, who wanted to expand his banking services into Shanghai.

No one asked Damon what lay on his horizon and he didn't say.

Washington, DC, perhaps? Maybe some other old employer would whiz him through the White House in their spare time?

Dessert was worth waiting for, and then it was time for Ruby to thank Russell for the marvellous meal, wish them all a Merry Christmas and see herself home.

She thought she'd executed a clean getaway as Damon rose to pull out her chair.

Until Russell insisted on everyone heading to the hotel foyer together, presumably so they could see her into a taxi, only by the time they got there Russell had rearranged events to his liking, in that everyone could fit in the limo, and his chauffeur would drive everyone home.

Ruby knew when to cut her losses and go with a superior plan, only by the time they arrived at Russell's high rise the plan had changed again.

Ruby didn't even see it coming until Russell alighted and helped Lena and Poppy from the car, and then leaned back down and asked Damon to see Ruby home, and by then the limo door was closing, and the limo—with her and Damon in it—was pulling smoothly away from the kerb.

'Old fox. He planned that,' she murmured, and Damon responded with a smile. 'And you let him.'

'My father has a chivalrous streak,' countered Damon. 'Surely you know that by now.'

She did know that. 'And you? What kind of streak do you have?'

'Right now I'm going to have to go with masochistic,'

he said with a twist of his lips as he leaned his head back against the black leather interior of the limo. Had Damon known how intimate this ride would be with the others gone and just the two of them in here now?

And then he turned his head towards her and the seat space she'd made sure to put between them seemed to disappear. 'I tried to answer your question,' he said quietly.

'I know.' And in doing so he'd got to her. Again. 'Did you think it would get you into my bed?'

'Not really, no.'

'Then why do it?'

'Maybe I just wanted to know what it felt like to be that open.'

'And what did it feel like?'

'Wrong.'

They lapsed into silence again, a brooding, swirling silence that complemented the black leather seats and the cavernous limo interior. Ruby rested her head back against the seat and closed her eyes against the pull of him. She'd wanted honesty from him. She hadn't realised just how much it would hurt.

'Maybe it'll get easier,' she offered quietly. 'Maybe you just need to find the right person.'

'Maybe.' But the word held a world of defeat in it, and Ruby opened weary eyes and turned her head and held his gaze.

She edged a little closer, moving slowly. It was the only way she knew to approach such a wild and wary thing. He didn't move towards her, but he didn't move away. Just watched in silence and when she set gentle

lips to his he shuddered in silence too, before pulling
slowly away.

'What was that for?' he whispered.

'That was for you. For trying, because I asked you
to, even if it didn't go so well. Consider it my Thank
You.'

'Oh.'

This time he was the one to initiate the meeting of
lips, and although he had no way with words he knew
exactly how to pour emotion into a kiss. Longing and
regret and she knew he still wanted her in spite of his
inability to be open with her, and it made her want to
cry.

'That was You're Welcome,' he whispered.

And then he kissed her again and she wound her
arms around his neck and his hands were gentle on her
waist as he drew her onto him, over him, and pressing
up into her with a sensuality she'd always known he
commanded.

Not just kisses any more but the slide of her body
against his and the rapid beating of his heart beneath
her hand. He had a connoisseur's touch and she had a
powerful need for that touch tonight. Did it really matter that she knew next to nothing about him and probably never would? She knew he wanted her—wasn't
that enough?

Passion fed and passion burned as their kisses grew
deeper and more urgent, and when the limo started to
slow and Ruby looked out of the window through glazed
eyes and saw her high rise up ahead she groaned, and
Damon groaned with her.

'Drive with me a while,' he whispered, and she knew

what he was asking and she'd resisted him before but there was no resisting him now.

Slowly, she lifted her hand to her headband and slid it from her head and dropped it to the floor. 'Yes.'

Damon reached for the intercom switch and said, 'Take us for a drive,' and the limo moved off.

Time enough now to loosen Damon's tie, and the buttons on his shirt, with her forehead pressed to his and their breath mingling as he slid the straps of her dress down her arms with gentle fingers.

'Tell me you know what you're getting us into,' he muttered. 'Tell me you know what you're doing.'

'I know what I'm doing.' While the top of her dress peeled away from her body and she drew his head down to the curve of her breast. 'So do you.' As her strapless bra came apart beneath his fingers and he claimed her nipple with his lips and set her to arching back and biting her own.

He explored every hollow and worshipped every curve and before too many minutes had passed he had her beneath him on the seat, half naked and wholly mindless as he moved inside her, every stroke a revelation.

'Tell me you can taste the truth in this,' he whispered. 'In me.'

'I do taste it.'

In the way he savoured her, honoured her, and in the way his touch made her tremble.

'Tell me you won't regret this.'

'Never. Damon, not ever.'

As the driver kept driving and Ruby and Damon got lost in each other.

* * *

It had to end eventually. Love-making always had to end. With Ruby climaxing in Damon's arms as he emptied himself into her. With Damon swallowing her cries of completion and groaning softly as her body grew boneless and his did too, and somehow she ended up stretched out on top of him, with Damon's arms around her waist keeping her there.

The interior of the limo looked like someone's messy closet. Her clothes would be here somewhere and she would get around to putting them back on soon.

But not just yet.

'That was...' Damon didn't seem to know how to finish the sentence '...a revelation.'

'I concur.' Ruby pushed herself up into a sitting position, still straddling him, still very, very naked. Damon's gaze fell to her breasts and his lazy grin turned lopsided.

'Here's a tip,' he said huskily. 'If you ever want to win an argument with me, just get naked.'

'Something to remember,' she murmured. 'Are we going to argue now?'

'No.' He slid his hand around the back of her neck and rose up to kiss the side of her mouth. He wasn't done with her yet, and the notion delighted her. 'Not right now.'

She couldn't seem to get enough of his touch. Of his kisses. 'So what shall we do?'

'Ladies' choice.' He leaned back against the seat, his slitted gaze not leaving her face as he began to harden against her once more.

'Good. Because, right now I just want to sit back and enjoy the ride.'

* * *

They found their clothes and put them on eventually. They made it back to Ruby's apartment building, and it was after one, and technically Christmas Day already, and Damon had places to be—like with his family— and Ruby had things to do, like go inside and figure out what she was going to do with Damon West for the rest of the undoubtedly short time he would be around.

He was as dishevelled as Ruby, but he got out of the car when it stopped at her door, and extended his hand for hers and brought it to his lips as she alighted from the limo with most everything in place, including her headband.

'Merry Christmas, Ruby.'

'You too,' she murmured, and took her hand back and headed quickly for the door before she turned around and held out her hand for him to join her. Only when she was safely inside the foyer and heading for the lifts did she look back and smile at what she saw.

Damon, leaning against the car with his hands in his pockets as he watched her retreat, and secrets or not she knew more of him now and she had not met with disappointment.

He didn't want true intimacy from her, and a wise woman accepted the things she could not change.

A wise woman took the gift of passion and pleasure that he *had* given her and cherished them for what they were.

Best Christmas present ever.

Damon West had as much self-awareness as the next man. He knew what he was good at, and seduction was one of those things. He knew what derailed him, and commitments of the personal kind headed that list. He'd set foot on the hackers' path at the tender age of twelve when he'd hacked into his school's academic database. At seventeen—with five more schools under his belt— he'd blitzed his exams, hacked the filter the department of education used to expose students of interest, and MIT had come knocking. He'd hacked into their system too and they'd sent him back a six-page mathematical proof of his predictability and offered him an education.

That education, and the one that had followed, had given him travel, a reason for being, and all the excitement he could handle and then some. All they'd asked from him in return was absolute discretion and a willingness to go anywhere, any time.

At twenty, he thought he'd found heaven.

At twenty-five he knew he had.

He would be thirty-three in January and as he headed back to his father's apartment with the scent of Ruby Maguire on his skin and the image of her naked and open for him dominating his mind, Damon West took the time to mourn the loss of the ordinary lifestyle he'd so willingly given up.

CHAPTER FIVE

CHRISTMAS Day started late for Ruby. Nowhere to be, no reason to get up. The two gifts beneath her tiny tree were ones she'd put there herself. A book on humanitarian imperialism—that one was supposedly from the cat. The other was a bottle of her favourite perfume. A light and woodsy scent to lift the spirits and brighten the day.

A Merry Christmas phone call came in from her mother before Ruby had found her way out of her sleepwear. A mother who sounded happy and content and who urged Ruby to come and stay a while in the New Year. A mother who asked if the courier had arrived yet, and sighed her exasperation when Ruby said not.

Ruby promised to ring back when they had.

A sashimi breakfast feast for a contented little cat followed. Freshly brewed coffee for Ruby and a butter croissant with fig and honey jam got her positively cheerful. The gourmet food hamper and the ridiculous peacock-feathered hair comb from her mother made her smile. *Shoulders back, Ruby,* she could hear her mother saying. *Chin up, there's my pretty girl.*

It had been very important to her mother that Ruby be a pretty girl.

Her father had been the one to encourage her to use her brains.

Ruby's mother had wanted to share custody of their only child once divorce had been imminent but, for reasons known only to him, Harry Maguire had been having none of that.

In the end Ruby's mother had taken the settlement money and run, leaving her daughter behind with the promise that she was always just a phone call away.

Better than nothing.

Better than a laughing, smiling father who'd disappeared one day without a word but plenty of money to be going on with.

Ruby had bought him a set of pewter chess pieces for Christmas this year—how stupid was that? The gaily wrapped parcel was burning a hole through the shelf in her bedroom closet and the child in her remained hopeful that her father would contact her today. The child in her would doubtless wait all day for her charming, laughing father to arrive.

Foolish Ruby.

Only a silly, hopeful child would put on a pretty azure sun frock and blow-dry her hair and pin it back with a peacock-feathered comb and make sure she had her father's favourite Scotch on hand and his favourite food in the fridge, and then sit on the lounge reading her book while she waited for Godot to arrive.

Part of her *knew* he wouldn't come.

But another part waited and waited some more.

The day loomed empty ahead of her, with nothing to do except wonder whether Poppy and Lena had liked their gifts and whether Damon liked his.

She'd shopped again on his father's behalf seeing as he'd taken to wearing the clothes they'd bought the other day. A lightweight travel bag that would be useless to anyone with more than a single change of clothes, and in one compartment she'd added a couple of pairs of the plainest no-name underwear she could find, and in the main compartment she'd placed a Panama hat. Everything the modern happy wanderer would ever need.

It was Lena who phoned through to thank Ruby for her gift-buying efforts, but it was Damon who got hold of the phone after that.

'Merry Christmas, Ruby.' Damon's voice came through smoothly polite. 'Your touch is everywhere here today—and we wanted to thank you for it.'

'Have the caterers been in?'

'In and gone, with a week's worth of leftovers in the fridge,' said Damon. 'Which is no reflection whatsoever on the quality of the food. The food was fantastic.'

'And your sisters liked the clothes?'

'They did. Now Lena's heading to her room for a nap, my father's heading to the study to disguise his nap as a work effort, Poppy's just started watching *It's A Wonderful Life* and I'm about to head out for a while.'

'Where?'

'Anywhere. Why? You looking for something to do?'

'What, and miss out on *It's A Wonderful Life*?'

'How many times have you seen it before? Trust me, you know how it goes. Downtrodden man reflects on his life, realises how many people depend on him and decides not to top himself. The End. And then you cry.'

'Still not sure we're living in the same universe, my

friend,' said the woman who'd just started a fiercely competitive chess game with a half-grown cat. 'What sort of counter offer do you have in mind?'

'A walk. Just to get some air. Doesn't necessarily have to be fresh.'

'Good thing too, this being the city,' she murmured. 'Chater Garden's not that far from you. There's greenery, topiary, a water feature or two... Ignore the concrete.'

'Sounds like I need a guide.'

'You really don't,' she said, smiling.

'But what if I want a guide?'

'Tell you what,' she said, feeling generous. 'What say I meet you at Chater Garden in half an hour? I'll be the one wearing the peacock feather in her hair.'

'One of these days I'll ask you why,' he murmured. 'I'll be the one in the Panama hat.'

Damon didn't know what had possessed him to seek out Ruby Maguire again today. Last night had been enough, more than enough to let him know that he should leave this one alone. Not for him a woman who could strip him bare. Never for him a woman who could access the secrets he kept in his soul.

Restlessness plagued him as he made his way to the park.

Tension rode him as he tried to figure out exactly what he would say to the woman who'd gifted him with something special last night. Maybe the words *whatever you gave to me, take it back* would be enough.

Just a walk in the park with a pretty woman on his arm and a burning desire to let her know that last night had been nothing more than a pleasant Christmas Eve diversion. That it didn't grant him any hold on her, or her on him. He wasn't sure he'd spelled that out last night.

He had a feeling he'd lost track of that particular notion around about the time he and Ruby had found themselves alone in the limo.

No regrets—he knew they'd covered that one.

But no promises? What exactly *had* he promised her last night that he shouldn't have? What had he given away?

Information? Of a certainty he'd revealed more than enough about his work, and he knew it, but he'd stopped, hadn't he? She *knew* his limits in that regard. She'd *accepted* them.

Had he revealed his total inexperience when it came to letting someone see him, really see him, for what he was? He probably had. Didn't mean he planned on doing it *again* in a hurry.

What else had he revealed in the back of that limo? A propensity for getting lost in passion? Well, if he had, Ruby had of a surety revealed the same. No crime there.

So why—as he watched her walk along the garden path towards him, in her pretty blue sundress with her tumbling curls pinned back with a peacock-feathered comb—did he feel so exposed?

Ruby Maguire's eyes were knowing as they met his. 'I figured as much,' she said wryly as she stopped before him. 'You're here to tell me that last night was a mistake. That I shouldn't expect a great deal from you. The word *nothing* comes to mind.'

'That about covers it,' he said gruffly.

'Well,' she said lightly, a vision of poise and loveliness and behind the pretty picture a brain that ran razor-sharp when it came to reading people. 'Seems to me you wasted your time in getting me here if that was the agenda, for it's nothing I don't already know. You over-played the light-hearted, carefree Damon on the phone, by the way, if you want to know what really tipped me off. It just wasn't you. Still...' she looked skywards and smiled '...it's a nice day for a stroll and I wanted to get out of the apartment. You don't mind if I use you as a distraction, do you?'

Was yes even a *possible* answer after such a gracious and glossy dismissal of his concerns regarding her developing some kind of unwanted attachment to him? 'No.'

He tipped his hat and held out his arm, and he even managed a self-mocking smile as she slipped her hand in the crook of his arm, and without a word they began to stroll.

'You excel at making things easy for others, don't you, Ruby?' he offered at last. 'And somewhere in the process you get exactly what you want. It's very impressive.'

'It's a gift,' she said dulcetly.

'Or a weapon,' he countered dryly. 'Where'd you hone that razor-sharp mind of yours, Ruby?'

'Harvard.'

It figured. 'Where did *you* study?' she asked.

Damon hesitated, and Ruby sighed.

'Never mind,' she said. 'I forgot who I was talking to. Although may I point out that sticking entirely to the immediate present when conversing with *anyone* is a lot like talking to a brick. Nonetheless, I shall endeavour to oblige and make it easier for you to keep your secrets to yourself. See that building to the West, overlooking the park?' She waved a slender hand in its direction. 'That's Hong Kong's legislative council building. It's one of the reasons there are so many political demonstrations and marches here in the park. As for the park's history, did you know that these grounds once housed the most hallowed of colonial institutions, the Hong Kong Cricket Club?'

'MIT,' said Damon tightly, and stopped Ruby's fact-spouting dead. 'I studied mathematics and computer programming at MIT.'

The hand resting in the crook of his arm tightened, and Ruby came to a standstill. Damon turned to find her regarding him with a mixture of frustration and puzzlement.

'What?' he said. 'You asked, I answered. I was just…'

'Filtering,' she said wryly. Which he had been. 'Trust me, Damon. I know this game. My father never talked much beyond the moment either. You'd have liked him, by the way. He could have certainly shown you a trick or two about sliding graciously past a question you're not inclined to answer.'

'How would he have slid past that one?'

'Oh, I dare say he'd have started spouting rhetoric about the measurement of man,' said Ruby with a smile. 'From there you might have swung through a deeply philosophical discussion of the education system or if he gauged you differently perhaps he'd have offered you a champagne and piled on the flattery as he guessed which of the top twenty learning institutes in the world *you* graduated from.'

'Have you heard from him today?'

'Why do you ask?'

Damon shrugged and realised he didn't have any good answer other than Ruby drew him in, even when he didn't want to be drawn, and got to him when he didn't want to be got. 'Maybe it's because I know what it's like to wait for word that never comes.'

'He hasn't been in touch.'

And then she leaned into him, butting up against his arm with her body as if she craved connection, and he knew that feeling and that shoulder shove because he'd used it on Poppy as a child. Remember me, it had been shorthand for. The one who cost us our mother by dint of being born. The one who never quite managed to shake his feeling of isolation, even within the arms of family.

So he did what Poppy used to do, and put his arm around Ruby's shoulder and hugged her to his side and kept her there. He could do that much for her. He did it without thinking.

'I really hoped he'd call, you know?' she said finally, with her arm around his waist and their footsteps in sync as they followed the path before them. 'So that I'd know he was okay. That he was alive. That's the worst part of all of this mess. The not knowing *anything*.'

He should have realised that a woman of Ruby's ilk would have thought past the most obvious reason for her father's absence from her life. That she would have considered all sorts of explanations for her father's disappearance, few of them palatable. 'You think there's been foul play?'

'I don't know,' she murmured. 'My father had many faults, don't get me wrong. Branding him a hero's just… dumb. But I always thought he cared for me, and the way he left—without even the slightest goodbye or heads up…it doesn't make sense. It doesn't feel right.'

'Maybe he was protecting you. You know the terminology, Ruby. Accomplice. Accessory after the fact.'

'He was smart enough to avoid all that and still say goodbye.'

If he'd wanted to. But Damon didn't say that and Ruby didn't go there either.

'So what do you think *did* happen?' he asked quietly. 'You think he could have been trying to stop the theft?'

'If I thought that, I'd have to prepare for the possibility that he's dead. I don't want to prepare for that possibility, Damon.'

'It seems to me you already have.'

'No.' Ruby looked to the sky and the skyscrapers that crowded into it. 'I haven't. Not yet. Maybe not ever. Not as long as there's hope.'

Not a fine Christmas Day for Ruby Maguire at all. In behind the peacock feathers and the smiles, Ruby Maguire was hurting.

'You know what you need this afternoon?' he said, and pressed his lips to her hair for good measure. 'A strictly temporary, don't read anything into this, distraction. Lucky for you, I'm a past *Master* at distracting people. As every last one of my school reports will attest.'

'Why, Damon West.' She sounded less morose already. 'Was that freely volunteered information?'

'I think it was. But don't distract me while I'm busy trying to distract you. I hear there's a hell of a roller-coaster ride around here somewhere.'

'Yes, but in order to get *on* it one has to plan ahead.'

'Or we could go and play on the midlevel elevators, that's always fun.'

'Well, if you're a two-year-old...'

'Golf!' he said, inspired.

'Spare me.'

'Shopping?'

Ruby Maguire rewarded him with a smile. 'I'm vastly impressed by your sacrifice, but no. Nothing much is open.'

'Swimming?'

'Maybe later.'

'Mah-jong?'

'But we'd need a third player.'

'Poppy'll play if we ask her. She might even know how.'

'Meaning you've never played?' asked Ruby delicately.

'No, but how hard could it be?'

'I like your optimism.' Her smile had widened. Her eyes held a hint of mischief. 'I suppose I could teach you the basics and then if Poppy wanted to join us she'd be most welcome. Were you to, say, enhance the speed of your learning experience by putting your money where your optimism is I would indeed be most delightfully distracted.'

'You have all the essentials?'

The peacock feather bobbed up and down vigorously as she nodded. 'Everything but your blank cheque.'

Ruby's apartment held its own when it came to luxury and location. Size wise, it only had two bedrooms, one of which she used as an office, but the lounge and dining area was plenty large enough for a crowd, and more than large enough for a fleecing.

'There's a kitten around here somewhere,' she said as she put her handbag on the side table and picked up the remote and switched the music on and drew the curtains back. Not Christmas tunes, heaven forbid, but rather a brother and sister duo whose music played light and ethereal and wormed its way into the soul one wisp at a time.

'You mean this kitten?' Ruby turned and there was the kitten, creeping out from behind the couch and venturing closer to Damon than he'd ever ventured to her without serious coaxing.

'That's him, and you're doing well. He's the wary type. I like to think he'll turn out to be a sweet and loving companion once we move past the outright mistrust stage but that's just pure and hopeful speculation.'

'Have you considered getting a dog?' asked Damon dryly as the little cat took cover behind the leg of the coffee table.

But Ruby wasn't quite mad enough to bring a dog to this city of sky rises and crowded concrete living. 'Not for here,' she said as she foraged in the fridge for the Christmas nibbles she'd stocked up on just in case, say, an army decided to drop in unexpectedly. 'Maybe if I lived on a ranch, or a tropical island. Australia…'

'Ever *been* to Australia?'

'Well, no. But I'm sure a dog could be very happy there. Its owner too.'

'Let me know if you ever want to try it some time,' he murmured. 'I have a beach house on the East Coast that I never use. You could stay there. No resident dog though.'

'Damon West, I stand corrected. You're not a homeless person after all.'

He smiled at that. 'Does it make you think better of me?'

'No, but your offer does. It's very generous. Also somewhat surprising. What if I were to discover some of those well-kept secrets of yours while I was there?'

'Well, you could try,' he said with supreme confidence as she set a jug of water and frosty glasses on the breakfast bar beside the food. 'We could have a little wager on it.'

'That's the spirit,' she said encouragingly and offered him a candied ginger. 'May I get you a drink? Inhibition-loosening beverage of your choice?'

'And if you miss out on a suitable job in Geneva you can always try the casinos in Monte Carlo,' he offered dryly. 'They'd have you in a heartbeat.'

'I'll keep that in mind,' she murmured, and he smiled his lazy smile and popped a candy in his mouth.

He reached for the hat on his head and set it on the breakfast stool next to him, making himself at home in her space, working his charm because she'd asked him to. Because she'd done enough soul-searching for today, and they could hammer out the details of their relationship another time, or just let it flow, considering that they both appeared to be on the same page when it came to knowing nothing permanent would come of it.

Didn't mean she couldn't appreciate and enjoy the gifts that he brought to her table today. The simple gift of being there. The rogue's gifts of distraction and entertainment. His hug for her earlier, the gift of human touch. His understanding of her predicament when it came to her father. He had family he hadn't heard from recently too.

'Have you heard from your brother?' One last serious question before she allowed herself to be seriously distracted.

'No.'

'Are you worried about him?'

'Lena is. I'm a little more inclined to give him some leeway. Jared's big on guilt at the moment because Lena nearly died under his command. Lena wants him home so she can tell him to get over it. My guess is that Jared's gone after the people who hurt her and that he'll be back when he can deliver up their heads on a plate and not before.'

'Oh.' What to say to that? 'It sounds...plausible.' If one discounted the fact that, out head-hunting or not, surely brother Jared would have found an opportunity to call home by now.

'I know how it sounds, Ruby. But we're used to not hearing from Jared for long stretches at a time. I'm not that worried about him. Yet.'

'Good,' she said sincerely. 'Here's to your brother getting his revenge and finding his way home.'

'You're not going to say he should leave it to the legal system?'

'Justice takes many forms, my friend. The legal system delivers but one of them.'

'They teach you that in law school?'

'No, that one comes with age and experience.'

'Imagine how cynical you'll be by the time you're sixty.'

'I know,' she said. 'Frightening. I have a feeling you're going to like mah-jong. It's a game of great subtlety. The wind blows and the probabilities turn. Dragons roar and the path ahead changes. Flexibility is the key. I'll show you the play, which you'll pick up fast, and I'll let you figure out the mathematical probabilities for yourself. Wouldn't want that fancy maths degree of yours to go to waste.'

'You're too kind.'

'I know.' She opened the case and watched Damon's gaze sharpen upon the tiles as most everyone's did when they first viewed the set. Pewter-backed jade, each piece exquisitely carved and painted and then polished to high gloss—each tile so perfectly matched to the next that there could be no telling them apart once they were face down.

'It's said this set once belonged to the emperor's favourite concubine and that she won many a concession from her lover when the tiles were played. I hope you don't mind if we play on a velvet cloth,' she murmured dulcetly. 'It's a very sensual experience. And of course it protects the pieces.'

Damon made no reply, just started in on his shirt buttons and then peeled it off and handed it to her. 'This being the shirt off my back,' he said. 'Take it. It'll save time.'

'It's also rumoured that a lot of games between the emperor and his concubine remained unfinished.' Ruby took the shirt from him and steeled herself not to ogle his very fine form. 'Now I know why.'

'Happy to do as much illuminating as you want on that score, Ruby. He was probably trying to distract her.'

'Well, I'm sure she appreciated his efforts,' she murmured. 'What a giver.'

Damon smiled, slow and lazy, and Ruby shivered, and not with apprehension. Something about this man called to her and it wasn't just his beautiful body and it certainly wasn't his zealously guarded mind. Maybe it was the yearning she sensed in his soul.

'C'mere,' he said, and Ruby went and gave herself over to him willingly, to the taste of him and the responsiveness of her skin beneath his touch. A fleeting kiss and then another as he teased her lips with his and made the ache inside her grow.

'Distracted yet?' he murmured.

'Very.'

She found places for her hands on his chest. A puckered nipple beneath one palm and the ridges of his stomach beneath another. 'Last night,' she whispered, 'was so...so...'

'Don't say disappointing.'

'Unexpected.' As he slid her hair comb from her hair and set his lips to the skin behind her ear. 'And unbelievably hot. I've been trying to figure out the why of it all morning.'

'I'm blaming it on the limo,' he whispered, thread-

ing his fingers through her hair and drawing her into an
open-mouthed kiss that as far as Ruby was concerned
destroyed his limo argument outright. 'All that forced
intimacy.'

'I'm thinking of blaming it on Santa,' she offered,
and closed her eyes the better to concentrate on the fire
in his touch.

'Not exactly a reasoned argument.'

Ruby countered by sliding her hand down until she
found the iron-hard length of him, deeply satisfied when
he groaned and surged against her hand and then in one
swift movement picked her up and planted her on the
table, her legs wide as he stepped in between them and
showed her exactly where he wanted that shaft to be.
'Better than yours, though. Where's the limo now?'

'What limo?' he muttered and his eyes were dark
with desire. 'Where's your bed?'

'Down the hall, first door on the right.'

By the time they got there Ruby's clothes were gone
and so were his, two of the hallway pictures were askew
and the walls had received a battering.

He gave himself so freely to pleasure, and Ruby did
too, until they were both bathed in touch and taste and
the heady scent of arousal, and then he rolled until she
sat astride him and he positioned her for his entry and
made it slow and glorious.

Ruby closed her eyes and wrapped her hands around
his forearms while he sat up and worked his clever lips
and tongue over her neck and throat. Piling distraction upon distraction and lacing it with an abandon she
couldn't resist.

There were no rules with this man. She wanted him

at her breast, and he took it with a groan and paid attention and made her scream. He kissed his way down her body after that, and he turned her on her back and took her hands and wrapped her fingers around the wrought-iron bed bars above her head and told her to keep them there and then proceeded to string kisses across her stomach and her hip, her thigh and finally her core, and he knew what he was doing, heaven help her he did, and she entreated him and cursed him in the same breath as he took her to a land far, far away.

There'd been a magical quality to last night's lovemaking that had taken Ruby unawares and turned the night golden, and today was no different.

He made her feel loved, and he made her feel beautiful as he let her ride out her climax and then entered her as if he couldn't wait a moment longer.

'Now you can touch me,' he whispered, and touch him she did, only she could never quite get enough, and her need built again, he made damn sure of that.

Need over reason, for how could reason explain this?

'Let go, Damon, just let go now. I'll come with you, I swear I will.'

And it was as if her words released the leash he'd kept on himself and stripped away every barrier. He shuddered hard and clung to her as he spilled himself deep inside her, and Ruby flew with him this time, not even half a heartbeat behind as together they found oblivion.

Just as she'd promised.

'The things you do to me,' he murmured as they lay on the bed, both of them on their backs, their bodies spent and separate but the connection between them running stronger than ever. He lifted his arm from his elbow down, made a fist and then stretched his fingers wide, and Ruby raised her hand to his and he threaded his fingers through hers. 'The concessions you wring from me.'

'I'd hardly call a thimbleful of honesty between lovers a concession,' she murmured lazily. 'Although maybe in your case I should. Maybe you should favour me with another example of your concessions, just so I can identify them in future.'

'Give me five minutes and I'll get right onto it.' He shot her a lazy, satisfied smile. 'Maybe ten.'

'Give me a memory from your childhood, something you don't usually reveal, and I'll give you anything you want.'

'Big promises, Empress.'

'Chances are I'll never have to deliver, Concession Boy.'

He closed his eyes. He shut her out. 'My mother died giving birth to me,' he said quietly. 'Not something I tell the world.'

Careful where your wishes take you, Ruby, she thought grimly, but it was too late to turn back now. 'That's understandable.'

Damon said nothing.

'Did your family hold it against you?'

'No,' he said. 'Never.'

Ruby let go of Damon's hand, the better to prop herself up on one elbow and look at him. But she slid her other hand in his the minute she could and he didn't pull away. 'I'm glad to hear it,' she said simply.

'Didn't stop me from spending most of my teens trying to push them away.'

'And then you got over yourself?' she asked hopefully, and he smiled wryly and brought her hand to his chest.

'Let's just say I finally figured out how much I needed them. And how much they needed me to come good. To make their loss worthwhile. To make it mean something.'

'Or, they could've just been waiting for you to stop beating yourself up over something you had no control over so that you could finally see how much they loved you. That'd work too. As an argument for persistence in the face of your rebellion.'

'The lawyer speaks.'

'Well, if reasoned argument isn't working for you, I dare say I could always try kissing you better. Provided of course that you tell me where it hurts.'

'My shoulder,' he murmured, his eyes dark and guarded, and she kissed his shoulder and he took a shuddering breath.

'My chest,' he said next and she kissed him above his heart and then she took his nipple in her mouth and Damon loosened his hold on her hand and the next thing she knew his hand was in her hair, the better to hold her against him.

'My side.' Little more than a rumble, but she heard him and she kissed him there, as he started to stiffen against her once more, ten minutes to resurrection be damned.

'Where else?' she whispered.

'You know where.'

'Say it.'

But he didn't say a word.

'Why, Damon West,' she said with a grin and slid her mouth another inch or two down his stupendous body. 'I do believe you're repressed. Who knew?'

'I am not repr—' he began warningly, and then she licked and made a meal out of him and he sucked in his breath and shut the hell up.

'Something on your mind?' she murmured long moments later. 'Because you'd tell me if there was, right?'

'Right,' he rasped.

'Liar.' She found the base of him and kissed him there and set her hand to him and he caught her hair up in his hands and strained within her grasp. 'This, by the way, is *my* concession to you and I do hope you like it. Feel free to distract me whenever you've had enough.' Damon groaned. Ruby licked.

'Is my hand too tight?' She slid it slowly up and down the generous length of him. 'Mouth too warm?' She slid that up and down the length of him too and interpreted his guttural groan as a no. 'Because you'd tell me, right?'

'Right.'

He let her pleasure him, for a time. And then he lifted her into his arms and slid inside her and Ruby could have cried at how right it felt to make love with this particular man, lose herself in him even.

But she didn't cry and she didn't say a word about how easily he could shatter her defences. Nor did she mention the decidedly inconvenient and somewhat frightening fact that she'd never felt this way with anyone before.

Ruby Maguire knew how to keep secrets too.

CHAPTER SIX

The aftermath of love-making wasn't always easy, conceded Damon. There could be awkwardness and boundaries to re-establish. Control to find. Leave to be taken, provided clothes could be found. So far, Damon had managed to find his clothes. Ruby hadn't even managed that, but then, she didn't have family waiting and wondering where the hell she was.

'What time is it?' she said.

'Four.'

'That late?' She sat up abruptly, every inch the dishevelled wanton, and the corners of Damon's mouth kicked in response.

'I'm taking that as a compliment.'

'And so you should.' Ruby slipped from the bed and found her dress, no awkwardness in her whatsoever and it helped ease his. 'Your powers of distraction are truly—' Ruby laid a hand over her heart '—*truly* stupendous.'

Damon smiled at her words and turned away and headed for the en-suite. There'd been a hell of a lot more than distraction going on here this afternoon, but if Ruby wasn't inclined to point it out then he certainly wasn't going to. Ruby—it seemed—had bypassed awkwardness and moved straight to the setting of bound-aries. Which was fine by him.

No promises and no regrets. They could do this. And then Ruby came into the bathroom with her dress on and leaned back against the bench as he splashed his face with water and took the hand towel she offered him.

'I need to get going soon,' he said, and wondered at his sudden reluctance to move.

'Want a lift?' And when he studied the towel instead of answering, 'I can drop you at the door?' He moved away from the basin and Ruby took his place, took one look in the mirror and gasped and then grabbed for her hairbrush. 'Boy, am I dropping you at the door.'

'You look fine.' He took the brush from her and stepped in behind her, setting brush to hair. His gaze met Ruby's in the mirror and it hit him like a train that he wanted this picture in his life. Wanted it with an intensity he usually reserved for his work. 'And you're welcome to come in.'

'No. Thank you, but no. If you're planning on at-tending your father's Boxing Day luncheon I'll see you tomorrow. If you're not...'

'I'll be there,' he murmured and handed her back her brush. 'I'll be at my father's until the thirtieth.'

'More information?' she purred. 'Why, Damon. You spoil me.'

'No, I don't.' But he wanted to.

'Anyway...' she said with a shrug that reminded him of the shrugs of his youth. The ones designed to make people think he wasn't hurting. 'Time to get you home.'

She drove him to his father's door. And then she smiled and blew him a kiss and drove away.

* * *

Russell West's inaugural Boxing Day luncheon had been Ruby's idea. An informal drop-in for business associates and friends, it started at midday and would go on until late as guests cycled through, staying for as long or as short a time as they wanted. The caterers were the best in the business and came complete with service manager and wait staff, which left Ruby very little to do but stay out of the way unless issues arose.

Instigator she might have been but host she was not. She left that to Russell and his family and could not fault any of them. Both Poppy and Lena were wearing the clothes she'd chosen for them. Both looked stunning—even if she did say so herself.

Ruby wore a simple ivory skirt and jacket with a violet camisole beneath. No lace. No frou-frou at all except for a tiny crystal-embedded hair clip to hold her hair up and out of her face. Her father's reputation preceded her these days, but she did her best to be unobtrusive in this type of company so that her presence would not reflect poorly on Russell.

No need for people to know how Russell had come by his recent social savvy. All they needed to know was that a new social circle had opened up and that it glowed with opportunity when it came to matching investors with developers, visionaries with the more practically minded, movers and shakers with those who could oil their way.

Damn right no one paid her any attention—everyone was too busy doing what they did best.

Ruby allowed herself a tiny smile. At least two major business deals would get stitched up here today. Maybe three. Not bad for a former corporate lawyer turned social PA.

'Ruby? Is that you?'

Ruby looked up at the sound of her name, her smile turning genuine as she recognised the speaker. 'Juliet! How are you? It's been too long. And you are *still* the most beautiful woman I've ever seen. I want your secret.'

'Flatterer,' said the other woman warmly as they exchanged kisses. 'Your father taught you well.'

'So true.' Ruby stood back and caught the other woman's hand. 'I heard you'd remarried. Renauld Lang, yes?'

'Yes.' Juliet's face softened. 'He's a good man, Ruby. A kind man. I got lucky.'

'You deserved to,' murmured Ruby gently. Juliet had been Ruby's father's lover once and had made the fatal mistake of getting serious about him, and befriending Ruby, and trying, bless Juliet's gentle heart, to make a place for herself in Harry Maguire's life.

It hadn't ended well.

'I know what they're saying about your father, Ruby,' said Juliet gently. 'And for what it's worth I don't believe a word of it. Harry was restless, and ruthless, and frustratingly enigmatic more often than not. But he wasn't a thief and he would *never* have walked away from you. You know that, don't you?'

'Sometimes I know it,' said Ruby with a wry smile. 'It means a lot to hear you say it.'

'Any time,' said the other woman gently.

'Ladies,' said a deeply delicious voice with just the right amount of wickedness in it. 'I'm doing the rounds on behalf of my father. May I interest either of you in a drink?'

Ruby looked up and her smile grew even wryer as she took in the elegance that was Damon all suited up and primed to behave. 'Juliet Lang, Damon West,' said Ruby. 'Juliet and I are old acquaintances. Damon and I are new acquaintances. Juliet, will you have a champagne?'

'Of course,' said the older woman.

'What about you, Ruby?' asked Damon.

'Thanks, but no. I'm working. I have a glass of water around here somewhere.'

Damon nodded and moved away and Ruby watched him go. She'd been trying not to watch him for the best part of the afternoon. The way he mingled easily and endured his father's pride in him with wry good humour. The way he drew daughters, wives and grandmothers to him like locusts to a plague.

Charmer, no question.

Be whatever someone wanted him to be.

'Impressive,' murmured Juliet.

'Very. But strictly short term.'

'Heartbreaker,' said Juliet warningly.

'Only if you let him be.'

Ruby smiled and found her glass, caught his gaze and sent him a silent and appreciative toast.

'Don't bait the man, Ruby. Didn't your father ever tell you not to play with fire?'

'He did,' said Ruby. 'But it's so much fun.'

She laughed with Juliet for a while and met her lovely husband, and then it was time to slip away and do the rounds of the powder rooms to make sure they were tidy and well stocked. Three bathrooms available to guests. Two off the atrium and living areas and another at the end of the hallway, past the guest bedrooms.

Ruby's shoes clickety-clacked as she made her way back down the hallway towards the mingling throng of powerful people, and then her shoes stopped their noise making midstride as a strong arm snaked out from a bedroom doorway and drew her inside onto carpeted floor. The bedroom door closed firmly behind her, and then Damon backed her against it and set his hands either side of her head and his lips to the curve of her neck.

'Damon, I'm working,' she whispered, even as her hands went to his waist and she tilted her head to allow him better access. 'What are we? Twelve?'

'I prefer to think of it as innovative,' he murmured silkily and then set his hungry mouth to hers, at which point all talking ceased for quite a while. More kisses followed. Delicate open-mouthed explorations that fed desire. Deep and drugging declarations of desire gone mad. Whatever this was, Ruby could no longer control it, and as for Damon…

'God, Ruby.'

He seemed bent on encouraging the insanity.

And then the doorknob turned and the door at her back began to open and Damon slammed it shut with the palm of his hand. Ruby stilled and stared at Damon, the fear of discovery heady when mixed with desire.

Who? she mouthed silently and Damon just shook his head and raised an eyebrow, but he didn't open the door and for that she was truly grateful.

The doorknob turned again and this time Damon frowned. 'Who is it?' he said.

'Lena.'

Damon grimaced, and his gaze cut from Ruby's face to the en-suite doorway.

Silently, Ruby ducked beneath his arm and made her way to the en-suite and carefully shut the door behind her. Damon's cue now, to open the door to Lena and guide her elsewhere so that Ruby could make her escape.

She heard the door open and Damon's guarded, 'What is it?' and Lena's exasperated, 'For heaven's sake, Damon. Let me in. What is *wrong* with you?'

'I was just coming back *out*,' said Damon, and in the relative safety of the bathroom Ruby nodded her agreement.

'Wait,' said Lena. 'I need to talk to you. Privately.'

Not good. Definitely not good.

'Now,' said Lena firmly, and, cursing silently, Ruby closed her eyes and leaned back against the wall to wait.

'Lena, not now. This really isn't a good time.'

But Lena wasn't listening and Damon stood back and let his sister into the room. Better to get it over with then, whatever it was, for Lena had that look on her face. The one that promised no mercy whatsoever for whoever had been stupid enough to irritate her in the first place to the point of explosion.

'Why didn't you tell me you had news on Jared's whereabouts?'

'What?' he said warily.

'Last night you told me you hadn't found a thing. Today Poppy tells me that you've already hacked into the ASIS database and found Jared's personnel record and pulled a coded file from the system that you now need Poppy to decode.'

'Lena, please,' he said urgently and pressed his fingers to her lips, something he should have done the moment she'd stepped in the room, only he'd still been dazed from Ruby's kisses and he hadn't even seen it coming. 'Not now.'

But she wrenched his hand away, eyes flashing. 'Why not? Am I too fragile to know the truth all of a sudden? Is that it?'

'Lena—'

'You *lied* to me. You sat there the other day and you lied to my face.'

'No, I told you I didn't have any information on Jared's whereabouts. I still don't.'

'Don't you *dare* pull that half-truth crap on me. Hacking might be your business, and secrecy your way of life, but I am your *sister* and this is Jared we're talking about. How could you? How could you shut me out? Has it not occurred to you that I might be able to help? That I might know ASIS operational systems and codes better than you?'

'Lena. Not. Now,' he said through gritted teeth.

'*Why* not now?'

And then the en-suite door opened and Ruby stood there pale but composed, and looking anywhere but at him.

'Probably because he doesn't want anyone overhearing your conversation,' she said quietly. 'So if you'll excuse me, I'm just going to…leave. Thanks, Damon, for the, ah, use of your bathroom.'

Smiling brightly, Ruby executed a hasty exit and shut the door firmly behind her.

'Oh, *hell*,' said Lena and stared at him in dismay. 'Damon, I'm so sorry—'

But Damon was already halfway out of the door.

He found her directing the wait staff with the precision of a conquering general. He stood back and watched, and let her do her thing and manoeuvre guests and charm her father. She hadn't fled, she had a job to do, and it suited Damon to stand and watch her do it while he planned how best to deal with a situation he'd never encountered before.

He went back to his room, with a bleak-eyed glare for Lena, who passed him in the hallway, where he filled his backpack with the things he would need and then returned to the main room and simply walked up to her in the kitchen, took her hand and headed for the door and to hell with what people thought. His father would get over it. His father's business friends and associates could think what they liked, and as for Ruby…

If she objected to his high-handedness she made no mention of it as she collected her work satchel from the cloak cupboard and strode through the apartment door he'd opened for her, with her hand still firmly ensconced in his.

Perhaps she was as glad to see the back end of the party as he was. Perhaps she had something to say. Time would tell, because she sure as hell wasn't saying anything now.

Such a fascinating face—the one she presented to him as they stepped into the lift and turned around to face the closing doors. Not classically beautiful—no Grace Kelly here—but those eyes could drown a man and her lips were the work of a master. A lovely, lively face, and if a man preferred it to classical perfection, well, that was his preference.

If a man wanted to walk blindfold off a cliff and entrust her with his darkest secrets, well…that was his business too.

They rode the lift in silence, all the way down to the car park and only when they were heading for her car did she finally choose to speak.

'So… I don't know much about hacking but I do know that the term *hacker* can have multiple meanings,' she began quietly. Careful words from a lawyer's mind. Ruby Maguire was thinking things through. 'What kind of hacker are you? Or perhaps the more appropriate question would be, to what *end* do you hack?'

'You cross-examining me, Ruby?'

'You planning on answering the question, Damon?'

Impasse.

'Because, please correct me if I'm wrong, but it sounded to me as if you hack to acquire information. Like your brother's whereabouts, for example.'

'That one's more of an unofficial side project detour…thing. Tiny. Really.'

'Right,' she drawled cuttingly. 'So the rest of your work relates to the *official* collection of restricted information. How very reassuring.'

'Shades of grey, Ruby,' he murmured and Ruby shot him a filthy glare.

'So you're a spy. An information thief, all jacked in, new millennium style.' And when he said nothing,

'God, Damon. Have you *any* idea how many ethical buttons this pushes for me? There *are* other ways of getting information. Legal ways.'

'Like, for example, you asking the FBI to share whatever information they have on your father? How's that working out for you, Ruby?'

'Shut up.'

'Second oldest profession, or so they say. It's not as if I'm breaking new ground here. Just newer ways of doing it. I work towards maintaining peaceful power balances between nations. How is that wrong?'

Ruby's steps had quickened, her chest rising and falling rapidly. Damon walked too, silence clearly the best option for now. How the hell had he got *into* this mess?

Headbands were the devil's work, he decided grimly. The next time he saw one he'd know to run.

'I knew you had secrets,' she said and fumbled through her satchel for her car keys. 'I chose to spend time with you anyway. But this… I've got to hand it to you, Damon. Even for me this is a whole new level of secrets and lies. I *knew* I should have stayed away from you,' she muttered. 'Why the *hell* didn't I?'

He had no answer for her there. 'You can't tell anyone, Ruby.'

'Yes, I gathered that,' she said, and raised a shaking hand to her head. 'Who else knows?'

'My immediate family. My handler. Now you. Six people in ten years.' It wasn't a bad effort. He didn't think it *too* bad a record.

'God.' She looked worried and so she should be. 'I won't tell anyone, Damon. You have my word.'

'And in an ideal world, your word would be enough,'

he said quietly, but this wasn't an ideal world. He needed to secure her silence and her loyalty. Bind her to him now, with whatever he had in hand.

'What if I said I could help you find your father?'

'*What?*'

'That's what you want, isn't it?'

'Yes, but…'

She didn't, or couldn't, finish her sentence. Typical lawyer. Always a But.

'I'm offering to contract out to you,' he continued. 'In return for your silence. You get news of your father. I acquire a hold on you I currently don't have. Everyone wins.'

'That's blackmail.'

'It's necessary,' he cut back hard. 'And at the end of the day you get to walk away, I get the peace of mind I need to let you walk away and the people I work for get to remain none the wiser as to what you know. That's worth something, Ruby. More than you know.'

'Well, aren't you chivalrous,' she murmured, and favoured him with a tight-lipped smile.

'I try.'

This discussion wasn't exactly going according to plan, decided Damon grimly. But then, nothing involving Ruby ever did.

'I'm trying to *protect* you,' he said curtly, and maybe Ruby heard the frustration in him for she eyed him uncertainly before looking to the car-park walls for answers, only there were none to be had there. He'd already looked.

'Or I could let my superiors know I've broken cover with you and let them deal with the fallout. They won't harm you, they'll recruit you. Like it or not, you won't have a choice. That's the value they place on the work I do for them, Ruby. The cost of maintaining my cover. And the reason I never wanted you to know any of this in the first place.'

'I knew you were trouble,' she said again. 'I knew.'

Again, Damon said nothing. It wasn't as if she were telling him anything new.

'How would you do it?' she said after a time. 'My father could be anywhere. How would you set about finding him? Where would you even start?'

'I'd access files various authorities have on him and get you to read them. See if what they have to say fits with what you remember. See if it throws up any ideas. And then we'll continue from there.'

'Couldn't you just…send me a report?'

'Sorry, Ruby. You don't get to stay clean while I get dirty for you. I want you with me.'

'And equally culpable.'

Damon shrugged. The short answer being yes.

She looked ready to weep but she tilted her chin and squared her shoulders. 'When do you need my answer on this?'

'Now.'

'And when would we do it?'

He gentled his tone and hoped for her sake she could handle this. 'Just as soon as we get you back to your apartment and get into different clothes.'

'What kind of clothes?' Ruby was willing to be distracted by the little things. It was a start.

'The kind that don't stand out.'

CHAPTER SEVEN

I<small>F</small> R<small>UBY</small> could press a rewind button she would.

This day would disappear for starters.

Russell's society luncheon would go.

She wouldn't go so far as to wipe Damon from memory completely but there were definitely things she would have done differently when it came to dealing with him.

Such as not push him for personal information he so clearly hadn't wanted to give.

And not allow herself to become so enamoured of the physical side of their relationship that she lost all sense of self-preservation.

Fooling around with Damon in his bedroom, with a party in full swing not six yards away. What kind of idiot behaviour was that?

She'd thought she could play with Damon without consequence. Use him, as it were. She really had thought she could be intimate with him and come away unscathed.

Wrong.

'First a father who may or may not be guilty of the biggest heist in banking history, and now a computer hacker for a lover,' she murmured, and a small cat peeked out from beneath her bed and regarded her solemnly. 'I'm really not having a good run. And what the hell kind of clothes does a person wear when committing a hacking offence?'

Damon had clothes in his backpack, or so he said. He'd retired to Ruby's bathroom to get changed.

Ruby tossed her jacket on the bed and began to rifle through her wardrobe. Jeans, they'd do. A black T-shirt she usually wore when cleaning things. Flat shoes... apart from the ones she wore around the apartment, and they were little more than slippers, flat shoes really weren't in her vocabulary. Almost-flat shoes, by way of a pair of black patent leather pumps with black and white spotted bows across the front of them, would have to do.

She put her hair up in a ponytail, left it ornament-free and returned to the lounge room in search of Damon, the man with the vagabond lifestyle, the secrets she didn't want to know, and a moral fluidity she couldn't even begin to comprehend.

Don't judge.

Why did she always have to judge?

Damon had his Christmas jeans on and a grey T-shirt and the battered black backpack slung across his shoulder now looked half-empty. She'd never seen him looking quite so downmarket before. Or so dangerous.

'Where are we going?' she asked tentatively.

'Out for some fast food.' He looked her over, frowned when he got to her shoes. 'Lose the shoes, Ruby. Or at least lose the bows.'

Fortunately for him, the bows came off without a great deal of persuasion and would go on again under the influence of superglue. 'Do I have to *eat* the fast food?' she said.

'It's tastier than it looks.'

'Only if you have the palate of a two-year-old.'

He smiled at that and some of the tension between them dissipated. 'It's my show, Ruby,' he said softly. 'Let's go.'

'Wait!' she said hastily. 'You don't want to talk about it first? Run me through what it is we'll be doing?'

'I'll talk you through it as we're doing it,' he offered calmly.

Ruby opened her mouth to protest, took one look at him, and shut it again without saying a word.

They walked from her apartment to the nearest train station. Just another young couple getting from one place to the next, foreigners but not strangers to Hong Kong or the mass transit railway service it provided.

Comfortable, as they found two free seats and Damon slung his backpack between his feet and laced her hand in his and smiled, before turning to look out of the train window into subway darkness, his thoughts his own.

'I should have bought a book,' she said lightly, and he fished his phone out of his pack and handed it to her.

'Take your pick.' And she took it because she was curious and scrolled though his offerings.

'No romance,' she said after a time and handed the phone back to him and earned herself a very level gaze. 'You said you'd explain what we were doing along the way. Why are we going to Kowloon?'

'To find an internet access point. One that tracks back to a public place.'

'Like a fast-food outlet?'

'Often they have internet access. Not that it'll do us any good. Too much surveillance. Not enough privacy.'

'So why are we doing the fast food thing at all?'

'I just like their coffee.'

He was deliberately messing with her head and from the glint in his eye he knew it.

'Once we get to Kowloon, we're looking for a combination of things within a short distance of each other,' he said quietly. 'A luxury hotel. A less than savoury hotel. And caffeine.'

'And then what?'

'And then we go to work.'

He found what he was looking for within five minutes of exiting the train station. Coffee stop at the fast-food place first, while Damon fiddled with his phone and largely ignored her. Normal behaviour for this part of the world, Ruby noted. Around here, mobile phones and miniature computers ruled supreme.

'All set?' he said, in less time than it took her to take two cautious sips of her surprisingly decent coffee. 'Bring it with you,' he said of her coffee. 'We're going to need a room.'

Not a room at the five-star hotel, however. No, Damon escorted her to a high rise nearby that boasted a bar on the ground floor, a hotel on the next, and several different categories of businesses after that, a brothel being one of them, given the nature of the girls lounging idly in the bar.

'One room, one night, a window facing the street, no company, no room service and no questions,' murmured Damon and handed a wad of Hong Kong dollars to the bruiser manning the reception desk.

'You got it,' said the bruiser and gave Damon a hotel swipe card and nodded towards the stairs.

'And another innkeepers' law bites the dust,' she murmured as they started up the stairs. Damon glanced at her, his gaze faintly mocking.

'Time to put the lawyer away, Ruby.'

'You don't say,' she countered grimly and stepped over a pile of what looked like discarded clothing on the stairs. 'Please tell me we're not staying here the night.'

'We're not staying here the night.'

Good news, because room 203 was charmless, airless and decidedly unclean. Ruby stood in the centre of the room sipping her suddenly mighty fine coffee and watched as Damon slung his backpack off his shoulder and withdrew a small laptop from within it. He set it on the bedside table beside the window and set its innards whirring.

'Pull up a chair,' he said, but Ruby didn't feel like sitting.

'Mind if I pace instead?'

'No pacing allowed,' he said. 'Sit.'

So she pulled up a chair and sat and stared at the computer screen, her heart beating too fast for comfort, and her eyes noticing the speed with which Damon's big hands flew over the keyboard. Logging into the internet somehow, without logging in.

'How do you know where to—? Oh, boy,' she whispered as all of a sudden they were somewhere within FBI-land and screen after screen of information was opening up in new windows, with Damon chasing them down, one by one, and entering string after string of code.

'Easy, Ruby,' he whispered, his eyes on the screen in front of him, his focus absolute. 'Relax.'

She wanted to ask him what he was doing and how he was doing it but she didn't have the breath for it.

'There's a rhythm to hacking, to navigating the information flow and pitting your wits against a security system built by another,' he said softly. 'For some, reaching their destination without detection is thrill enough. Others, they only want to destroy. For some of us, the destination is just a portal to a bigger game and it's a game based on power and knowledge and balance on the grandest of scales. That's my game, and it's more dangerous than you know. I need your silence on the issue, Ruby.'

'Believe me, you have it.'

'Not yet I don't.'

A blur of information. So fast; all of it too fast for comprehension. A download option.

Damon's hands falling away from the computer keys.

Ruby's breath coming rapid and strained, adrenalin coursing fiercely through her body as she stared at the little arrow on the screen that Damon had placed atop the download link.

'Your turn.'

Damon's voice low and husky as he transferred that intense focus to her face.

'It's the FBI's file on your father.'

Time slowed down to crawling as Ruby stared first at Damon and then at the screen. 'I, ah—I'm not—sure. Oh, *hell*,' she whispered, because she wanted that information and Damon had made it so easy for her to just reach out and take it.

'Or we leave the information where it is, I tell my handler I've blown my cover with you and we see how that unfolds.'

'No.' Not with her father's file sitting there just begging to be taken. 'My father's whereabouts in return for my silence. I get it, Damon. And I agree to your terms.' Her hand moved. The download began. Her choice, and she wore that knowledge like a stain.

'Guess I'm not as principled as I thought,' she said faintly.

'Who is?' muttered Damon, his focus back on the screen.

The file took an agonisingly slow ten seconds to download, and then Damon was back at the keyboard, fingers flying.

'You're getting out of the FBI pages now, right?' she said.

'Right.'

And straight into the British intelligence system, and Ruby's stomach lurched and her pulse rate soared all over again. 'Hell of a ride,' she said but he was gone again, skimming through supposedly secure cyberspace with an ease that made her gasp.

Another download link, but no agony of hesitation this time for Ruby. They were done and gone, with a swiftness she found hard to comprehend. All the way out this time. Two files stored on a USB the size of a thumbnail. Laptop off and opened up with a tiny screwdriver. One of the motherboard components replaced. Fifteen minutes from start to finish, and they were

walking back down those shabby hotel stairs and hand-
ing the door card over to Reception.

'Any decent cheap *yum cha* restaurants around here?'
he asked the man, and got directions and nodded, while
Ruby sweated and smiled and tried to resist the urge to
flee.

'Please tell me we're not going back there,' she said
when they were two shopfronts away and Ruby was
walking faster than she'd ever walked before, every
nerve ending buzzing and every neon sign a thousand
times brighter than it had been fifteen minutes ago. She
ran her hands up and down her arms, mildly surprised
she didn't give off sparks. 'We're not, right?'

'Right.'

Damon's pace had quickened too. Ruby was practically skipping. 'So…where *are* we going?'

'*Yum cha?*'

'Are you serious?' He couldn't possibly be serious.
He was.

'Not *yum cha*,' she said. 'I wouldn't be able to sit
still. I'm feeling…'

'Wired.'

'Exactly.'

'It'll pass.'

'Yes, but *when*?'

'Soon,' he said with a kick to his mouth that warned
her she was amusing him.

'Look!' She pointed to a shopfront across the road.
'Chinese massage. They're very relaxing. We could
have one of those.'

'It's a brothel, Ruby.'

'Oh.' Ruby took a closer look. 'Brothel. Good pickup. Maybe I just need to go back to the apartment and go for a swim. Soothing. Tactile. Potential to expend energy. Plenty of energy happening here at the moment, Damon. Possibly a little too much.'

'Breathe, Ruby.'

'I am. It's not helping. I really need to get rid of some of this energy *now*. You are so hot when you're hacking, by the way. Who knew?'

'The things I do for you,' he murmured, and swung her into an alleyway and pinned her against the wall, his mouth mere millimetres from her own. 'Settle down, Ruby.'

'Or what?' she whispered, just before she snaked her hand around his neck and drew him down for a hot, open exploration of his mouth. Plenty of energy happening between them at the moment. Enough tactile stimulation to make her forget her own name.

Damon groaned and the kiss turned incendiary. Energy released only now the concern was that they'd both go up in flames.

'You'll get us arrested,' he murmured, with a nip for her mouth as he wrapped his hand around her wrist, dragged it away from his neck and set them walking again. 'Time to get you home, Ruby. Now.'

'Authority has always *really* worked for me,' she said breathlessly and meant every word. 'Seriously, who doesn't love a man who knows how to take charge? An expert in his chosen field. How did you get into this field, by the way? I'm assuming it wasn't part of any school study curriculum.'

'It was something of a calling.'

'Ah. Junior hacker, were you?'

'Not now, Ruby.'

'I'm thinking school database, assessment marks in need of rearranging…'

'I was doing them a *service*. Pointing out the holes in the system.'

'Of course you were. How old were you at the time? Fourteen? Fifteen?'

'Twelve.'

'What a brat.' Two more steps and Ruby stopped dead. 'Damon, I think I've found a solution to the energy crisis. See that clothes shop on the other side of the road? It's open.'

'I see it,' he said. 'But isn't it a little Hello Kitty for you?'

'You mean it's a shop for teens? I can do teen wear.' Ruby nodded vigorously. 'I'm a felon. I can do anything.'

'Technically, you're only an accessory.'

'Wrong. The skills were yours but I think you'll find I'm a first-degree principal, which is what you intended all along. You had to draw me in. Make me part of it so that I wouldn't talk about it. Which I won't. Ever. When do I get the files?'

'You don't. You get to read through them when you're ready, take from them what you can and then I destroy them.'

'I'm ready,' she said, and the glance he cut her told her more plainly than words his thoughts on her readiness for anything.

'No, really. I am. I am fully aware that these are not the sort of files you want to have hanging around. I should look at them soon.'

'When you're ready,' he said, quietly inflexible. 'You're not ready.'

'It's this heady life of crime. It's frying my brain.'

'It'll pass.'

'The pertinent question still being *when*?'

'Soon.'

'You have no idea how *alive* I feel at the moment,' she said. 'Do you feel alive too?'

'Yes.' With more than a hint of amusement about him.

'Does it ever get old for you? The ha—your work?'

'No,' he said and finally his smile came wide and unguarded. 'No, this never gets old.'

They made it back to Ruby's apartment eventually. Damon insisting they only take a short train hop and then a taxi the rest of the way home. Perhaps he wanted to make sure no one was following them and a tail was easier to spot in a taxi, but Ruby didn't ask and Damon didn't say. She asked him if he wanted a drink once they reached the kitchen—manners, Ruby—and when he said yes she asked what would he like and he said Scotch if she had it.

'Good choice,' she murmured and poured one for herself too, before setting a bowl of peanuts on the counter, and eyeing the backpack he'd placed on the stool next to him with a mixture of apprehension and longing.

'I may not be ready, Damon, but there's no way in hell I'm going to settle until I know what those files say about my father,' she told him, and he nodded and unzipped the pack and pulled out the computer and set it up to go before turning the computer around to face Ruby.

'Have at it.'

'Okay, Ruby,' she said more to herself than anyone else. 'You can do this.'

And opened the first file.

Fifteen minutes later she was none the wiser as to where her father was or what had happened to him.

'The bank's investigation team got called off by the FBI. The Feds referred it to the British, and as far as British Intelligence is concerned they're not pursuing it at all. And what the hell is an A48?'

'Road map co-ordinates?' Damon offered. 'The AK 47's second cousin? A road in Britain?'

'Is it really?'

'I think so.'

'Maybe he's there,' she said glumly and handed him the computer. 'Read them or delete them. There's precious little there that I didn't already know.'

'We can search again.'

'No,' said Ruby emphatically. 'I don't think I could stand it. I did what you asked of me, Damon, and I don't regret it but I certainly don't ever want to do it again. I'm a felon but I'm free. I haven't found my father but at least no one's found him dead. That's *good* news. I'm willing to embrace the no-news-is-good-news policy today. As for you and me...' Ruby's whiskey-coloured eyes reflected a guardedness he'd never seen in them before. 'I overheard something I shouldn't have about you, Damon, and I paid the price and now we're square. Aren't we?'

'Yes.' They were square.

'And as much as I've enjoyed getting to know you, the work you do scares me, Damon, and the life you lead you lead alone. I will think of you with pleasure and I will think of you with hunger but it's time for you to leave.'

'Hunger?' he queried softly.

'Don't dwell on it,' she told him wryly. 'Hunger's manageable. You're not.'

He knew it. 'Mind if I get changed? My suit's in your bathroom.'

'Chameleon.' But she said it with a smile. 'Go. Get changed. Break my heart all over again when you come back out wearing a Savile Row suit and a gotta-be-going smile. I'm a felon. Tough. Worldly. Brave. I can handle it.'

She was making it easy for him again. Easy for him to do what he knew he should do. Walk away.

Just him and a hatful of regrets.

'I'm heading to Australia in three days' time,' he said.

'Enjoy.' She didn't know why he was telling her this and it showed. Time to enlighten her.

'Come with me.'

'Pardon?'

'Come with me.' Nothing but impulsiveness on his part and astonishment on hers. 'I have a house on the beach and a few weeks free. You could stay there while you figure out what it is you want to do next. We could just...swim.' Or sink.

Probably the latter.

Ruby eyed him narrowly. 'You just want to keep an

eye on me. Make sure I don't go spilling your secrets where I shouldn't. You're obsessing about me knowing what it is you do.'

'Only a little.' Only a lot.

'Well, stop it or you'll go blind,' she told him heatedly. 'You. Can. Trust. Me. Which is more than I can say for you.'

He took a step towards her and watched her scramble off her barstool fast and put out a hand as if to ward him off. 'Damon,' she began warningly. 'We are so close to finishing this. Don't mess with the plan.'

'There's a plan?' Damon reached out and touched her hair, wove silken strands of it around his fingertips, and finally, as if she would break beneath his touch, set his lips to the edge of her mouth. 'Come with me,' he whispered. 'Forget the plan.'

'You scare me, Damon.' But she kissed him as if she was starving for him and he kissed her and knew he was insatiable for her in return.

'I'll try not to.'

'And you'll fool me into thinking that you care.'

'Maybe I do,' he whispered and slid his hands to her buttocks and picked her up, and she wrapped her legs around him and made him groan. 'Come with me.'

Fifteen minutes later, as she climaxed round him for the second time, he said, 'Ruby, *please*.'

And she said, 'Yes.'

CHAPTER EIGHT

DAMON tried to slip back into his father's apartment un-noticed. No chance of that with two older sisters sitting in wait for him as they watched whatever they were watching on the TV. That was the problem with sisters who'd done double duty as substitute mothers over the years—they saw everything. Especially those things he didn't want them to see.

Poppy spotted him first as Lena was sitting with her back to the door, but Lena turned around and called him over and offered him a glass of wine.

No point trying to avoid them for they'd only follow him, so he anteed up and he sat his butt down.

Lena would take point, she always did, but only a fool would discount the effectiveness of Poppy when it came to stripping him bare.

Lena waited until he had his wineglass in hand and his thoughts in order before starting in on him, which meant she was either very tired or going soft.

'So,' she said, and fixed him with the mother stare. 'You and Ruby Maguire?'

'So?' he said in turn. 'Neither of us are in another relationship. Why shouldn't we?'

'You've known her for all of *two days*.'

'Five.'

'Does she know what you do?' asked Lena caustically.

'Well, she does *now*,' he replied in kind. 'Which part of *later* did you not understand?'

'Which part of stop being so bloody secretive do *you* not understand?'

'It's just habit.'

'No, it's a convenient way of keeping people at a distance, is what it is. Your whole way of life is designed to keep people away. Even family. Even me. I won't have it.'

'I'm getting that.'

And all of a sudden Lena looked close to tears.

'We failed you, didn't we?' she murmured. 'Jared and Poppy, and me. We let you pull away, and stay away, for far too long and now you can hardly find your way home.'

'I'm home,' he said desperately. 'I'm right here.'

But she shook her head and the smile she sent him was strained. 'No more lies, Damon. Not when it comes to Jared and whatever you might find out about him. Promise me.'

He did not want to promise that. 'Lena, I—'

'Promise.'

'All right.' He shook his head. 'All right, I promise. Satisfied?'

'Not quite,' she said as if moving on to the next insurmountable object. 'What happened with Ruby?'

'Nothing much.' Give or take a momentous decision or two.

'Can you trust her?'

'Put it this way, if I can't, I'm f—'

'Got it,' said Poppy primly and he and Lena shared a smile of amusement.

'Good,' he said blandly and set his wine down on the coffee table. 'Is that it for the interrogation?'

'Not quite,' said Poppy and Damon sighed. Poppy's turn.

'How much do you like her, Damon? Maybe this unanticipated openness with Ruby can be a good thing. Room—if you want it—for a relationship to grow.'

'No,' he said. 'What would I do with a relationship? Besides destroy it. Drag Ruby around the world with me? Pull her into the life? No.' He stared broodingly at his wineglass. 'Ruby started out as a distraction, nothing more. Now she's even more of a distraction, but as for anything permanent? No.'

'That's three nos in a row,' murmured Lena. 'That's a lot of nos.'

'She's coming to the beach house with me,' he offered reluctantly. No point trying to hide it. They'd find out soon enough.

'That's interesting,' said Lena. 'Has Damon ever taken a woman to the beach house to your knowledge, Poppy?'

'No.'

'No. That's two more nos, just in case anyone's counting.'

'I have to be able to trust her,' he said grimly.

'So how does that work?' asked Lena. 'You're just going to keep her there until you do? Could take a lifetime, Damon. Knowing you.'

'I think it's a good idea,' said Poppy. 'Give them more

time to adjust to Ruby knowing that little bit more about Damon than she should. Besides, the trust will come. I'm sure of it.'

Poppy was a sweetheart and an optimist. Damned if Damon knew how she'd come to be part of this family.

'And maybe we can help. Maybe if we sat down with Ruby over a drink or two and some girl talk we could make it seem more…normal. Nothing to concern her. You never bring your work home. You never let us near it. You're really very noble and protective where that's concerned.'

'I took her hacking with me,' he said curtly.

'You what?' said Poppy incredulously.

'You *idiot*,' said Lena.

And the conversation was mostly downhill from there.

A week and a half later Ruby made her way to Sydney and from there to Ballina near Damon's house on the coast. Her work for Russell was done. She'd left the little cat in the care of her next-door neighbour's six-year-old daughter in exchange for letting her neighbour's parents use her apartment during their two-week holiday stay in Hong Kong. It was an arrangement that seemed to suit everyone, including one tiny standoffish cat.

Nothing to hold her in Hong Kong now and nothing planned except for a week or two of sand, sea and Damon, and she didn't know what to expect from him, other than surprises. She didn't know why she was here except that somewhere between meeting him and agreeing to this, she'd lost her brain.

What kind of woman flew halfway around the world

to visit a man who'd enchanted her and then warned her not to expect anything from him? A man for whom secrets and hacking and blackmail were everyday events? Or at least regular events.

Why had she *ever* said yes to this?

You're in love with him, said a little voice but Ruby rejected the notion outright.

I am not!

Then you're besotted by him, said the little voice, and this much she had to concede.

The sex is very good, yes.

You're going to try and change him. Turn him into a good boy.

Not sure that's possible. Anyway, he's not entirely bad. Espionage is a time-honoured profession. Heroic even.

He's a thief, Ruby.

He works to preserve the power balance between nations. He aims to protect. He was trying to protect *me* from the consequences of knowing too much. That's very honourable.

Silence from the stalls.

Win for Ruby.

But as she stepped through the arrival doors of the small regional airport and spotted Damon and her body melted and her wits turned to water with nothing but a glance from those midnight-blue eyes, the little voice spoke again.

You are so utterly gone on this man. Accepting him for what he is. Defending his less-than-stellar decisions. Not even wanting to tweak him. Put your own life on hold just to be with him. What's that if not love?

It's not *love*. It's just…exploration.

And you're irrational. Ladies and gentlemen of the jury, I rest my case.

But Ruby wasn't listening any more, she was too busy walking towards Damon.

He stood well back from the crowd, with his back to a wall and his hands in the pockets of a pair of calf-length cargos. He looked more tanned than he had been at Christmas. His white T-shirt—like his cargos—had seen better days.

Beach wear, one supposed. Casual and comfortable.

Ruby's wardrobe rarely ran to casual, comfortable beachwear. Tennis garb on Rhode Island was about as casual as she got. Mainly because, without fail, across all the years of her upbringing, she'd never not been on show. At her father's side. As her mother's daughter. Appearances mattered.

She had a feeling that appearances didn't matter much to Damon.

'I like your headband,' he said when he reached her.

Or maybe they did.

'It's very restrained for you,' he said next.

Which was true, because she'd gone for a plain white band to match her uncrushable white travelling shirt and jacket and her equally uncrushable lemon-coloured miniskirt. Sometimes synthetics were the only way to go.

'I like your tie,' she said in return, and his eyes warmed and he leaned down to greet her with a casual kiss, the kind that got bandied about between friends.

'You came,' he said next. 'I wasn't sure you would.'

And suddenly the air between them crackled with everything they *weren't* saying.

'I said I would.'

'Still...' Damon shrugged. 'People change their minds.'

'Have you?' Best to get it over with, if Damon had indeed changed his mind about the wisdom of her visiting him here.

'No,' he said quietly. 'I'm in if you are.'

'I'm here,' she said simply. 'And I'm not here under duress.'

Damon's smile came slow and sweet. 'Welcome to Australia, Ruby. How are you liking it so far?'

'Sydney Harbour's far more beautiful than in its pictures and the vibe so far is   ' she spared a glance for his superbly fitting T-shirt '—relaxed. I may not have packed the right clothes.'

'Lucky for you we have shops. Or you can just borrow some of mine.'

'You mean you have more than one set?' she queried archly.

'I have a few sets at the house. C'mon, let's get you there. From there we'll hit the beach. You'll like the beach.'

Damon's vehicle was some sort of utility four-wheel drive. Unprepossessing. New-car clean. Nothing to write home about.

His beach house, on the other hand, completely enchanted her. Split level, the rooms wrapped around a central Balinese-style pavilion area, and the ceilings soared, and windows were everywhere.

There were guest rooms and games rooms, sitting

rooms and entertainment halls. An open-plan chef's kitchen and a garden that offered lushness and privacy and invited exploration. A narrow path ran from the other side of the outdoor pool, over a smattering of sand dunes, and wound its way down to the beach. The beach stretched for miles on either side, waves crashed ebulliently on the sand, and the ocean beyond the waves stretched clear to the horizon.

Casual, comfortable living didn't *come* any more luxurious than this.

'It's beautiful, Damon,' she said as he set her luggage down and turned towards her.

'It's easy to kick back here,' he said quietly. 'Be as formal or as informal as you like. As elegant or whimsical as you like.' He offered up a tiny smile. 'Just be yourself. This house will hold you; enjoy whatever you bring to it, even. And so will I.'

Now *there* was a welcome to set a heart to fluttering. She'd forgotten just how easily he could charm her when he wanted to. 'You speak as if this place is alive.'

'It is. The minute I walked through its doors I knew I had to own it.'

'Impulsive.'

'Or maybe I just know what I want.'

'Well, there's that too.' And she couldn't fault it.

'If you find any girl stuff here, it's Lena's,' he said. 'She's been staying with me up until a couple of days ago.'

'Got it. Thanks for the heads up,' said Ruby. 'How is Lena?'

'Frail. Not nearly as strong as she wants to be.'

'She didn't strike me as weak, Damon. Even in Hong Kong. Begs the question of what she used to be like.'

'Amazing,' he said simply. 'She was amazing. She sends her regards, by the way, and she left you a basket full of bath stuff and creams for you to use during your stay. It's in your room.'

'I'll have to thank her.'

'There's a housekeeper who comes in a couple of times a week. I had her prepare a bedroom for you.'

'Oh,' said Ruby, and eyed him uncertainly. 'Thank you.'

'Doesn't mean I don't want you in my bed, Ruby. Just that there's a room you can call your own as well. I asked Lena if that was the sort of set-up you might prefer. She said yes.'

Lena said.

Thanks, Lena.

He headed towards a wide wooden bowl and dropped his keys in it and took something else out of it.

'I'm screwing this up, aren't I?' he said and ran a hand through his hair for good measure. 'It's just... I've never brought a woman here before. I wanted to do it right. Lena warned me not to push you into anything you weren't ready for. Apparently I can be a little too persuasive for my own good. I've also been ordered not to wear you out, get you sunburnt, drown you or take you hang-gliding.'

'Oh,' she said faintly. 'Hang-gliding.'

'You'll love it. Seriously.'

'Chances are I *won't*,' she murmured and Damon grinned. 'I'm a guest, Damon. You're meant to be indulging me, not trying to kill me.'

'Yeah, Lena mentioned that too. She also mumbled something about best behaviour, picking up wet towels, keeping regular sleeping hours and not gaming on the computers half the night, and, oh, she said to tell you good luck. Sisters are wonderful, aren't they?'

'I don't know, I don't have any,' she said smoothly. 'Are we done with the household warnings yet? Any locked rooms I must never enter? Broom cupboard I should never open?'

'By all means open the broom cupboard,' he murmured. 'Wouldn't want to deprive you of the joy of household chores.' His smile turned wry and his eyes grew serious. 'It's all right, Ruby. There's nothing here you can stumble over when it comes to my work. I never bring it home and I never let it touch the people around me. That time in Kowloon with you was the exception, not the rule. It won't happen again.'

'Fine by me,' she answered quietly, and turned her attention to her luggage and smiled up at him with a false sunshinery her mother would have been proud of. 'I bought a gift for your household,' she said, and withdrew from her hand luggage the duty-free Scotch and champagne she'd purchased at the airport. 'There's caviar *somewhere* in there too. I seem to have developed a taste for it. That would be your fault.'

Damon smiled and held something out towards her in return. 'For you,' he said.

It was a headband. A cluster of fresh frangipanis twined around a solid frame, only on closer inspection the frangipanis were made of porcelain.

'Oh, yes.' Ruby made no effort to hide her pleasure

as she slipped off her old headband and replaced it with the new. 'That'll work.'

It was then that he kissed her. A meeting of lips that came fleeting at first, and then he returned for more and this time he savoured her.

He did that, she remembered belatedly.

He had a way of sliding into a moment and savouring whatever it might bring.

'Well, hello,' she murmured when their lips parted. And thank God. 'I've been wondering where you were.'

'I was giving you space.'

'Little hint for when we next meet,' she said, and punctuated her remark with the rasp of her tongue across his lower lip. 'Presents are good, presents are wonderful, but as far as space is concerned…I don't need it.'

Ruby smiled and wove her hands through his hair and let him drag her against his hard, rangy body. 'Though I am very aware that I *do* need a shower,' she protested as he slid her jacket from her shoulders. 'I'm straight off the plane.'

'Contrary, Ruby.'

'Well, yes. Surely you hadn't forgotten already?'

He had such busy hands. They slid beneath her skirt, and the next thing she knew he'd leaned back against the low-slung sofa and lifted her up, and her knees were finding purchase on it the better to plaster herself against him.

Damon's thumb slipped between her panties and stroked.

Ruby gasped and he ate it straight from her mouth. She pushed forward and they toppled over the back of the sofa and onto the cushions and it didn't matter any more that she'd wanted to shower, she needed to feel Damon's touch on her skin and his lips caressing hers.

'I dreamed of you,' she told him as he ran his hands over her thighs and positioned her exactly where she wanted to be. 'You were lawless. Bad. And I wanted you even more because of it.'

He took her mouth again and this time his kiss held a hint of savagery in it. 'I have ethics,' he whispered. 'Boundaries. I can even be hospitable when I really put my mind to it. You'll see.'

His questing fingers slipped beneath the boundaries of her panties again and Ruby shuddered with need of less boundaries and more contact. He dipped a long finger inside her and Ruby gasped her pleasure and she held his hand in place and closed her eyes the better to concentrate on his touch.

'I dreamed of you, Damon. Lord, how I dreamed of you.'

'I dreamed of you too,' he murmured as she dealt with the buttons and the zip at his waist and took him in hand.

'What was I doing?' she whispered as she slid her panties aside and positioned him for entry.

'This.' His voice guttural as he surged up inside her, his hands at her waist, vicelike as he held her in place. He slowly withdrew, and then rocked up into her again. 'You were doing this.'

They swam in the surf much later in the day, and then showered together and she used the bubbles Lena had left for her on him, and after that he sat her down at the kitchen counter in her underwear and fed her a toasted BLT sandwich on sourdough with mayonnaise.

He was handy in the kitchen—not fussy about what he put together but competent nonetheless. He put things away when he was done with them. He knew where things lived.

Definitely a point of difference between Damon and the rest of the men in her life. Missing fathers and step-fathers and the like. Staff inhabited kitchens in their world—not them.

'Have you ever surfed before?' he asked her later that afternoon as they sat on the sand and watched the waves come crashing in.

'I've skied before,' she said lazily. 'I have very fond memories of a winter in Switzerland where I was a fearless snowboard queen of the mountain.'

'I'm very impressed,' he said. 'Then what happened?'

'Then we went to live in Bahrain.' A fond sigh escaped her. 'I learned to drive in Bahrain.'

'Please don't tell me you learned to drive in a racing car unless you want to see me weeping with envy.'

'Of course I didn't.' She stood up, brushed sand from her rear. 'I learned to drive in a Hummer in the desert. My instructor's name was Carl. Carl set my girlish heart aflutter with his commando impersonation but, alas, he wasn't much of one for reckless endangerment. Even in a Hummer.'

'Surfing could be a little sedate for you,' said Damon in reply. 'If the wind picks up this afternoon we'll break out the kiteboards.'

* * *

Surfing was not sedate. Nor was the kitesurfing they attempted later that afternoon. The hang-gliding they did the following day didn't qualify as sedate either. There was more swimming. More love-making. And for Ruby, plenty of naps and lazing about in between the next action-man adventure.

Damon didn't nap. Not ever. He slept well through the night—when they slept—and needed no rest whatsoever during the day.

He wasn't one for television unless it was as background to whatever else he happened to be doing at the time. He cooked. He charmed. He rarely sat still. Even when sitting in his computer room he did ten things at once and all of them at warp speed.

When he ate, he liked to do it standing at counters. He could do a restaurant meal—he'd managed it in Hong Kong and he managed it again when they went into Byron Bay for dinner one night—but it wasn't his preference.

If there was a pool nearby he'd be in it. A pool table in the room and he'd be at it. The ocean and the toys he took to it could hold him for hours. Making love could also garner his undivided and sustained attention.

For now.

A suspicion formed in Ruby's mind about the type of kid he'd been, based on the man he'd become. How hard it must have been to educate a boy who couldn't sit still and whose mind worked that much faster than anyone else's. How hacking would have been such a natural fit for him given he'd had to sit at a computer and cut a snail's pace through all the schoolwork anyway.

Damon's lifestyle choices made far more sense to her now. His work kept him focused, delivered up the adrenalin he craved and kept him on the move. New places, new people, a world's worth of distraction— chances were he needed all those things in order to be content, and always would.

Not a man to plan a settled, predictable life around, but then, he'd never once suggested doing so.

'You're hyperactive, aren't you?' she asked him one night as he put together a late-night fruit platter that neither of them wanted, and tried—with limited success—to watch a movie with her.

Damon shot her a wary glance before deciding that the platter needed some biscuits.

'That's one label,' he offered up finally. 'There have been others.'

'Like what?' And when he didn't reply, 'Let me guess. Intellectually gifted, easily bored and distracted, physically reckless. How am I doing so far?'

'You're very astute.'

'ADD?'

He wouldn't look at her. Had to dump a load of mango peelings down the garbage disposal instead.

She took that as a yes, and gave up on ever getting to the end of the movie. Time to leave the sumptuously comfy lounge and take her bare feet and her stripey boy-leg panties and vest over to the kitchen counter instead. His side of the counter, mind. They were way past having a bench in between them.

Mango slices had rapidly become a favourite snack of Ruby's. She selected one, ate it, and smiled when a freshly wet hand cloth landed with a splat on the bench beside her. 'Thank you.'

She'd need that later. It wouldn't do to have sticky hands once she started running them all over Damon's irresistible flesh.

'So how do you feel about flying to Sydney tomorrow for a couple of days' exploration?' she said next. Change of subject, after a fashion. No change of craving for this man detected. 'I hear there's a bridge there to climb. The internet tells me there's a racetrack on offer too. Maybe we can rustle up a car or two and a pair of willing instructors to ride shotgun and have ourselves a little wager on the outcome? I can't let all that experience on Bahrain's international circuit go to waste. Because I did get there eventually. I may not have mentioned that earlier. Memories of Carl weeping inconsolably over his Hummer's split gearbox casing may have distracted me.'

'You destroyed a man's gearbox?'

'Well, not on *purpose*. Good thing I was wearing my buzzy bee headband at the time, otherwise he may have taken one look at me and seen red.' She picked up another mango slice and offered it to him. 'Mango?'

'You don't have to scatter your conversation for me, Ruby. Or give me a hundred and one conversation threads to choose from. I can follow a one-track conversation just fine,' he said quietly. 'Labels and all. And, yes. Doctors diagnosed me ADHD as a kid.'

Ruby frowned. 'Were you medicated?'

'There was medication,' he said. 'Wasn't easy, getting me to take it.'

'Rebellious.'

'I didn't need it. I can control it. I can be still. You don't need to indulge me by offering up adventure trips to Sydney whenever you think I'm getting bored.'

He sounded irritated and looked defensive. Apparently this was contagious.

'Is indulging you such a sin?' she argued mildly. 'And here I thought it was part of being a good house guest. Sometimes I indulge you, sometimes you indulge me. And sometimes we leave each other alone. Given that you've been indulging my every whim for the past few days I figured it might be time to ante up.'

Ruby ate the mango piece, seeing as Damon's mouth was set in a tightly closed line. She wiped her sticky fingers down his shirtfront and pushed him aside so she could get to the tap and rinse her hands.

'I wasn't *judging* you, Damon. I'm trying to *understand* you, and every time I think I come close you put up another wall.' She rinsed her hands and shook the excess water off them with a decidedly annoyed flick, before turning around and running smack bang into a wall of simmering manhood. She poked a pointy finger into Damon's well-exercised chest. 'It's very irritating.'

'Is that so?' he said silkily.

'Yes.' Another poke for the immovable object. 'And stop trying to distract me with sex.'

'I thought you liked the sex.'

She loved the sex. She was fast approaching the conclusion that fighting with Damon and then making up with him could well lead to incandescently memorable sex. 'That is not the point.' Another jab, only this time he caught her hand and flattened it against his chest.

'What is it we're doing here, Damon? Getting to

know each other? Indulging in a no-strings-attached, short-term affair where getting to know each other better is not a requirement? Are you trying to decide whether you can trust me to keep your secrets? What? Because I can't play this game if I don't know the rules.'

'There is no game,' he said quietly and redirected her hand to his heart. 'No rules either. Just an automatic defence against a criticism I've worn my entire life.'

He could break her heart too, whenever he wanted to. Distract her so that she never pushed too hard when it came to the question uppermost on her mind. The 'where are we going with this' question. The 'what the hell am I still doing here when you won't even let me know the simplest things about you' question.

'I don't have *all* the symptoms of ADHD,' he said gruffly. 'I can focus when I want to. I think before doing. I can be still.'

'Really?'

'I can.'

'But you don't need to be, do you? You've organised your life so you don't have to be still, and that's fine too. Plenty of other people organise their lives that way too. I've spent my entire life surrounded by gifted, driven, workaholic risk-takers who wouldn't know how to rest or be still if their lives depended on it. Your father's one of them. My father was another. Stepfather number three too, although he enjoys coming home. That's what my mother does—she makes him enjoy coming home.'

'There are women who still do that?' He looked intrigued.

'Yes,' she said pleasantly. 'I'm not one of them. I want a career.'

'Couldn't you do both?' he murmured silkily.

'Could you?' she asked in kind. 'Would you?'

'We're circling the relationship question again, aren't we?'

'Yes.'

'Not sure I have that much to offer you, Ruby.'

Not what Ruby wanted to hear. 'I thought you might say that. This house, is it yours free and clear?'

'Yes.'

'Any others?'

'A downtown apartment in Massachusetts.'

'Nice. Any other dependants I don't know about? Ex-wives? Children? Goldfish?'

She'd won from him a tiny smile. 'No.'

'So apart from your work—which you never bring home—you're actually pleasantly unencumbered.'

'Are you judging my suitability as a *spouse*?'

'Yes. You seem to think you have little to offer in that department. I'm presenting an alternate view. Where were we? Ah, yes. Your family seems sane enough—the ones I've met. I'm going to give them a tick.'

'You just don't know them well enough yet.'

'How many times a week would you want to have sex?'

Damon blinked. Then he smiled. 'A lot. Surely that's a strike *against*,' he murmured silkily.

'Depends on the woman,' she offered in counter. 'The timing. The mood. I'm going to go out on a limb here and vouch for your expertise. How many times a week would you cook?'

'Depends where we were.'

'Good answer,' she said with a nod. 'Any health is-sues? Genetic peculiarities? Apart from the ADHD of course. That one's already noted.'

'No.'

'So far, so good, wouldn't you say?' she said and speared him with a glance. 'Alas, there is still your in-ability to let anyone ever get close to you to consider. That one's proving problematic.'

'Do tell.'

Oh, she intended to. But not right yet.

'You know it was my father who taught me how to judge people,' she said lightly. 'He made an art form out of figuring out what makes people tick. Discovering their weaknesses, testing their strengths. His verdict would be that you undervalue yourself, by the way. He'd wonder what the hell happened to make you so insecure about being you. Then he'd play you to his advantage, but that's a whole other story that I really don't want to get into right now. Suffice to say that he taught me well and that I know a little something about reading people. Judging them. Playing them, even, but that's a whole other story that we probably don't need to dwell on either.'

'Maybe later,' he said with a hint of his old smooth-ness.

'Maybe never,' she countered and his grin came quick and free.

'What is it you're trying to say to me, Ruby?'

'What I'm *trying* to say is that I may be judging you, Damon, but I do not find you lacking. You have many fine qualities. You have plenty to offer. What I'd also like to get on record is that I don't need any lavish promises from you. I don't necessarily need a spouse. But if you *are* interested in exploring some kind of continuing relationship with me I do have one demand.'

'You'd make a wonderful divorce lawyer,' he murmured. 'What is it?'

'I want you to let down your defences and let me see you. The real you. No obfuscation. No distractions. No best behaviour. Just you.'

He didn't seem to know how to take her words. What to do with them or say in return. Wary man. Heartbreakingly vulnerable man underneath all the layers.

'So… I'm about to get naked and wet in that gorgeous pool over there,' she said and sidestepped him neatly. 'Care to join me?'

Ruby didn't wait for Damon's reply, just headed poolside and started shedding clothes. She glanced back over her shoulder at him.

'You did say that if I ever wanted to win an argument with you all I had to do was get naked, right?'

'Right.'

Damon hardly recognised his own voice, it cracked and wavered like a pubescent boy's.

'You are so *hot* when you're being cautious,' she said with a siren's smile. 'Gives you a totally unfair advantage.'

'Says the naked woman standing in water up to her waist.'

'Just so,' she said archly. 'Why is your shirt still on?'

'Beats me.' He dragged it up and over his head. Let it drop to the ground.

'Better,' she murmured appreciatively. 'Shirtless and brooding is a good look for you. Almost as good as naked and lost in the moment. Want to come and lose yourself in the moment with me, Damon?' No teasing in her now, just a longing directed straight at him.

'I just did,' he said and went to join her.

CHAPTER NINE

HEADING Sydneyside suited Damon. He and Ruby could—and did—play hard here. They had a suite overlooking Circular Quay but they didn't spend much time there. Out and about was Ruby's preferred state of being while in Sydney and, for all that Damon often accompanied her, she had no problem heading one way and waving Damon in the other direction if their interests diverged.

She had a confidence he envied. She knew how to be herself, and it was a contrary and fascinating self indeed. *Never* sloppy in appearance. Analytical when it came to the behaviours of others. He could see her as a lawyer. She had the shrewdness.

And the capacity to argue either way.

'I mentioned you to my handler,' he said over breakfast on their third morning in Sydney. They were down at the Quay, sitting in a sidewalk café, with the sun shining brightly and another day of exploration in front of them, give or take a job interview for Ruby and a work appointment for him.

'You what?' said Ruby.

'I figured it was time I told him I wanted to see a bit more of you.'

'Much as I am bowled over by such a hugely romantic gesture, couldn't you have told me first?'

'I need to get back to work soon and I need to know how careful I'm going to have to be. I asked him if anyone had you under surveillance on account of your father and the chances that he might get in contact with you.'

'And what was the answer?'

'He said no. According to his sources—and they're extensive—you've never been under surveillance. Not even in the days following your father's disappearance.'

'Maybe they're understaffed,' she muttered sourly.

'Seems unlikely. He asked me if I wanted him to do some more digging about your father. I said I'd take care of it.'

'You already have.'

'I thought I might take another look. See if there's something I missed.'

'Like what?'

'I don't know yet.' But he was beginning to have his suspicions. 'Could your father have worked in intelligence?'

Ruby's surprise was instantaneous. 'Where did *that* come from?'

'The bank handed over an eight-hundred-and-seventy-two-million-dollar recovery investigation to the Feds, the Feds handballed it to British Intelligence and the British backed off. Maybe your father belongs to someone else. You've said more than once that he was a master at reading and manipulating people. A man who kept secrets. It'd fit.'

Ruby frowned and lifted her sunglasses to the top

of her head. The better to see him or the better for him to see her. Wordlessly demanding a more secure connection between them and getting it too. She was full of tricks like that.

'As far as I know, my father only ever worked in finance,' she said cautiously.

'Would your mother know if he'd ever been involved elsewhere?'

'I doubt it.'

'Might have been why she bailed.'

'No, that would be because of the infidelity and my father never being where he said he was going to be, or doing what he promised to do,' countered Ruby dryly.

'Must've been some childhood.'

'My father did his best to be there for me,' she said. 'Usually he succeeded. But not always. Enough, Damon. You're barking up the wrong tree. My father was a merchant banker not a spy.' She dropped a kiss on his cheek and made to leave his company for an appointment with the senior partner of an Australian-based law firm. 'I need to get to this appointment. I'll tell you about my woefully overprivileged upbringing another time.'

She kissed his other cheek and drew back to stare at him searchingly before offering up another kiss, this time for his lips. 'Be good. Don't dig. Not on my behalf. I have enough trouble accepting that you dig on behalf of other people.'

He accepted the kiss she placed on his other cheek with a faint smile.

'What happens if they offer you a job?'

'There is no job. I'm just fishing and so are they.'

Damon watched her walk away, admiring the sway of her hips and the curve of her slender calves. 'Let me see you. The real you,' she'd said to him only three days ago. Today she'd told him to be good and not dig. As far as he was concerned that was a bit like telling a shark not to swim.

Ruby would have a job offer within the hour, he predicted.

He'd have more information on her father within the hour too.

And then they would look at each other again and see what came of that.

Damon found another coffee shop and this one had everything he needed. He checked in with the home office, a routine ping and nothing more.

A different café next and another easy public access point and this time Damon turned his efforts to discovering somewhat more about Ruby's father and the missing millions. FBI records turned up a referral of the case over to the British Intelligence Service. Their records turned up nothing but dross.

On a hunch, he wormed his way into yet another database. Deeper and deeper still, as his coffee sat untouched on the table beside him, the painted wall at his back giving him all the privacy he needed. His senses stayed with the coffee crowd but he gave his mind over to the language in his head, and the pathways opening up for him on screen, no telling where they would lead.

The lure of the unknown, a siren song he'd never been able to resist. A failing, some would say, but he'd never been any different and if indeed it was a flaw, he'd done his damnedest to turn it into a useful one.

Two minutes in and no fixed destination in mind, just a name and a suspicion. A database to search through and eventually a hit. A record of employment, collated not by employer but by counterparts with a need to know. He sipped at his coffee as he waited for the download. Time enough to read it later.

This lot had a reputation for knowing when their security had been compromised. They wouldn't know who, and they wouldn't know what he'd been after once he'd had his way with the memory interface, but still…

Time to go.

He gave the waitress a smile, left a tip on the table…

He had an uneasy feeling about this one. A notion that he should have left this particular stone unturned, and it mixed with the rush of the run and made him want to lengthen his stride in the way of a man in a hurry.

Easy now, no problem here.

Just a little light reading for later on.

Ruby was already back at the suite when Damon returned just on lunchtime, several forms of transport behind him, his computer sporting some brand-new motherboard components and his reading up-to-date.

Fascinating reading. King hit on his maiden run. Knowledge was power and power was useful. Provided you knew how to wield it.

Damon far preferred leaving the wielding part of the process to others.

Problem: Harry Maguire had been a key asset for

the British Intelligence Service when it came to monitoring—and occasionally enabling—money laundering throughout South-East Asia. Why British and not American? No idea. Maybe they'd simply been the ones to get to him first. Regardless, he'd been on the payroll for over thirty years.

Thirty years. Before Ruby. During Ruby. And he'd never said a word.

Next problem: Harry had been monitoring a sensitive money-laundering deal when he'd disappeared. A deal the British had not wanted to see go through. General consensus had it that Harry was dead but no corpse had been forthcoming so nobody knew for sure.

Damon's immediate problem: what to tell Ruby?

Right now he was leaning heavily towards telling her nothing.

Ruby smiled when she saw him and indicated an already open bottle of champagne on the kitchenette counter.

'You got the job,' he said.

'I was offered the job.'

'Did you *take* the job?'

'I'm letting them know.'

'Where's it based?'

'Hong Kong.'

'Handy.'

'Not for someone who's looking to start afresh. My father cast a long shadow in Hong Kong, Damon, and not just because people think him a thief. I'm tired of tripping over it.'

Damon said nothing.

'I also wouldn't have access to the resources and

community a main office would offer,' she continued thoughtfully. 'Mentoring. A cohort to learn from, and with. They want me to fly solo in Hong Kong. I could do that for myself.'

'You could access the company's resources online,' he said mildly. 'Computer conferencing to take care of the mentoring and working together business.'

Ruby's eyes narrowed thoughtfully.

'Not that I'm trying to influence you. But it could be done. Leaving you with a certain autonomy when it comes to running things your way.'

'Why, Damon West. Are you calling me a dictator?'

'Course not,' he said with a shake of his head as he crossed to the counter and filled the champagne flute she'd left there for him.

'Liar.'

Damon grinned and tilted his glass her way. 'Here's to choices and what we make of them. Congratulations on being offered the job, whether you take it or not.'

'Thank you,' she said graciously and held out her glass for a refill. 'Don't mind me, I'm still debating the offer. I'll be debating the offer for days and your power to distract me will be fully tested. What did you get up to this morning in my absence?'

'Nothing much. Bit of sightseeing,' he said offhand.

'Ah.'

Ruby didn't ask for details. And Damon didn't say.

Damon took Ruby's preoccupation with career planning as a signal to do a little career expansion of his own. He acquired a contract to design a network security system for a corporate customer. Work that he could do from the beach house and make a start on straight away if Ruby didn't mind.

Ruby didn't mind. She'd decided to face the complexities of her burgeoning relationship with Damon on a day-by-day basis. No planning required. No stressing about her and Damon's future allowed.

Besides, the reality of Damon's work process was highly entertaining.

Damon worked in a room full of computers with half a dozen programs running at once, and he did it in ten-minute bursts while wearing board shorts and a tan.

Not exactly office-trained was Damon.

In the absence of a whole lot else to do, Ruby set her sights on conquering kitesurfing. Her stomach muscles would thank her once they'd stopped protesting, and Damon's work pattern meant that every fifteen minutes or so she could hand the rig over to him and take a break.

At which point her stomach muscles would thank her on the spot.

'Lunch time,' he said as he came down to meet her at water's edge for the umpteenth time that morning. 'And we have visitors.'

'Who?'

'Lena and Trig.'

'Trig for trigonometry?' she said as she unbuckled the harness, more than happy to be done with it for the day.

'Trig for trigger-happy,' he said, and unclipped the kite lines and gave her a breezy grin.

'Oh, that's comforting,' she murmured. 'Friend of yours?'

'Friend of Jared and Lena's, mainly. We grew up next door to each other. Jared and Trig joined the service together. Lena joined up a year later. Longest year of Lena's life,' said Damon. 'Mine and Poppy's too.'

'So has Trig heard from Jared?'

'No, but he's got a lead on where he might be.' They started up the beach, Damon loaded down with gear and Ruby's aching muscles happy to let him carry the lot.

'He's come to you for help?'

'Yeah, but not the kind of help you're thinking. Trig wants to depart on a little fact-finding mission. Lena's determined to go with him.'

'That doesn't sound like a particularly smart idea.'

'Can I quote you on that?'

'Only if you want me to wear Lena's everlasting animosity.'

'Point taken. I'll keep you in reserve, counsellor.' And then they were at the house pavilion and it was smiles and introductions and greetings, with Ruby acutely aware of her tangled hair and the salt on her skin.

Damon and Trig moved over towards the garden tap to rinse off the kite-surfing rig.

Ruby turned to Lena and thanked her kindly for the welcome-to-the-beach-house lotions and potions and then slid on into a polished how-do-you-do and a lovely-to-see-you.

'You're looking well,' said Ruby, a substantial exaggeration given Lena's extreme slenderness, but no woman needed reminding that she'd looked better yesterday. 'I, on the other hand, look like a hoyden. Give me five minutes to shower and change and I'll be back.'

'Take ten,' said Lena with a smile. 'The boys'll talk kite-board rigs for at least that long.'

'Leaving you to do what? Entertain yourself?'

'Leaving me to mock them,' said Lena. 'It's a pattern we're all familiar with. Go. Wash off the salt. Put on the visitor clothes—I can see you want to. Besides, Trig's already compared you to half the Victoria's Secret Angels. I want to see the look on his face when you do your corporate princess thing.'

'The corporate princess is gone,' said Ruby. 'I bought myself some beach clothes.'

'Should be interesting,' said Lena. 'One of these days you're going to have to give me some fashion advice. The compliments I get whenever I wear the clothes you bought for me have been amazing.'

'I have two words for you,' said Ruby. 'Persian Pink.'

'Never,' said Lena with a gamine smile that made her truly beautiful. Oh, the things people never saw when they looked in a mirror.

An *oomph* and a thump from somewhere over near the tap caught Ruby's attention and she turned to find Damon in possession of the garden hose, apparently intent on cooling the trigger-happy one down. Trig, in turn, seemed equally intent on gathering up the hose line and strangling Damon with it—both of them grinning like sharks. 'Are they always like this?'

'Not *always*. Trig probably shouldn't have been staring at your arse. I did warn him.'

'About my bum?'

'That Damon was serious about you.'

'What makes you say that?'

'You're here, aren't you? And Damon's all happy and relaxed on the inside as well as on the surface. That's rare.'

Ruby eyed Lena uncertainly. 'You can tell all that just by looking at him?'

'Can't you?' said Lena with the beginnings of a smile. 'Oh, all right. Maybe I'm imagining things. Seeing what I want to see. But he's certainly very possessive of you, and making no apology for it with Trig. That's an excellent sign of attachment. Damon protects what's his. Always has. Usually with a complete disregard for his own safety that can be scary to watch.'

Possessive. Serious. Lena's words whizzed by, with Ruby scrambling madly to keep up. *Disregard for own safety. Scary.* Ruby backing up to ask the obvious question. 'Possessive how? As in if I even look at another man sideways he'll strangle me, possessive?'

'Not quite, although I wouldn't say he'd be entirely *happy* were you to look at Trig sideways.'

Neither, it seemed, would Lena be happy. Ruby stifled a smile. 'Duly noted.'

'All I was meaning,' said Lena repressively, 'is that if you were ever in danger, Damon would protect you with everything he had, including his life. For example, he pulled Poppy out of a rip once, when they were little. Saw her in trouble and swam like a demon to get to her, got caught in it as well and then swam like two demons to get them out. I thought they were both going to die.'

'Brave though.'

'Made an impression, I'll give him that.' Lena eyed

her speculatively. 'Damon used to avoid his I'll-die-for-you dilemmas by not laying claim to much. Wonder what he's going to do now?'

'Hopefully, stay alive,' said Ruby dryly. 'As for your claims about Damon laying claim to me, I think I'll just tell you I have no idea what you're talking about and go and have me that shower now.' Ruby took a step towards the back of the house and then turned around to assess once more the wrestling tangle of well-muscled limbs. 'They're not going to kill each other *now*, are they?'

'No, Damon knows Trig was only winding him up by studying you. He's made his point. Now they're just saying hello.'

'Right.' That was hello. 'Australian thing, is it?'

Lena just smiled.

Ruby returned to the fray some fifteen minutes later, wearing a pretty little cropped and layered silk camisole, heavy on the plums and pinks, ivory hipster trousers, bare feet, and her purple butterfly headband. She'd taken the time to blow-dry her hair and apply a touch of make-up. Visitors were visitors after all. No need to disrespect them by not making an effort.

Trig stared at her as she approached them, his grin wide and his gaze unholy. Probably her lack of shoes. Could be the butterfly.

Damon stared too, eyes narrow upon her bared midriff.

'Looking a little possessive there, boyo,' Trig murmured to Damon.

'Just feeling my way,' responded Damon evenly, and

then went and spoiled all that lovely nonchalance by shooting Trig a dirty glare. 'You're not feeling *anything*.'

Ruby's smile widened. 'I just couldn't find a *thing* to wear,' she said to Damon when she reached them. 'You might have to take me shopping.'

'I am *so* impressed,' said the aptly named Trig. 'What else does she do? Besides bait you.'

'I could tell you but you'd weep,' said Damon, and turned to Ruby. 'We're trying to convince Lena to stay here and concentrate on getting better while Trig goes looking for Jared.'

Family politics. Never, ever—on pain of death—get in the middle of it.

Particularly if you weren't family.

'How's that working out for everyone?' she said cautiously.

'You're a lawyer. Reason with her,' said Damon.

Oh, yes. This was going to end well.

'So… I'm guessing we've moved past delicacy, in terms of approach?' asked Ruby.

'Delicacy's not something we employ around Lena,' said Trig. 'Lena considers it a weakness.'

Okeydokeythen. Ruby ignored Lena's mutinous expression in favour of asking the obvious question. 'Lena, in your honest opinion, will you slow Trig down?'

'No,' said Lena.

'YES.' This from an extremely frustrated Trig. 'Lena, you have no idea how much I worry about you these days. Stay here with Damon and Ruby. Get well. *Get out of my goddamn head!*'

'Why would I want to be in your head?' Lena yelled back. *'There's nothing in there but testosterone.'*

'I don't know, Damon,' said Ruby dubiously. 'She looks fighting fit to me.' And in a voice she knew would carry, 'How long did you say they'd been married?'

That stopped them.

Lena scowled. Trig glowered.

Damon headed for the fridge in order to hide his smirk and returned with two beers and a bottle of white wine. 'I'll get glasses.'

Ruby smiled. Delicately. And watched him go. Watched him return and pour wine for Lena and slide it across the countertop, and pour one for her too, before distributing the beer. While the silence droned on.

'Far be it from me to want to take charge of this discussion,' she began calmly, and suffered Damon's extremely level gaze in silence, 'or take sides, but, Lena, it does seem to me that the gentlemen have a point. What if you end up having to move quickly because you're in danger? What if you have to run? Could you?'

Trig opened his mouth to say something. Ruby silenced him with a glance. 'Lena?'

'I can run,' said Lena in a thin hollow voice.

'Lena, you can barely *walk*,' countered Trig savagely. 'Don't you dare downplay your injuries to me. I was the one who pushed your *guts* back into your body.'

'I can run,' said Lena. And then went and spoiled her insistence with a fat and silent tear.

Trig fled, taking his beer and Damon with him. Out to the barbecue area where they set about unearthing a four-foot stainless-steel barbecuing wonder from its coverings.

'Looks like they're starting lunch,' said Ruby.

'I'm sorry,' said Lena as she wiped her tears away

with her fingers only to have more replace them. 'I'm not myself. I just want—'

'To be yourself again and find your brother. I know.' Ruby reached across the counter, covered Lena's hand and squeezed. 'It's okay.'

'No, it's *not* okay,' said Lena. 'I never cry. Especially not in front of Trig.'

'Because... Why not?'

'Because he'll never let me live it down.'

'Oh, I don't know,' said Ruby. 'Looks like a man hell-bent on forgetting the past few minutes to me. You want to know what else I think?'

Rhetorical question.

'I think you're terrified you might not recover from your injuries as well as you might like, and I think those two clowns out there are terrified right along with you. I think that regardless of what you want to do, what you *need* to do is take it easy on your body and listen to the clowns for once.'

Ruby smiled and the circus continued. 'Besides, Trig's not going anywhere unless you agree to stay here. I'm guessing he's saving that little titbit up for when all other forms of persuasion fail. What would you rather have him do, Lena? Babysit you or go look for your brother?'

Trig left. Lena stayed. And the following morning Ruby began to turn her mind to her future. Her two weeks were almost up and, much as she'd delighted in them, she couldn't stay on here indefinitely and neither would Damon.

Charming he remained, but Damon was getting restless.

The system design work he'd taken on currently held his attention but Ruby was under no illusions that he was about to forgo his covert work and his travelling lifestyle and become a model citizen. The jobs Ruby had taken to looking at all required her to commit to a particular course of action and stick to it. They all expected her to base herself somewhere for two to three years and stay there.

Ruby pushed the latest company structure and advancements file she'd been reading away from her with a sigh. Lena was at the kitchen bench making fruit smoothies for them both. Lena did not like being coddled and she'd just finished a workout in the pool that had left Ruby quietly terrified that Lena was going to overdo it and land herself back in hospital.

'I'm no medical expert,' said Ruby as Lena walked slowly towards the table, a smoothie in each hand. 'But have you considered that doing physio three times a day when the doctor recommends you only do it once might be doing you more harm than good?'

'Stop fussing,' said Lena. 'I'm fine. But seeing as we're being reflective, have you considered where Damon fits into all these work options you're contemplating?'

'Why do you think I'm rejecting them all?' Ruby took a glum sip of her smoothie. 'Have you any idea how hard it is to make plans that will accommodate your brother in my life?'

'Well, have you tried making them *with* him? That might help.'

'Ow,' said Ruby. 'Sarcasm. Don't you think that if I'd wanted to engage Damon on the topic I'd have done so already?'

'Maybe. Maybe not,' said Lena. 'You might be waiting for him to say *I love you*. Which he does, by the way.'

'And you know this how?'

'Observation.'

'I see,' said Ruby dryly.

'The thing is, Damon spends a lot of time thinking he's not worthy of love,' continued Lena earnestly. 'Pushing it away. He might not know how to say it. He might have to follow your lead. And you can lead, Ruby. You're very good at it.'

'Are you suggesting that I say it first?'

'That's exactly what I'm suggesting.'

'I'll keep it in mind,' said Ruby coolly. 'As long as *you* bear in mind that *I love you* is not an easy thing to say—and mean—no matter who's doing the talking.'

'I've overstepped my boundaries, haven't I?'

'You have.'

'Sorry. Bad habit.' Lena looked dismayed.

'You're here. The relationship is playing out in front of you and you want to smooth your brother's way. You're forgiven,' said Ruby, and meant it. 'But let me give you a little background information about me and the way I was raised.

'My father was a man of many secrets and even more agendas, none of which I was privy to. I loved him but I didn't know him. I adored him but I was never quite sure when he was being truthful and when he was lying through his teeth. Hell, I don't even know if he loved me. If he's alive and well and living off a mountain of stolen money and has no intention of contacting me ever again, I'm going to have to go with no.'

'That's quite a background,' said Lena with a grimace.

'Now enter Damon,' said Ruby. 'A fascinating, complex, glory of a man with a head full of secrets and a job that requires him to keep them. A man so used to keeping people *out* that getting him to reveal even the tiniest thing about himself requires a patience and perseverance I'm not sure I possess. And then just when I think I can't do this, he turns around and bares his soul for me—not his secrets but his soul, and I get lost in him, Lena, so lost it scares me. And he gets lost in me.'

Ruby's headband came off, and this time she left it off as she ran her hands through her already beach-swept hair.

'If this is love, it's not a comfortable, easy love,' she said. 'If this is honesty, it's going to take some getting used to.' Lena's sympathetic gaze cut to some place just over Ruby's shoulder. 'And if that's Damon I'm going to freak.'

'I just remembered a doctor's appointment,' said Lena. 'A really long one.'

'Lena.' Damon's quiet, measured voice confirmed the worst. 'No need to get up, though it'd be nice if you'd butt out.'

He came into view, a dangerously attractive man wearing long shorts and a simple grey cotton T-shirt that looked anything but simple on him. He held out his hand to Ruby, his ocean eyes stormy. 'Walk with me.'

It wasn't a request.

They headed for the beach path, Damon leading and Ruby in his wake once they got there, but he did not let her hand go and he did not slow his stride. He kept walking once they reached the water's edge.

Walking off a mad, one of her favourite nannies-of-old would have said. Better a walk than broken toys. And once Ruby had finally calmed down enough to be coherent, she'd say, 'Okay, Ruby Lou, talk. Who's wounded you most mortally now?'

That particular question had always been a prelude to a conversation about anger and wilfulness and how to manage both. The nanny would bring out her sewing kit and together she and Ruby would analyse the insult and Ruby's reaction to it and at the end of the conversation there would be a funny, pretty headband for Ruby Lou to wear.

'What can't you have?' Nanny Laura would say as the headband went on.

'My way all the time.'

'And why can't you have it?'

'Because other people have feelings too.'

'There's my considerate girl.'

A memorably grounded nanny, that one, though she hadn't lasted long.

But the lesson had sunk in and Ruby did her best to think of other people's feelings too.

Damon had feelings, ones that ran fathoms deep.

And Ruby had wounded them.

'How much did you hear?' she asked when they were halfway along the beach and the silence had reached suffocation point.

'Damon, stop. Please.' She planted her feet in the sand at the water's edge and tugged on his hand. 'I'm asking you to stop walking while I explain.'

She felt the pull of his hand against hers and held on tight. He could do this. Be still for her. And she could try and mend the damage done. 'How much did you hear?'

'All of it, Ruby.'

He turned to look at her, and she could see that exercise hadn't calmed him down any.

'All of it. Starting with my sister trying to explain away my faults and finishing with you saying you're too scared to take a chance on me.'

'I didn't say that,' argued Ruby. 'I said I needed time. There's a difference. I *am* taking a chance on you, Damon. What do you think I've been doing? I'm just not sure what happens next, that's all, and I'm not pushing you for answers. Dammit, Damon! You've made no mention whatsoever about where you're going or what you plan to do once these two weeks are up. You're playing us day by day and close to the chest and so am I. Isn't that what you *want*?'

Damon smiled mirthlessly. 'Apparently not.'

'Then what *do* you want? Because I'm willing to have this conversation if you are. I just didn't want to be the one to start it.'

'I want to talk about what comes next,' he said gruffly. 'Where you're going. Where you want to go. The things I have to do and the things I can change to suit myself. Or suit us.'

Damon took a deep breath and reached out to tuck a flyaway strand of hair behind her ear. 'No headband.'

'I left it on the table.'

'I know love and trust doesn't come easy to you, Ruby. It doesn't come easy to me either. But I do want to be with you. Make some changes so that I *can* be with you, at times. If that would suit you.'

It was a start.

CHAPTER TEN

THREE days later, on the back of some rather haphazard planning, Ruby went back to Hong Kong. Damon joined her a week later. Living with her, loving her, and watching her try and make up her mind on a new career path and permanent location with a smile on his face and a patience that surprised her.

When she'd gone round in circles a few times he weighed in with reasoned argument.

If she liked it in Hong Kong why not stay on here for a while?

Forget her father's actions, they were not hers to own and if people couldn't see that they were fools.

At least in Hong Kong she already knew who her friends were. The ones who'd stood by her when things had gone bad. The ones who kept in contact with her and valued her company.

An advantage over starting afresh, he'd said.

He could see things very clearly when he wanted to, could Damon. Ruby's respect for him grew, along with her dependence on making decisions *with* him rather than without.

Eventually, she decided to make Hong Kong work for her for now. The Australian-based law firm still hadn't filled their Hong Kong position. Plenty of room now for some negotiation of terms. One week every month a trip back to the Sydney office to consolidate the work. Formalised mentorship facilitated by computer conferencing technology. And free rein to do things her way when it came to setting up shop.

And if the decision sounded as if it was based in part on Damon's solid reasoning that Hong Kong would prove a useful base for them both, well, maybe it was.

Damon too was looking to rent office space in Hong Kong. Build up a legitimate network development service for small businesses. Employ a manager. A couple of technicians. Lend a hand every now and then. Keep his head in the game. Go legit with at least some of his work.

It sounded good in theory.

Whether he would have enough focus to actually step up and *do* it was anyone's guess.

Days whizzed by and Ruby took to talking to the cat again.

A vastly friendlier little cat, for little girls were apparently very good at sneaking through a little cat's reserve. The cat, who now went by the name of Jao, now had two homes to choose from, and one he retreated to when he wanted peace and solitude and the other home he favoured when he wanted to play.

Not bad for a no-name scrap of mistrust and misery.

'Fall on your feet, don't you?' she told Jao, who'd developed a habit of taking a fast and clawless strike at her ankles from beneath the overhang of the kitchen bench. 'Just like Damon.'

Damon who'd been looking at office space but neglecting to pay attention to the contractual leasing terms of the office space chosen. Damon didn't have the patience for it. Ruby did. Also a vested interest in not wanting him to expire of frustration before his venture into the world of small-business ownership had even begun.

'Damon's going to need a *very* switched on business manager,' she said to the little cat as she marked for signing the leasing arrangement he'd decided to go with.

'Damon's well aware of that,' said a voice, and Ruby looked up from the papers and saw Damon coming towards her, fresh from the shower with only a towel to keep him company.

'You couldn't afford me,' she said, and favoured him with a very appreciative smile. 'Besides, I've decided to take the Hong Kong job. Even if I only do the initial set-up and then pass the position on to someone else. That corner suite we looked at yesterday would be perfect.'

'The ground-floor corner office with the too big reception area, too small a workshop and the little courtyard? The one you told me was on the border of Triad territory?'

'Yes,' said Ruby serenely. '*Border* being the operative word. Between *two* opposing Chinese corporations, actually. Authorities tend to steer clear and that is of benefit to a lawyer with a client base of asylum seekers, many of whom have not had pleasant experiences with authority.'

'Get each side to throw in a day guard and lockdown parking facilities for your wheels and I might even agree,' he said as he picked up the pen and scrawled his signature beside every cross. 'You'll be dealing with desperate people, Ruby. You're going to have to take precautions.'

'I know. And later on I want to pick your brains when it comes to securing computer files and whatnot. Maybe I can be your first customer.' She picked up the paperwork and waved it in his face. 'Next time, *read* it.'

'Why? You already have.' He dropped a kiss on her lips and forestalled further comment. 'You know, you're lucky to have me. I haven't mentioned locking you up and not letting you out of this apartment ever again *once* during this conversation.'

'Nor will you if you have any sense of fair play at all. When it comes to courting danger, each to his own.'

'The family's going to say it's my fault you went dark side,' he continued morosely. 'They'll say I encouraged you.'

Ruby smiled. 'And they'd be right. Am I going to have to get undressed in order to win this argument?'

'You've already won it. Besides, I need to change the topic,' he murmured, and let his bottom lip drag against hers before sliding his lips across to her ear. 'I have to go to Eastern Europe for work.'

Ruby drew away swiftly and fixed him with an unfriendly gaze. 'I *knew* you were buttering me up for something.'

'No, you didn't. You thought I was just being my usual charming self.'

This was true. Not that she had any intention of saying that aloud. '*When* are you going to Eastern Europe?'

'Today.'

Ruby nodded. Thumped him in the chest with a none-too-gentle fist. 'How long have you known?'

'Ten minutes.' He glanced at the microwave clock. 'Fifteen.'

'When are you coming back?'

'A week?' Damon shrugged. 'It's hard to say. Hopefully a week.'

'Will you call and let me know?'

'No contact. You know how this goes, Ruby. We've talked about it.'

Yes, but talking wasn't doing. Ruby glared at him afresh. 'Make sure you bring me back a present. At least then I'll know I've been in your thoughts.'

'A headband?'

'Yes,' she said and lifted her chin. 'A headband for reasonable, considerate, loveable little Ruby, and I'll give you fair warning. Regardless of my *inherently* forgiving nature, I do have a temper, and certain actions have been known to trigger it.' Her hands had gone to her hips. 'Keep your secrets when it comes to your work, I don't want them. As for our personal affairs, I don't like being manipulated and I resent being lied to. Are we clear?'

'Ruby, you're the classiest and most effective manipulator I've ever seen. How come I can't even *practise* on you?'

'I'm not joking, Damon. Don't ever play me that way.'

'I won't.'

'Promise me.'

'Ruby, I won't.'

And Ruby believed him.

Another week. No word from Damon, but then he'd warned her not to expect it. Ruby stayed busy and somewhere along the way she realised she wasn't fretting about Damon and the things he might be doing. Shades of grey and each to their own, and Damon would go about making the world a better place his way and Ruby would try and make the world a fairer place her way, and who was to judge which was the right way?

If Damon ever wanted a muse when it came to his work and the ethics involved he would get one. Label him a hero or brand him a thief. She could argue either way.

Ruby leased the corner office suite. Made a few changes. The walls would not be grey but ivory. The furnishings would be comfortable and not pretentious. Her new neighbours wondered what she was up to. She had flyers printed up listing the company's services. Obtained flyers and posters from charities and services that she thought her future clients would find useful. Word got around. Her new landlord stopped by.

Yes, she was Harry Maguire's daughter.

No, she had no idea where the money was, or her father for that matter.

Yes, she was opening up a law office specialising in migration, and yes, indeed, she would be most interested in having the local security service stop by her offices on their nightly rounds. Day rounds too, if they existed. It would be money well spent.

And Damon stayed away.

Day three of week two of his absence and Ruby's office walls were now ivory and she'd moved on to furnishings. Work desks and office chairs. A wooden table and benches and potted greenery for the courtyard. She started the hunt for a receptionist. At least three languages, she told the dressmaker three doors down. With written proficiency in two. Preferably someone who lived locally but wasn't closely affiliated with any of the Triads.

The dressmaker knew of someone who might be interested in part-time work. Very smart boy. The son of one of her regular clients. Chinese Korean.

And then just like that, Damon was back. Standing in the doorway of her new office, a bunch of purple orchids in one hand and a gaily wrapped package in the other.

'Two presents,' he said. 'I thought I might need them.'

'So true,' she said, and then Ruby was in his arms and Damon was twirling her round and kissing her with an intensity that belonged to him alone.

'Miss me?' he whispered when she finally broke free.

'Like crazy.'

'Feel like taking the afternoon off?'

'Only if you can get two desktop computers, a scanner/printer/fax and a notebook here and set up by nine tomorrow morning.'

Damon handed her his tributes and pulled out his phone. Two minutes later it was organised.

'Tell me you're impressed,' he said.

'Show off.' But she kissed him again and it was quite

some time before she turned her attention to the opening of gifts. 'I could get used to this.'

'That's the plan.'

'Truffles from Belgium,' she said in approval of the exquisitely boxed handmade selection. 'Very nice.'

'And this,' he said, and dangled a heart shaped pendant on a silver ribbon from his fingertips. Silver filigree that swirled an intricate path around a heart of red Murano glass.

'Damon, it's gorgeous,' she said with unfeigned enthusiasm and set about putting it on. 'Venice?'

'Still full of bridges and rising water.' He fingered the pendant at her neck. 'Guess what I discovered when I walked through the door and you looked up and smiled at me as if Christmas had come early?'

'That I like presents?'

'That Lena was right about one thing and wrong about another.'

'Lena's right and wrong about a lot of things. Which things are we talking about?'   •

'Love,' he said quietly, his gaze intent on hers. 'I love you, Ruby. And you don't have to say it first and you don't have to say it back if it's not your way. I just wanted you to know how I feel about you these days.'

Ruby stared at him wordlessly, still clutching the pendant he'd given her, the heart currently residing around her neck. She opened her mouth to say those three little words back to him but those words, they simply wouldn't come.

'I've missed you so much,' she said weakly. 'I'm so glad you're back.' Her next words came out in a panicked rush. 'I'm still working on the love thing.'

'It's okay, Ruby. Not everyone jumps off cliffs the way I do. Not everyone wants to.'

'I want to,' she said earnestly. 'I do. I'm standing on the cliff edge and I've just watched you leap off it and my heart is in my mouth for you, and my knees are shaking, and why the *hell* didn't you wait for me, Damon, so we could have done this together? Because now I'll have to jump off that cliff all by myself.'

'No, you won't,' he said with a wry smile. 'I'll jump with you, Ruby. Any time you're ready. First time's always the hardest. Next time might not be too bad at all.'

'Next time *wait for me*,' she commanded fiercely and then drew him to her and wrapped her arms around him and simply held him close and tried to clamp down on her fear of saying those words and meaning them and then not having them be enough. She squeezed him tightly and pressed her lips to his cheek and then the side of his mouth and then she kissed him full on the lips and felt him shudder in return. 'What's it like?' she whispered because she really had to know.

'Oh, you know,' he said raggedly and rested his forehead gently against hers. 'Freefall.'

Life with Ruby in Hong Kong held a fascination for Damon. Ruby got things done with a speed and attention to detail that entranced him. She made his world move with a brightness and lightness he couldn't explain but what it meant was that he could stand utterly still in the middle of it.

And be completely content.

And then Ruby's solicitor phoned through one morning and asked her to drop by the office, and a tremor slid through Damon's shiny magic world. A premonition, if you like, that Damon's sins might be coming back to bite him.

Ruby's feelings for her father were complicated.

Hell, *Damon's* feelings for her father were complicated.

For thirty years Harry Maguire had played the game and kept his secrets in and his daughter out. Thirty years.

Damon didn't know whether to hold him up as a role model or pity him for being so blind.

Damon drove them to the solicitor's offices while Ruby fretted. As soon as they arrived the assistant took one look at them and sent them straight in.

Harry Maguire's solicitor was gimlet-eyed and silver-haired. An old college friend of her father's, so Ruby had said, and there was something in the way the man eyed him and shook his hand as Ruby introduced them that made Damon wonder who exactly this man was and whether he'd known of Harry Maguire's alternate life and whether he knew more than he should about Damon's.

The pleasantries seemed to go on for ever and then the solicitor sat them both down and headed for the other side of the desk and pushed an A4 envelope across the desk towards Ruby.

'This was delivered this morning but before you open it you need to prepare yourself for bad news.'

'How bad?' said Ruby.

'There is a death certificate in there, Ruby,' he said gently. 'I've had it verified. I'm sorry. Your father's dead.'

Ruby barely flinched. Half expecting it, thought Damon. Not sure what to think, feel or do.

'How?' she said threadily, and left the envelope untouched. 'And when?'

'It's hard to say.' The solicitor cleared his throat. 'British Intelligence found his body two days ago. Their report is extremely brief. The coroner's report lists both the time of death and the cause of death as unknown. Harry's body is currently in a London morgue. I can arrange to have it sent on. Anywhere you like.'

'New York,' said Ruby faintly. 'There's a family plot in New York and burial arrangements are in place there. I'll have to phone home. I'm just assuming…'

Ruby put her hand up as if to straighten her headband but she didn't have one on. Her hands went in her lap after that. 'I'm hoping the family will allow him to be buried there. He was blood, even if he was a disgrace to them.' Her chin came up. 'If not I'll make other arrangements. Start a new family plot.'

Loyal to the end. For Ruby there was no other way.

'Your father's assets and accounts have been unfrozen,' said the solicitor, taking back the envelope and unloading it, seeing as Ruby hadn't done so. He found the paperwork he wanted, passed it over to her and this time she took it. 'I have your father's will here, and now that we have a death certificate we can get started on—'

'Did they recover the money?' asked Ruby.

The solicitor frowned. 'British Intelligence makes no mention of it. Anyway, there are no surprises when it comes to your father's will. You're his sole beneficiary. I can start—'

'So they didn't clear him of the theft,' said Damon.

'No, but the release of his assets would suggest—'

'Why don't you ask the British to release Harry Maguire's employee number?' suggested Damon grimly. 'That should clear a few things up.'

'Young man…' The solicitor sat back slowly in his chair and steepled his fingers. '*That* is a very unusual suggestion. One has to ask oneself what could be gained by such a request. May I suggest that the answer would be very little?'

'Oh, I don't know,' drawled Damon. 'What's a daughter's belief in her father's essential goodness worth? What's the knowledge that a man spent thirty years protecting his daughter from the dangers his intelligence work engendered actually worth? What's a man's reputation worth, for that matter?'

'Not a lot,' said the solicitor softly, and rested his head back against his chair, his impenetrable grey gaze fixed on Damon. 'In the grander scheme. Perhaps it's a matter of perspective.'

'Yes,' said Damon agreeably. 'Perhaps it is.'

'Stop,' said Ruby shakily. 'Both of you, *stop*!'

Now the solicitor turned his gaze on Ruby and Damon could have sworn he saw a flicker of grief cross the older man's face. The solicitor sighed, tapped his fingertips together several times, as if coming to a decision.

'Your father was a great asset to us all, Ruby,' said the solicitor, and Damon's eyes narrowed at the other man's choice of words. 'But I fear the restoration of his reputation would prove far too costly for all concerned, including you, and also—if I may be so bold as to dispense a warning—your very intriguing young Mr West. You need to let this go.'

The wily grey fox stood up and went to the door. Opened it to signal the end of their audience with him.

'I'm sorry, Ruby. I've already done everything I can,' he said as she reached the door, her face blank and her eyes stark. 'Your father knew the risks.'

The drive back to the apartment took for ever. Ruby stared out of the window. Damon drove and tried to keep his attention on the road. He shouldn't have said anything. Or saved it for another day. *A never day*, a voice in his head whispered quietly. *You knew this information was going to remake Ruby's world.*

But the way Harry Maguire had been dealt with enraged him and recklessness and fury had taken care of the rest.

So he had cut a path through all the lies and delivered up to Ruby some small semblance of truth and a father she could be proud of. That was what he'd been trying to do. That was what the solicitor who wasn't just a solicitor had been trying to do too.

Deliver up Ruby a father she could be proud of.

Surely they had done the right thing?

Ruby stood straight and silent in the lift on the way to their apartment. She could barely get the key in the lock and flinched when Damon went to do it for her.

'I'll *do* it,' she snapped, so he let her, and strode in after her, already knowing he wasn't going to like what was coming up next.

'Would you like something to drink?' he said as she

dumped her satchel on the kitchen counter. 'Brandy? Scotch? Cup of tea?'

'No,' she said. He could hardly hear her. 'How long have you known?'

'Ruby—'

'How long have you known?' Oh, he could hear her now.

'Known what?' He didn't intend insolence, God help him he did not. Just clarification as to what exactly they were talking about.

'That my father was dead!'

Good. Easy stuff first. 'I found out today. Same time as you,' he said soothingly.

'And how long have you known that he worked for the British Secret Service?'

Now the difficult part.

'Since Sydney.'

'Sydney,' she echoed faintly. 'All that time and you never said a word.'

'I didn't know what to say.'

'How about *Ruby your father was a spy and he's probably dead*?'

'Are you sure you wouldn't like a drink?' he said a touch desperately. 'Pretty sure I'd like one.'

'I trusted you!' Her voice cracked on the word *trusted*. 'And you lied to me. You went after that information and you found it and never said a goddamn word until it suited you to do so! Why now? Why couldn't you have just let it be?'

'Because hacking's what I do,' he raged back. 'It's part of who I am, for better or for worse, and because it annoyed me that they had no intention of restoring your father's reputation to you. What good to you is a corpse and a lifetime of unanswered questions? At least now you know what he did and why he died. He wasn't a thief. He didn't abandon you. He did everything he could to *protect* you. Isn't that worth something?'

'Yes, but can't you understand what I've *lost*?'

'Your father,' he answered doggedly, feeling for all the world as if he were back at school. 'Your view of him. But surely this view is better?'

'A *lifetime* spent not knowing him at all, Damon.'

'That's not true. You did know him, Ruby. Just not that part. Everybody keeps secrets.'

But Ruby just stared at him and shook her head. 'Not like he did. Not like you.'

'But I didn't goddamn *keep* your father's secret,' he roared. 'I told you! Not immediately. Not without a hell of a lot of soul-searching, but I told you, and I knew you'd hang me for it and I *still* told you. Because I thought it would *help* you deal with your father's death. Because I love you. What the hell else do you want from me?'

'I want you to leave.' There was no give in her. Just a blistering fury focused directly at him.

'Ruby—' Damon shook his head. 'No. You're in shock.'

'I want you to leave.' Tears had joined the fury and they lashed at him and stripped him bare.

'Ruby, please.' Surely she would see reason soon, wouldn't she? She could *always* argue both sides of a debate. 'You don't want to do this.'

'No, I think I do. Get out. Getoutgetout*getout*!'

Damon stalked to the room they shared, shoved a

handful of clothes and his notebook in his backpack. Time to go, only this time he didn't want to go.

One more. He'd give it one more try.

Back out to the open-plan area to find Ruby with her elbows on the kitchen counter and both hands in her hair. She looked up as he approached and her eyes were wet and haunted but her mouth was tight and grim.

'Ruby, I'm sorry,' he said. 'For the way this played out and my part in it—I'm sorry.'

'I know,' she replied and nodded and tried to smile through her tears. 'I know you are, but it's not enough. Of all the things I've lost today, what hurts the most is losing my faith in you.'

CHAPTER ELEVEN

IT TOOK Ruby three days to find any sort of equilibrium at all. Three days' worth of misery and sleeplessness, exhaustion and tears. Self-realisation was a painful thing.

Word got out that her father was dead and then came the requests for media interviews—which she refused—and the curiosity of just about everyone she came into contact with—which she couldn't do anything about.

She notified the family, including her mother, made preparations for her father's body to be sent to New York. It had been Ruby's mother who'd argued most strongly for Harry to be buried in the family crypt. The answer had been a vehement no in the beginning and then Ruby's mother had got on the phone to every single one of them and two hours later the answer had been yes.

Maybe her mother had known that her husband had worked for a secret intelligence service all along, but Ruby never asked and her mother didn't say.

People kept a secret for a reason. Chose to share it only when that reason no longer existed or the benefit of exposing the secret outweighed the cost.

Something Damon had been trying to tell her, thought Ruby guiltily. Only she hadn't had the heart to listen.

Hadn't had the brain to sift through the incoming information and separate gold from dross.

You're in shock, he'd said, and she'd known even then that he'd been being generous in his estimation of her.

Irrational.

Mean-spirited.

Scared.

Those were the words he could have used.

Lashing out because life wasn't how she wanted it to be. How old was she? Four?

Where was a sensible, sewing-basket-toting nanny when you needed one?

Ruby had walked and walked some more and the mad had finally worn off. All she had left was sorrow and a growing fear that she couldn't make things right with Damon. That he'd seen her in all her insecure glory and had finally had enough.

It was time to go and find him but he wasn't in Hong Kong. Not staying with Russell, not gettable by mobile. Gone, because she'd screamed at him to leave. There'd been no reasoning with her and Damon had known it.

He could be anywhere.

So who would know? Lena? Worth a try. A phone call.

A difficult one, and Ruby knew it was mad but she found an old polka-dot headband and brushed her hair and put it on, and make-up too, and then surveyed herself in the mirror.

'There's my considerate girl,' she murmured and blinked back sudden tears. 'Now go and apologise.'

'Damon's at the beach house,' said Lena when Ruby asked her. 'What the *hell* did you do?'

'I watched Damon put his heart, his career and then our relationship on the line because he thought it would help me to deal with my father's death,' she said quietly. 'And I called it betrayal.'

Lena said nothing for quite some time and then sighed. 'Damon doesn't know the meaning of the word *self-preservation* when it comes to protecting the people he loves. I did warn you.'

'I know,' said Ruby, and closed her eyes. 'And I get it now.'

'Do you love my brother, Ruby?'

'I do,' she said, altogether terrified that it was too little too late. 'And I need to tell it to him straight.'

'Then I suggest you get on a plane and get yourself over here. There's a front-door key stuck in a crack between the laundry door window frame and the wall,' said Lena. 'And, Ruby? Don't take too long. My brother's hurting. Makes me want to hurt you.'

It only took Ruby a day to get to Byron. She hired a car at the airport, got out the map and tried to remember the way to the beach house and eventually found it, still as beautiful as ever.

She knocked on the door and waited. Rang the door-bell and knocked and waited again.

Nothing.

Eventually she found the key and stepped inside, feeling like a trespasser and a thief, and no gorgeous soft furnishings or open pavilion could take that feeling away from her. And then she saw Damon out on the kiteboard and her heart rate tripled again.

How long would she have before he came in? Time enough to get her props in place?

Sliding the house key in the bowl by the door, Ruby chocked the front door open and started bringing things in.

The sea had always been a favourite playground of Damon's. It swallowed up all the energy a person could throw at it and then sat there, mouth wide open, and dared a man to offer up just that little bit more.

Poppy hated it with a fear she couldn't shake but Damon embraced it. Soar or dive, his body rejoiced and his soul got fed and the bleakness that dogged him these days went away.

But he had to come back in eventually, and when his arms were aching and his legs close to breaking he skidded back in over the sand and brought the parachute down and kitted out and started the walk back up to the house, gear in hand.

The first thing he saw was the headband. It hung off the tap he always used to wash the gear. Misty pink and moss green, a timid gumnut baby peeking out from between the folds, and Damon instantly forgot all about the hosing down of toys. Instead he slid the headband from the tap and, clutching it tightly in his hand, high-tailed it through the garden towards the house. 'Ruby?'

She wasn't in the pool and she wasn't in the pavilion. 'Ruby?'

Damon tossed the headband on the low coffee table that stood in the centre of the pavilion and that was when he noticed the envelope. He backed up. Picked it up. It had his name on it. He didn't open it. Maybe she was in the kitchen.

Nope. Now he opened it.

'I'm sorry,' it said. Only it did it in a hundred different languages, some of them numerical, and filled the entire page.

She wasn't in his bedroom either.

Or any of the other bedrooms or bathrooms and she wasn't in the games room.

He found her in the computer room, with her back to him as she sat at his main console, and every last one of his monitors showing the blue screen of death. She wore a pale pink halter dress, and her black work satchel leaned haphazardly against her chair.

Damon leaned against the doorframe and crossed his arms, mainly to stop them from reaching for her. He cleared his throat.

She didn't turn round, just leaned sideways to read from some sort of textbook that she'd propped open with the edge of his keyboard. She kept her fingers poised over the keys.

'Ruby, what are you doing?'

Ruby straightened slender shoulders but she didn't turn round. She'd put her hair up in some sort of elaborate bun and the clip that held it in place had little pale pink hearts all over it. He had no objection to the hearts but he wanted to see her face.

'I'm hacking your computer,' she said and raised a hand towards the back of her neck to capture a stray strand of hair and give it a twirl.

'Right.'

Damon felt his lips begin to curve.

'How's that working out for you?'

'Not good.' She leaned sideways to study the book again. 'I may need lessons.'

He moved closer until he stood behind her. He breathed her in deep but he still didn't dare touch. Instead, he curled his hands over the back of her chair and peered over her shoulder. 'What is it you want to do?'

'Apologise,' she said. 'And leave a message. A really big one. Full screen. Unerasable.'

'Which would you rather use?' he said. 'Polymorphic or metamorphic code?'

'Can I have both?'

'How long have you got?'

'Hopefully a lifetime,' she said. 'But the message has to go up now. Good thing I brought backup.'

Ruby shut the book with a snap and reached down into her satchel, withdrawing a heart-shaped piece of glossy red contact paper. She leaned back in the chair, her skin brushing against the backs of his fingers and her hair bare millimetres from his chin. She put French-manicured nails to the pointy end, peeled the backing away from the contact and then slapped that big fat red heart up right in the middle of his state-of-the-art computer screen.

'That's cheating,' he said.

'Sue me.'

She pulled a felt-tipped pen out of her satchel next and tugged the lid off with a snap. Damon saw the size of that square-tipped sucker, and wondered if she had any intention whatsoever of staying within the lines. 'Ah, Ruby?'

'What?' She leaned forward and started writing across his heart. Big bold capitals that filled it to the brim.

RUBY LOVES DAMON. (permanently)

'Never mind,' he murmured, and waited, and this time she turned around and the silent entreaty in her eyes cut a path straight to his heart, no code required.

'Damon, I'm sorry,' she said. 'My father's secrecy... His whole secret life felt like a betrayal of my life and the relationship I thought I had with him. I couldn't distinguish between his secrets and yours. All I could see was lies and betrayal. I was too blind to see that everything you'd done you'd done for me. To protect me.'

'I shouldn't have gone after the info on your father,' he offered gruffly. 'I knew you didn't want me to. I did it anyway. If I hadn't, none of this would have happened.'

'And I would never have truly known my father.'

Ruby took a deep breath and her chest rose and fell. She tilted her head, not quite a nod but a tiny twitch of resolve.

'What I did to you, and said to you, and screamed at you, was wrong. I'm so sorry. It won't happen again. I won't let it. Can you forgive me?'

'You had a bad day, Ruby. I can't see there being any others like it. And, yes, if you need my forgiveness you have it.'

'I need it,' she said. 'Almost as much as I need to tell you I love you. Because I do love you, Damon, and if you give me the chance I will spend the rest of my life telling you I love you, and showing you that I do, and jumping off tall cliffs with you.' Ruby's eyes began to shimmer. 'If you still want me to.'

'I want you to,' he said quietly. 'And I promise you this. I will never lie to you, Ruby. I will always love you. And as for secrets—'

She put her fingers to his lips and shushed him. 'Keep your secrets, Damon. I trust you.'

He kissed her fingertips and began again doggedly. 'As for secrets, I promise you—'

'Shh,' she whispered, softer still, and replaced fingertips with teasing lips that brushed his briefly and then drew back just a fraction. 'I don't need your promises either, Damon. I only need you.'

'—that I will always tell you and share with you—'

'Shh.' Ruby punctuated her demand with a lingering kiss. 'I love you.'

'—everything—'

'Shh!' Another kiss and this time the stroke of her tongue.

'—I can!' he finished, and drew his head back, even as he drew her into his arms. 'Are we arguing?'

'What? No! I was just trying to—'

'I'm pretty sure we are,' he murmured silkily. 'Arguing, that is.'

'No, we're not,' she said, eyeing him uncertainly.

'*And* we seem to be at something of an impasse,' he continued, and then he slid his hand up her arm and tugged gently on her halter tie and comprehension finally dawned.

'You're right,' she said with a sultry, knowing smile. 'We're arguing. It's terrible. Dear me, what *shall* I do?'

'I have an idea,' he murmured, and picked her up and whirled her round as she peppered his face with kisses. 'How would you like to win it?'

* * * * *

BLAME IT ON THE BIKINI

BY
NATALIE ANDERSON

Natalie Anderson adores a happy ending, which is why she always reads the back of a book first. Just to be sure. So you can be sure you've got a happy ending in your hands right now—because she promises nothing less. Along with happy endings, she loves peppermint-filled dark chocolate, pineapple juice and extremely long showers. Not to mention spending hours teasing her imaginary friends with dating dilemmas. She tends to torment them before eventually relenting and offering—you guessed it—a happy ending. She lives in Christchurch, New Zealand, with her gorgeous husband and four fabulous children.

If, like her, you love a happy ending, be sure to come and say hi on facebook/authornatalica and on Twitter @authornataliea, or her website/blog: www.natalie-anderson.com.

For Dave, Dave and Gungy:

Thank you so much for giving up time in your precious weekends to help construct "The Plotting Shed"— without that wonderful room of my own I don't think Brad and Mya's story would ever have been finished!

I truly appreciate your kindness and generosity

(and that of Bridge and Kat for kid duty!!!)

CHAPTER ONE

CAN I get away with it?

It was harder than you'd think to take a picture of yourself in a small, enclosed space wearing nothing but a bikini. Biting back the giggle, Mya Campbell peered at her latest effort. The flash had created a big white space over at least half the screen, obscuring most of her reflection, and what you could see was more dork than glam.

With a muffled snort—a combination of frustration and laughter—she deleted it and twisted in front of the mirror, trying for another. Her teeth pinched her lower lip as she glanced at the result—maybe the skinny-straps scarlet number was a step too far?

'Is everything okay?' the clearly suspicious sales assistant called through the curtain, her iced tone snootier than her brittle perfect appearance.

'Fine, thanks.' Mya fumbled, quickly taking another snap before the woman yanked back the curtain. She needed to get it away before being—ah—busted.

Both she and the assistant knew she couldn't afford any of these astronomically priced designer swimsuits. But that long-suppressed imp inside her liked a dress-up and it had been so long and if she were to have such a thing as a summer holiday, then she'd really love one of these little, very little things…

Giggles erupted as she tried to send the text. Her fingertips slipped she shook so hard. She was such an idiot. Typos abounded and she tapped faster as she heard the assistant return.

'Are you sure you don't need any help?'

She needed help all right. Professional help from those people in white coats. Too late now, the soft whooshing sound confirmed her message had gone. And she couldn't afford this scrap of spandex anyway.

'Thanks, but no, I don't think this style is really me.' Of course it wasn't. She tossed the phone into her open bag on the floor and began the contortions required to get out of the tiny bikini. She caught a glimpse of herself bent double and at that point she blushed. The bikini was basically indecent. Would she never learn that bodies like hers were not built for tiny two pieces? She'd bend to pull off her shoes at the beach and instantly fall out of a top like this. Not remotely useful for swimming. She'd have to lie still and pose, and that just wasn't her. Mind you, a summer holiday wasn't for her this year either.

And never in a million years would she send such a picture to anyone other than her best friend and all-around pain in the butt, Lauren Davenport. But Lauren would understand—and Mya didn't need her answer now. It was a 'no' already.

Brad Davenport looked at his watch and stifled the growl of frustration. He'd had back-to-back cases in court all day, followed by this meeting that had gone on over an hour too long. He watched the bitterness between the parents, watched eleven-year-old Gage Simmons seated next to him shrivel into a smaller and smaller ball as accusations were hurled from either side of the room. The boy's parents were more interested in taking pieces out of each other and blocking each other instead of thinking about what might be best for their son. And finally Brad's legendary patience snapped.

'I think we can leave this for now,' he interrupted abruptly. 'My client needs a break. We'll reschedule for later in the week.'

He glanced around the room and the other lawyers nodded. Then he glanced at the kid, who was looking at the floor with a blank-slate expression. He'd seen it many times, had worn it himself many times—withdrawing, not showing anyone how much you hurt inside.

Yeah, it wasn't only his client who needed a break. But Brad's burden was his own fault. He'd taken on too many cases. Brad Davenport definitely had a problem saying no.

Twenty minutes later he carried the bag full of files out to his car and considered the evening ahead. He needed a blowout—some all-physical pleasure to help him relax, because right now the arguments still circled in his head. Questions he needed to ask and answer lit up like blindingly bright signs; every item on his to-do list shouted at him megaphone-style. Yeah, his head hurt. He reached for his phone and took it off mute, ready to find an energetic date for the night—someone willing, wild and happy to walk away when the fun was done.

There were a couple of voice messages, more emails, a collection of texts—including one with an attachment from a number he didn't recognise. He tapped it.

Can I get away with it?

He absorbed that accompanying message by a weird kind of osmosis, because the picture itself consumed all his attention. He could see only the side of her face, only half her smile, but that didn't matter—he was a man and there were curves in the centre of the screen. Creamy, plump breasts pushed up out of the do-me-now-or-die scarlet bra she'd squeezed into. Brad swore in amazement, his skin burning all over in immediate response. The picture cut off beneath her belly button—damn it— but he really couldn't complain. Her breasts were outstanding—lush curves that made him think…think… Actually no, he'd lost all ability to *think*.

Can I get away with it?

This doll could get away with anything she wanted.

Startled, but happily so, he slid his fingers across the screen to zoom the picture, adjusting it so it was her partially exposed face he focused on now. She was smiling as if she was only just holding back the sexiest of laughs.

Brad stilled, his heart hiccupping as disbelief stole a beat. There was only one person in the world with a smile like that. Slowly he traced her lips. Her upper lip was sensual—widening, just as the bone structure of her face widened to those sharp, high cheekbones and wide-set green eyes while her lower lip was as full, but shorter; it had to be to fit with that narrow little chin. And between those slightly mismatched lips was that telltale gap between her two front teeth. It had never been fixed. Her whole body was untainted by cosmetic procedures, indeed any kind of cosmetics.

Mya Campbell. Best friend of his wayward sister, Lauren, and persona non grata at the Davenport residence.

In that minute that Brad thought about her—the longest stretch of time he'd *ever* thought about her—a few images from the past decade haphazardly flashed through his head. Glimpses of a girl who'd been around the house often enough, but who'd hidden away whenever he or his parents were home. Who could blame her? His parents had been unwelcoming and patronising. Which of course had made Lauren push the friendship all the more. And Mya had come across as less than impressed with those in authority and less than interested in abiding by any of the normal social rules. The two of them had looked like absolute terrors. And the irony was that Mya was the most academically brilliant student in the school. An uber-geek beneath the attitude and the outrageous outfits. That was why she was *at* the school; she was the scholarship kid.

He'd only ever seen her dressed up 'properly' the once. She'd still looked sullen, exuding a kind of 'cooler-than-you' arrogance, and frankly at the time he'd been otherwise distracted by a far friendlier girl. But now he saw the all-grown-up sensuality. Now he saw the humour that he'd heard often enough but never been privy to—never been interested enough to want to be privy to. Now he saw what she'd been hiding all this time. Now the heat shot to his groin in a stab so severe he flinched. And she'd sent him...?

No. He laughed aloud at the ridiculous thought. Mya Campbell had *not* just sent him a sexy summons. She didn't even know he existed—other than as her best friend's big, distant brother. Hell, he hadn't seen her in, what, at least three years? He tapped the screen to bring it back to normal—correction, completely amazing—view. No, this playful pose wasn't for him. Which meant that certified genius Mya Campbell had actually made a mistake for once in her life. What was he going to do about it? Crucially, where was Mya now?

Questions pounded his head again, but this time they caused anticipation rather than a headache. He tossed the phone onto the passenger seat of his convertible, ignoring every other message. He put his sunglasses on, stress gone, and fired the engine. Now the night beckoned with a very amusing intrigue to unravel.

Can I get away with it?

Not this time.

The music was so loud Mya could feel the vibrations through her feet—which was saying something given her shoes had two and a half inches of sole. But she was used to the volume and she had enough experience to lip-read the orders well enough now. Shifts six days a week in one of the hottest bars in town had her able to work fast and efficient. The way she always worked. No matter what she was doing, Mya Campbell was driven to be the best.

Her phone sat snug against her thigh in the side pocket of her skinny jeans, switched to mute so it didn't interrupt her shift. The duty manager, Drew, frowned on them texting or taking calls behind the bar. Fair enough. They were too busy anyway. So she had no idea whether Lauren had got the pic or what she'd thought of it. Though, given Lauren was welded to her mobile, Mya figured there'd be an answer when she got a spare second to check. She grinned as she lined twelve shiny new shot glasses on the polished bar, thinking of Lauren's face when she saw it. She'd be appalled—she'd always shrieked over Mya's more outrageous 'statement' outfits.

'Come on, gorgeous, show us your stuff!'

Mya glanced up at the bunch of guys crowded round her end of the bar. A stag party, they'd insisted she pour the trick shots for them, not her sidekick, Jonny, down the other end of the bar. She didn't get big-headed about it—truth was Jonny had taught her the tricks and she was still working towards acing him on them. It was just these guys wanted the female factor.

She'd mixed three for them already and now was onto the finale. She enjoyed it—nothing like lighting up a dozen flaming sambucas for a bunch of wild boys who were megaphone loud in their appreciation. She flicked her wrist and poured the liquid—a running stream into each glass. Then she met the eyes of the groom and flashed him a smile.

'Are you ready?' she teased lightly.

The guys nodded and cheered in unison.

She held the lighter to the first shot glass and gently blew, igniting the rest of the line of glasses down the bar. The cheers erupted. She glanced at Jonny and winked. She'd only recently mastered that one, and she knew he was standing right where one of the fire extinguishers was kept.

Grinning, she watched them knock the shots back and slam the glasses onto the bar. Some barracked for more but she already knew the best man had other ideas. Her part in their debauched night was over; they were onto their next destination—she didn't really want to know where or how much further downhill they were going to slide.

'A thank-you kiss!' one of the guys called. 'Kiss! Kiss!'

They all chanted.

Mya just held up the lighter and flicked it so the flame shot up. She waved it slowly back and forth in front of her face. 'I wouldn't want you to get hurt,' she said with a teasing tilt of her head.

They howled and hissed like water hitting a burning element. Laughing—mostly in relief now—she watched them mobilise and work their way to the door. And that was when she saw him.

Brad *High-School-Crush* Davenport.

For a second, shock slackened every muscle and she dropped the lighter. Grasping at the last moment to stop it slipping, she accidentally caught the hot end. *Damn.* She tossed it onto the shelf below the bar and rubbed the palm of her hand on the half-apron tied round her waist. The sharp sting of that small patch of skin didn't stop her from staring spellbound schoolgirl-fashion at her former *HSC*. But that was because he was staring right at her as if she were the one and only reason he'd walked into the bar.

Good grief. She tried to stop the burn spreading to her belly because it wasn't right that one look could ignite such a reaction in her.

Back in the days when she'd believed in fairy tales, she'd also believed Brad would have been her perfect prince. Now she knew so much better: a) there were no princes, b) even if there were, she had no need for a prince and c) Brad Davenport was nowhere near perfect.

Although to be fair, he certainly looked it. Now—impossible though it might be—he looked more perfect than ever. All six feet three and a half inches of him. She knew about the half because it was written in pencil on the door-jamb in the kitchen leading to the butler's sink, along with Lauren's height and those of their mum and dad—one of the displays of Happy Familydom his mother had cultivated.

Topping the modelicious height, his dark brown hair was neatly trimmed, giving him a clean-cut, good-boy look. He was anything but good. Then there were the eyes—light brown maple-syrup eyes, with that irresistible golden tinge to them. With a single look that he'd perfected at an eyebrow-raising young age, he could get any woman to beg him to pour it all over her.

And Brad obliged. The guy had had more girlfriends than Mya had worked overtime hours. And Mya had done nothing but work since she'd badgered the local shop owner into letting her do deliveries when she was nine years old.

She tried to move but some trickster had concreted her feet to the floor. She kept staring as he walked through the bar, and with every step he came closer, her temperature lifted another degree. This despite the air-conditioning unit blasting just above the bar.

He was one of those people for whom the crowds parted, as if an invisible bulldozer were clearing the space just ahead of him. It wasn't just his height, not just his conventionally handsome face with its perfect symmetry and toothpaste-advertisement teeth, but his demeanour. He had the *presence* thing down pat. No wonder he won every case he took on. People paid attention to him whether they wanted to or not. Right now Mya wasn't the only person staring. Peripheral vision told her every woman in the bar was; so were most of the men.

She needed to pull it together. She wasn't going to be yet another woman who rolled over and begged for Brad Davenport—even if he was giving her that *look*. But why was he giving *her* that look? He'd never looked at her like that before; in fact he'd never really looked at her at all.

Her heart raced the way it did before an exam when she was in mid *'OMG I've forgotten everything'* panic. Had she entered a parallel universe and somehow turned sixteen all over again?

'Hi, Brad.' She forced a normal greeting as he stepped up to the space the stag boys had left at the bar.

'Hi, Mya.' He mirrored her casual tone—only his was genuine whereas hers was breathless fakery.

It was so unfair that the guy had been blessed with such gorgeousness. In the attractiveness exam of life, Brad scored in the top point five per cent. But it—and other blessings from birth—had utterly spoilt him. Despite her knowing this, the maple-syrup glow in those eyes continued to cook her brain to mush. She ran both hands down the front of her apron, trying to get her muscles to snap out of the spellbound lethargy. But her body had gone treacly soft inside while on the outside her skin was sizzling hot. What was she waiting for? 'What can I get you?'

He smiled, the full-bore Brad Davenport charming smile. 'A beer, please.'

'Just the one?' She flicked her hair out of her eyes with a businesslike flip of her fingers. That was better— the sooner she got moving, the more control she'd regain. And she could put herself half in the fridge while she got his beer; that would be a very good thing.

'And whatever you're having. Are you due a break soon?' He stood straight up at the bar, not leaning on it as most of the other customers did. In his dark jacket and white open-neck shirt, he looked the epitome of the 'hotshot lawyer who'd worked late'.

Mya blinked rapidly. She *was* due for her break, but she wasn't sure she wanted to have it with him around. She felt as if she was missing something about this. It was almost as if he thought she'd been expecting him. 'It's pretty busy.'

'But that stag party has left so now's a good time, right? Let me get you a drink.'

'I don't dri—'

'Water, soda, juice,' he listed effortlessly. 'There are other options.' He countered her no-drinking-on-the-job argument before she'd even got it out.

Good grief. Surely he wasn't hitting on her? No way—the guy had never noticed her before.

These days Mya was used to being hit on—she worked in a bar after all. The guys there were usually drinking alcohol, so inevitably their minds turned to sex after a time. Any woman would do; it wasn't that she was anything that special. Naturally they tried it on, and naturally she knew how to put them off. She deliberately dressed in a way that wouldn't invite attention; her plain vee-neck black tee minimised her boobs and the apron tucked round her hips covered most of her thighs in her black jeans. She did wear the platforms, but the extra couple of inches helped her ability to look customers in the eye.

She still had to look up to Brad. And right now he was looking into her eyes as if there were nothing and no one else in the room to bother with. Yeah, he was good at making a woman feel as if she were everything in his world. Very good.

'I'll have some water,' she muttered. There was zero alcohol in her system but she really needed to sober up. Not to mention cool down. She swallowed, determined to employ some easy bartender-to-customer-type conversation. 'Been a while since I've seen you. What have you been up to?'

'I've been busy with work.'

Of course, he was reputedly amazing in the courtroom, but she bet his work wasn't all he'd been busy with. The guy was legendary even at school. She and Lauren had been there a full five years after him and there'd been talk of his slayer skills. Lauren had been mega popular with all the older girls because they wanted to get to him through her.

'You need to get away from the bar to have a break,' he said once she'd set his drink in front of him.

Actually she quite liked that giant block of wood between them. She'd thought herself well over that teen crush, but all it had taken was that one look from him and she was all saucy inside. But there was a compelling glint in his eyes, and somehow she didn't manage to refuse.

As he shepherded her through the crowd, she steeled herself against the light brush of his hand on her back. She was *not* feeling remotely feminine next to his tall, muscled frame. She was *not* enjoying the bulldozer effect and seeing everyone clear out of his path and him guiding her through as if she were some princess to be protected. Surely she couldn't be that pathetic?

The balcony was darker and quieter. Of course he'd know where to find the most intimate place in an overcrowded venue. She pressed her back against the cold wall. She preferred to be able to keep an eye on the punters, and it gave her unreliable muscles some support. But in a second she realised it was a bad idea because Brad now towered in front of her. Yeah, he was all she could see and there was no way of getting around him easily.

The loud rhythm of the music was nothing on the frantic beat of her pulse in her ears. But he must be used to it—women blushing and going breathless in his company. She hoped he didn't think it was anything out of the ordinary.

'Will you excuse me a sec?' she said briskly. 'I just need to check a couple of messages.'

'Sure.'

She slipped her hand into her pocket, needing to fill in a few of her fifteen minutes and catch her breath. Besides, the imp in her wanted to know Lauren's reaction to the photo she'd sent. But there were no messages at all—which was odd given Lauren's tech-addiction. She frowned at the phone.

'Did you need to make a call?' he asked quietly.

'Do you mind? It won't take a second.' And it would fill in a few more of the fifteen minutes.

'Go for it.' Brad lifted his glass and sipped.

Mya turned slightly towards the wall and made the call.

'What did you think?' she quietly asked as soon as Lauren answered.

'Think of what?'

'The pic,' Mya mumbled into the phone, turning further away so Lauren's big, bad brother couldn't hear. 'I sent it a couple of hours ago.'

'What picture?'

'*The* pic.' Mya's heart drummed faster. She glanced at Brad. Standing straight in front of her—a little too close. His eyes flicked up from her body to her face. She didn't want him listening, but now she'd looked at him, she couldn't look away. Not when she'd seen that look in his eyes. It wasn't just maple syrup now. It was alight with something else.

'I haven't received any pic. What was it of?' Lauren laughed.

'But I sent it,' Mya said in confusion. She'd heard that whooshing sound when the message had gone. 'You must have got it.'

'Nup, nada.'

Mya's blood pounded round her body. Sweltering,

she tried to think. Because if that message hadn't gone to Lauren, then to whom had it gone?

She stared up at the guy standing closer than he ought and gradually became aware of a change in him. His eyes weren't just alive with the maple-syrup effect; no, now they were lit with unholy amusement. Why—?

Impossible.

The heat of anticipation within Mya transformed to horror in less than a heartbeat. And to make it worse, Brad suddenly smiled, hell, his shoulders actually shook—was the guy *laughing at her*?

'I definitely haven't got it,' Lauren warbled on. 'But I'm glad you rang because I haven't seen you in...'

Mya zoned out from Lauren, remembering the rush in the change room, the way she'd been giggling and not concentrating, the way her fingers had slipped over the screen...

No. Please no.

Lauren's voice and the noise from the bar all but disappeared, as if she'd dived into a swimming pool and could hear only muted, warped sound. Her stunned brain slowly cranked through the facts while the rest of her remained locked in the heat of his gaze.

Her contacts list automatically defaulted to alphabetical order. She'd never deleted all the contacts already on it either—and it was an old phone of Lauren's. No doubt her brother's number had been programmed in a long, long time ago. And *B* came before *L*. So first in the phone list?

Davenport. Brad Davenport.

CHAPTER TWO

Mya ignored the fact that Lauren was still babbling in her ear and jabbed the phone, shutting it down. She shoved it back in her pocket and tossed her head to get her fringe out of her eyes. 'It seems my phone's died,' she said with exaggerated effervescence. 'Can I borrow yours?'

Brad's silent chuckle became a quick, audible burst before he summoned the control to answer. 'Really?'

She nodded vehemently, pretending she couldn't feel the rhythmic vibrating against her thigh.

'But your phone is ringing.'

Yeah, there was no pretending she couldn't hear the shrill squawks over the beat of the bar music.

'What is that?'

'It's a recording of dolphins talking to each other,' she answered brightly before hitting him with a bald-faced lie. 'But while my ringer is working, the person on the other end can't hear me.'

'Maybe you hit mute.'

'Look, can I use it?' She dropped all pretence at perky and spoke flatly. Oh, she wanted to curl into a ball and roll behind a rock. Now. This was why he was here tonight. What had he thought? Surely he hadn't thought the picture was meant for him and he'd come to her? As if she'd called him?

Mya bit back hysterical laughter. Teen Mya would have loved Brad Davenport to hunt her down for a hook-up. Adult Mya had learned to avoid sharks. And of all the people she had to mistakenly send a picture to, it had to be her best friend's brother? Her best friend's completely *gorgeous*, speed-through-a-million-sexual-partners brother?

Brad held her gaze captive with his warm, amused one. 'But my phone cost a lot of money and I don't like the way you're holding that glass of water. I don't think my phone can survive the depths.'

Was the guy a mind-reader? Of course she wanted to drown the thing—she'd drown Brad himself if she could. Or better still, herself.

How could she have made such a mistake? This ranked as the most mortifying moment of her life. Why had she gone with the scarlet bikini with the see-through sides?

'How come you have my number anyway?' he asked lazily, confirming the worst.

'This was an old phone of Lauren's.' Mya groaned. 'She passed it on to me.'

'One of the ones she lost and made Dad replace?'

Hell, that would be right. For a while there Lauren had made her father pay—literally. 'She told me he'd given her a new one and she didn't need this one any more.' She didn't like the frown in Brad's eyes.

Yeah, she was the bad influence, wasn't she? The one who came from the wrong side of the tracks to lead Lauren astray. Did he think she abused her relationship with Lauren to get things? Lauren's parents had thought that. Indeed, Lauren *had* tried to give Mya things. Mya had refused to take most of them. The little she had, she'd hidden from her own parents. She didn't want them feeling bad that they couldn't afford those kinds of gifts—indeed any. Even then Lauren had tricked her into taking this phone and she'd taken nothing since.

And now? Now there was no dignity left in this situation. 'Would you please delete it?' she asked. Yeah, begging already.

'Never.'

Incredibly, his instant laughing response melted her but she couldn't be flattered by this. She just *couldn't*. 'It wasn't meant for you.'

'More's the pity,' he said softly. 'Do you often text pictures of yourself in underwear to your friends?'

'It wasn't *underwear*,' she said indignantly.

His chin lifted and the sound of his laughter rang out, crashing and curling over her like a wave of warmth. 'It's a bra.'

But Mya couldn't float in that tempting sea. 'It's a bikini.'

He shook his head, his brown eyes teasing. 'Sorry, Mya. It's a bra.'

She was still too mortified to be teased. 'I was in a swimwear store. I wanted Lauren's opinion on it. It was a bikini.'

'There were see-though bits.' He gestured widely and half shrugged. 'There was underwire. Looked like a bra to me.'

'You'd know because you've seen so many?' She tried to hide, but felt her blush rise higher.

'Sure,' he chuckled. 'And for the record, yes, you can definitely get away with it.'

Brad watched Mya closely and couldn't bring himself to take the polite step back despite knowing the

doll was embarrassed beyond belief. But no way in hell
was he ever deleting that image. She was gorgeous—
far more gorgeous than he'd realised. The picture had
been the teaser, but seeing her like this now? All flushed
and snappy, pocket-sized but bright-eyed—he was beyond intrigued.

Her hair was swept into a ponytail. Now he remembered the colour had frequently changed. She and Lauren
had spent for ever in Lauren's room, giggles emanat-
ing as they did outrageous things to their hair. Though
right now, instead of hot pink and purple, Mya's hair colour looked almost natural—a light brown with slightly
blonde streaks round the front. Her wickedly high cheekbones created sharp planes sloping down to that narrow
little chin. Those teeth and that impish smile broke the
perfection, yet were perfect themselves. The all-black
ensemble was unusual for her but it didn't hide her body.
Despite her slender limbs and pixie face, she wasn't boyishly slim. Her jeans were painted on, and the apron
around her hips didn't wholly hide her curvy butt. As
for those breasts… Plumped up by the bikini/bra in the
picture, they'd been so bountiful they'd spilled over the
edges. Now, disguised under that plain black tee, their
silhouette was minimised. But no simple cotton covering could fully hide the softness that seemed sinfully
generous in proportion to her small stature.

His heart drummed a triumphant beat. Blood pulsed,
priming muscles. Because he'd seen the way she'd
looked at him—the flash she hadn't been able to hide
when he'd first walked into the bar. There'd been that
pull, that instinctive reaction. He knew the signs—the
second glances, small smiles, the heightened colour.
The sparkle in the eyes, the parting of the lips. Brad
Davenport also knew his worth. He knew he had a body

that attracted a second glance—oh, and the cynic in him knew most women would never forget his trust fund. So he was used to being wanted and he knew when a woman wanted him.

Now the tip of her tongue briefly touched that too-wide top lip and then she bit back her smile. Yeah, she still had that gap between her two front teeth.

With just a look she'd had those stag-party guys competing to catch her close and hold her. Only she'd held them off with a few words and a hint of fire. And he wasn't thinking of the lighter flame.

Brad's entire body was on fire, and for the second time that night he gave in to impulse. He took her glass from her and put it on the table next to his.

'What are you doing?' A breathless squeak.

'We're old friends,' he said softly. 'We should greet each other properly.'

'I wouldn't have said we were *friends*.' Her voice wobbled.

He smiled at the sound. He'd stirred a small response from her, but he wanted more. And he was used to winning what he wanted. Before she could say anything more, he stepped close and caught her mouth with his.

She instantly tensed, but he kept it light. When the stiff surprise ebbed from her body—pleasingly quickly—he lifted his head a fraction and stepped closer at the same time. He flicked his tongue to feel her soft lips, tracing their uneven length, and then sealing his to hers again and tasting the delight inside her mouth. And then she kissed him back and that fire exploded. Man, Mya Campbell was a hell of a lot hotter than he'd ever thought possible.

For a split second Mya wondered if she were dreaming. Then the heat blasted into her and she knew not even *her* imagination could come up with this. She held her head up without even realising—no thought of pushing him away. Because the guy did wicked things with his tongue—sweeping it between her lips. Deeper and deeper again. Caressing her mouth as if it were the most delicious pleasure. She softened, opening more. And he stepped closer, taking more, *giving* so much more.

His chest pressed into hers. She could feel how broad and strong he was. It was a damn good thing she had the wall behind her—she was sandwiched between two solid forces and it was utterly exquisite. His mouth was rapacious now. His body insistent. Like yin and yang—hard versus the soft. And yet there was tension in her body too, that fierce need for physical fulfilment unfurling inside.

She slid her hand over his abs, the heat of him blazing through the white cotton shirt. She could feel those taut muscles and shivered at the thought of them working hard above her, beneath her—every way towards pleasure.

Her rational mind spun off into the distance while her senses took centre stage, demanding all her attention. She all but oozed into him, utterly malleable, his to twist and tease. And he did—grinding against her, kissing her mouth, her jaw, her neck and back to her mouth. She threaded her fingers through his hair, opening yet more for him.

His hand slid to the curve of her hip, lower still to her butt. He spread his fingers, pulling her hips closer to the heat of his—so she could feel his response even more. A moan escaped as she felt his thick erection pressing against her belly. So hot, so soon, this was just so crazy.

But all thought vanished as his other hand slid up from her waist, cupping her breast. She momentarily tensed, anticipating the pain—she was too sensitive for touch there. But his fingers stilled, not following through on their upward sweep; a half-second later he moved again to cup her soft flesh, avoiding her nipple. Good thing, as both were overloading already just with the pressure of his chest against hers. She relaxed against him again as she realised he somehow understood. Instead he pressed deeper—his tongue laying claim to her mouth, his body almost imprinting on hers.

And despite this oh-so-thorough kiss, she wanted so much more than this.

She moved restlessly—tiny rocking motions of her hips. It was all she could manage given how hard he was pinning her to the wall. But with every small movement she drew closer and closer to the hit of ecstasy that she suddenly needed more than anything else in the world.

It wasn't a kiss; it was a siege—he'd encircled her and demanded her surrender. It hadn't taken her long to cave at all. Her fingers curled instinctively into his cotton shirt as wicked tension gripped her. Almost at breaking point—the convulsions of ecstasy were a mere breath away.

'Excuse me!'

Mya froze and she felt Brad's arms go equally rigid. She pulled back and met his eyes—he looked as startled as she felt.

'Mya, you're way over your break time.' Drew, her boss, snapped right beside her. 'What do you think you're doing?'

All but stupefied, Mya turned and stared at her boss. She literally didn't know. Couldn't think. Couldn't answer. She was still trying to process the chemical reaction that had ignited every cell while in Brad's embrace. But as she looked at the extreme irritation on Drew's face, reality rushed back. Her boss was furious. Panic slammed the door shut on the remaining good vibes—she couldn't afford to lose this job. What on earth *had* she been thinking?

'Drew, I'm so sorry,' she said in a breathless rush, stepping further away from Brad. 'I wasn't aware of the time. I didn't—'

'No kidding,' Drew interrupted rudely, her scrambled apology having no effect on his temper. 'This is—'

'My fault.' To Mya's horror, Brad coolly interrupted Drew. 'I distracted her.'

Drew turned his glower on Brad. But within a second his expression eased a fraction as he got a good look at the man now stepping up in front of him.

Mya watched the two men square off. All of a sudden Brad seemed both taller and broader as he moved to put himself partly between her and Drew. Oh, this wasn't good—she really didn't need Brad interfering; she was on the line as it was. She could handle Drew herself without any macho-male stuff.

Brad sent her a quick glance but seemed oblivious to her wordless plea to shut the heck up and back off. Instead he turned back to Drew.

Mya held her breath but then Brad smiled—that big, easy smile, with just a hint of the 'born-to-it-all' arrogance. 'My name's Brad Davenport.' He extended his hand as if it were not in the least embarrassing that he'd just been caught kissing the brains out of Drew's employee when she should have been working. 'I want to hire out your bar.'

'Drew.' Mya's manager paused a moment and then shook Brad's hand. 'This is a popular place. I'm not sure you'll need the whole bar for one small party.'

'It's not going to be a small party. I want the whole

bar,' Brad answered calmly. 'Obviously we'll pay to secure absolute privacy for the night.'

Mya watched the change come over Drew as he as-
sessed Brad's worth. It didn't take much to know the
clothes were designer, the watch gold, the self-assurance
in-built...

'I'm sure we can come to some arrangement.' Drew's
demeanour changed to sycophantic in a heartbeat.

'I'm sure we can.' Brad smiled his killer smile once
again. 'It should be good. This place has an atmosphere
I like.'

Mya watched the Davenport charm in action as he
arranged a meeting time with Drew. He got everything
his own way *so* easily. Utterly used to doors swinging
open—and women's legs parting on sight of that smile
too. And while she was totally relieved he'd just saved
her neck from the block, she was also irritated with the
ease with which he'd done it. The man had everything.
Money, looks, brains, charm. Had he ever known what
it was to have to fight for something? To really have to
work for something? Mya knew what it was to work,
hard.

'You have two minutes,' Drew said to Mya, as if he
were an emperor granting a favour to a lowly serf. 'Then
back behind that bar.'

'Of course.' Mya nodded as he disappeared into the
crowd. Then she turned back to Brad. 'I'm afraid you're
going to have to follow through on that meeting.'

'I'm looking forward to it.' Brad didn't look at all
bothered. 'I think a night here could be fun.'

Mya chose to ignore the hint of entendre in his expression. 'Have you got a reason to party?'

'Who needs a reason?' Brad shrugged.

'Because life's just one big party?'

He merely chuckled and then stepped closer. 'I'm sorry we were interrupted. Things were getting interesting there.'

But that close call had firmly grounded Mya. 'Things were getting out of hand,' she corrected, opting not to look any higher than his collar. 'I'm sorry about that. You took me by surprise.'

'Wow,' Brad said after a pause. 'I'm intrigued to think what it'll be like when I give you fair warning.'

Mya shook her head and stepped away. 'You're not getting another chance.'

She felt his hand on her elbow turning her back towards him. His hand slipped down her arm to take her fingers in his.

The touch made her look up before she thought better of it. His surprisingly intense expression incinerated her but she hauled herself from the ashes of easiness. Mya liked sex, but she preferred it within the context of some kind of relationship, not the one-night-stand scene Brad was champion of. And she was steering well clear of *any* kind of entanglement for the foreseeable future. Long-term future. She had too much else to do—like work, study and occasionally eat and sleep.

Also, this man had always had everything too easy. She'd just seen him in action—twice already tonight. He wasn't having her that way again. She truly had just been caught by surprise, and her response to him was simply a reflection of his expertise and her lack of any physical release in the last while, right?

The swirling frustration and embarrassment inside her coalesced and came out as temper. 'You thought that picture was a booty call, didn't you?' She called him out with sarcasm-coated words. 'From a woman that you haven't spoken to in at least five years?'

'Have we ever spoken?' He laughed off her accusation. 'I thought you and Lauren just paraded around fake-Goth-style and giggled behind closed doors. Interesting to think what was really going on behind those doors given the pictures you send each other. Thinking about it, you two went to prom together, didn't you?'

'With her boyfriend,' Mya answered.

'Oh, a threesome.' Brad laughed harder.

'If you remember, she tried to get you to take me.'

'Oh, yeah.' His eyes widened as he thought about it. 'That's right.'

Unlike him, Mya had *never* forgotten what for her had been the most mortifying moment of that night. He'd been home from university. He'd had some silvery-blonde girlfriend with him. Tall and sleek, she'd had the obligatory blue eyes and the label clothes and the 'born to it all' attitude. Mya had hated her on sight. The girlfriend had spent most of the time spread on a sofa being kissed to glory by Brad.

'You were wearing one of Lauren's dresses,' he said slowly.

'Yes.' She was amazed he'd now remembered that detail. Mya had butchered one of Lauren's many formal dresses. A soft, pretty pink dress—never a colour she'd normally wear. She'd taken to it with a pair of scissors and completely cut away the back and secured it with long, trailing ribbons. She'd been aiming for a soft romantic look.

It was the dress that she'd hoped might garner her the attention she'd thought she'd wanted. All she'd wanted to do was fit in—to be popular and accepted. To be just like the rest of them and *not* different for once. She'd wanted it to all be easy. But it was never as easy as a change of clothes. Make-overs didn't change the person underneath. She hadn't just been sixteen and never been kissed. She'd made it all the way to eighteen and first-year uni before that honour had fallen to a fellow student who'd seemed sweet enough until he'd had what he wanted.

But back at that night of the dance, she'd had the whole prom fantasy. What wallflower schoolgirl didn't? The one where the hottest guy in school asked her to dance and it was all perfect and ended with a kiss. Or the super-hot brother of the best friend asked her? Yeah, she'd been such a cliché. And she'd felt like a princess for all of five minutes, until Brad had ignored her. She'd been pretty and dressed up and hadn't even been able to turn the head of the most sexually hungry male she knew back then.

'You were too busy wearing that blonde to answer at the time,' Mya said dryly.

The dimple in his cheek deepened. 'Yeah, that's right.'

He hadn't appreciated his younger sister's interruption. Mya had seen the raw lust in him, the tease, the firmness with which he pulled the girl onto his lap—his strong arm wrapped around her waist, his confident hand close to her breast. And for a few minutes, she'd wanted to be that girl. Now for five minutes she had been. And it was better than any fantasy.

Mya sucked up her stupidity and turned her self-scorn towards him instead. 'That's all irrelevant anyway. What's really the issue here is how pathetically horn dog you are. You get a look at a woman in her *bikini* and you're suddenly hot for her? When you've never so much as looked at her in the last decade?'

Amusement still burned in his eyes. 'You were a child a decade ago.'

'It's still pathetic.' And frankly, insulting.

'Maybe that prom night isn't so irrelevant at all.' His smile widened. 'Did you have a crush on me back in high school? Your best friend's older brother?'

She gaped.

'Because,' he leaned closer and drawled outrageously, 'you wouldn't have been the only one.'

Hell, the guy had an ego. Unfortunately what he'd said was true. There were several girls who'd done the faux-friendship thing to Lauren just to get close to her brother. Mya shook her head and denied him anyway. 'Girls that age are at the mercy of hormones just as boys are and they fixate on the nearest object. Their fixating on you was probably more a matter of locality than your attractiveness.'

He grinned wolfishly. 'So if it wasn't me your hormones fixed on, then who?'

'I didn't have the time.'

'Everybody has the time.' He moved closer as his voice dropped to an intimate whisper. 'Who did you used to dream of?'

'No one.'

'So rebellious on the outside, such a square inside.' He shook his head.

Mya gritted her teeth.

'No wonder you erupted with one touch—you've been repressed too long.'

Mya couldn't answer because that was actually true. She'd been without too long; that was the reason she'd inhaled his touch like an attention-starved animal.

'Did you wish I'd said yes to Lauren and taken you to the ball? Is that why you're trying to cut me down now? Did I burst your love-struck teen bubble?'

He was so close to the mark it was mortifying. But she'd never, ever admit it. 'I'm sure you've burst many poor girls' bubbles, but you never burst mine.' Mya willed a languid tone. 'Fact is I've always seen through your charm to what you really are.'

'And what am I?'

'Selfish, spoilt, arrogant. Insufferable.'

'Is that all?' He paused a moment. 'You don't want to add some more about how unattractive you find me?'

Very funny. 'You're so up yourself it's unbelievable.'

'But you still want me.' He breathed out and then laughed. 'You're never going to be able to deny it. Not when you kissed me like that.'

'You were the one who kissed me.' Cross, she licked her extremely dry lips.

'It started that way but within two seconds you were clawing my shirt off.'

'I was trying to push you away.'

The rogue laughed harder. Mya pulled her hand free of his grip and strode back through to the bar. She got behind it and found he was right there in front of her, waiting to be served—and still annoyingly amused.

'You have to go now,' she told him firmly, determined not to let that smile affect her. 'I have work to do.' She pulled out a chopping board, some lemons and a knife to prove it.

'No.' He shook his head. 'I need you more than ever now.'

Yeah, right. He'd never needed her before. And while she didn't want to think he'd kissed her on a whim, the fact was he had. He'd never wanted to kiss her before, remember? The guy who had his pick of every woman in every room in the world hadn't noticed her until she was hardly dressed. It really didn't do much for her ego. And even less for his character. It showed he was simply attracted to the lowest common denominator—bared flesh.

He shook his head in mock despair. 'You suspect my motivation.'

'Your reputation does precede you.' She maintained her cool. 'And all you've said and done so far tonight merely confirms the worst.'

'Actually, Mya, I really do need you.' His expression went serious. 'I'm not just going to hire out the bar. I'm going to hire you.'

CHAPTER THREE

'I'M NOT interested.' Mya was telling herself that over and over but her body wasn't listening. Her pulse still pounded, her ears still attuned to every nuance in his words. But her ego was piqued. He'd kissed her only after seeing her breasts in a skimpy bikini—and now he wanted to *hire* her? For what exactly?

'Sure you are.' He winked. 'I have to have a party now and you're the perfect person to organise it for poor helpless me.'

She shook her head. 'Poor and helpless are the antithesis of what you are. You don't need anyone, let alone me.'

He grinned, obviously appreciating the unvarnished truth, but behind the smiling eyes she sensed his brain was whizzing. Yeah, the guy was wickedly calculating. And far too together already after the kiss that had shattered her. She needed to keep her guard well up.

'Lauren's finished her degree,' he said.

Momentarily thrown by the change in topic, Mya blinked. Then she nodded, but said nothing. If she hadn't been such an idiot, she'd have been a lot nearer to finishing her degree too.

'For a while there it didn't seem likely she'd even finish high school let alone a university degree,' he added.

He was right. When Mya had started at that school,

Lauren's wild streak had been on the verge of going septic and that hadn't been in the perfect Davenport family plan at all. They were all graduates with successful careers—and expected Lauren to achieve the same. Whereas Mya was the *only* one in her family to have finished school. She was supposed to be the first in the family to finish a degree too. Honours no less, having won a prestigious scholarship. Except she'd screwed it up, and now she doubted that she'd ever deserved it. But she'd finish her degree all on her own account—independence was now everything to her. This time she was taking the lead from Lauren. So she nodded. 'She defied everyone's expectations and did it. Brilliantly too.'

There was a pause and she couldn't help glancing at him. And then they both laughed at that one unbelievable aspect of Lauren's success.

'It's more than a little ironic, don't you think?' he said, his face lightening completely. 'That she almost dropped out and now she's going to be a teacher?'

'She'll be a dragon too, I bet.' Mya bit her lip but couldn't quite hold back the chuckle. 'Super-strict. She won't put up with any illegal nail polish.' Back in the day, Mya and Lauren had broken more than the nail-polish rules. Their favourite look had been purple splatter.

'So we'll have the party for her. It's as good an excuse as any,' Brad said confidently. 'Exam results are out. It's not long until Christmas. Many of her friends are going overseas and won't be back for her graduation ceremony next year. She's worked hard for a long while.' He faced her square on again. 'So we'll surprise her.'

'You're going to have it as a surprise?' Mya asked. 'You want me to distract her?' She'd be happy to sneak Lauren out and be there for the big surprise moment.

But he was shaking his head. 'I want you to organise it.'

Mya's enthusiasm burst like a kid's balloon encountering the prick of a needle. Of course he did. He had to have this party but she'd be the one copping all the extra work to get it ready? Her ego suffered another blow—and more importantly she just didn't have the time to do it. 'Isn't partying *your* area of expertise?'

'Darling, I've never *planned* a party. I *am* the party.' He mimicked her emphasis.

'Oh, please.'

'Who better to arrange it than my sister's best friend? I said I'll hire you. You'll be paid.'

She bridled. 'I'm not taking money from you. I'm her *friend*.' The thought of him paying for her services irked her. She'd always put in an honest day's work but the thought of *Brad* owning her time spiked her hackles.

'I'll get in a planner instead.' He shrugged.

Now she was even more ticked. He was too used to getting everything his own way. 'You think you can just throw some money on the table and have some flash event happen? Lauren wouldn't want some impersonal, chic party put together by cutesy PR girls she doesn't even know.' Mya shook her head. 'Wouldn't it mean more to her if *you* put in some personal effort? She doesn't like cookie-cutter perfection.' Lauren had had so many things bought for her—by impersonal secretaries. She liked the individual—that was part of what had drawn her and Mya so close.

He looked sceptical. 'You think I should choose the colour scheme and the canapés?'

'Why not?' she asked blandly.

'You're not tempted by an unlimited budget and licence to do anything? Most women would love that, right?'

'I'm not like most women. Nor is Lauren. You should organise it—it's your idea.' She sent him a cutting glance. 'Or are you too selfish to spend time on her?'

He laughed. 'Sweetheart, every human on this planet is selfish,' he said. 'We all do what's ultimately best for ourselves. I am doing this for very selfish reasons and not many of them to do with Lauren herself. It's mainly so *I* don't have to deal with my mother's hand-wringing and a frozen dinner out with my parents to celebrate Lauren's graduation. And so *you* don't get in trouble with your boss and take it out on me. Does that make me a bad person?'

Heat ricocheted round her body like a jet of boiling oil as she saw the intense look in his eye. He didn't want her to think badly of him? And he *was* doing this to prevent her from getting in trouble. 'No,' she conceded.

'You have to help me,' he said softly.

That was one step too far. 'We wouldn't be in this position if you hadn't kissed me.' She tried to argue back but felt herself slipping. 'You created this problem. You don't need me.'

'Do I have the names and numbers of half her friends? No. I don't know all her university mates the way you do. Of course I need your help.'

Silent, she looked at him.

'*I'm* thinking of Lauren. Are *you*?' he jeered.

She sighed. 'For Lauren's sake, I'll help. But you're not paying me.'

'What a good friend you are,' he teased.

'I am, actually,' she declared.

'We all do what is best for *ourselves*,' he murmured with a shake of his head. 'Wasn't insisting I be actively involved in the planning really because *you* wanted to spend more time with *me*?'

She gaped—how did he turn that one around? 'No. I'm only thinking of Lauren.' She vehemently denied that tendril of excitement curling through her innards at the thought of spending time with him. He had an outsize ego that needed stripping. 'You think you're irresistible, don't you?'

'Experience has led me to believe that's often the case.'

His eyes were glinting. He might be laughing, but she suspected part of him meant it. *Outrageous* wasn't the word. The guy needed taking down a peg or forty. 'Not in *this* case.'

'No?' He chuckled, radiating good humour. 'So that blush is pure annoyance? Then you've nothing to worry about, right? We can organise Lauren's party together because you can resist me no problem.'

Could she resist him? For a second Mya wondered and then her fighting spirit came to the fore. Of *course* she could. 'No problem at all.'

He leaned closer. 'I'm sorry I haven't seen much of you in recent years.'

'Maybe you should have turned up to a couple of Lauren's birthday parties.'

He winced, hand to his chest. 'I was overseas.'

She knew he'd studied further overseas before coming back and setting up his own practice. 'So convenient. For work, was it? You learned well from your father.'

'Meaning?'

'Doesn't *he* use work for emotional avoidance too? Earns millions to buy the things to make up for it.' Lauren had been given so many *things* and none of them what she'd truly yearned for.

The laughing glint vanished from Brad's eyes. 'Formed a few judgments over the years, haven't you?'

Mya realised she might have gone more than a little far. 'I'm sorry, that was out of line. I'll always be grateful for the kindness your parents showed me,' she said stiltedly, embarrassed at her rudeness.

But he laughed again, the devil dancing back in his eyes. 'Their *kindness*?'

Okay, maybe he did remember the ultra-frosty welcome she'd got for the first year or three that she and Lauren hung out. 'They didn't ban me from their home.' Even though she knew they'd wanted to. Now they realised they owed Mya something.

'Don't worry about it. I know even better than you what a mess it was.'

He'd certainly left home the second he could. Mya had been the one who'd spent every afternoon after school with Lauren in that house. She and Lauren hid up in Lauren's suite, laughing and ignoring the frozen misery downstairs. The false image of the perfect family. 'But Lauren's the one who's made the conscious effort to be different from how she was raised.'

'You're saying I've not?'

Mya shrugged. 'You're the mini-me lawyer.'

'You do know my father and I practise vastly different types of law. I'm not in his firm.'

Blandly she picked up a glass and polished it. That didn't mean anything.

'What, all lawyers are the same?' He snorted. 'I don't do anything he does. I work with kids.'

She knew this, and at this precise moment she point-blank refused to be impressed by it. 'You think your save-the-children heroic-lawyer act somehow ameliorates your womanising ways?' Because Brad *was* a womaniser. Just like his father.

'Doesn't it?'

See, he didn't even deny the charge. 'You think? Yeah, that's probably why you do child advocacy,' she mused. 'To score the chicks by showing your sensitive side.'

He laughed, a loud burst of genuine humour that had her smiling back in automatic response.

'That's an interesting take. I've never really thought about it that way.' He shrugged. 'But even if it does give me some chick-points, at least I've done something with my life that's useful. Is igniting alcohol for party boys useful?'

She shifted uncomfortably. Serving drinks was a means to an end. But she managed a smooth reply. 'Helping people relax is a skill.'

His brows shot up. 'I'm not sure you're that good at helping guys *relax*.'

She met his gaze and felt the intensity pull between them again.

'Are you still at university or are you finished now?' He broke the silence, looking down and toying with the pile of postcards on the edge of the bar.

'I'm there part-time this year.'

'Studying what?'

'A double degree. Law and commerce.'

'Law and commerce?' he repeated. 'So you're going to become a greedy capitalist like my evil father and me?' He laughed. She didn't blame him, given her stabbing disapproval mere seconds ago. 'You're enjoying it?'

'Of course,' she said stiffly.

'And the plan?'

'A job in one of the top-five firms, of course.'

'Speciality?'

'Corporate.'

'You mean like banking? Counting beans? Helping companies raid others and earning yourself wads of cash in the process?'

'Nothing wrong with wanting to earn a decent wage in a job where you can sit down.' She walked away to serve the customers she'd been ignoring too long. Her need to achieve wasn't something trust-fund-son over there could understand. She needed money—not for a giant flat-screen TV and a house with a lap-pool and overseas jaunts. She needed a new house, yes, but not for herself. For her parents.

She was conscious of his gaze still on her as he sat now nursing something non-alcoholic and taking in the scene. As she glanced over, she saw his eyes held a hint of bleak strain. Was it possible that behind the playboy façade, the guy was actually *tired*?

But he didn't leave. Even when the bar got quieter and they'd turned the music down a notch. In another ten minutes the lights would brighten to encourage the stragglers out of the dark corners. Mya felt him watching her, felt her fingers go butter-slippery. She kept thinking about the kiss; heat came in waves—when memory swept over control. She couldn't stay away when he signalled her over to his end of the bar.

'I've been thinking about the drinks for Lauren's party,' he said easily. 'It would be good to offer something different, right? Not just the usual.'

So that was why he was still sitting there? He was party planning? Not surreptitiously watching her at all?

'There you go, see?' Mya said brightly, masking how deflated she suddenly felt. 'You'll organise a brilliant party. You don't need me.'

'I need your expertise,' he countered blandly. 'I don't think I can ignite alcohol.'

No, but he could ignite other things with a mere look. Mya pulled her head together and focused on the task at hand. 'You want me to come up with a couple of Lauren-inspired cocktails?'

'They're the house speciality, right? So, yeah, make up some new ones, give them a cute name, we'll put them up on the blackboard.' He chuckled. 'Something that'll be good fun to watch the bartender make. Definitely use a bit of fire.'

'And ice,' she answered, then turned away to scoop crushed ice into a glass and wished she could put herself in with it. How could she be this hot? Maybe it was a bug?

'What would you use to make her cocktail?' he asked idly. 'What kind of spirit is Lauren?'

She took the question seriously. 'Classic bones, quirky overtones. A combination that you wouldn't expect.'

She turned her back to him and looked at the rows and rows of gleaming bottles. Reached up and grabbed a few and put them on the bar beside Brad. Then she poured. 'Her cocktail would need to be layered.' Carefully she bent and made sure each layer sat properly on the next. 'Unexpected but delicious.' She smiled to herself as she added a few drops of another few things. Then she straightened and looked at him expectantly.

He just held her gaze.

Finally she broke the silence. 'You don't want to try it?'

He studied the vivid blue, orange and green liquid in the glass in front of him. 'Not unless you try it first. It looks like poison to me. Too many ingredients.'

'I don't drink on the job.' She smiled sweetly. 'Are you too scared?'

'Don't think you can goad me into doing what you want,' he said softly. But he picked up the glass and took a small sip. He inhaled deeply after swallowing the liquid fire. 'That's surprisingly good.'

'Yes,' Mya said smugly. 'Just like Lauren.'

He grinned his appreciation. 'All right, clever clogs, what cocktail would you put together for me?'

Oh, that was easy. She picked up a bottle and put it on the bar.

He stared at it, aghast. 'You're calling me a boring old malt?'

'It needs nothing else. Overpowering enough on its own.'

'Well, you're wrong. There's another like that that's more me than a single malt.'

'What's that?'

'Tequila. Lethal, best with a little salt and a twist of something tart like one of your lemons.'

She rolled her eyes.

'And what are you?' He laughed. 'Brandy? Vodka? Maudlin gin?'

'None. I don't have time.'

'You should make time. You shouldn't work so hard.'

'Needs must.' She shrugged it off lightly. 'And you have to leave now so I can close up the bar.'

'Have lunch with me tomorrow. We can brainstorm ideas.'

She should have said yes to organising the party on her own. Why had she thought he ought to have active involvement? 'I'm at class tomorrow. I'm doing summer school.' She'd be in summer school for the next three years.

'Okay, breakfast, then.'

She shook her head. 'I'm working.'

'This place is open all night?' His brows lifted.

'I work in a café in the mornings and some other shifts that fit around my classes and the bar work.'

'And you work here every night?'

'Not on Sundays.'

'Where do you work on a Sunday—the café?'

She nodded, looking up in time to see his quick frown. She rolled her eyes. Yes, she worked hard; that was what people did when they had to. Eating was essential after all.

'Why didn't you take a summer internship?'

She turned and put all the bottles back in their places on the shelves. The summer internships at prestigious law firms in the city were sought after. Often they led to permanent job offers once degrees were completed. But she wasn't going there again, not until her final year of study and she'd recovered her grade average. Not to mention her dignity. 'I need to keep going with my studies and, believe it or not, I earn more in the bar.'

'You get good tips?'

'Really good.' She rinsed her hands again and wiped down the bench.

'You might get more if you let some more of that red lace stuff show.' He glanced down the bar. 'One thing we are going to do for the party is have better bartender outfits. You'd never guess what you wear beneath the undertaker's uniform you've got going on in here.'

Heat scorched her cheeks again. Once again, why had she picked that wretched scarlet bikini? He was never going to let her forget it. 'This is what we all wear in the bar. It's simple, efficient and looks smart.'

'It's deadly dull and doesn't make the most of your assets. Not like that red underneath it.'

'It's not underneath it.'

'You took it off?' He looked appalled. 'Why on earth did you take it off?'

'It was a *bikini*,' she said, goaded. She closed her eyes and breathed deep to stop herself laughing. His wicked smile suggested he knew she was close to it anyway. She looked at him. Not at all sorry he had to shell out however many tens of thousands to hire the most popular bar in town outright for a night during the busiest time of the year.

'Why do men get so fixated on lacy underwear?' she asked aloud. 'Don't you know sexy underwear is no indicator of how far a woman is prepared to go?'

'You're saying you'll go further than what your boring day-bra might indicate?' he said mildly.

'No!' she snapped.

'So you do wear boring day-bras?'

Oh, the guy was incorrigible. But, heaven help her, she couldn't help but laugh. So she'd see him some saucy talk, and raise him some flirt. She nodded with a secret smile. 'No lace.'

'Why's that?' The corner of his beautiful mouth lifted.

'No boyfriend to buy me some,' she flipped tartly and stalked away, letting the clip of her high heels underline her reply.

'You wouldn't let some guy buy you frills,' he called after her. 'You're too independent for that.'

Very true. Interesting he understood that. But she swung back to face him because she didn't want him thinking he knew it all. 'Actually it's just that they're uncomfortable.'

'They are?' His gaze lowered again.

'No woman can wear those things for more than five minutes.'

'No woman in my presence would need to.'

She ignored the comeback and cooed instead. 'I'm very sensitive. Lace hurts.' She watched his expression with amazement. Was he actually blushing? She smirked, pleased she'd finally managed to push him off his self-assured pedestal.

'How sensitive?' He walked down the side of the bar so he was close to her again. 'Can they cope with touch?'

That was when she realised his flush wasn't from embarrassment but arousal. Her body clenched, drenched in fire. 'No.'

'No?' he asked, surprised. The flush on his skin deepened.

She was burning up with a blush to match.

'Hmm. That sensitive, huh?' He looked thoughtful. 'What other bits are too sensitive?'

She couldn't look away from the teasing intimacy in his eyes. The intense drive of his words melted her. She hadn't meant this to get so personal. She'd been out to tease him. Only her too-sensitive bits were shrieking right now, liquefying in the heat he was conjuring—his words locking her in a lit crucible.

'Must make it difficult for you,' he said softly. 'I bet you pull away. You can't just go with it.' He looked at her speculatively. 'Just the way you pulled back from me before.'

She was so hot, her soul singed by words alone. She couldn't even answer. Because in truth? He was right.

'Seems to me you need some practice coping.'

She shook her head. 'I'm not inexperienced.' And

she definitely didn't need to get any more experience by playing with him.

His mouth curved in disbelief. 'Aren't you?'

Well, okay, she wasn't as experienced as *him*. She lifted her head proudly. 'I've had boyfriends.' Jerks, the pair of them.

'Yeah, but you've never been with me.'

'And you're that amazing?' she asked, managing a tone of utter skepticism, which was quite something given her wayward hormones were shrieking that *yes, he was that amazing!*

His expression was pure intent. 'You'll have to wait and see.'

'You're so obnoxious.' She recovered her sass, more determined than ever to shoot him down. 'Why would I want to have sex with a guy who's been with every other girl in the city?'

'Not *every* other girl,' he protested. 'But I don't see anything wrong with sharing the love,' he added. 'If you have too much sex with one woman, she starts to get funny ideas. Better to have sex with too many women. Safer.'

'Oh, real safe.' She rolled her eyes. But he wasn't denying it. Brad Davenport wasn't a commitment kind of guy. He was a playboy.

He reached across the bar and ran a finger down her arm. Electricity sparked every millimetre of the way. She saw it. He saw it. There was no denying it. So she didn't.

'This isn't anything more than lust.' She turned and literally burrowed out more ice from the freezer.

'So what?' he calmly said behind her. 'It's still worth exploring.'

'Even if I agree there's chemistry, I'm not sure I can

bear to feed your over-bloated ego by saying yes.' But the feeling the guy could inspire with just a look?

'You'll always regret it if you don't,' he insisted.

'And probably regret it if I do.'

'Damned either way, then,' he said with a laugh. 'You might as well have the good moment and enjoy it.'

'Moment?' She suppressed the squeeze her muscles had in response to his laugh. 'As in singular? What are you going for here, some orgasmic snuffle?'

'You don't need to worry. I'll take care of you.'

'I don't need anybody to take care of me,' she denied, affronted.

'Really?'

Narrow-eyed, she watched him draw closer. It seemed to her there might be an imbalance of attraction here. Was it all about her wanting him? Or was the chemistry as insane for him as it was for her?

'Maybe you don't. But you keep thinking about that kiss,' he said. 'I can tell.'

She was shaking her head already but when she went to deny it he put his finger back on her mouth.

'You can't hide it. I see it in your eyes. It's the same for me,' he said simply. 'I want to kiss you again.'

'Brad—'

He straightened. 'I accept that you're saying no, for now, but don't deny that the desire is there.'

'I haven't kissed anyone in a while.' She shrugged. 'What happened before was merely a reaction to that.'

He shook his head. 'You were every bit as into it as I was. You're as "all or nothing" in your approach to life. It's just that you go for nothing and I go for all.'

'Have you ever managed nothing?'

'I am right now.'

'Really.' Not a question, more an expression of disbelief. 'Almost two hours with nothing?'

'Nothing,' he said, as if it wasn't an experience he was enjoying. 'Not so much as an eyelash flutter since you.'

Mya chuckled and this time she reached across, clasping his wrist as if she feared he was about to have a heart attack. 'How are *you* coping?'

'Moment by moment.' He clapped his hand over hers. 'But I'm quietly confident.'

'Quietly?' she mocked. She leaned across the bar again and gave him some advice. 'You shouldn't hype yourself up so much. It'll end up a disappointment.'

'What orgasm was ever a disappointment?'

She tried so hard not to blush. 'Is that all it is for you? The momentary thrill?'

'It's pretty much up there, yeah,' he drawled. 'I won't lie.' He lifted her hand with his and pressed her palm to his heart. 'I fancy you.' He paused. 'Now, can you speak with the same kind of honesty?'

For a moment she couldn't answer as she absorbed the strong, regular thud of his heartbeat. But while the moments of orgasm might feel good, it was the moments afterwards she was more worried about. She curled her fingers into a fist and pulled away from him. 'I'm not on trial here.'

'You're a coward,' he accused. 'Is having fun so wrong?'

Mya answered with absolute honesty. 'Not wrong. Inconvenient.'

'Never inconvenient. You need to sort your priorities.'

She shook her head and laughed. 'Oh, no, I have my priorities *exactly* right.'

No burst of heat was going to blow her balloon off course.

CHAPTER FOUR

THE next night Brad watched Mya stride into the all but empty bar like a bounty hunter on a hot trail. A satchel hung over her shoulder, she'd poured herself back into the black jeans, and her fiercely swept up hair all spelt *business* to him. The bar wasn't officially open yet, but she was here to work, and anyone watching would know it.

No Messing Around Mya.

He bit back the amusement, because he was going to mess with Mya. He knew he had to play it carefully or she'd block him the way she'd blocked all those other guys at the bar. But he knew the party was a brilliant idea, and having to work with her to plan it? Genius. Because he hadn't felt heat in nothing but a kiss in for ever. The chemistry between them had kept him awake and rock hard all hours. He'd never felt the thrill of the chase like this. Then again, he hadn't *had* to chase like this. He watched closely to see her reaction when she saw him but her face remained an expressionless mask—too expressionless. Now, that took effort.

Good. If she had to work hard to hide her reaction to him, that meant her reaction was extreme. As was his to her. But he wasn't going to hide it. No, he was all about having fun and being up front.

'Hi, darling,' he called, hoping to raise a spark.

She didn't answer until she'd reached the bar and then it was with a mocking coo. 'Have you forgotten my name? I'm Mya.'

'I can't call you "darling"?' He propped an elbow on the broad expanse of highly polished wood.

'I'm suspicious of men who rely on pet names.' She moved to put the bar between them. 'I wonder if it's because they can't remember the name of the woman they're with.'

He smiled, enjoying the way she was so determined to put him in his place.

'You've been guilty of it, haven't you?' She raised her brows and said it as a statement of fact, not a question.

He always remembered a woman's name at the time, but a few months later? Yeah, he'd better plead the fifth. With growing disappointment he watched her wind the apron round her waist, hiding how well her thighs were shown off in the spray-on jeans.

'We're not open yet.' She turned to face him. 'So I can't serve you.'

'It's all right.' Brad nodded at his half-empty glass. 'Your boss already has. I've been talking with him about the party. Saturday after next. That okay for you?'

Her teeth worried her lower lip as a frown creased her forehead. 'I'll need to talk to Drew. I'm rostered to work that night.'

'Not any more. It's already sorted. You're there as a guest, not a bartender.'

That little frown didn't lighten. 'Yes, but—'

'You work every night,' he interrupted. 'You're not going to take a night off for your best friend's surprise party?'

'Of course I am.'

'Then there's no problem, is there?'

'No, but you didn't need to arrange that for me.' Her vibrant green eyes rested on him, still frustratingly cool.

Was that what bothered her? Him interfering? Fair enough. 'I thought it would help,' he explained honestly. 'I wanted your boss to understand that he couldn't call on you at all that night and that I was willing to pay for extra staff.'

'And that's wonderful of you,' she said through a smile that couldn't be more fake. 'But I can handle my own requests for a night off.' She suddenly looked concerned more than cross. 'But it's very soon and very close to Christmas. You'll have to work quick to make sure people are free that night.'

'They'll be free.' Where the food and drink were free, people turned up.

'You'll need to get invitations out.' She pulled a rack of glasses from a dish-drawer beneath the counter and began stacking them onto another shelf.

He grinned, happy that she was being overly efficient. He hoped it meant he was under her skin. 'Can't I just send a text?'

'You want the whole world and his dog to turn up and drink the place dry?' She turned and gave him a pointed look. 'You'll need to have a list of bona fide invitees on the door at the very least. But you should do proper invitations.'

'Right, okay.' He nodded as if her every word were law. 'And personalised, right?'

'Right.'

Actually she was right. Lauren wasn't a store-bought-stationery kind of woman. Mya wasn't either. Brad had spent all last night wondering just what kind of woman Mya was.

'Maybe you should do the actual invitations?' he suggested. 'You're good at taking photos and stuff. You have a real eye for composition.'

She sent him a withering look before turning back to stack the glasses. 'I don't have time. I can come up with the guest list and get you some contact details, but you're going to have to put it all together.'

'Okay, I can do that.' He sighed. 'What are you thinking of? Gilt-edged cardboard things?' Never in a million years.

She flattened him with another killer cool stare. 'I think Lauren would prefer something a little more original than that.'

'I'll get to thinking, then,' he answered mock meekly.

She eyed him suspiciously this time before her gaze lifted to something behind him and brightened. 'Nice of you to turn up, Jonny,' she called. 'Everything's ready.'

'I knew I could count on you.' The tall guy who'd just walked in winked at her. 'But you need the music.' He stepped behind the bar and the relentless, rhythmic thud began.

Brad watched Mya instinctively move in time to the beat. With her natural rhythm and grace and fiendish determination, not to mention her sharp tongue and challenging eyes? He was dying here. And he wasn't getting anywhere very far, very fast.

The bar opened and the stream began. Offices weren't shutting for at least an hour yet but these people were ready to party. He didn't want to leave. Instead he watched half the other punters eye her up just as he was doing.

She and the Jonny guy made a good combo. Jonny, tattoos on display beneath the sleeves of the regulation black tee, was tanned and tall where she was pale and petite. Brad watched them banter their way through the cocktail preps. Her competitive streak was right to the fore. It amused him seeing the clinical way she observed the guy. He saw her flicking her wrist in practice, mimicking the movement of the master.

'You're almost as good as he is,' he said when she came to his end of the bar in a quiet moment.

She didn't pout at the honest assessment. Mya wouldn't want false flattery. She was too straight-up for that. 'Give me another week or two and I'll be better.'

Brad smiled. She wanted to be the best?

'The protégée wants to whip the master, but I'm not going to let that happen.' Jonny slung his arm along Mya's shoulders.

Brad immediately felt an animal response, his skin prickling at the sight of another man touching Mya—since when did he have hackles?

'Oh, it's going to happen and you know it.' Mya flicked Jonny's arm off as easily as she'd flicked off the flirty guys from the stag do the night before. 'You're running scared.'

Both Brad and Jonny chuckled and watched her swagger to a waiting customer.

'You've been teaching her?' Brad asked Jonny.

Jonny nodded. 'She's a quick learner. Focused, driven, plus she's been practising. That's how she got the job here in the first place.'

'And she wants to work here because?'

'It's the most popular bar in town.' Jonny looked at him directly. 'We get good clientele with a lot of money to spend. So we make good money. With her looks and the skill to match, she's popular.'

'Why do you help her out? You're not threatened by her?' Brad texted some mates, determined not to turn into some sad stalker type who just sat there and stared at his fixation. He certainly didn't want to feel this needle as he watched the byplay of the two bartenders. It couldn't be jealousy, could it? Never.

Jonny laughed. 'Wouldn't you rather work with her than some guy?' he pointed out with a sly smile. 'We work well together—people like the competition. Some like to look at her, others like to look at me.' He turned back to the bar and bluntly summed it up. 'It's all for the show and to help them spend their money.'

And Mya needed the money. She'd mentioned the tips last night. She could earn more here than on an internship? Even though the internship would progress her career. Brad frowned as he remembered what little he could about her. The girl his parents had been so disapproving of had actually become the Dux of the school—carrying off the elite academic prizes. It had only been because Mya was going to university that Lauren had decided to go too. So surely she was doing as well at university? By rights she should be bonded to some corporate firm already, with a scholarship in return for five years of her working life. Instead she was flinging bourbon around a bar and working back-to-back shifts between the club and a café while squeezing in summer school as well. Something had gone wrong somewhere; the question was, what?

Mya wished Brad would go do his thinking elsewhere. She'd spent all night trying not to think about him, and here he was the minute she'd walked into work. She tried to retain coordination as she checked round the tables making sure all were clean and had the necessary seating arrangements, but she felt his eyes on her.

She'd gone overboard in her reaction to learning he'd

cancelled one of her shifts, but the truth was she couldn't afford to lose a night off work. As it was she worked the bar job and a café job in the daytime. But it wasn't just a silver spoon that Brad had been born with; it was a whole canteen of cutlery. He might work, but it wasn't because he needed the money. He had no idea what it was like for people on the wrong side of the poverty line. And he was so used to getting his own way she was now ridden with the urge to argue with every one of his suggestions.

She walked back to the bar. She'd gone uber-efficient when she'd seen him sitting there. It was a way of working off the insane amount of energy she seemed to be imbued with. It didn't help that he was so gorgeous wearing dark jeans, a belt that drew every eye to his lean waist and a red tee so faded it was almost pink—only Brad could put on pink and make it masculine sexy. Pure ladybait.

Eyes locked with his, she reached for the knife to slice more lemons. Her skin sizzled as he openly looked her up and down.

'You never used to dress so monochrome,' he commented thoughtfully.

He remembered that? Mya had never worn normal in the past, but she didn't have the time to make her crazy outfits any more.

'Needs must,' she said briefly. If she didn't have the time to do something properly, she preferred not to do it at all, so all the fun she'd once had in creating something from nothing had been put away. Lauren had never worn the latest in fashion either—another thing that had brought them together back at school. She too turned her back on the consumerism of the day, and together they'd done it with style. Mya knew how to sew. She could turn a rag into something unexpected—deliberately setting out to make a statement with her clothing.

He glanced up and grinned at her. 'Still touchy?'

'I didn't sleep well.' She sliced quickly.

'Nor did I. I kept looking at your picture on my phone.'

She paused, eyes glued to the knife. No way could she dare look at his expression this second. 'I don't want to know what you were doing with my picture.'

'I never looked at you that way before.'

Oh, like that was meant to make her feel better?

'I'm aware of that,' she snapped. 'It was not 'til you saw the bikini.'

'No, I was otherwise occupied. I'm sorry about that in a way. But to be honest it was a good thing. You weren't ready for me then.'

'I'm not now,' she lied, snapping the knife down on the chopping board, ignoring the way the lemon juice stung her burn.

'Oh, you hold your own,' he said. 'And you know it.'

Her phone vibrated against her leg. She frowned and pulled it out. But it wasn't a text; it was a reminder from her calendar.

Oh, no.

'Are you okay? You've changed colour.' Brad raised his voice. 'Mya?' He asked more sharply. 'Bad news?'

She tried to smile but couldn't force the fear far enough off her face to manage it. How *could* she have made such a mistake? She had everything on file, had due dates highlighted *and* underlined, but she'd been too busy dreaming up exotic cocktails and daft names to christen them in the past twenty-four hours to check. In other words, she'd been having too much *fun*.

She'd been so distracted she'd said yes to the extra

shift at the café when they'd called last minute, forgetting to check her diary just in case. She'd figured it was
better to keep fully occupied and thus ward off dangerous, idle-moment thoughts. Brad-type thoughts and re-
plays of an unexpected, crazy kiss. She'd been distracted
by imaginary conversations with a guy. About a *party*?

As a result, the assignment due tomorrow for her
summer course had slipped her mind. She'd not done it.
She'd not even *half* done it. She hadn't done nearly the
amount of research and reading she should have. She
was playing everything close to the wire at the moment,
every minute screwed down to either work or study, and
last-minute deadlines had become the norm in recent
weeks—so long as she had the info she needed. Mya
was good enough to wing it. But just winging it wasn't
good enough for her. She wanted to ace it. She wanted
her perfect GPA back. She wanted her perfect control
back. She didn't want to be sleepless and thinking saucy
thoughts at inappropriate hours of the day. She was *such*
a fool to let herself be distracted. Especially by Brad
Davenport. She drew a deep breath into her crushed
lungs. No more distraction.

'Nothing I can't manage,' she lied and brought the
bottles back to the line-up of shot glasses to pour more
cherry-cheesecake shots for the trio of babes at a nearby
table who were wearing 'so hot right now' dresses and
drinking in the vision of killer-in-casual Brad.

'Really?' He watched her with absolute focus, as if
he had no idea that he'd caught the undying attention of
every woman in the building. But he knew it already—
it was normal for him.

She nodded and looked down to concentrate on pouring the vodka in the glasses, not trusting herself to speak
again without snapping at him. Suddenly she was too

stressed to be company for anyone, and his utterly innate gorgeousness irked her more than was reasonable.

He put both palms on the bar and leaned closer. 'Mya?'

That underlying note of concern in his deep voice didn't help her combat the melting effect his mere presence had on her bones. His observation of her made her butter-fingered—not good when she had to flip two glass bottles at once in performing-seal fashion. Smashing the spirits would see the dollars coming out of her pay packet. 'I need to concentrate.' She offered a vaguely apologetic smile. 'We'll have to talk about the party later.'

'Sure.' He eased back and flashed her a smile that would easily have coaxed her own out had she looked long enough.

But she resolutely kept her eyes on the glasses as she fixed the cranberry layer in them, because she was not allowing him to distract her any more. She put the shots onto a tray, lifted it and slowly walked out from behind the bar, to carry them to the divas. They were all looking over her shoulder, checking out Brad.

'You know him?' one of them asked in an overly loud whisper as Mya put the tray on the table between them. 'He's single?'

'Permanently,' Mya answered honestly. She glanced around and saw he hadn't moved. Worse he had a smile on, not his usual full-strength-flirt one, but a small twist to the lips that somehow made him even *more* attractive. It was so unfair the way he could make hearts seize with a mere look. She turned back to the pretty women. 'But he loves to play.'

And no doubt he'd adore three women at once. Maybe if she were to see him go off with the trio for some debauched night, then she'd blast away the resurgence of this stupid teen crush and be able to concentrate wholly on the wretched assignment she had ahead of her.

One of the girls stood and went over to talk to him. Mya went straight back behind the bar and tried not to pay attention to the high-pitched laughter. But she knew it was exactly two and a half minutes until he joined the women at their table. Mya decided to let Jonny serve them from then on.

She ignored the way the women leaned forward and chatted so animatedly. She ignored the laughter and smiles that Brad gave each of them. Most of all she ignored the way he tried to catch her eye when she walked past a couple of times. Peripheral vision let her know he looked up and over to her; she refused to look back. She had far more important things to think on. And then she was simply far too busy. People began pouring in as the sun went down but the night warmed up.

'Jonny, if I don't take my break now, I'm going to miss it altogether.' She leaned across to beg him.

'Go now.' He nodded. 'Pete and I can handle it.'

She grabbed the oversized ancient laptop she always lugged round in her satchel all day and took it out to the small balcony Brad had led her to the other night. She didn't really know why she'd brought it with her—it wasn't as if she'd somehow type on her feet as she worked her shifts at the café and then the bar.

Her heart sank as she scrolled to the relevant document. The cases were all cited, but she'd have to try to get copies of them to read them in full. What library was going to be open at midnight? She didn't have the Internet in her small flat as she couldn't afford the connection. She didn't even have a landline. She'd have to go to a twenty-four-hour café with wireless access and try to do it from there. Downloading fifteen cases? Oh, she was screwed.

She'd hardly started the first paragraph when Drew came out and caught her hunched over at a corner table.

'You can't sit there studying. This is a bar, not a library,' he grumbled. 'It's not the right look.'

It was the last thing she needed—her control-freak, this-place-must-maintain-its-cool-image boss coming down on her.

'It's my break—surely I can read?' She looked up at him. Didn't he get how desperate she was?

'Not there, you can't,' Drew informed her coolly.

To her horror, tears were a mere blink away. She shut her laptop and stood. Swatting up screeds of legalese in the dark alley outside didn't inspire her but if that was what she had to do, she'd do it. It was going to be an all nighter anyway. Followed by the brunch shift at the café tomorrow. How could she have screwed everything up—*again*?

She walked out past the queue forming at the door and into the night, desperate despite the fact she'd only have a few minutes at most before Drew hunted her out. While the summer sun's heat still warmed the air, it was now dark. Hooray for the safety torch on her keychain; she'd be able to read the fine-print text on the step at the back entrance of the bar.

'Big essay?' Brad had followed her, gazing at the ancient computer in her hand.

She nodded glumly, her stomach knotting again. 'Due tomorrow and I've not done it and I don't have half the case law I need,' she confessed.

'Tomorrow?'

She winced. Did he have to hammer home her incompetence? 'I need to read up.' In other words, she needed him to go back inside and keep chatting to those women.

'How long's your break?'

'Twenty minutes.'

'You can't possibly concentrate here.' He frowned at the giant recycling bin into which they threw all the empty bottles. Yeah, the sound of smashing glass was regular and went well with that thudding bass beat coming through the brick walls of the converted warehouse.

'I can concentrate anywhere.' If she had the info she needed.

'And do an assignment in twenty minutes? You might be brilliant, Mya, but you're not a magician.' He frowned. 'How come you don't have the case law?'

'I did an extra shift at the café today,' she said. 'I forgot about the assignment.'

'You have too much on.'

'Yes, so I need to work now,' she said pointedly. But he didn't take the hint. Instead he cocked his head and came over all thoughtful.

'I've got access to all the legal databases. Including the subscription ones at my place,' he said.

The ones that cost money to print each article from? The ones that held the case law she hadn't been able to download because she'd done the extra shift at the café? The ones she couldn't get to because the libraries were closed at this time of night?

He pondered another moment. 'Skip your break and ask Jonny to cover the last of your shift. You know he'll do it. He owes you for setting up alone tonight. Come home with me. You can print off all you need and work all night.' He stepped closer, pressing the best point, decisive. 'I'll help you.'

She folded her arms, using her laptop as body armour, mainly to hide the way her thundering heart was threatening to beat its way right out of her chest. 'This isn't a family law assignment.' She tried to play it cool and not collapse in a heap of gratitude at his feet. Or a heap of lustful wishes.

'I covered commercial in my degree too, you know. You're not the only one with dibs on brilliance. I got straight As.'

Of course he did; he was that perfect. And she wasn't. She no longer had the brilliant label at law school. She shook her head. 'I can't cheat.'

'You're not going to,' he growled. Stepping close, he put his hands on her shoulders. 'I'm not going to write the assignment for you,' he said firmly, as if she were a kid who had to have the simplest thing explained to her twenty different ways. 'Consider me your law librarian.'

Mya just stared. Feeling the warmth from his firm hands, and seeing his fit frame up close, she felt as if he were like an ad for all-male capability and virility. He was also the least likely librarian she could ever imagine.

He laughed and stepped closer. 'I used to work in the law library as a student. I'm very good at searches.'

'You *never* worked as a librarian.' That she just didn't believe.

'Okay, library assistant,' he clarified, all humble integrity mixed with that killer charm. 'Great job to have as a student.' His wicked grin bounced back. 'I got to meet all the cute girls, and their names and addresses were all on there on the system already.'

'So you abused your position?' Mya drawled, trying to cover the way she wanted to abuse his closeness now and lean against him.

'You're accusing me of wrongdoing?' He shook her and she nearly stumbled that last step right into his arms.

'How come you're so down on me? All I'm trying to do is offer you a little help.'

She kept her balance. She didn't like having to accept help.

'Just some space and some computer access.' He held out the offer as if it were as innocent as a plate of homemade cookies.

While access to those databases would be awesome, what she really couldn't resist this second was his charm. 'Okay, I really appreciate it,' she breathed out in a rush. 'But I don't want to put you out.'

'You're not putting me out.' He let go of her shoulders and turned to walk back down the alley. 'And I promise I won't bother you.'

He didn't have to *do* anything to bother her. He only had to exist. And the nearer he was, the worse it was. But she was just going to have to control that silly part of her body because she had an essay to write.

'Relax and go finish your shift,' he said, leading her past the queue and back into the crowded bar. 'You'll get the info you need and you've got all night to nail it.'

Yeah, but it wasn't the assignment she was thinking of nailing.

CHAPTER FIVE

As MYA went back to mixing concoctions behind the bar, she surreptitiously watched Brad head back to the three beautiful women. Okay, so he was just helping her out with her schoolwork. There was nothing more to his offer. That was fine, perfect in fact. Then a couple of his mates turned up and he introduced the babes to them. Then—Mya couldn't help but notice—Brad stepped back from the conversation. And every time she glanced over—purely to see if their glasses needed refilling, of course—he was watching her. Time and time again their gazes met. And the thing was, he wasn't even giving her the full maple-syrup look, but it had the same effect anyway.

Yeah, she still wasn't over the fact that he was the hottest man she'd ever laid eyes on. It seemed there was a part of her that would always want him, no matter what else she had going on or how much of a player he was.

And had he made the computer-access offer to win her over and into his bed? Possibly. Did that matter? Not really. Because she wouldn't be sleeping in his bed. She'd be getting her assignment written.

It was just before 1:00 a.m. before she could get away—early, as Brad had suggested. Brad's two mates and the three babes had already left the bar, so he was waiting alone, having swapped from drinking beer to soda water hours ago. He straightened from the wall he was leaning against as she neared, her heavy satchel over her shoulder.

'Your place is really only a few minutes away?' she asked, determined to stay matter-of-fact and not crawl up against him and beg him to take her to bed and have his wicked way with her so she'd mindlessly fall into sleep the way she ached to.

He nodded.

Sure enough, just down the road and around the corner from the row of eclectic shops and bars in the more 'alternative' area of town was a street of small, old villas. Every single one of them had been stylishly renovated and looked gorgeous and no doubt cost a mint.

'Why do you live here?' It was nothing like the exclusive suburb in which he'd grown up with the massive modern houses and immaculate lawns.

'I like the mix in the neighbourhood.' He shrugged. 'Lots of good restaurants nearby and it's central.'

'You don't cook?'

'Not often,' he admitted with a flash of a smile.

She waited by the potted rosebush on the wooden veranda while he unlocked the villa and put in the code for the security system. And she knew he was wrong. She couldn't possibly concentrate here, not with him around.

'Let me give you the tour,' he said as he led her the length of the wooden-floored hallway.

'I don't need to see your private things.' She regretted this now. She'd have been better off winging the assignment by cobbling together an average essay with reference to just the few textbooks she had in her flat.

'Yes, you do. Otherwise you'll be curious, and if you're curious you won't be able to concentrate.'

She managed a smile. 'Because all women are curious about seeing your room?'

'Of course,' he said. 'Kitchen and lounge are this way.'

They faced out to the back of the house, the garden not visible this time of night. For a guy who didn't cook, he still had all the mod cons in the kitchen. She stayed in the doorway, really not wanting to take in the atmosphere of being in his personal space.

'Guest bathroom this way.' He brushed past her as he stepped back out to the hall and opened a door on the other side of it. 'Then there are a couple of spare bedrooms. One is my office. The other is a library and workroom for my assistant.' He opened the door opposite.

She didn't go into his office but into the one he'd said was the library. She wouldn't have guessed he'd have a library certainly not such a varied one.

'You have a whole bookcase of children's books.' She read the spines. She recognised so many she'd read in her hanging-out-at-the-library days when she'd avoided all the other students. Avoided the teasing. That was where she'd met Lauren—who'd been ripping a page out of a book she could have afforded a million times over.

'I work for children,' he answered briefly. 'I got a bulk lot from a second-hand store.'

Internally she laughed at the way everything was shelved in the 'right' place. Clearly he hadn't been kidding about his library-assistant job. She pulled one from the 'teen-read' shelf and flicked it open. Inside the front cover a name had been written in boyish scrawl—Brad Davenport. Second-hand store, huh?

She smiled. 'That was my favourite for years. I read it so many times.'

'Uh-huh.' He took the book off her.

'Did you cry at the end?' she asked.

He smiled but didn't confess.

'I did every time,' she admitted with a whisper.

Still he didn't give it up.

'You don't want me to know that you're a marsh-mallow inside?'

'I'm no marshmallow,' he answered. 'I have them here for the look of it. Generally the kids only come here to meet and talk with me so they're not so nervous in court. I'm not their counsellor or anything. I'm merely their legal representative.'

'But they're your books.' And the kids he was sup-posedly not that close to drew pictures for him that he put on his walls?

His reluctant smile came with a small sigh. 'I like to read.'

'And you like kids?

'Sometimes.' He drew the word out, his voice ring-ing with caveats. 'But I have no interest in having any myself.' He put the book back. 'There are enough out there who've been done over by their dipstick parents.'

'You think you'd be a dipstick parent?'

'Undoubtedly.'

She smiled.

'I think parenting is one of those things you learn from the example you had,' he said lightly. 'I didn't have a great example.'

'So you know what not to do.'

He shook his head. 'It's never that simple. I see the cycle of dysfunctional families in my office every day. Now—' he moved back out of the room '—the last room is my bedroom.'

Mya hovered in the doorway, really not wanting to intrude as the sense of intimacy built between them.

He turned and saw her hesitating and rolled his eyes. 'I promise not to pounce.'

She stepped right into the room. He had the biggest bed she'd ever seen, smothered in white coverings. It would be like resting in a bowl of whipped cream. Definitely not a bed for pyjamas; there should be nothing but bare skin in that.

'Why is it so high?' she asked, then quickly cleared her throat of the embarrassing rasp that had roughened her voice.

'I'm tall.'

'You wouldn't want to fall out of it, would you?' If she sat on the edge of it, her feet couldn't touch the floor. 'It's like Mount Olympus or something.'

There was no giant TV screen on a table at the foot of the bed. No chest of drawers for clothing. No bookshelf. No, it was just that massive bed with the billowing white covering demanding her attention.

'Nice to know I inspire you to think of Greek gods.'

She sent him a baleful look. It was unfair of him to start with the teasing again when she had a whole night of work ahead of her. She was tense enough with unwanted yearning. But she couldn't resist pulling his string a touch—wishing she really could. 'What do I inspire you to think of?'

His gaze shifted to the left of her—to that bed. 'Better not say.'

'Don't tell me you're shy?' She laughed.

'I don't want to embarrass you.'

Oh, it was way too late for that. 'I mistakenly sent you a picture of myself in a half-see-through bikini. I don't think I could be more embarrassed.'

'That was just an image. I couldn't touch you.'

Her breathing faltered, her pulse skipped quicker at

the thought of where and how he was thinking of touching her. And when. Now? Mere words banished the chill she'd felt before as heat crept up her cheeks and across her entire body.

A half-smile curved his lips. 'You like a little talk, don't you? For a woman who's planning to spend the rest of her life counting beans, you have to get your thrills somewhere, huh?'

'There's nothing wrong with chasing financial security.' She chose to ignore the suggestion she might like a little sauce talk.

'Strikes me you chase all-over safety. Which isn't something I can give you,' he warned, leaning close. 'You're not entirely safe with me.'

'Now you tell me, when you've got me alone in your house.' Her insides were melting—that part of her had no desire to be safe right now. It was a dangerous game and one that was so irresistible.

'In the middle of the night.'

She turned and looked at the pretty design on the lower part of the wallpaper. Not just normal wallpaper, but almost a mural. Good diversion. 'The room came like this?'

'No, I chose it.' He let her pull back from the brink.

'You did?' It made the room like a grotto—with that big bed in the middle and the soft-looking white pillows and duvet. 'Okay, you chose it with women in mind.'

'No, I liked my tree house when I was a kid. Remember that?'

She did remember the old hut up high in one of the ancient trees at his parents' house. She and Lauren had been banned from it. It had been padlocked and everything. His escape from the magazine-spread-perfect house. Lauren had got her escape by banning her mother from her room.

'This gives me the same feeling of peace.' He walked towards her. 'And women don't sleep in here.'

Yeah, right. 'Because you have a separate bedroom for your seduction routine? One with boxes of condoms and sex toys?'

'I don't need sex toys,' he boasted with a self-mocking smile. 'And you've already seen the spare rooms. One's my office, one's my library.'

'So what, you're celibate?' She let her eyebrows seek the sky.

'I prefer to sleep-over at their houses. It makes the morning-after escape easier.'

She shook her head but couldn't help the laugh. 'You're bad.'

'No, I'm good. It's easier for both of us. Women tend to be more relaxed in their own environment.'

'Do you even make it to the morning, or do you sneak out while she's still asleep?'

'I never *sneak* out.' He walked a step closer still. 'There's nothing like starting the day with sex. I leave her recovering in bed after that.'

'And dreaming of another encounter that will never happen.' Mya desperately clung to some kind of mockery but all she could think about was kissing him, about starting the day with sex—with him.

'Why ruin a beautiful memory?' He smiled. 'One perfect night is all that's required. More just gets messy.'

She suspected just the one with him would get messy for her. Her one and only one night had been hideous the next day.

'Now,' he said softly, so close in her personal space now her pulse was frantic. 'You can either work in my office or the library. You've got your laptop.' He glanced at the dinosaur beast in her bag. It weighed a ton but still had a word-processing program that worked. That was all that mattered. 'Let's go with my office.' He made the decision for her. 'I'll pull up the cases you need while you get reading. And my computer is faster in there than the one in the office. You can type up your assignment on that—be better for you ergonomically.'

Mya dragged in a shaky breath, determinedly so *not* disappointed he hadn't kissed her, and followed him to the office.

There was really only one reason why Brad had offered to help Mya. One carnal, driving reason. But now she was in his house he fully regretted it. Her scent tormented him. The light sweetness overlaid with the tart lemon from the bar. Yeah, that was Mya. He switched on the computer with deliberately calm movements. In truth, he wanted to spin in his seat and grab her, have her over his desk in a second and kiss every inch of her skin. Here, in his bed, the kitchen, everywhere. He had the sinking feeling she'd haunt his house for ever if he didn't get her out of his system.

But there was no doubt she was waiting for him to make his move. His playboy reputation had all her barriers up, and though he knew he could eventually get her to say yes, he didn't want to be that predictable. He didn't want her thinking she knew all there was to know about him. Because she didn't. He wasn't *that* out of control. He didn't *want* to be that out of control. And he wasn't that shallow—at least he hoped not. So he bit back the raging lust and concentrated on the case searches instead.

He quickly read the list she pulled out. It wouldn't take him that long.

She had her textbook out and was making notes already. He smiled as he watched her discreetly while logging in to the online databases. She was so natural with her hair tied back and her pen in hand, ready to take notes as she read—fast. She'd eased right into it, looking more relaxed and at home than he'd ever seen her in the bar, for all the effort that she put in there. And that was the difference, he figured: there it was a big effort, whereas this—reading, studying, thinking—was effortless for her. And natural.

'You really like corporate law, or is it about the earning potential?' he couldn't resist asking when he was about halfway through the list.

She lifted her head and met his eyes for a too-short moment. 'I really do like it.' She looked at the pages. 'Does that surprise you? I like the challenge. I like figuring out the rules. I like the power in negotiation.'

He nodded but couldn't help thinking she was holding something back. Her drive was so strong.

'You think I'm shallow?' She looked up again and this time he saw the flicker of insecurity in her eyes. It mattered to her what he thought of her?

'No,' he answered honestly. 'Different people enjoy different things. Different people have different things driving them.'

She nodded, but to his disappointment didn't open up more.

'Why are you doing summer school?' He couldn't help asking. 'Why do you work so many shifts? Aren't you on scholarship?'

'Not any more.'

'Why not?'

Mya took in a deep breath. She never usually discussed this—but telling Brad might be a darn good idea. It might help keep her focused around him. 'I failed.'

His fingers stopped on the keyboard and he swivelled in the chair to face her. 'You finally flunked an exam? Don't worry about it—everyone does sometime.'

Somehow she didn't think he had. 'I didn't flunk one. I flunked them all. Finals last year I completely crashed.'

'What happened?' His eyes widened.

Yeah, it had been a shock to her too. She'd always been the super-bright one. The rebellious but diligent student who was there on sufferance because she dragged the school's academic rankings up single-handedly.

'What happened?' he asked again when she said nothing. 'Your family? Is everyone okay?'

'It was nothing catastrophic.' She turned away and began underlining random sentences with pencil. 'It was embarrassing.'

'So what happened?'

She really didn't want to go into it but going into it would put the ice on any hot thoughts—hers and his— and she wanted to get through this night without being tempted. 'I met a guy. I thought he was, you know, the *one*.' Now she was blushing with embarrassment, because she'd been so naïve. 'But he totally wasn't. He broke up with me two days out from exams and I…handled it badly.' It was mortifying now to look back on, but she'd been hurt. She'd finally thought she'd found a place to fit in, and she couldn't have been more wrong.

'What a jerk breaking up at exam time.'

She nodded. 'He was. But I was an idiot. A big idiot.' Because she'd gone out and made everything worse.

'How big?'

'I went out and got really drunk.'

'Oh.' He was silent a moment. 'Did something bad happen?'

'Not bad. But not that great either.' She glanced at him. 'My own mistake and I've learned from it.' The responsibility lay with her. She was the one who'd lain in bed crying her eyes out. She was the one who'd gone out and got drunk to try to forget about him and ease the pain. She was the one who'd brought home some random guy and slept with him just to feel wanted. She'd woken up the morning of her first exam with a dry mouth and a sick stomach and an inability to remember the name of the man in her bed. She'd been mortified and ashamed and sick. Hung-over and bleary-eyed, she'd not even made it past the first hour of the exam. The one that afternoon she'd turned up, signed her name and walked out again. The last exam she'd actually tried to do something on but had panicked halfway through and walked out. Her supervisor had called her in when the results came out. Had asked what had happened, had wanted her to get a doctor's note or something because her performance was so shockingly below her usual standard. Below anyone's standards. But she could never have done that. It was her fault, her responsibility.

She'd fed from the scholarship fund long enough. All her secondary schooling, now half her university degree. No more. She was making her own way in the world—and paying her own way. Nothing mattered more than gaining financial independence, by getting a good job. And if it meant it took longer for her to finish her degree working part-time, so she could live, then that was just the way it had to be.

'What have you learned?' Brad asked.

She turned and looked at him directly. 'That I can't let

anything or anyone get in the way of my studies again. Definitely no man, no relationship.

'That's why you don't want to get involved with anyone? That's why it's inconvenient?'

'That's right.' She nodded, denying the other reason even to herself. 'I'm busy. I'm working at the bar every night and at the café on the weekends. I've got lectures midweek and assignments and reading to do in and around that. I just don't have time for anyone or anything else.'

'You can't let one bad experience put you off for ever.'

'Not for ever. Just the next couple of years.'

He frowned. 'But you get time off over Christmas, right?'

'From lectures but I have assignments and I have shifts right the way through.' The public holidays paid good money, and patrons were more generous tippers too. 'I'm not interested in anything.'

'Not a great quality of life for you, though, is it? All work and no play.'

'It's not for ever,' she said again.

'No? How many years are you off finishing your degree?'

'Part-time it's going to take me three. That's with taking summer papers as well.'

'So no nookie for you for another three years?' He shook his head, looking appalled. 'That's more than a little tragic.'

'Sex isn't the be-all and end-all,' she said with more confidence than she felt.

'It's up there. Without sex there can be no life.'

'We're not talking biology here.'

'You're going to be miserable,' he warned.

'I'm not. I'm going to achieve what I want to achieve.'

'With no help from anybody.'

'You understand, right?'

'No, I don't.'

Startled, she looked at him.

'I don't see why it has to be that miserable.' He turned and met her eyes. 'No such thing as balance with you, is there?'

'I have to do what I have to do. And I'm not into the casual-sex scene.' She cleared her throat, trying to hold the blush at bay as she remembered that mortifying morning. 'I learned that too. I don't want a fling. But nor do I want a relationship right now. I have too much else to do.'

'All or nothing,' he murmured.

'Right now it's nothing,' she confirmed.

He looked at her, brown eyes serious. 'Okay.' He held her gaze. 'Message received loud and clear.'

She said nothing. He turned back to the computer and pulled the list of cases nearer. Mya watched his fingers fly over the keyboard. Serious, focused.

That was it? She'd told him as explicitly as she could that she didn't want an affair and he just accepted it?

Because here was the thing—she was still totally hot for the guy. How could he be so focused when she was dying of desire? She'd gone for honesty and he'd taken it. He'd backed right off. But instead of feeling any kind of relief, she felt *more* wound up. She'd been so sure he'd make some kind of move. She'd been so sure she'd say no. Only there were no moves from him, and only *yeses* and *pleases* circling in her head.

She couldn't believe her madness. Her brain had been lost somewhere between here and the bar.

He stood and picked up the pages as they came out of the printer and put highlighters and sticky notes in front of her. She almost laughed. It seemed the guy was as much of a stationery addict as she was.

'It's all vital for doing an assignment.' He winked. 'I'm off to make you some coffee while you get started.'

He'd left the documents open on screen so she could cut and paste quotes as necessary. Hell, he'd even opened up a documents file, named for her, and saved the other cases he'd downloaded. She stared at them, not taking in a word, just waiting.

Five minutes later he put the steaming mug in front of her and stayed on the other side of the desk.

'I'm turning in now. There's more coffee in the machine in the kitchen, fruit in the bowl, chocolate on hand too. Stay as late as you like. Don't go walking out there at some stupid hour of the morning.'

'I can't stay the whole night.' There was just no way.

'It'll probably take you all night to get the assignment done anyway. No point in taking unnecessary risks.' He walked back to the doorway in jeans and tee—she noticed his feet were now bare.

'Thanks,' she said rustily. 'Really appreciate this.' And was so disappointed when he disappeared down the hallway.

She stared at the screen. All this info was at her fingertips. All she had to do was read, assimilate, process, write. It wasn't that hard. She'd done enough essays to know what her lecturers wanted and what it was she needed to get that extra half grade.

But the house was silent.

Acutely aware of his presence under the roof, she sat stupidly still, listening for sounds of him. Imagining going to find him—imagining sliding into that mountainous cloud of a bed and...

She'd pushed him away and it had worked. For *him*.

She still wanted what she couldn't have and with that she'd lost her ability to concentrate. That was a first. She glanced at the big printer on the table behind her. Half a tree's worth of paper and twenty minutes later she was ready to leave.

'What are you doing?' he asked just as she'd tiptoed to the front door.

She whirled around. What was she doing? What was *he* doing standing there almost completely bare? Only a pair of boxer shorts preserved his modesty and even then they were that knit-cotton variety that clung rather than hung loose. And speaking of things being *hung*...

She burned. 'I can't work here.' It was a pathetic whisper.

'You're sneaking out.' He crossed his arms. It only emphasised his biceps. It was so unfair of him to have such a fit body.

'I didn't want to wake you.'

'How are you planning on getting home?'

'I can walk.'

'It's after two in the morning.'

'I walk home from the bar all the time. I have a safety alarm. I walk along well-lit streets. I'm not stupid.'

His jaw clenched. 'Take my car.'

Could he make it worse for her? 'No, that's okay. I'm fine walking.'

'It's not fine for anyone to walk home alone this time of night. Take my car.'

She sighed. 'That's very kind of you, but I can't.'

'You have a real issue accepting help, don't you?' he growled.

Possibly. Okay, yes, particularly from him. His whole 'friendly' act was confusing her hormones more. 'I can't drive,' she admitted in a low voice. 'I've never got my licence. I've never learned to drive.'

For a second his mouth hung open. 'Everyone learns to drive. It's a life skill. Didn't your dad teach you?'

Her dad didn't drive either. That was because the accident at the factory years ago had left him with a limp and unable to use his right arm. He'd been a sickness beneficiary ever since. Living in a house that was damp, in a hideous part of town that was getting rougher by the day. She was determined to get her parents out of there. She owed it to them. 'You're assuming we had a car,' she said bluntly. They couldn't afford many things most people would consider basic necessities, like a car and petrol or even their power bill most of the time.

'Okay.' He turned and strode back to his bedroom. 'I'll drive you.'

'You don't have to do that,' she called after him, beyond frustrated and embarrassed and frankly miserable.

'Yes, I do.'

'I didn't want to disturb you.'

'It's way too late for that.' He returned, jeans on, tee in hand. 'I'll drop you home.'

She needed him to put the tee on, and she really needed him too. She'd had such sensual thoughts in the past hour she was almost insane with it.

But he read her fierce expression wrong. 'Don't you dare argue with me any more.'

He opened the front door and waited for her.

To her horror her eyes filled and she quickly walked out. She was too strung out to argue. She'd not admitted to anyone the struggle she'd been having. Not even to Lauren. But she was so tired. The relentless shifts, the constant pressure of squeezing in assignment after assignment, of fitting in lectures around work, of desperately trying to get the highest of grades every time, of never, ever getting enough sleep. But it was something she alone had to deal with. And she certainly couldn't lose more time or sleep fantasising about him.

CHAPTER SIX

BRAD'S tension didn't ease as he unlocked the car and opened the passenger door in the middle of the night for her. For someone so independent, her inability to drive threw him. They lived in New Zealand. Everyone drove here. And she shouldn't be walking home alone night after night after work at the bar. She was so pale; the amount of work she had on bothered him. It didn't help that he'd lumbered her with this party as well. He was thoughtless. And, yes, selfish.

Because all it had been about was him stealing time with her. He'd wanted her—and any excuse would do to get that time. But now? Now he really was concerned.

'I'll teach you to drive,' he said, putting his car in gear and pulling out into the quiet, dark street.

'Thanks all the same but it's not necessary. I live centrally. I walk to work. I use public transport—it's better for the environment.'

'You're happy to learn bar tricks from Jonny,' he pointed out, annoyance biting at her refusal.

'I wouldn't want to damage your car.'

His body tautened to a ridiculous degree, urging him to pull over and kiss her into silence. Into saying yes—to this, to anything, to *every*thing. He wanted her more than he'd ever wanted a woman. Who'd have thought that a picture could have affected him like this?

No. It wasn't just the picture. It was every time she opened her mouth and shot him down while eating him up with her eyes. If they ever got it on, it would be mind-blowing. He knew it. But that wasn't happening. She wasn't into flings and he wasn't into anything else and he was man enough to back off. He'd drop her home now and go out tomorrow night and find a new friend to play with.

But the idea left him cold. Instead, he went back to thinking about her.

'About Lauren's party.' He revved the engine while waiting at another infernal red light. The ten-minute drive seemed to be taking for ever. 'If it's too much for you—'

'It's not too much.' She interrupted him and he heard the attempted smile in her voice. 'I just got behind on this one assignment and I'll get that done tonight. At home. I want to help. I can do it. Just to the left here is fine.' She pointed out her apartment.

'I haven't thought much more about it.' He hadn't thought about the party at all. He'd spent all his spare moments imagining the delicious things he'd do to Mya the minute she let him.

She turned to face him as he cut the engine. 'The cocktails will be fun. Just get in a good band and a DJ and good food. It'll be fine.'

He flicked on the interior light so he could see her properly. 'You wouldn't be lowering your standards for me, would you?'

The colour ran under her skin but she kept on her smile as she shook her head. 'I'd never do that. I still expect the best.'

Brad grinned despite his disappointment. She'd have got the best. Her automatic, instant refusals of anything he offered? They pricked his pride. He wished she'd come to him, wished she'd be as unable to resist their chemistry as much as he seemed unable to.

'I really don't know how to thank you.' She clutched the door handle, her eyes wide and filled with something he really wished was desire.

'I can think of a couple of ways.' He couldn't help one last little tease.

'You've a one-track mind, haven't you?' she teased right back, but she looked away from him, drawing a veil over that spark.

The devil in him urged to press her for a date, but he already knew her answer. She was either working or studying, every waking minute. So he let her go and drove home in the darkness. But once there he remained wide-awake and restless and *hot*. Nothing was going to happen between them, but that hadn't diminished the ache and the hunger. Lust. He'd get over it. But as he sat in front of his computer, the sky lightened and he got to wondering whether she'd finished her assignment. Whether she was working her shift. Whether she was okay. And then he realised he wasn't going to be able to rest until he knew for sure that she was.

Mya knew that if she could survive tonight, she could survive anything. She showered to refresh her system but it was a bad idea. The warm water made muscles melt and her mind wander into dangerous territory. She flicked the jets to cold. Then she dragged herself to her desk and pulled out the piles of paper and opened her ancient laptop. She had four hours. She didn't have time to lust after anyone.

Finally she got in the zone. She read—fortunately she was fast at it—assimilated, analysed and wrote, fingers thumping the keyboard. Her phone alarm beeped at seven forty-five just as she was finalising the formatting. She packed up and sprinted to the café. There was Internet access there. She grabbed a coffee and hit Send on the email. Her assignment was safely en route to her lecturer's inbox. She straightened and stretched out the kinks in her back from hunching over her keyboard. Exhaustion hit her like a freight train. Only now she had to put on an apron and start making everyone else's coffees.

Two hours later she switched her phone to mute and put it in the cubby so she'd no longer be bothered by the zillion messages she was receiving. Brad had sent the invites to everyone about the same time she'd sent the assignment to her lecturer. She'd never expected he'd follow through so quickly or with such impact. She should have known better. Brad Davenport was all about impact.

She'd been impressed by the slick black-and-white mysterious message that had spread over the screen of her phone when she'd clicked on it. Yeah, she'd been fielding texts and calls all morning with people wanting the inside deal on what the plans were for the party—all excitement and conjecture. Because the Davenports were the ultimate in cool. Stylish, unique and rolling in it, and anyone who was anyone, or who wanted to be someone, wanted this invite. She'd answered honestly that she hadn't a clue what was planned but that they'd better be smart enough to keep it secret from Lauren. Mya had threatened them with a prolonged and agonising social-death sentence should anyone spoil the surprise.

Her shift crawled to its end. She was almost in tears

with relief and at the same time ready to drag herself across town. She'd doze in the bus on the way. The last person she expected to see just outside the café door was Brad.

'What are you doing here?' Was she so tired she was hallucinating?

'I thought I'd give you a lift home. You must be exhausted.'

Not a hallucination, he was real. Looking so strong and smiling, and she wished she didn't have any stupid scruples.

'I'm okay.' She was so tired, it was harder to control her reaction to his proximity and the urges he inspired.

'You got it done?'

She nodded, glad he'd reminded her of her work. 'Thanks for coming in but I'm not going home. I'm having lunch with my parents.' She was due there this minute.

'I'll give you a ride.'

'No, it's fine,' she hurriedly refused. 'I take the bus.'

He looked at her. 'I can give you a ride.'

'Shouldn't you be working?' She really didn't want him taking her there.

'I'm due a lunch break too.'

'But—'

'Can you stop saying no to me in everything?' he asked. 'I'm offering as a *friend*, Mya. Nothing more.'

She opened her mouth and then shut it again as she registered the ragged thread of frustration in his voice. He must be tired too—that invitation would have taken some time on the computer. Had he not slept a wink either?

'You don't have to do this,' she said softly ten minutes

later as they headed towards the motorway that would take them right across town and to the outskirts.

'Don't worry, I won't embarrass you.' He reached over and gave her knee a teasing squeeze. 'I won't tell them you like sending people racy pictures of yourself.'

She managed a light laugh but her discomfort mushroomed as she realised he was going to see the worst.

'Are *you* embarrassed?' he asked quietly. 'You don't want me to see your home?'

'No,' she argued instantly. 'But you wouldn't be the first person to look down your nose at my neighbourhood. We come from totally different worlds, so don't act like you're all understanding and down with it. You can't ever relate.'

'Your shoulders aren't broad enough for a chip this big.'

'Oh, it's a chip, is it? It's just me being oversensitive?' She twisted in her seat to face him. 'What would you know? Have you ever faced the judgments and expectations from each side of the economic divide? Girls from the wrong side of the tracks like me are only good for a fling.' Never marriage material. That was how James had treated her. At first he hadn't known. He'd been attracted to her academic success, but when he'd found out about her background, he'd run a mile. 'All *you've* ever wanted from women like me is sex.'

'All I've ever wanted from *any* woman is sex,' he pointed out lazily. 'It has nothing to do with your family background.'

About to launch into more of a rant, she stopped and mentally replayed what he'd said. And then she laughed.

'I mean really—' he winked '—you don't think you're taking this too seriously? We're in the twenty-first century, not feudal England.'

She shook her head. 'Twenty-first century or not, the class system operates. There's an underclass you know nothing about.'

'Don't patronise me,' he said. 'I'm not ignorant. I'm aware of the unemployment figures and I've dealt with worse in my work. You've got no idea of the dysfunction I see. I can tell you it crosses all socioeconomic boundaries. Sometimes the worst are the ones who have the most.'

'Yeah, but you don't know the stress financial problems can bring.'

'That's true. I don't have personal experience of that. But I'm not totally without empathy.'

'And salary doesn't necessarily equate with effort,' she grumped. Her mother worked so hard and still earned a pittance. That was why she'd insisted Mya study so hard at school, so she'd end up with a job that actually paid well. And Mya wanted to work to help her parents.

'Mya.' He silenced her. 'I know this might amaze you, but I'm not that stupid or that insensitive.'

She put her head in her hands. Of course he wasn't. 'Sorry.'

She heard his chuckle and let his hand rub her shoulder gently—too briefly.

'I'll let you away with it because I know how tired you are,' he said.

But her discomfort grew as they neared. He'd been right—she didn't want him seeing it. She was embarrassed. Embarrassed she hadn't done something sooner to get her parents out of there. She should have done so much more already. 'You can just drop me, okay?'

'Sure,' he answered calmly. 'They must be impressed with how hard you're working at the moment.'

Mya chewed her lower lip. 'They don't know.'

'Don't know what?'

'Don't know anything.'

'That you work at the bar, the café or that you're not at uni full-time?'

She shook her head. 'They don't know I lost the scholarships. They don't know I'm at summer school. They can't know. Can't ever.' She felt tears sting. Stupid tears—only because she was tired.

He took his eyes from the road for too long to stare at her. 'And you're that stressed about them finding out?'

'Of course I am. Watch the traffic, will you?'

He turned back to stare at the road, a frown pulling his brows. 'I think you should tell them.'

Her breath failed. 'I can't tell them. They're so proud of me. It's…everything.'

'They'd understand.'

They wouldn't. She'd be a failure. She didn't ever want to let them down. She didn't want disappointment to stamp out the light in their eyes when they looked at her. 'You don't get it. I'm the only one to have even finished school. They're so proud of me, they tell everyone. I can't let them down now. This is what I am to them.' It was all she was.

'Everyone stuffs up sometimes, Mya. I think they'd understand.'

'They wouldn't. And I couldn't bear for them to know. It alienated me from the others. My cousins, the other neighbourhood kids… They gave me a hard time then. I don't want more of a hard time now. I don't want my parents disappointed. Life's been tough enough on them.'

She'd been bullied as she walked across the neighbourhood in her school uniform—the only kid in the block to go to a school with a uniform. Taunted—told she'd become a snob, torn down. *Freak. You think you're better than us?*

She hadn't thought that. She knew just how hard those in her 'hood worked—or worked to try to get a job. Sure, a couple hadn't. A couple had gone off the rails in the way Lauren had once threatened to. But she knew better than anyone that snobbery worked both ways. In the one hand she'd carried the hopes and dreams of her parents; in the other she'd been burdened with the spite and jealousy of others. She didn't fit in here any more, but she sure hadn't fitted in with her new school either.

And now she was held up as the neighbourhood example—her cousin's five-year-old daughter had said she wanted to go to uni and be just like her. She couldn't let them down.

She'd had opportunities others hadn't had and she'd squandered them on a man who was so removed from her own sphere—that elite, born-to-it world that she'd never once felt comfortable in. She couldn't let them know what an idiot she'd been. And she couldn't be that naïve girl again. This damsel was doing her own rescuing. No man, no fairy-tale fantasy, would come between her and her studies.

'How will you get home after lunch?' he asked as they neared her home.

'Same as always.'

She knew he was looking at the gang symbols graffitied on the fences they passed. The lush greenery of the affluent central suburbs gave way to unkempt, sunburned brown grass and bare dirt. The old-looking swing-set in the park and the new activity set that had already been defaced, litter spilling from the bin. She knew what he was thinking; she thought it too. The neighbourhood wasn't just rough; it was unsafe and was worsening. Her resolve firmed. She was getting her parents out of here as soon as she could.

They were sitting on the porch when Brad turned into the driveway. The two-bedroom government-supplied house had been modified so her father could walk in easily. He didn't rise as Brad stopped the car, but her mother hurried over. Brad got out of the car and greeted her with his intensely annoying polite manners. Mya watched her mother blink a couple of times, watched his full impact on her—that overpowering charm. And she helplessly watched him accept her mother's invitation to join them at lunch. All done before she'd even said hello.

When Brad walked into the house, he was shocked—but not for the reasons Mya might have thought he might be. He'd seen way smaller, emptier properties. No, what shocked him was the wall in the lounge.

It was smothered in the evidence of Mya's achievements. There were certificates everywhere. Certificates going back more than a decade—from when she won spelling competitions at age six. Competitions far beyond her years at that. There were newspaper articles citing her academic successes. There were pictures of her in her uniform. Pictures of her accepting cups and prize-giving. But there were no pictures of her playing.

Proof of their pride in her was everywhere and he realised she hadn't been kidding about the pressure. No wonder her identity was so bound up in performance—*perfect* performance. But surely her parents weren't so success obsessed for her that they'd disown her if they knew she'd failed? She was their only child.

'Brad's a lawyer. A tutor at university.' Mya walked in with her father, who was leaning on her arm. 'He's been helping me with my studies this year. He just gave me a ride because I was running late to get here.' She bit her lip and looked at Brad as if worried she'd made a slip in mentioning law school given she was supposed to be on holiday.

'She doesn't need my help, you know.' Brad went with her story with an easy smile. 'She's just trying to make me feel useful.'

The sad thing was he liked feeling useful to her. Even if in truth he wasn't.

'She's a genius.' Even as he was saying it, he realised he was buying into the Mya-brain-box worshipping—doing it as badly as her parents. Talking her up until she was terrified of failing. Mya, who needed no help academically because she was such a star. Never-fail Mya. Never *dare* fail.

So he switched. 'But she works really hard at it.'

He encountered a beseeching green gaze just at the moment her mother's proud tones came from the other side of the table.

'Mya always works hard.'

Brad worked hard himself then, keeping the conversation light—and away from work. Mya was abnormally quiet and giving him keen looks every so often. It bothered him she was so nervous—what did she think would happen? Did she trust him so little? He wouldn't let her down and give her away.

'I hope it wasn't too bad my staying.' He finally apologised for butting in when they were back in his car and driving towards town. 'But I really enjoyed it.'

'It was hardly your usual restaurant standard,' she answered brusquely.

'You couldn't get fresher than that salad,' he pointed out.

That drew a small smile. 'It's the one thing he likes

the most but tending the garden takes him a long time.
He has chronic pain and he gets tired.'

'It was an accident?'

'In the factory years ago.' She nodded. 'He's been on
a sickness benefit since. Mum does the midnight shift at
the local supermarket.' She sighed. 'So now you know
why I want to get the big corporate job.'

He nodded.

'I want to move them somewhere else. Somewhere
much nicer.'

'I can understand that.' He paused. 'You really care
about what they think of you, huh?'

'Don't you care about what your folks think of you?'

He laughed beneath his breath. 'It no longer matters
to me what either of them think.'

'No longer? So it used to?'

'When I was a kid I wanted to please Dad.' He
laughed—the small kind of laugh designed to cover up
real feelings.

Mya didn't want him to cover up. 'But you don't any
more?'

'I'm really good at my job and I enjoy it. What he
thinks is irrelevant.'

'What did he do?'

'He didn't do anything.'

'I'm not stupid either, Brad.' She turned in her seat
to study his profile directly.

'So you know what he does.' Brad trod harder on
the accelerator and gave her the briefest of glances. His
warm brown eyes now hard and matte. 'Buys his way
out of anything.'

'What did he buy his way out of for you?' Mya asked
quietly.

Attention. It was all about attention. For him. For

Lauren. He'd once asked his father to come and see him in a debating contest of all things. Sure, not the most exciting of events, but he'd been fifteen years old and still young enough to want his father's approval. At that time he'd wanted to *be* his father. A brilliant lawyer, top-earning partner in his firm with the beautiful wife, the yacht, the two kids and the dog.

'I caught him.' Brad surprised himself by answering honestly.

'Doing what?'

'Betraying us.' He glanced at Mya. She'd revealed a part of her life that she preferred to keep private and that she wanted to fix. He wanted her to know that he understood that. So he told her. 'I wanted him to come to see me in the debating final when I was a teen. But he said he had an important meeting he couldn't get out of. I won and went up to show him the medal.' He'd gone up to his father's office, excited with the winning medal in hand, anticipating how he'd quietly hold it up and get the smile, the accolade. Instead he'd discovered that the very important meeting his father hadn't been able to wriggle out of had been with one of the junior lawyers. Fresh from law school, whether she was overly ambitious or being taken advantage of, Brad didn't know and no longer cared.

'The meeting was with a trainee,' he said. 'She was on her knees in front of him.'

'Oh, Brad.'

His father had winked. Winked and put his finger to his lips, as if Brad was old enough—'man' enough—to understand and keep his sordid secret. His scheduled screw more important than his own son. And the promises he'd made to his wife.

So many dreams had shattered that day.

The anger had burned like acid as he'd run home and hidden in the damn tree hut that he hadn't built with his father, but that his father had paid some builder to put in for the look of it.

Brad decided never to be a lawyer like his father. It would never be a father-and-son firm as his father had always envisaged. No insanely high billing rates for Brad. He'd turned to the far poorer-paying child advocacy in direct retaliation to his father. He had the trust fund from his grandfather. He was never going to be short of money. So there was something more worthwhile that he could do. Something that would irritate his accolade- and image-driven dad.

But eventually he realised his father really didn't give a damn what he did. Brad just wasn't that important to him. His gestures might be grand, but they were empty. Just purchases. There was a missing element no true paternal love. All his father was, was hungry for success, money and women—and for maintaining that façade of the perfect family in society.

'I thought Mother didn't know,' Brad scoffed lightly. 'I thought I was protecting her.' Brad had kept that bitter secret for months, feeling all kinds of betrayal— for himself, his sister and his mother.

'But she did,' Mya said.

He nodded. 'We have an annual barbecue at home for all Dad's staff. And that trainee turned up all confidence and Mother greeted her *so* politely. So knowingly. Coolly making it clear to her that while Dad might screw the secretaries, he'd never leave his wife.'

His mother was as selfish as his father. She wanted what she wanted and was happy to put up with the inconvenience of having a faithless husband. Money and status mattered more than truth. She was so busy projecting the perfect image. That was the moment that Brad decided not to help her project that image any more. That was when he removed himself from home as much as possible. He'd gone off and found his own fun—with his own rules.

He looked at Mya. He'd never told anyone that. Not anyone. Had lack of sleep got to him too? And, yeah, he regretted mentioning any of it now he saw what looked like pity in her eyes. He didn't want pity, thanks very much; he had it all under control. He was more than happy with the way he managed his life.

'I'm never going to marry,' he said firmly. 'I'm not going to lie the way they both do.'

'You don't think a long-term relationship can work?'

'Not for me.'

'You're not willing to take the risk?'

'Why would I? I can get all I want.' He smiled, acting up the playboy answer again. And he figured the women in his life got what they wanted too. Which wasn't really *him* but the things he could give them—good sex, fancy dinners, a flash lifestyle. And fun. 'I care about my work. I like to have fun. I like my space. I like it uncomplicated.'

'Easy.'

'Is that so wrong?'

'No,' she said softly. 'Not if that's what both parties want. And understand.'

He trod on the brake and turned to look at her. 'I don't do relationships, Mya. I do fun and flings and nothing more.'

'Message received loud and clear.' She echoed his words of the night before, calmly meeting his stare.

He felt sorry, tired, resigned. 'So this…chemistry between us,' he said slowly.

'Goes nowhere,' she answered. 'It's just one of those things, you know—the friend's older brother...'

'The sister's best friend.'

'We're such a cliché,' Mya acknowledged with a lift of her shoulders. He'd have believed she was amused had her laugh not cracked at the end. 'We've seen too many movies. And you know how it is— you always want what you can't have.'

'We'll be friends.' He did want to remain in contact with her.

She hesitated. Too long for his liking. 'We'll do this party for Lauren.'

And after that? Back to zero contact? It would be for the best. But it wasn't what he wanted at all. He still wanted her to the point of distraction. He'd just have to get over it. Another woman maybe?

He gripped the steering wheel with psycho-killer strength. Appalled with her schedule, he dropped her to university for an hour's lecture knowing she then had to go straight back to the bar for another night's shift. Despite the scratchy feeling beneath his eyelids, he found himself driving to his parents' house. He vaguely tried to remember when it was he'd last been there, and failed. But now was a good time. His father would still be at work and his mother would be at some meeting. He avoided both the house and them as much as possible.

'Hello?' he called out just in case as he opened up the door and disarmed the alarm.

No answer. He took the stairs. His and Lauren's rooms were still neat, still as they'd had them when they were growing up. On a separate floor to their parents, at opposite ends of the hallway from each other, with guest rooms and bathrooms in between. The physical distance was nothing on the emotional distance between the entire family. And though he and Lauren had grown a little closer as adults, the gap between parents and children had only widened.

His mother had read a home-organisation book at some point in one of her obsessive phases, and all their personal things were stored in crates, neatly stacked and labelled in the back of their wardrobes. Schoolwork from decades ago. When was he ever going to go through that? When would anyone? But it wasn't his room that he'd come to grab stuff from. It was Lauren's.

Because that photo of Mya at her parents' house had reminded Brad that, at one stage in her turbulent teen years, *Lauren* had taken hundreds of photos. For a long time she'd preferred the magic of the old-style camera before messing around with digital. The old playroom had been converted into a darkroom for her, their parents eager to do anything that might hold Lauren's interest in a topic that was actually palatable to them—not like boys and underage clubbing. It had long since been converted back into a study but the boxes of prints remained in Lauren's wardrobe.

He sat on her bedroom floor and flicked through them, his heart thudding harder and harder as he worked through the piles. Lauren's best friend, the natural model for Lauren's photographic phase. It had been the two of them against the world, right? The rebel and the reject—the kid who'd not been included by anyone at the hellish, snobby school they'd gone to. Except for Lauren.

Though it was subtle, Mya had changed. The planes of her face had sharpened, those high cheekbones, the big green eyes were able to hold secrets now. In her teen years the attitude was obvious. The resentment, the defensiveness. But so was the joy, effortlessly captured in every other photo—that pixie smile, the gleam in her eyes.

Often she had a battered library book in her hand. Every other photo it seemed Lauren had snapped while Mya was unaware—and she was so pretty. The ones where she *was* aware were funny. The madness of some of the pictures made him laugh—terrifying teen girls.

He'd gone to university as soon as he turned seventeen and missed much of this part of Lauren's life. It had been a relief to get out of the house. At the time he'd been too selfish to think of his sister. He'd thought she hadn't known but of course she had. He'd discovered that in their tennis sessions. It was the great unacknowledged truth, how unhappy and dysfunctional their perfect family unit really was. The affairs of his father, the obsessive illness of his mother. They all retreated behind the façades they'd chosen for themselves. His father the distant workaholic, his mother the busy do-good wealthy woman, his sister the tearaway who acted out for any kind of attention. What was left for him but the playboy role?

He paused over one photo. Mya in that prom dress. He should have taken a better look at her in it back then. Then again it was probably better that he hadn't.

She was leaning against the wheel of a car, parked on a lawn that looked as if it hadn't seen a mower in a few months with ratty weeds. With broken headlights and the weeds around the wheel, that car was going absolutely nowhere any time soon. Yeah, that'd be the car she hadn't learnt to drive in.

Brad put that picture to the side and shuffled through some more. He thought about taking the whole box home to look through at leisure but that was a step too far into stalker territory. He flicked through the pile more quickly—Mya wearing some mad hat, Mya draped in what looked like an old curtain. Mya in another dress apparently butchered and sewn together. He looked at the commonality in the pictures. Lauren's pictures of Mya in Mya's crazy—brilliant—creations. So many different things and so out there.

He flipped through them, faster and faster. She'd not always worn black. She'd always worn outrageous. Uncaring of what society might think. She'd made them herself, made that massive statement—'here I am, look at me...'

Where had that fearless girl gone?

Why had she turned herself into a shadow? Now in nothing but black, slinking round as if she hoped she couldn't be seen. Why didn't she want to be seen? Where had the crazy fun gone? She'd grown into a pale, worried woman. A woman who worked too damn hard. Brad held the picture and looked at the smiling face, and slowly his own smile returned as it dawned on him.

It wasn't Lauren who needed a party. It was Mya.

CHAPTER SEVEN

BRAD was lost in thought when his sister thumped his shoulder.

'What was that for?' He frowned, rubbing his biceps more from surprise than pain.

'What's wrong with you?' Lauren asked.

'What do you mean?'

'I mean those two women just swished past you with hips and bits wiggling and you didn't even look at them. Plus I almost beat you today, which has never happened in our whole lives.'

Seated at the tennis-club lounge, Brad felt more confused than ever. 'What women?'

Lauren's mouth fell open. 'Are you sick?'

Okay, he had been somewhat distracted this morning. 'I've got a tough case on.' He offered a genuine excuse. Gage Simmons was truanting again and still not speaking to his psychologist, and the idea of his parents coping with a mediation conference was a joke.

'Isn't that even more reason for you to scope out some action?' Lauren said sarcastically. 'That's your usual stress release, isn't it?'

Once upon a time it had been, sure. But he hadn't looked at another woman in days—there was another consuming his brain space. 'Have you seen much of Mya recently?'

'*My* Mya?' Lauren's pretty nose wrinkled. 'Not much. Why?'

'I ran into her recently,' Brad hedged. Seemed Mya hadn't told Lauren about the mis-sent photo. Good.

'Where?'

'At that bar she works at.'

Lauren nodded and sighed. 'She works all the time.'

'Mmm.' Brad knew if he left the space, Lauren would fill it.

'It was her birthday last month and she couldn't even come for a coffee with me, she was so crunched between work and study,' Lauren said.

Bingo.

'Seems a shame for her.' Brad hesitated, unsure of how to put his idea forward without his sister guessing what it was he'd really wanted. 'Your birthday is coming up soon and you'll get your mitts on all your money.' Her trust fund would be released. 'We'll have to have a huge party.'

Lauren shrugged. 'I don't want it.'

'The party or the money?'

'The money,' said Lauren.

Brad paid proper attention to his sister for the first time all morning. 'What do you mean you don't want it?'

'I'm going to give it away.'

'What? Why?'

Lauren shrugged and looked self-conscious. 'I want to make a difference. You make a difference.'

Brad smothered his groan and at the same time felt affection bubble for his scamp of a kid sister. 'It's easier for me to do that when I don't have to worry about how much I earn in my job. I can afford to take on the pro bono cases, Lauren. I couldn't do that as easily without the trust fund.'

'That's what Mya said too.' Lauren frowned. 'But look at her, she's so independent.'

'Yeah, but she's not having much fun with it. Life should include some fun, don't you think?'

'We all know what you mean by that.' Lauren rolled her eyes and giggled.

'Not just that. Some simple fun too, you know—party fun.' Brad stretched his legs out under the table. 'What are we Davenports good at?'

'Not that much.' Lauren sipped her lemonade through her straw.

Brad raised an eyebrow. 'But we are. We're really good at putting on a show, right? Let's put on a show for Mya.'

'Mya?' Lauren breathed in so quickly she choked on her drink. Coughing, she asked him the dreaded question. 'You're not going to mess with her, are you, Brad?'

He shook his head. 'No.'

'Hmm.' Lauren didn't look convinced. 'She's not as strong as she seems, you know. She's actually quite vulnerable.'

'Are you telling me to stay away?' Brad managed a smile.

'Would it make any difference if I did?' Lauren asked point-blank. 'I just don't think it would end well. Things don't end all that well for your women, and Mya's had enough of that.'

'Don't worry.' Brad grinned, though his teeth were clenched. 'She's like a sister to me.' What did she mean things didn't end that well for his women? 'And this is because I have a venue I need to do something with for a night.'

'A venue?' Lauren leaned forward, and Brad smiled for real this time. Yeah, his sister had always liked a party. 'So what were you thinking?'

'How's this for a plan?'

Mya got used to the random calls and quickly got in the habit of checking her phone for texts every five minutes. They were short queries about the tiniest details that most people would never think of. One thing to be said for Brad, he was thorough. Very thorough.

In the mornings now he came to the café and ordered a coffee. He never stayed more than ten minutes or so, always moved away when she got busy and had to serve someone. She spent the rest of the day looking forward to her shift at the bar.

Because now he turned up there early every night and urged her to do her worst in creating another cocktail or shot before the crowds came in. She loved the challenge and got the giggles over the often awful results. It didn't matter if she made something that tasted hideous. They laughed about it—with him naming them outrageously. His word play had her in hysterics. He made suggestions; she ran with them. Together they came up with some bizarre mixes that actually worked and many, many failures. But with Brad, failing was more fun than not. And while they worked on it in that calm twenty minutes or so before the crowds appeared, they talked.

She admitted more about her parents' troubles and told him about her cousins who lived around the corner. He listened and then, in turn, 'fessed up more about his parents, and occasionally referenced his work. She knew he was incredibly busy; sometimes he came in looking drained but he always switched 'on' as soon as someone spoke to him. But she knew he went back home after their cocktail-mixing session to do more work. It was why he never drank more than a mouthful of whatever they'd mixed. But mostly they laughed—teasing about everything from taste in music and TV shows to sports teams, and swapped stories of wild, fun times with Lauren.

Mya laughed more in those few minutes each day than she had all year. But fun as it was, it was also slowly killing her because her teen dreams were nothing on the adult fantasies she had now about Brad Davenport. He was so attractive, so much fun and yet so serious about the silliest of things for the party. His concern over the finest of details was so attractive.

In days he became a constant in her life—the one person she saw most of aside from her workmates. It was only for a few minutes, but they were the highlight. And then there were all those texts and the never-ending playlist suggestions for the DJ.

Three days before the party, in between her shifts at the café and the bar, Mya was studying at the library. Her phone vibrated with a message from Brad.

Where are you?

She chuckled at over-educated Brad's inability to use any abbreviated text language. She was similarly afflicted. So she texted back her grammatically correct reply and went back to her books.

She didn't know how long it was before she glanced up and saw him standing at the end of the nearest row of books. 'What are you doing here?'

'It's my natural home.' He winked as he walked nearer.

'But you of all people should know you're not allowed food in the library.' She gave the paper bags he was carrying a pointed look.

'No one will see us.' He jerked his head and sneaked down the stacks away from the study tables and well out of range of the librarian's help desk.

'Brad,' she whispered. But in the end there was no choice but to follow, and she'd come over all first-year giggly student in the library in a heartbeat.

In the narrow space, surrounded by thick, bound books, he opened the bag and pulled out a couple of pottles and put them on a gap in the shelves.

'What is this?' she asked, intrigued.

'Chocolate mousse.'

Of course it was; why had she even asked? But she did, and she had to ask the even more obvious. 'You want me to try them?'

'Yes, they come in these cute little cups, see?' he whispered. 'Which do you think, mint or chilli?'

'You are taking this far too seriously.' She shook her head, but licked her lips at the same time. Yum. She took a tiny bit on two teaspoons and tried them. 'They're both really good. I think Lauren would like—'

'Which do *you* like best?' he interrupted, his gaze boring into her.

Mya's skin goosebumped while her innards seared. She'd missed that look these past couple of days—that full-of-awareness-and-forbidden-desires look. She'd thought he'd gone all friendly and party efficient and had forgotten that kiss altogether—or didn't think it was worth anything. Now all she could think of was that kiss and how much it had moved her and that maybe, just maybe, he was thinking of it too.

'Why does it matter what I think?' She didn't have to try to whisper now. Her voice had gone completely husky. 'This is for Lauren, not me.'

'She'll like what you like,' Brad insisted, stepping closer. 'Come on, tell me.'

She'd never had lust-in-the-library fantasies. Until now. And right now, all she wanted was for Brad to kiss her again in this quiet, still space.

'You've gone red,' he said. 'Was the chilli-chocolate too hot?'

'Must have been,' she muttered.

He was looking at her mouth. Could he please stop looking at her mouth? Did she have a huge gob of mousse on her lip? Because he looked as if he wanted to *taste*, and she wanted him to, very much.

Mya had never felt so hot.

But Brad missed her scorching thoughts. 'Mint it is, then.'

She nodded. Just. 'You've really got into this,' she said, trying to pull herself together as he replaced the lids on the pottles and put them back in the bag.

'I've discovered my latent party-planning talent.' The smallest smile quirked his mouth. He glanced at her and caught her staring. 'So you're all set up to bring her?'

'It's all sorted.' Mya nodded. She'd arranged it with Lauren a few days ago. But now that the party was so close, she felt irrationally ill at ease—even unhappy. She'd be glad when it was over, wouldn't she? She wasn't sure any more. But the worse feeling was the jealousy—she was envious of how much effort he'd gone to for his sister. Which was just mean of her.

She walked away from him, hiding from his intent gaze, back out to the table she'd been studying at. Hopefully he'd leave right away. But he didn't. He pulled out the seat next to hers, sat and flipped open his iPad, hooking into the university's wireless network.

How was she supposed to study now? He didn't get

that when he was around, her brain shut down and all she could think of now was lewd behaviour in the library. She coped for less than five minutes and then she spoke without thinking.

'Did you ever get it on in the library in your librarian days?'

He shot her a startled look.

'I mean—' she felt her blush growing '—that'd be the kind of thing you'd have done back then, right?'

She trailed off as his intense look grew. He slowly shook his head.

He hadn't? *Really?* She'd have thought that Mr Slayer like him would have…but no. He hadn't. Nor had she, of course. And now here they were…

Oh, hell, why did that excite her all the more?

She looked at him and decided honesty was the best policy. 'I can't concentrate on my study when you're around,' she mumbled. 'At the bar, the café, it's different. I don't need to think as hard as I do here. But I can't *think* with you…' She trailed off.

He didn't say anything, just looked at her with those penetrating eyes. He hadn't moved in the past ninety seconds. She wasn't sure if he was even still breathing. Mya felt even hotter than before but now there was a huge dose of embarrassment twisted into her inner furnace as well. She'd all but admitted she still fancied him. But the fact was now she fancied him more than ever. And he'd gone all *buddy* on her.

'Maybe it's best if we work out any last-minute plans over the phone or something,' she said quickly, trying to recover. 'It would be easier, don't you think?'

Slowly he blinked and then seemed to see straight through her. 'That's what you want?'

'That would be for the best,' she squeaked.

He remained still for a very long moment, still watching her. And then he whispered, 'What are you going to wear?'

She froze; like his look, his question breached the boundaries from friendly to intimate—but she'd done that herself already. Now she felt she'd plunged off the edge of a cliff and was swimming in darkness. Who knew which direction the safe beach was? 'I'm not sure.'

'Not black,' he said quietly.

'Probably.'

'No,' he muttered. 'Give me that at least.'

'Okay.' Mya could hardly swallow and her skin was doing that hot-and-cold tingly thing again. 'You've done such a great job,' she said softly, aiming for that conversation-closing platitude—that she meant with all her being. 'She's going to be so thrilled.'

'You think?' His smile lanced her heart. 'I hope so.'

Suddenly he stood, not pausing to pack away his gear, just shoving it into his case as he left.

Instantly she felt bereft. But it was for the best. She looked down at the black-and-white text in front of her— the case names and details she had to understand and memorise. She didn't see any of them. She sighed and blinked to refocus. The sooner the party was over, the better.

He didn't text the day of the party. He didn't need to, of course; he had everything planned to the nth degree. But he'd got her thinking. She wanted to get dressed up. Really get dressed up in a way she hadn't in years. *Her* kind of dressing where she'd been as loud and unconventional—deliberate, girly. Everything unexpected. She'd been in the black jeans so long she'd almost forgotten her old style. But she didn't have any money for anything new and had no time to make anything.

Yet there was one dress she could wear. She shied away from the thought—it would be so obvious, wouldn't it? But she could adapt it, she could wear a wrap or a cardigan or something to dress it down a little...she could get away with it. Maybe.

She went to her parents' house and picked it up, smiling to herself throughout the long bus-ride. She realised she was more excited about seeing him than she was about seeing Lauren's reaction to her surprise.

Once dressed, she went to Lauren's as she'd arranged for their 'girly night out'—their first in ages.

'Look at you!' Lauren squealed when she greeted her at her door.

'Ditto.' Mya laughed at how glamorous Lauren looked.

'Where should we go first?' Lauren asked, her eyes sparkling.

'I promised Drew I'd drop something in at the bar. Is it okay if we go there first?' Mya spun her line.

''Course!'

Mya sent the 'we're coming' text as they climbed into the taxi. All the way there she kept up an inane patter about one of her regular café customers—not Brad. Mya's heart thudded as they swept up the steps. Kirk was on the door and he winked as they walked up and he swung the door open for them.

There was a moment of silence. Then a collective scream.

'Surprise!'

The cacophony of almost a hundred people screaming momentarily deafened her, but Mya chuckled. The glitter confetti bucketing down on them might have been a touch OTT but that was all the more fun. She gazed at Lauren for her reaction.

Only then she noticed that Lauren was looking right back at her with a huge grin on. And then she heard the crowd chanting.

'Mya! Mya! Mya!'

'What?' Mya gazed round in confusion.

Then—who knew from where—a gong sounded and they all screamed again in unison.

'Happy Birthday, Mya!'

Mya clapped her hand over her mouth and shook her head.

'This is for you,' Mya tried to tell Lauren.

'Uh-uh.' Lauren shimmied closer with a wicked smile. 'Fooled you. We all fooled you.'

Shocked, Mya stood immobile. She didn't even breathe—only her eyes still functioned, sending images to her brain. And OMG they were all in on it. Jonny was laughing, her varsity mates. Even Drew was grinning. Her fellow baristas from the café were here. They'd all fooled her. They were all here for *her*.

It seemed Lauren had breathed in giggle-gas as she laughed delightedly, putting her arm along Mya's shoulders.

'But it's not my birthday.' Mya's mouth felt as if she'd been at the dentist for a ten-hour procedure and she had all that cotton-gauze stuff still clogging it.

'You never had a birthday party because you were working.' Lauren laughed more. 'So we took matters into our own hands.'

We.

Mya looked into the smiling crowd once more. Her mouth automatically curved into an answering smile even though she was still in shock, still couldn't believe any of this.

Then she saw him. Brad.

And heaven help her he was all in black—black suit, black tie, black shirt. It emphasised his height, his eyes, his aura of simmering sexuality. The tailored tuxedo a perfect foil for her recycled old prom outfit. If they were a couple, they couldn't have planned it better. Except they weren't and they hadn't.

But he'd planned it—this whole party. Had it been a set-up right from the beginning? What did he mean by all of this? Was this mere seduction? Or a gesture of kindness? Her heart thudded so fast she thought she might faint.

He strode forward from the throng of people and pulled her into a quick hug. 'I changed my mind about the party once we got to talking,' he whispered into her ear. 'I thought it would be more fun to have a party for you.'

Her fingers touched his smooth jacket briefly, the contact with his body *far* too brief. He pulled back and looked at her for a split second, a shot of truth in his gaze—serious, sweet sincerity.

So all the things he'd asked her about hadn't been for Lauren, but for her? No wonder he'd wanted to know which mousse *she'd* preferred. She blinked rapidly, emotion slamming into her. Pleasure, disbelief, gratitude, confusion.

She went cold again—and hot. She wanted this, she appreciated this, she did. But part of her wanted to escape as well. Part of her wanted to be alone.

Okay, not alone. She wanted to be with Brad.

* * *

Brad had lost all ability to move the moment he saw her. For a snatched moment of time his heart had stopped, his muscles froze solid, his brain shut down completely. When his system started again, it sped straight to a higher rate than usual. Adrenalin coursed through his veins and desire shot straight to his groin. Yeah, that was the part of him most affected. He drew a deep breath and forced his body to relax. Mya had made it more than clear it wasn't happening. And that was fine. He was man enough to handle rejection. Except she didn't look as if she was saying 'no' now. Her green eyes were wide and as fixed on him as his were on her. He'd known all along she was attracted to him, but determined not to have a hot affair. He could respect that. He was a man, not an animal, and all this tonight really hadn't been about trying to make it happen. Only now he finally saw it—the surrender in her eyes, the seduction.

The *yes*.

She was in that dress. That damn beautiful pink prom dress, with her breasts cupped high and ribbons trailing down her bare back. His attempt to hold back his body's reaction began to falter. When she looked at him like that? His muscles bunched, rigid with the urge to push her three steps back to the wall and screw her 'til she screamed. Nothing sophisticated, nothing smooth. Just a wild-animal moment to assuage the white-hot lust consuming him.

But they were in a roomful of people and that wasn't the show he had planned for them. And it wasn't what she truly wanted either. She had her other priorities and he could respect them, right?

The only way he'd get through the night alive was to stay away from her and focus on his host duties. He'd been crazy taking this on, on top of his overfull caseload. He'd challenge Mya for her 'world's most busy' title. But he'd done it. And that look on her face had been worth it. Now he could only hope she appreciated the other things he had planned for the evening. But jumping her wasn't on that list.

Mya was aware of Lauren watching her so she forced her gaze off Brad's tall frame as he disappeared back into the throng. 'This is unbelievable.' She smiled at her best friend.

'So good.' Lauren grabbed her hand. 'Come on, I heard a rumour about crazy cocktails.'

They were there—listed on a chalk-board with Jonny standing behind the bar rolling his eyes over the contents. Mya grinned and ordered the only alcohol-free option—she needed to keep her wits about her.

A crowd formed around her—friends she hadn't seen or been able to have fun with in ages, workmates with whom she'd never been able to just hang out. Conversation was fast and snatched and fun, and she tried so hard not to keep watch for Brad. She was determined to enjoy this—the first party ever thrown for her.

But an hour or so into it, the lights suddenly dimmed dramatically.

'What's happening?' Mya leaned close to Lauren as the music switched so suddenly nothing but fierce drumming hit max volume.

'I have no idea.'

Mya stared transfixed as about twenty black-clad figures swooped in, suddenly clearing a path through the crowds and pushing giant black boxes around the floor. The drums continued while the shadows put some kind of construction together.

Brad, looking sexier than a man had any right to be,

was suddenly lit up from an overhead spotlight and appeared taller than ever. She realised those black-clad figures had created a small stage of sorts that extended down the middle of the room. Mya, like everyone else in the place, was stunned into immobility.

'If you don't mind, everyone, there's something we need to do tonight.' Brad's voice boomed out. He had a microphone?

The black cloths that had been covering the windows behind him dropped, revealing two giant screens. The spotlight went off Brad while on screen an old-style countdown reel played. The guests joined in counting down. As they got to one the entire bar went pitch-black.

In the pregnant pause, Mya leaned in to Lauren. 'When did he set this up?'

'You're asking me?' Lauren giggled. 'He didn't let me in on this bit. I just had to get you here.'

'You know we're here to celebrate Mya's birthday tonight. But the thing that you and I all know, but that Mya doesn't quite believe yet, is that not only is she an amazing academic and gifted cocktail creator, she's also an artist. And so for tonight, we're turning this place into an art gallery and seeing what other marvellous things Mya has done.'

'He's *what*?' Mya asked, clapping her hand over her mouth to hold back the shriek.

Now she understood what the stage really was—a runway. And walking along the runway now were models. Slim, gorgeous girls in black bikinis and boots, modelling her hats, her accessories, her dresses that she'd created in her teen years and in the first couple of years at university. Where the hell had he got them all from?

She turned to Lauren, who held her hands up in

the classic 'don't shoot' pose and shook her head at the same time.

She glanced at Brad and couldn't contain the crow of delighted laughter. *Naturally* he'd found a way to get bikini-clad women on the scene. The crowd cheered and clapped, and she couldn't blame them as the leggy beauties strutted the length and Brad gave a running commentary on each item.

'There was a time in Mya's life when we all looked forward to seeing what it was she was wearing—the accessories, the clothes, sometimes the shoes.'

Everybody laughed as a picture of silver-marker-decorated gumboots flashed up on the screens.

'She moved into this world of recycled clothing, making new from the old, turning someone else's rubbish into art for herself. Maximalist, statement clothing. More than clothing. It was wearable art.'

Mya gazed at both stage and screen, her heart swelling. He'd created a multimedia display—a live modelling show interspersed with images from the past flashing up on those giant screens and a soundtrack made up of her fave teen beats. She pressed her freezing palm to her hot forehead. All those DJ picks he'd texted her. The really cheesy ones she'd sent back. He'd made a music mash-up and photo montage, and it was all so embarrassing and wonderful at the same time.

'Of course, she designed for men as well,' Brad said as the tempo of music changed.

Oh, my. Mya's jaw dropped and she gripped Lauren's hand, giggling now. Because she'd *never* designed anything for a guy. But there was an extremely buff guy up there now in nothing but black boxers and some sort of butchered baseball cap. She hadn't designed it for a man, though one could wear it, of course, but it had just been for the fun of it. And the tie that was now being displayed by another guy with very little else on, that had been her school tie that she'd redecorated in a rebellious fit one day. But that mega-buff guy in nothing but black boxers really knew how to show it off.

'So come on, everyone, give it up for Multifaceted Mya.'

Oh, no, someone had switched the lights on her. Literally shone the light on her, and some gorgeous thing came down to where she sat with Lauren. It was the buff guy with the cap. Nothing but the boxers and the cap. Mya looked over at Brad and saw his mouth twitching with amusement as he spoke.

'While Mya makes her way to the runway, here are a couple of stills from the collection where we can see her talent at her best.'

Mya froze on her seat. He couldn't be serious—she had to walk up there? And OMG there were huge photos of her up on those screens?

The black-clad male model extended his hand to her. She had no choice but to take her turn down the damn runway with the hot stuff at her side.

'Let's face it,' Brad concluded. 'The lady has an abundance of talent.'

Everyone in the place was on their feet and cheering.

Mya looked at Brad and saw his smile. Tender, a little mocking—self-mocking perhaps—but genuine. It pierced straight through the last thin layer of defence she had left and exposed her to the full glare of his attraction. In every cell, all the way to her toes it hit—how gorgeous he was.

He wasn't just sexy and funny and handsome. He was nice, thoughtful and caring. It was a side of him she'd never wanted to acknowledge. She'd preferred to keep him in the slutski spoilt-man stereotype. Mr Superficial Playboy. That was the easy way out. But the truth was he was utterly outrageous, utterly unashamed and yet utterly kind.

The lights came back on, and Lauren came up as the bar music resumed.

'It was all her idea.' Brad curved his arm around Lauren's shoulders and drew her close.

'That's not true.' Lauren shook her head firmly.

'Lauren found everything.' Brad gave his sister a sharp look.

'He came up with it when we were playing tennis at the club the other week.'

'It was supposed to be a party for you,' Mya said, too shaky inside to look at Brad at this moment.

'I don't need a party.' Lauren shrugged. 'I go to parties all the time.'

'I'm getting you back for your birthday,' Mya promised.

Lauren just laughed as one of her boys claimed her for the dance floor.

'How did you do all this?' Mya asked Brad, her mouth dry and still not looking at him.

'I had help,' he confessed. 'With the catwalk and the lighting and the music and stuff.'

Mya shook her head and looked across the room. 'Where did you find all of it?'

'My mother's itemised storage system. Lauren had kept them all.'

Well, it had mainly been Lauren's clothes Mya had messed with. The only thing Mya had kept was the dress she was now wearing.

'And you called on all your girlfriends to model for you.' She felt overwhelmed. 'Why did you do it?'

'I found some of the pictures of you,' he said softly.

'You and your pictures.' She stole a quick glance at him.

His mouth had twisted into a wry smile and that soft expression was in his eyes. 'None as good as the one you sent me, but ones Lauren took when you guys were mucking around a few years ago. You were so bold and so creative. Why have you given all that up? You have real talent.'

'No,' she scoffed, totally downplaying it.

'Didn't you just see that standing ovation?'

'You set it up.' She couldn't resist the urge to lean closer to tease him. 'All those beautiful models and all their glorious skin?'

Her words drew a reluctant smile to his lips. 'All that aside, you really do have talent,' he insisted.

'I appreciate this, so much,' she said softly, her throat aching because it was such a kind thing he'd done for her. 'But I don't have time to do that any more. It was a hobby. Life has moved on from that stuff.'

She blinked as bleak frustration dimmed his eyes. 'Mya, you don't *have* a life.'

'I do,' she argued, quiet but firm. 'And I'm lucky enough to have friends.' Ones who cared. She might even dare put him in that category after tonight. Except, grateful as she was for this night, she didn't want to lock him away in that neat and tidy box.

Something flashed in his eyes and was almost immediately blanked out. All that remained was resignation—she felt it too.

He smiled as another guest walked up to talk to them. It was that charismatic smile of his, yet strangely devoid of depth. Despite the excessive heat of a crowded club-floor on a hot summer's night, Mya's skin cooled as if

the first spears of winter had bitten their way through
the hot warehouse bricks. His walls were back up; that
automatic charming gleam hid the honesty in his eyes.
It felt as if she'd lost something precious.

Brad watched her mingle, the gnawing feeling inside
worsening with each minute that she laughed and in-
teracted and clearly had fun. She was having a great
time, but it wasn't enough. He was used to getting what
he wanted—easily. Giving up what he wanted wasn't
nearly so easy. Especially when she looked at him with
that expression in her eyes—the one that told him he
could have what he'd wanted more than anything these
past couple of weeks.

But successful though it may be to a point, this night
was also a failure. She'd appreciated his effort, but she
hadn't understood it. He wanted her to understand she
had so much more to offer the world if she'd just give
herself a chance, if she just let go of all the burden she
took on and let herself be free. She should be doing
the things she loved, not just doing things *for* those she
loved.

The realisation hurt and with that came the worse
hit—he cared too much about where she was at and
what she was doing. When he looked at her now, there
wasn't just that stirring in his groin—there was an ache
in his chest.

He liked her—too much to mess around with her.
Things don't end all that well for your women. While
he wasn't sure he agreed with Lauren's statement, he
wasn't taking the risk with Mya. He could get her to say
yes, but she wasn't cut out for a fling, and he didn't want
more than just that. Even if he did, she wasn't ready for

that in her life. She had her other priorities and that was fine. The only thing to do, right now, was walk away.

So he did.

CHAPTER EIGHT

IT MIGHT have been one of the best nights of her life, but Mya wanted the fireworks to finish it off. She didn't want to be the wallflower walking home alone tonight as she had all those years ago at that miserable prom.

She glanced around. Lauren was flirting with yet another guy—she'd been collecting them throughout the night. Several other friends were propping up the bar getting outrageously hammered with her lethal cocktail mix. Others were up on the catwalk having a dance-off to the hits of their teen years. It was a crazy-fun night.

But Brad had quietly slipped off into the dark—alone. He hadn't said goodbye to her or anyone. He'd flipped a wave at Lauren but he hadn't even looked at Mya.

That wasn't good enough.

Did he think he could do this for her—send her insides into such a spin—and then walk away?

Tonight had been her one night off in months. And didn't she deserve pleasure in it—pleasure for *all* the night? Didn't she deserve a treat? It wouldn't be like that mess-up last year when she'd thought she could handle a night of nothing but physical fun and had failed. This time she knew what she was doing—and she *knew* Brad. She even liked him. But not enough to cause confusion. She'd read the rulebook, was certain she could handle herself on the field. This time she already knew the score. And while there was that hint of insecurity about her performance, she figured Brad wouldn't be all that bothered. Ultimately all she'd be was another notch to him, right? But *she* would have the best sexual experience of her life. He'd teased that it would be, but she knew to her bones he'd follow through. She simply couldn't resist—not for one night.

So she blew Lauren a kiss and waved.

Her feet moved of their own accord, fast, determined, sure. She was stone-cold sober but in a blink she was there already—standing at his front door. Before she could take a breath and think better of it, she hammered the door so hard her knuckles hurt.

He opened it sooner than she expected. He'd lost the jacket but was still in the black shirt and trousers and, oddly, a cleaning cloth in his hand. He stared at her— saying it all with just that wild-eyed look—surprise to desire in a heartbeat. Only then he closed his eyes and bent his head. Sudden nerves paralysed her. Insecurity drowned her moment of boldness.

'Are you going to let me in?' she asked, her voice pathetically breathy even to her own ears. So much for chutzpah.

He looked up and she saw nothing but raw emotion in his eyes—not just desire, but torment. It was reflected in his stance too as he blocked her entry, his hand gripping the door. 'You know what will happen if I do.'

Relief shot into her belly, bursting into flame on impact. 'Yes,' she said. 'That's why I'm here.'

'But—'

'I don't want a relationship, and I don't want a fling. But I've changed my mind about the one-night thing.'

He swallowed and then stepped to one side. She

walked in, holding her head high while her blood fizzed round her body. She went straight to the place she'd fantasised about for weeks. The cover was stripped back, the light switched on—the brightness harsh on her eyes after the moonlit walk here.

'What happened to the vase?' The mess on the floor surprised her.

'Accident caused by frustration.' He watched her as if he was afraid she'd disappear if he blinked.

'You're not usually clumsy.'

'I'm not usually frustrated.'

She paused. If he was 'frustrated', why wasn't he happy to see her here now? 'Why are you feeling bad?' she asked softly, stepping closer. 'It was a great night. I loved every second of it. Everyone else did too.'

'This isn't why I did it.' He spoke low and rough. 'I just wanted you to have some fun.'

'I did,' she answered. 'And I'd like some more.'

'Lauren said not to mess with you. That you're fragile.'

Shock hit, embarrassment soon followed and both burned. What else had Lauren said? 'Do I look fragile to you?'

'Not on the outside, but that vase didn't seem that fragile either and it still broke when I dropped it.'

'You're not going to get the opportunity to drop me,' she said. 'I only want what's left of tonight. I don't want anything more. I'd never expect promises from you. I understand that.' There were only a couple of hours of darkness left. A couple would have to be enough. 'And you know I can't give more either. This isn't going to be anything more for either of us. This is just tonight.'

He walked nearer. Intensity sliced into her as she saw the look on his face, the raw, unrestrained desire honed in on one focal point—*her*. Excitement swept over her and she backed up until the backs of her thighs hit his bed and she sat on the edge of it.

She gazed at him—unashamed in her admiration. He was so much taller, stronger. And looking at her like this? So lethal.

She realised that until now he'd kept a leash on his desires, letting her think she'd controlled this thing between them. But he could have pulled her to him any time he'd wanted. His potency was strong enough to render her will useless. She wanted to be his. But just as violent was the desire to have him ache for her in this same extreme way. Impossible, of course. Hence the one night.

'Are you sure?' he asked as he moved to within touching distance.

'Yes.'

'I like you.' He frowned as if that wasn't a good thing. 'I want the best for you.'

She just wanted to enjoy this attraction—and end up free of it. 'Then give me the best.'

He smiled, his eyes lighting up.

'Don't tease me any more,' she begged. She needed him to come nearer, to stop talking, to make her feel as if she wasn't about to make a massive fool of herself.

'But it's all about the tease.' A glimpse of humour.

'You know what I mean.' She wanted it to be fast. She wanted to get the release, to be freed from it. For it to be over.

He stepped close. The brilliant thing about the height of his bed was that she didn't have to crane her neck too far to look at him. With a single finger he traced the hem of her dress—now rucked up to just over her knees. She couldn't believe he wasn't moving faster already. But instead he put his hands on her pressed-together knees and exerted the smallest pressure.

'Let me in, Mya.' His gaze didn't leave her face. 'Let me in.'

Mya trembled at the cool command. He seemed to be asking for more than access to her body. 'I am.' She swung her legs wide.

'No.' He bent and his lips brushed her neck. 'If we're doing this, then I want everything tonight.' He ran two fingers down her cheek; the slight pressure made her turn her head. He whispered into her exposed ear. His words a caress, an intimacy. As if he'd somehow accessed her soul. 'How much do you want this?' His lips brushed the whorls of her ear. 'It better be as much as I do because otherwise you might not be able to keep up.'

'You're that fabulous, huh?'

'I just want to be sure we're on the same page for this evening. Because it ain't over.'

'I'm not fat and I'm not about to sing,' she said with a hint of her old defiance.

'What about screaming?' He leaned closer until there was nothing but a whisper of air between them. She could feel the heat radiating from him, and her own emotions burned.

Tired of talk, tired of waiting, Mya wanted action. She lifted her chin and laid one on him.

For a moment Brad lost control of the situation. For someone who supposedly suffered extreme sensitivity, Mya could give a blisteringly hard kiss. Her fingers threaded into his hair, holding him there while beneath his mouth hers was lush and hungry. Startled, he gave it to her—the full brunt of the want that had burdened him these past weeks. He dived deep into her sweet

mouth, tangling his tongue against her equally raven-
ous one. He pressed harder until he felt her trembling
and moaning already.

He eased it back a bit, put his hands on her face, cupping those beautiful cheekbones with gentle fingers and
pulling back just enough for their lips to barely be clinging. 'I have no intention of bruising you,' he said quietly.

That nagging feeling that she was holding back
wouldn't leave him. What held her so reserved? While
she smiled and joked with the bar patrons and Lauren's
boys, there was that distance that he'd seen no one
breach. He wanted to be the one who broke all the way
in.

So while there was a time and a place for hot and
hard, quick and rough sex, this wasn't it. She wanted it
that way. He knew she did. She was desperate to have
him to have the release. And for it to be over. Because
there was that part of her that was mad with herself for
wanting him as badly as she did. She didn't want to be
another of his conquests. She didn't understand yet that
she *wasn't*.

Because there was his own confounding desire for
her to come to terms with. He hadn't realised it was possible to want a woman this much. He'd craved sex before. Of course he had. But that had been sex. That had
been about getting the pleasure and the release. This was
about her. This was about seeing her shaking and out of
control and filled with ecstasy. This was about seeing
her weak with wanting him, with her unable to stand—
only being able to lie on a bed and beg for him to come
to her. Oh, yeah, the submissive fantasies were a first.

And now he had her—lying back on his bed with
that dress even more rucked up, giving him a glimpse of
lace-covered treasure. He tensed every muscle to fight

the urge to dive straight in. Heat tightened his skin; he felt as if he were on the rack—stretched well beyond his usual limitations. And now she forced him closer than he'd like. Pushed him to intrude deeper than he normally would. Yes, he wanted it all from her.

He quickly stripped himself and then straddled her on the bed and let the ribbons slide through his fingers as he loosened them enough to pull the bodice of the dress down to bare her beautiful, bountiful breasts.

She shivered before he even touched them. He let his fingers trace near to their precious peaks, so slowly and gently—watching to see how she coped. She moved restlessly beneath him. He bent closer, traced his tongue around the tight, rosy nipples and blew warm air over the tips of them.

She shuddered.

'Too much?' he asked softly.

She shook her head, her chest rising and falling quickly. He carefully cupped her soft flesh, let the centre of his palm touch her nipple. She shuddered again and arched her back, pushing her breasts deeper into his hands. He pushed his hands together, pushing her breasts together, letting her nipples peep over the top of his cupped hands. Beautiful. Big and beautiful and so responsive. He blew on them again. And then so carefully bent to brush his lips over them.

'Oh, no,' she whimpered.

'Okay?' he murmured, caressing them ever so softly.

She nodded and arched towards him again so he kept up the slow, wet caresses.

Her hips rocked now and he smiled at her giveaway reaction. Did she want the same treatment down there? He sure as hell hoped so. He stripped away her small briefs and then kissed his way down her flat stomach, his own excitement uncontrollable as he neared her most intimate curves. He'd dreamed of this for so long, he could hardly believe it was real now. But she was warm and writhing and tasted so hot. Her response deepened, her movements wild.

The pleasure of seeing her so wanting was more satisfying than anything in his life. He peeled her legs further apart, tasting her glistening femininity, holding her hips firmly so she couldn't escape him as she stiffened and then began to convulse. He sucked on her most sensitive nub and then buried his tongue inside her, quickly reaching up to cup her breasts and cover her nipples—diamond hard now, they pressed into his palms. He applied more pressure and tasted the reward as she came hard and loud, screaming for him.

He breathed hard, flicking his tongue to see her through the aftershocks and then he moved quickly. But his fingers were all thumbs as he tried to get the condom on.

'Damn,' he muttered. Desperate, the need to drive deep within her the only thing circling in his head.

Now. Now. Now.

His lungs burned, his heart thumped—and he'd not even started. He was going to embarrass himself at this rate.

'Can I help?' she teased.

'No,' he snapped hoarsely. Instantly feeling bad about biting her head off.

But she laughed. A throaty, sexy laugh as if she knew just how he was feeling.

It was all right for her—she'd had her first orgasm. Finally he was sheathed. He knelt and gazed at her. His gaze fixed on the cherry-red, too-sensitive nipples, low-

ered to her pink, glistening sex and then he looked up
into her glowing eyes.

His heart seized.

Her laughter faded. 'Brad?'

Her voice lifted a notch, the return of excitement even
though she perceived the threat. Oh, yeah, he had plans.
He leaned over her, relishing using his size to dominate
her. But she wasn't intimidated. Not her, no—her smile
returned. Those wide, uneven lips parted and revealed
that sexy-as-hell gap. All petite, fragile, strong woman.

Take. Take. Take.

So he did. Peeling her legs further apart, he took
position, his aching erection pressing against her slippery, sweet entrance. So hot for him. Meeting his gaze
unflinchingly, her breasts rising and falling fast as she
waited for him to finally take her.

And he did—surging forward to encase himself in
one swift movement. But he was almost obliterated as
he felt her clamp around him for the first time. He closed
his eyes, clenched his teeth, locked still to stop the instant orgasm before he'd begun any kind of rhythm. That
just *wasn't* happening.

He breathed hard, pushing back the blissful, delirious
fog, refusing his release until he'd seen her too strung
out to scream any more. And finally he moved, slow,
back and forth, circular. Stopping to caress her breasts,
her neck, her lips. Teasing, nipping, sucking—savouring
every inch of skin he could access while locking himself
inside her. And it was good. So damn good.

'Please let me come, please let me come,' she begged
him, writhing again, her face flushed and her skin damp.

Victory sang in his veins as he slowly claimed, withdrew and reclaimed his place right in the core of her. Her

clenching, soft heat offered unutterable joy as much as it did wicked torment. And he was too ecstatic to care about the implications of the one thought hammering in his head.

Mine. Mine. Mine.

Breathless, pinned beneath his marvellous weight, Mya called to him. How could he bear it so slow? Wasn't he dying inside for the release? How could he hold back from coming inside her so long? Didn't he want to drive himself into her the way she ached for him to— furious and fast and hard?

Oh, hell—was it her? Was she not good enough at this for him? She certainly didn't know any tricks or anything much beyond the basics. And this was sex at its most basic, with him above her, no fancy positions or toys. She knew no tricks—was probably the most apathetic lover he'd ever had. All she'd been able to do the past half-hour was lie there and moan.

He slipped his palm beneath her bottom, pushing her closer so he could thrust even deeper into her, and all self-conscious thought was obliterated in the ecstasy of his onslaught. There was nothing she could do but absorb his decadent attention.

She tensed as that unbearably tense pleasure rebuilt in her. He pushed closer, closer. Her body tautened, her muscles, nerves, heart all strung out, locking onto every part of him she could. She was no longer begging, no longer coherent. Just gasping, grasping for that final step into oblivion. And then screaming. He tossed her into that river of delight. Sensations tumbled over and over— bliss shuddering through her in spasm after spasm. And she clung to him through it all as if he were her life raft as well as the source of the surge.

She gasped again as the last tremor shivered through her and she regained enough strength to sweep a hand down his sweat-slicked back. His skin burned, the muscles beneath flexing and rigid. She turned her face into his neck, wanting to hide how raw her emotions were. How close she felt to him in this moment.

With a feral grunt he pulled her head back so her mouth met his. A hungry, uncontrollable kiss. His tongue pummelling as fast and relentlessly as that other part of him was. Something broke free within her, that desire to *hold* onto him. To hold onto him so tight because he'd given her something so precious. She sucked on his tongue the way her sex was—tightly squeezing. Not letting him go. Stroking him back. A slick friction that set fire to her senses again.

He tore his mouth from hers, arching and shouting as his release ripped out of him. Her body quaked as she received it, intensifying her own pleasure to the point where she could bear no more.

It took a few moments for Brad to realise he'd blanked out and was slumped over her. Their bodies were stuck together—hot skin, locked limbs. Hell, could she breathe? He propped himself up on his elbows and looked at her.

'Wow.' She nodded slowly. 'Okay. I can see why.'

It wasn't quite the comment he'd wanted. That hadn't been his usual wham and bam and 'let's do it three times again, ma'am'. Physical and fast and fun. He didn't know what had got into him with this so-slow-you-think-you're-going-to-die-from-bliss intensity.

'You sure proved your point.' She swallowed.

He might have managed to laugh that off if he weren't so winded. Slowly, reluctantly, painfully, he withdrew from her warmth and rolled to lie beside her. He kept his eyes closed, holding back the exposed feeling. Because that had been so far from his usual behaviour that he couldn't comprehend it.

That hadn't just been sex. He didn't really know what it had been, but he knew it was not just sex. Part of him wanted to flee the scene immediately. Another part of him was stirring back to life, hungry for a repeat. How could the gnawing ache be worse now than it had been before?

'I'm sorry for being so useless,' she murmured.

He flashed his eyes open and lifted his head. *'What?'*

To his amazement she'd gone bright red, more flushed than when she'd been in the throes of passion and about to come. 'I just lay there.'

He really did laugh then—and it was all genuine. 'No, you didn't.'

She'd sighed and moved in subtle, uncontrollable ways that had nearly driven him out of his mind. And she'd held him. He'd had the most incredible feeling when she'd held him.

He pulled her close. But sleep didn't claim him as quickly as it did her. Instead he lay still fully attuned to the signals of her body, his embrace tightening as her body relaxed into sleep. He'd never struggled to get to sleep after sex before. But he'd never had sex like that before either. He tried to process it, his body humming, his mind replaying fragments, sending flashes of memory to senses already overloaded and struggling with oversensitivity. Almost an hour later, still nowhere near sleep, he slipped away from her. In the moonlit kitchen he poured a glass of water. He drank, trying to wash away the fever and regain his laid-back, carefree attitude. But the cool water didn't dispel the growing sense of discomfort and confusion.

The best moment of his life might also have been the biggest mistake.

CHAPTER NINE

MYA woke early, panic clanging louder than an electronic alarm plugged into subwoofer speakers. Warm, sweat-dampened skin where they touched. Time to get out of here. She slipped out from his hot embrace, ultra-careful not to wake him because there was something she had to do first.

Quietly she found her phone and got it ready. Just as he stirred, she threw the sheet back and captured him in all his morning glory before he could blink.

'Now we're even.' She laughed and teasingly waved the phone at him, determined to hide the ache pulling down her heart—from herself most of all.

He blinked and a slow, naughty smile spread over his face—the return of the charmer. 'Damn, you should have told me.' He stretched. 'I could have posed better for you.'

He could *never* have been posed better. He looked like the Greek god he'd joked about.

'I'll delete this when you delete the picture of me,' she offered. But it was a lie. Even if she trashed it from her phone, she couldn't ever wipe this image from her brain.

'I'm never deleting that.' His laughter rumbled, rippling muscles over his taut, bronzed chest. 'I've sent it to my computer. It looks brilliant on a big screen.'

Oh, she should have known. 'You're a perv.'

'And you're an amateur. You think I mind you having a photo of me like this?'

'Well.' Mya sniffed. 'I guess half the city's women have seen you like this, so, really, it's nothing that personal, is it?' She had to remind herself who she was dealing with—and all that this had been.

'Miaow,' he said and then reared up on the bed, moving towards her like a tiger on the prowl. 'Why don't we make a movie instead? Come here and star in it with me.'

The sight of him on all fours was almost enough to tip her over the edge, but she dug in her heels. 'You really are a perv.'

'Come on, back to bed.' He knelt right up, the most X-rated fantasy Mya had ever seen. 'It's early.'

'And I have work to get to.' She really *had* to get out of here.

'You're kidding.'

She shook her head.

'Be late. Call in sick.'

Oh, no, she wasn't letting him tempt her. It was finished. 'You know it's over. The mystery is gone—the wondering of "what'll we be like"—now we know. Now you can go back to your three-women-a-week lifestyle and I can get on with my studying.'

There was a moment, the briefest of pauses when she wondered what he was going to say. He looked away, hiding his expressive eyes, and he flung back on the bed. 'It's only three when I'm on holiday.' He rested his head on his arm and looked even more like a Greek god reclining.

And all Mya could think was how he'd said there was nothing like starting the day with some good sex. She closed her eyes and forced away the whisper of temptation and the vision of one very aroused Brad. She had a shift to get to. She pulled her crumpled dress back on, hoping it was early enough for her not to get caught doing the walk of shame home.

'You can borrow some of my clothes if you want,' he said unhelpfully.

No. That would mean she'd have to see him again to return them, and there was no way that was happening. There was no way she was indulging again. It was going to take long enough to forget how incredible he was as a lover.

She didn't regret last night. But it had been so good she almost did.

'I don't think they'd fit but thanks all the same.' She turned her back on him so he couldn't see her mega blush.

There was no reason for them to see each other again after this. He'd had what he'd wanted now and so had she. It was over. Outside work hours she'd be back to nothing but study, and he'd be back to saving kids during the day and romping his way around the city at night. It was one night and it was over.

Four days later her eyes hurt and she was exhausted but two coffees and a sugary doughnut saw her through the first two hours of her shift at the café. She'd already agreed to stay on and do a double shift before going straight to the bar. Desperate to fill every moment of her day. Study wasn't enough —it was in silence, and in silence her mind wandered. She needed noise and relentless activity.

Sex was sex, right? It was fun and physical, the release was great, and then it was over. Nothing more to it. So why was she so damn fixated on him?

Drew looked up when she finally got to the bar. She was running late from the café, but to her surprise he wasn't grumpy; in fact he smiled at her as if she were his employee of the week.

'We have another private function tonight,' he said. 'In the VIP room.'

'We do?' Another person had hired out part of the place for some outrageous price this close to Christmas? 'Who's the client?'

'Same guy as last time,' Drew answered. 'Brad. He specially requested Jonny. Double rates.'

Mya's insides went solar-hot and her outsides ice-cold, while her heart soared and then dropped in the space of a second. He was supposed to be out of her life—in fact, he *was* out of her life. He hadn't contacted her; she hadn't contacted him... But now he was coming to her place of work but didn't want to see her? He'd asked for *Jonny*?

She didn't know whether to be mad, glad or amused.

'Trouble is,' Drew said, 'Jonny cut himself today. His fingers are all bandaged up and he'll be off the rest of the week. Are you up to serving the private party?'

'Do I still get double rates?' Mya asked.

'I'll have to check with the client.'

Mya flicked her fringe out of her eyes and got down to prepping her cocktail trims. 'Don't worry, I'll check with him.' Her blood quickened as both anger and anticipation simmered. Why hadn't he wanted *her* to tend his bar, hmm?

Half an hour later, she walked into the small room that could be roped off for VIPs or small private functions. 'Hi, Brad,' she said coolly. 'You've offended me.'

'I have?'

'You don't like my cocktail skills any more?'

'I didn't think you'd want me to pay for your time.'

He turned on the smiling charm immediately—but then leaned a little closer to where she now stood setting up the small bar. 'I thought you might prefer not to have to see me.'

She shrugged. 'It wouldn't matter to me.' She carefully placed glasses. 'Maybe I could do with the money.'

'And that wouldn't bother you?' He watched her closely.

'You'd be paying me to pour drinks,' she answered with some sass. 'Not anything else. And you're offering to pay Jonny more than the going rate?'

'To secure the private space I had to. I didn't think you'd want me to treat you as a charity.'

'But you wouldn't be, would you?' she asked coolly.

He studied her, a small smile playing around his way-too-luscious lips. Yeah, there was the problem—she now knew exactly how skilled that mouth was.

'I can be professional,' she said—to herself more than to him.

'Can you?'

'Sure, can't you?'

His smile deepened. 'I'm not at work. I'm here to have fun and flirt with the bar staff.'

'You wanted to flirt with Jonny?' She laughed. 'I'm sorry to disappoint you, but Jonny is off sick. You're stuck with me.'

He looked at her.

'Am I worth double?' she asked him and tilted her head on the side.

'You do know what you're doing, don't you?'

'Stirring a cocktail, yes?'

'You're stirring, but not just the cocktail.'

'We can still be friends, right? Isn't that what you said?' she said archly.

That was before they'd slept together.

'Of course.' He inclined his head and walked to greet the first person coming through the door.

Mya watched the guests arrive and insecurity smote her—there were women here, seriously hot women. Smart ones too. Lawyers, the lot of them. And it was so dumb to feel threatened when she was ninety per cent on her way to being a lawyer too. And even if she weren't, she still didn't need to feel any less worthy than them.

Yet she did. The years of conditioning at that school had shaped her—that she should feel grateful for having that opportunity. That she shouldn't stuff it up. That her drop-kick family background meant she'd never be fully accepted by the social strata that most of these people came from—as James had pointed out.

She watched Brad laughing with one of the women. Oh, no, maybe that was why he hadn't wanted her to work the bar—had he been sparing her because he was here with another woman? Why hadn't she thought of that?

Brad knew all the guys were checking her out. It had been a dumb idea to come here, but he'd thought he could pull it off if Jonny had been doing the work. Then Brad could pop into the main bar and snatch a few words with Mya and see how the land lay. Only now she was right in front of him, smiling, joking and teasing with them all as she served them.

And all he could do was watch like some lovelorn pup hoping for any kind of bone to be thrown his way. Some small scrap that might show she wanted him again. It was more than his pride that was stung. Did she really not want another night with him? Had that truly been enough for her? He didn't believe it—was egotistical enough not to. All he needed was some proof. And to get that, he figured he just needed to get a little closer to her.

Mya fully regretted saying she'd do this. He was more handsome than she remembered, more fun with his wicked smiles and sharp words. And now she was assailed by images of sneaking him into the cupboard or some dark corner in the alley and having her wicked way with him. Quick and frantic and fabulous.

And to make it worse, he'd now taken up residence right beside her and was watching her every move with the full-on maple-syrup glow. Brad Davenport on full throttle. She fumbled with the bottle and was annoyed to glance up and see him suddenly smiling as if he'd won the lottery.

'Not on your game tonight?' he drawled. 'Or is it because you can't concentrate when I'm near?'

She stopped what she was doing—but couldn't stop her blush. 'Don't be mean.'

His brows hit the ceiling. 'I'm not the one who was mean—you're the one who said one night only,' he whispered harshly as he leaned over.

'You only *do* one night,' she whispered back.

'Not necessarily.' He leaned against the bar. 'Maybe I can do unpredictable.'

Mya clutched the neck of the bottle with damp fingers and tried to joke. 'Would you be saying this to Jonny?'

He didn't bother to reply, just kept those burning brown eyes on her.

'Why didn't you ask for me?' she added.

'Can you honestly say you wouldn't have got mad if I did? Can you honestly say you'd be happy for me to pay for your time no matter the context?'

She poured herself a tall glass of water. Damn, the guy actually understood her.

'I'll walk you home tonight,' he said.

'You're hoping for a good-night kiss?' She squared her shoulders and asked straight out.

'I'm concerned for your safety,' he replied, his eyes twinkling.

'Really?'

'Partly. Mainly I want more than a good-night kiss.'

'Do you?' she asked softly. 'What do you want?'

He didn't answer with words—just that look.

Mya turned away while she still could. 'I'll get Pete to come in and finish serving you guys, and I'll meet you out the front at closing time.'

To her pleasure, he was waiting as she'd asked, at the very end of the night.

'Where do you live?' he asked.

'Tonight?' she said. 'I'm staying at your place.' She walked up to him but he took a step to the side and back, out of reach.

'I'm not touching you now,' he muttered. 'If I touch you now we'll be all over each other in the nearest shadow and I don't want to do that.'

'You don't?' Her confidence surged at his words.

He closed his eyes. 'I don't want it to be sordid.'

Delight and desire filled her, topped off with relief. All that pleasure was smashed away by the need that pierced her a second later. She walked faster. 'It wouldn't be.'

He stopped on the footpath behind her. 'Mya.' A warning, a plea, a demand.

She turned her head to look back at him and smiled.

Then she walked faster still, her body slick and ready. 'It would be fun.'

As it had been the night of her party, she seemed to fly rather than walk. Her feet skimmed over the concrete. There was no alcohol in her system, yet she was in a haze as if she was under the influence.

She was under the influence of *him*.

She realised he was breathing faster than normal, and he was fit. The walk home hadn't exactly taxed him. Something else was bothering him—the same thing that was bothering her.

She walked up the narrow path to his villa. Under the veranda they were shrouded in darkness the streetlamps couldn't penetrate. The scent of the rose in the pot by the door was sweet and fresh. She stood in front of the door, like an impatient cat yowling to be let in, while he stood behind her.

'I can't get the key in the lock,' he muttered, nuzzling her neck. 'Don't go getting all Freudian on that.' He chuckled with a groan.

At least they were almost inside his home. He hauled her closer, crushing her against him. She melted into his hot strength, almost delirious with ecstasy already. Yes, this was what she wanted—more of him. *All* of him. And she was too desperate now to wait a minute longer. On the darkened deck, no one could see them from the street. So Mya, bolder than she'd ever been in her life and on the brink of ecstasy because he wanted her as much as she did him, pulled her jeans down. She didn't get them very far, wiggling her hips side to side to tug them as far as she could, but she only made it to mid-thigh. She'd hooked her knickers with them, and despite the warmth of summer, the air on her bared butt was cool. She pressed back to feel the rough denim of his jeans against her.

He swore, pithy, crude, hot.

She looked over her shoulder as she put her hands to the cool paint and arched back, letting her butt grind against his pelvis.

He swore again, explicit and thrilling, and curled a strong arm around her waist, his other hand scraping the key in the lock. Finally he got it and turned the handle. He lifted her with that one arm and took the two paces inside. He turned them both and slammed the door, stepped forward immediately, his hands gripping hers and lifting them higher on the wood so they were above her head.

His feet moved between hers, pushing hers wider apart. But they couldn't go that far the way her jeans were only pulled to her mid-thigh. It excited her all the more—she wanted to be pinned by him again. It had been all she'd been able to think of for days. He leaned against her from behind, holding her still as he unzipped his jeans. She pressed her palms to the door herself, rubbing to feel the blunt head of him so near to entering her slick heat.

'Hell, Mya.' He cursed again. 'I want you...'

She heard the sharp rip, felt his movement behind her. A second later his hands circled her thighs. His fingers met in the middle, touching her intimately. She heard his roughly drawn breath as he felt how wet she already was. His fingers returned to her inner thighs, holding her tight now, and he thrust in hard. No preliminaries, just raw heat.

She gasped, shocked and delighted and desperate all at once. She put her hands on the door, bracing and giving leverage to push back on him and take him deeper.

He moaned and immediately pressed his mouth to her shoulder to muffle the sounds of ecstatic agony.

Heat beaded all over her body. Her breath burned in too-short bursts. More moisture slicked where she needed it most, easing his sudden, forceful invasion.

He circled his hips and then thrust hard all the way home again, surging into a quick, hard, breathless rhythm. A coarse word of bliss rapidly transformed into a groan and he paused his rough thrusts into her. 'Damn it…you can't possibly come this way.'

'Oh, yeah?' But she could, she was almost there already. Desperately turned on. 'Don't you dare stop.'

He lifted her, flattening her against the door. Literally screwing her to it. A good thing given her legs were trembling so much they couldn't hold her up because she was so close to orgasm.

He forced his fingers between her and the wood, and for a second they stroked, as if to ensure she was as turned on as she declared. She pressed against his hand, trapping it, stopping the tease. Then arched her back as much as she could.

'Brad!'

He growled and withdrew his hand, slamming it against the wall by her head as he thrust hard again. 'I want you so much.'

She squeezed her eyes shut, breathing hard as his words struck like hot stones into her soul and his body rammed once more into hers. She felt his rough jaw against her cheek; the blunt demand inflamed her body.

She could hardly move her mouth to form the words. 'More,' she confessed. 'I…want you. More… More.'

It became a mantra and then a scream as the sensations skidded, becoming convulsions that twisted through her. Her hands curled into claws as she shook.

She ground her hips round and round between him and the wall. Both immovable forces. With a harsh groan he resisted her attempts to milk him. His hands gripped her hips, holding her still as over and over he stroked as if trying to get deeper and deeper within her, as if he too couldn't bear for it to be over just yet. His need shocked her. The same need that had summoned her here, making her ignore both caution and reason.

'Oh. *Yes*.' Her own primal reaction to his demand was an orgasm so strong she would have fallen to the floor had he not held her so tightly.

His fingers dug as the answering cry was ripped from him.

Breathing hard, he slumped against her, still pinning her to the wall, his head falling to her shoulder. She felt the harsh gusts of breath down her back as he held her close. She appreciated the contact—the comfort—as if he too needed the time and the proximity to process what they'd just shared.

And then he moved, lifting her into his arms and stomping a few feet into his spare room—the library. He sank into the big armchair, holding her in his lap.

Their eyes met in the dim light. He smiled at her and then kissed her. She kissed him back. The slow, tender kisses that they'd skipped in their haste for completion.

'We're doing this again,' he said quietly.

How could she deny him anything when he was so skilfully stirring her body into blissful submission? 'A couple more times,' she muttered, barely able to think.

'More than a couple.'

Okay, she could see the attraction in that for her, but what about him? 'What's in it for you?'

He laughed silently, but she felt the vibrations all around her. 'You have to ask, after *that*?'

She'd never thought of herself as a skilled lover or any kind of sexual goddess. 'That other guy told me I was lousy in bed,' she admitted. 'And given James had just dumped me, I thought he was right.'

'You're kidding,' Brad groaned. 'You're amazing. That was unbelievably amazing.'

The glow he'd already lit inside her burned brighter. 'Is this not normal for you?' she teased.

He stilled. She could sense him deliberating over his reply. She looked away, studying the shelf of books as if she could read the titles in the gloom.

He took her chin in firm fingers and turned her so she had to look him in the eye again. 'No. It's not.'

She felt her cheeks burn but he wouldn't let her turn her head away.

'That other night? And tonight?' he said softly. 'Best sex of my life.'

'No,' she whispered. She didn't want him to flatter her with false praise.

'Do I have to print out a certificate before you'll believe me?'

She chuckled.

He was the one shaking his head now. 'You don't have to get the awards, you know. You don't need accolades to be certified attractive. All you have to do is smile.'

How could she not smile when he said things like that? 'Another confession?' she whispered. 'It was the best sex of my life too.'

He smiled.

'But this can't be anything,' she added quickly.

'I don't think we need to label it, do we?'

'It's only for a little while.' Only until she had her desire for him under control. If she didn't put her heart on the line, she'd be fine.

He shook his head. 'Don't you get it? We can't put limitations on this because we'll both want more if we do that. You always want what you can't have. And we both have that fighter within who wants to defy the rules.'

'So what do you suggest—no rules?'

'No rules.' He leaned over her and whispered. His hand teasing the soft skin of her inner thigh. 'And if you like, no boundaries.'

Mya stared at him, incredibly tempted. He meant physical boundaries. She knew that. 'None at all?'

He lifted his shoulders.

Her heart thudded so hard. 'All or nothing?'

'Anything you want me to do, sure, I'll do.'

'You're offering to be my love slave? You'll do whatever I want?' She couldn't help but smile at that idea.

He nodded. 'You take pleasure from me and I'll take pleasure from you.'

He was offering a licence to thrill. 'What if I don't want to do something you ask me to?' she asked curiously.

His expression deepened and he ran a gentle finger down her arm. 'I think you'll want to.'

She touched her tongue to her lip. Yes, she figured she would.

His fingers tickled as he suddenly grinned. 'I wasn't actually thinking of anything that kinky,' he teased. 'But maybe you were.'

Colour heated her cheeks. 'What I think of as kinky you probably think of as tame,' she muttered defensively.

'You can ask me for anything,' he murmured.

She nodded. 'It's not the right time for a relationship for me and you never want one…but for now—'

'There's just now.' His arms tightened around her and he stood, carrying her down to his room.

Mya reached out and switched on the light as they passed it.

'I love this wallpaper.' She gazed at the green vines climbing the white paper. 'It still stuns me you're into floral.'

'It's not floral,' he said firmly, planting her on the bed and tugging off her jeans. 'It's jungle.'

'*That's* floral.' She rolled onto her stomach and pointed to the small vase on the bedside table filled with sweet-smelling summer roses.

'Women like flowers,' he said blandly, bending to kiss the small of her back.

Oh, he might talk all sophisticated loverman, but it wasn't quite as it seemed and she knew it. 'No, you had flowers there that first time I visited, and you didn't know I was coming.'

'I'm always prepared for an overnight female guest.' He emphasised the tease with a nip of his teeth.

'No.' She rolled to face him and grabbed a fistful of his shirt to pull him onto her. 'You prefer to sleep at their houses so you can do the "quickie and exit" in the morning. The only reason *I'm* here is because you know I'll leave early. You know I'm not going to linger and make for an awkward morning-after moment.' She met his darkened gaze and determinedly ignored the way his fingers were stroking closer and closer to her nipple. 'So the flowers are here because you like them. Furthermore—'

'There's more?'

'Oh, there is. I have all the evidence for this case. You grow the roses in your garden.'

'Okay, so I grow the roses,' he admitted. 'Are you going to tease me about it?'

'Of course not.' She rubbed her fingers against his stubble. 'They're beautiful.'

His amusement turned wicked. 'I get pleasure from watching something bloom. I appreciate form, nature's "curves".' His hand slid over her hips and between her thighs.

'You can try to hide behind some sexy talk, but the fact is *you're* talented. You really care about your roses.'

'I really like curves.' He burrowed down the bed more. 'I like pretty pink flowers too.' He pulled her knees apart. 'And you're right, I like to look after them.' He bent and kissed her there, his tongue circling in ever-teasing strokes, before sliding inside.

Mya had given up on her analysis the moment he touched her. Her eyes closed as sensation rippled out from deep within her. He turned her on so quickly.

When she was wrung out and panting he rose, wearing the smile of a victor. She wound her arms around his waist and pulled him close.

'Mmm,' he groaned appreciatively as she wriggled beneath him. 'I've discovered a liking for clinging flowers.'

'What about carnivorous ones?' She arched swiftly and ate him whole.

But later as she tumbled towards sleep in his arms she reminded herself exactly how long this fling was going to last. Brad might have said no limitations, but as far as she was concerned it was for one week and one week only. She only had two lecture-free weeks over the Christmas break. The first was his, the second was for her assignments and exam study. There'd be no room for him in her life from then on. Abstinence had failed; an overdose had to work. One week of indulgence.

CHAPTER TEN

SHE came to him every night. And every night it was the same but different— variations on a theme. So many, many wonderful variations. He delighted in his deepening knowledge of her—he sought to learn what she liked, what made her shiver, the slow discovery of all her secrets. But finding enough time to see her was hard. Frantic sex followed by sleep followed by more frantic sex before she left for work. He sometimes had lunch with her—a snatched ten minutes before he was due in court or before she had a lecture. Ten minutes wasn't enough. He went back to the bar in the early evenings but then left to get more work done— and to let her work.

There wasn't enough time. Mya grasped the few moments they had but it felt like the glitter from the party impossible to catch and hold. Just an ephemeral, beautiful shimmer. So she was determined to make the most of it. Brad seemed more intent than ever on 'just having fun' too—as if he was also aware of how brief this would be.

She stretched in his big bed, slowly and so reluctantly coming awake after what felt like only five minutes' sleep. She could hear him talking—dozily she listened to one half of an incisive discussion on some point of law. She smiled as she snoozed. He sounded so authoritative—which he was on this, of course—quoting from case after case, and given that she could hear he was pacing down the far end of the hall, she knew he was recalling those cases from his own memory, not that of a computer. Geek. Question was why he was talking so early in the morning.

She sat up and looked at her watch. It wasn't just early in the morning—it was still the middle of the night. She'd really had only a little more than five minutes' sleep.

She slipped out of bed and wrapped a towel round herself and tiptoed down the hall. She could see the light in his office was on, and she paused in the doorway. He stood at his desk, his hair a crumpled mess, unshaven, circles under his eyes, still on that difficult call.

She took a step back and went back to the bedroom, not wanting to eavesdrop. But in the silent house, his voice carried—his concern was obvious. She waited a very long time for him to return to bed. But even though he'd stopped talking quite some time ago now, he still didn't come down the hall. So she got up again—concerned.

From in his office doorway, she saw him sitting at his desk, his face a portrait of worry. She'd noticed before how tired he sometimes looked when he thought no one was watching. The animated, charming façade slipped on when people talked to him. She didn't want him to feel as if he had to put that mask on for her. She understood now that he covered up with the charm factor. Why did he feel the need to maintain the image? When he claimed to hate that manufactured perfection in his parents' home? In a way he was as guilty of it as they were.

But then he closed his eyes and put his head in his hands.

'Brad?' She swiftly walked into the room, round the side of his desk and put her arms around him. It was an instinctive, caring gesture. Nothing sexual, just the comfort of a hug. 'What's wrong?'

For a long time he said nothing. But then there was a sigh and a mumble. 'Christmas is bad for most of my kids.'

My kids. The word meant much. She softened inside. He cared deeply, but he didn't like to display it for everyone. 'Something's happened?'

'Gage has run away.'

Mya bit her lip. Two days out from Christmas? Things must be bad. 'Who's Gage?'

'A client. His parents split a while back. He's been shuttling between them for a few years, but it's never been easy. His father had a new partner on the scene but they've split up recently.' He sighed. 'What's worse, do you think? Being fought over, or not being noticed or wanted at all?' He glanced at her. 'Or being expected to carry the expectations and dreams and ambitions of generations?'

She shook her head. 'It depends.'

'It does,' he said tiredly. 'I should have spotted there was something badly wrong,' he added quietly. 'I should have seen it. I knew he'd been truanting. I knew he hadn't been talking to the psych. But I—'

'You're not his parent.'

'I'm his advocate. I should know what it is he wants.'

'And do you?'

He stared sightlessly at the desk. 'I'm not sure. He's on the run but if I were to guess I'd say he'll head to his dad's ex. She's been the one there. But she lives in another town now. She wasn't married to the guy. She's not a guardian. In theory she has no legal claim to Gage.'

'But if he wants to stay with her, if she wants him— can you help them?'

'Maybe. That's if he is heading there, if he is okay.' He looked worried. 'Not all stepmothers are wicked.'

And not all playboys were heartless.

'It's really sad,' she said.

He nodded. 'And if he doesn't turn up soon, he's only going to make it harder for himself to get what he wants.'

'I'm sorry, Brad.'

He rubbed his forehead, as if he could rub away the stress. 'You should go get some sleep.'

'Not without you.' There was one thing she could give him—the one thing he'd wanted from her. It wasn't much, but it was all she had, and she wanted to give him comfort now. She didn't know how she was going to do it, but after Christmas she was walking away from him. She'd been such a fool to think she could handle this. 'You do an incredible job,' she whispered. He was an incredible person.

'Not good enough,' he muttered. 'Not this time. I should have spotted it, Mya. Hell, I hope he's okay.'

'He will be.' She hugged him tighter. 'Don't feel bad,' she urged. 'You help so many people. You'll help him too.'

Worry burdened Brad—burned inside him. Because he feared Mya was wrong—on several levels. 'I do this job to make myself feel good. To pretend to myself that I have helped out in some way,' he confessed. 'But do I really?' He shrugged. 'Who knows?'

'Of course you do,' she said vehemently. 'You're hugely talented and you give that talent to the most vulnerable. You're generous.'

'Mya,' he muttered, trying to claw back some cool. To joke his way out of this intensity the way he always did. 'I thought I only did counsel for child to score chicks?'

'I don't think you're as selfish as you like to make out that you are.'

Oh, but she was wrong. He knew he was selfish. He'd been told it many times by women. And they were right. 'I'm not very good company tonight.' He felt uncomfortable—felt vulnerable with her this moment. He wanted to pull it back in. His chest ached. Maybe he was coming down with summer flu. 'I don't feel that great,' he muttered, too tired to hold that last fact back.

'I know.'

He turned and looked at her—beautiful, bright, *sweet* Mya, whom he wanted so much from and yet who couldn't give it.

Wasn't it ironic that the game-changing woman for him didn't want the game changed? He'd positioned himself as her bed-buddy—painted himself into a corner as her 'good-time guy'. And was that so bad? A few minutes of fun here and there in an otherwise hardworking life? He was the king of quick'n'fun, wasn't he? With the same woman for once, yet what difference did that really make?

It made all the difference. Tonight it hurt.

Because he cared for her a lot more than he'd like, and the reality was he didn't stand a chance. There was no room in her life for him. Her parents came first and that was fair enough. He'd played the playboy role too well for too long for her to see him any other way. He supposed it served him right. But this second he was so wrung out, he was at the point where he'd take all he could get. And so he tried to pull it back on again—

his playful tease. 'Is there something you wanted?' he drawled.

But she didn't respond with the same kind of light amusement. 'Yes, there is.'

She didn't tease him with her wishes or do a pretend strip to reveal her polka-dotted panties and mismatched cotton bra. Instead she looked serious. 'Tell me what you want me to do.'

He coughed; it felt as if something were crushing his chest. A crazy, over-the-top reaction. This was hardly the first time a woman had asked him to reveal a sexual fantasy. But he didn't want a fantasy tonight. He just wanted Mya. 'I thought I made it clear you didn't have to do anything other than just be for me.'

'No. You've done what I wanted you to do so many times. Now it's your turn. I'm yours. What would you like me to do?'

He didn't answer. Frankly, he couldn't think with the way she was looking at him with all the promises of the world in her eyes and the sweetness in that unique smile.

'No ropes?' Finally, she teased. And her laughter tied his tongue—and his heart—the way no real binds ever could.

All he wanted was for her to welcome him the way she always did. All he needed was to see how much she enjoyed being with him; her response told him she was as enthralled as much as he in the passion between them. He ached for that total embrace, the softness in her body. Yeah, her embrace alone was enough. Her absolute acceptance. He took her hand and pulled her closer.

'Cover me,' he whispered.

Deliverance finally came as she draped her warm limbs over his.

CHAPTER ELEVEN

SHE never got back from the bar until the early hours of the morning. Brad loathed the thought of her walking home alone, but she refused to let him pick her up after work, arguing it was too late for him. She wouldn't pay for taxi fares—certainly wouldn't let *him* pay for them. According to her, her scream-in-a-can and night-school self-defence moves were enough protection. Not for Brad they weren't. She didn't know it but he'd paid Kirk, the bouncer, to walk her home these past couple of weeks. He'd even concocted the lie for Kirk to tell her—that he'd moved into the city and walking her wasn't far out of his way. Mya hadn't argued much, which made Brad suspect she wasn't completely convinced about her self-defence skills either. It made his blood sizzle that he could only help her if he did it secretly.

His blood sizzled more because of the intensity with which he *wanted* to help her. It was crazy. And even crazier was that here he was, awake way beyond midnight, waiting to hear the sound of the key in the lock. Since when had he *ever* given a woman a key to his home?

He'd seen how tired she was today. She'd had two coffees for breakfast this morning. He knew she'd get something to eat at the café—and more coffee. Then she'd gone straight into her shift at the bar. She'd get more sustenance there too. But what the woman needed was some sleep. She needed to take better care of herself. He needed to take better care of her. He hated how hard she worked. And he hated how it had been his fault she'd had so little sleep last night—and not from energetic bedroom games but talking. Off-loading all his troubles about Gage. He didn't feel comfortable about that either. It was time to ease back a bit, get them back into the playful groove. Lighten it up the way he liked it. But his mood was bleak—worried about Gage, worried about Mya, and, frankly, worried about himself and his ability to handle it all.

Eventually he heard her arrive, her heels clipping along the hallway. He rolled onto his stomach and closed his eyes, feigning deep sleep—too late to switch the light off.

'Brad?'

A stage whisper that he ignored. He counted his breathing, trying to keep it deep and regular.

She touched his shoulder, and he braced to stop the flinch as her fingertips stroked. She had a soft touch, but not shy. He made the counting in his head louder so he wouldn't smile. The thing she needed most right now was sleep, not an hour getting physical with him.

'Brad?'

He was *asleep*; hadn't she got that already?

She sighed. The edge of disappointment nearly broke his resolve. He'd make it up to her tomorrow. He'd disable her alarm and let her sleep late. Then he'd wake her slow—morning sex was the way to start the day, and they'd never yet managed it in any kind of leisurely fashion. And Christmas morning meant the café would be closed.

She walked a couple of paces away. He carefully opened his eyes and saw her back was to him. He could see the weariness in her shoulders, in the way she rubbed her forehead as if there was a residual ache there before she began to undress. He wished she wouldn't work as hard as she did. He wished she'd damn well let him help her out. She could drop one of her jobs; he'd see to it that she didn't starve.

He was so busy thinking he didn't notice that she'd turned around. Or that he was supposed to be out like a light.

'You're awake.'

He snapped his eyes shut but he knew it was too late.

'Brad!'

Busted. 'I was asleep.'

'You were pretending to be asleep!' She sounded outraged. 'Why were you pretending to be asleep?' She supplied the answer before he could even open his mouth. 'You didn't want to have to perform tonight? You're lying there feigning sleep like some unfulfilled spouse trying to avoid duty sex?'

'Mya—'

'Are you bored already?'

It was the hurt behind the indignance that got him moving. He shot out of bed. 'Does it look like I'm bored?'

His erection was so hard it hurt, his skin pulled tighter than ever before. All he wanted to do was bury himself deep in her heat and find the release. He wanted those sensations that only she could give, to steal away all the thoughts that tormented him, to be as close as they'd been last night with nothing between them.

'If you didn't want me to come tonight, all you had to do is tell me.' She ignored his evidential display.

'I want you to come.' And yes, he meant that in the teenage double-entendre way.

'Then what are you doing pretending you're asleep?' Arms folded, foot tapping, she waited.

He sighed. He was a condemned man. His answer would annoy her but she wouldn't let him get away with not explaining himself to her. 'I thought you needed some sleep.'

Her jaw dropped.

'Look at you,' he said. 'You're exhausted.'

'The shadows beneath my eyes are a turn-off, is that it?' she queried—not hiding the hint of hurt. 'You're not doing a lot for my ego here.'

'Mya,' he said coaxingly and reached for her.

She pulled back out of reach. Totally put out. 'I work two jobs and study on top of that, so exhaustion is normal. I'm sorry if I can't live up to the high-gloss appearance of your usual lovers. Maybe you need to stick to ladies of leisure.'

'Mya.' He tried to laugh it off, gesturing at his erection. 'It's perfectly clear your appearance is still lethal for me.'

She wasn't buying it. 'You can't tell me you didn't pull some all-nighters when you were studying. It's normal student behaviour.'

'Not every assignment, I didn't.'

'Well, bully for you for being more organised than me.'

'No one can be more organised than you. Your problem is that not only are you studying, you're working two jobs. That's not a normal workload.'

'In my world it happens all the time. You do what you have to do.'

'Yeah, but *you* don't have to do that much.'

'I do if I need to eat.'

'Why not let me help you?'

She whirled away from him. 'You don't need to help me. All I want from you is—'

'Yeah, okay. I got it.' He didn't want to hear what *little* she wanted from him. He'd made the bed. But now the bed wasn't enough for him.

What was wrong with him? He'd never turned down sex. Ever. If a pretty woman was offering, he was on it. Easy come, easy go and a good time had by both.

She'd wanted to ravish him, and he'd lain there like a log. And ironically harder than a piece of petrified wood. He'd definitely come down with some kind of mind-altering fever. And now she was halfway down the hallway again.

'You're not leaving,' he stated, striding after her.

'I'm not staying where I'm not wanted.'

'You're wanted. You *know* you're wanted. All you have to do is look at me to know you're wanted.'

'That's just a normal state of being for you.'

White-hot fury ripped through him because this was *not* normal for him.

She turned in time to read his expression and suddenly shook her head. 'Don't make this complicated.' She kept backing up the hallway. 'I think I'll spend tonight at my place. Catch up on my beauty sleep.' A pointed look. 'And I need to get to my parents' place early in the morning. We can get together next week.'

He caught up to her in a couple of quick strides. He

pulled her against him and kissed her until she was panting. And so was he.

'You couldn't look more beautiful than you do right now,' he said.

When her attention was riveted on him. When desire filled her eyes and blood pounded in her lips and she was seconds off breathing his name.

But that hurt look in her eyes grew—dimming that light. 'You just don't like me walking out on you right now. But you started it.'

'What I don't like is how hard you're working. Why not work smarter instead of harder?'

'What is that piece of management-mag speak supposed to mean?'

'Get just one job. A better job. Get an internship at a firm.'

She shook her head.

'You could clerk for me over the summer.' It was the worst thing to suggest; he knew it before he'd even opened his mouth but he couldn't stop the words.

'I'm not a charity case. I'm tired of charity. I want to do it myself. I want to deserve it myself.'

'You do deserve it,' he argued, his volume lifting along with his frustration. 'You're super smart. You've got amazing grades. Any firm would want you.'

'You only do because of this…connection,' she said. 'It's the sexual equivalent of the old boys' network. Only because you know me. I'd rather send my CV out and get a job on my own merit.'

'Okay, fine. Will you send your CV to my firm?'

'Of course not.'

'So you're doing the opposite. Because we do know each other, you won't work with me?'

'We couldn't. I couldn't.'

'Why not? We'd make a great team.'

She just stared at him.

'Everybody makes connections, Mya,' he said, his body clenched with frustration. Wanting to shake sense into her some way or another and knowing already that he was doomed to failure. She was so *damn* obstinate. 'That's why they have networking groups. Young lawyers, young farmers, young fashion designers. People have mentors. It's normal.'

'You set up on your own,' she argued. 'You turned your back on any help your father could offer.'

He drew a hard breath. 'You know I had my reasons for that. And I still had help. I might have turned my back on my father's help, but I still had his name.' He sighed. 'And to be honest I know that helped. It helped that I had money.'

'It helped more that you'd won all the prizes in your year at university. Your own merit, Brad. I want to do the same.'

'I still had help,' he ground out through his teeth, hating to have to admit it, but knowing it was the truth.

'Well, I'll get my lecturer to write a reference or something.'

'So it's just me you won't accept help from?'

'I'm not using our personal relationship for professional gain.'

'So we have a relationship.' He pounced.

'No,' she denied instantly, swallowing hard. 'This is a fling. Stress relief.' Mya stared at him in all his naked glory. What was the man thinking? Why was he changing the rules—why was he offering for her to work with him? As if that were possible? What did he think would happen when he decided he'd had enough of sleeping with her? No way could she take this from him.

'Look, I made the mistake of going for one job based on a relationship already. I'm not doing it again. James had suggested I apply for an internship at a particular firm last summer.' She'd been thrilled when they'd both been accepted. 'But then he found out some of my grades and I took him home to see my parents…and it was like he turned into a different person overnight.' It wasn't until later that she learned how average James's grades really were. 'But his grades didn't matter because he was getting a job at the most prestigious accountancy firm in town anyway because his dad was a partner there. Meanwhile I spent my first pay packet in advance buying clothes that might possibly be acceptable to work there, but after he broke up with me, and just before those exams, the company withdrew the offer, saying they had no need for so many interns. So no, I'm not trusting any job offer based on any kind of connection other than merit. I'm not having any kind of relationship interfere with my future.'

'So you have to earn everything yourself? You can't accept a gift? I only have money thanks to *chance* at birth. You can't take anything from me?' he asked, completely frustrated.

'That's right.' She wouldn't take anything from him. Because what he was offering wouldn't ever be enough. 'I need to earn it myself.'

'You have to be so independent, don't you? You have to be the best,' he said bitterly. 'So insanely competitive you're on the brink of a breakdown from the sleepless nights and caffeine overdoses. Well, why don't you go

ahead and study yourself to death? Then work yourself
to death and become a corporate lawyer.'

'Is that such a crime?'

'It is when you have huge talent in another area.'

She rolled her eyes. 'Don't go there.'

'You should make time for your wearable art. It's
important to you. You should be happy as well as successful.'

That wasn't what was going to make her happy.

'It's something you're so good at,' he continued. 'You
should take the opportunity. You should put your work
out there.'

'I can't.'

'You'd rather not compete at all rather than come
second?' He shook his head. 'Is being the best *so* important to you?'

'Success requires sacrifice,' she said firmly. 'What
would you have me do, Brad? Give up all I've worked
so hard for, to try and scrape a living selling some recycled tat? That's not realistic. It's not going to happen.
Yes, I love doing that but I also love the law.'

'So strike a *balance*.'

'I can't yet.'

'You won't ever,' he said, going quiet. 'There'll always be something else you feel you have to achieve.
Your parents wouldn't want you to live like this. Your
parents want you to be happy.'

'Don't talk to me about what my parents want. I know
what they *need*.' And she was the only one who could
help them.

'You don't. You can't face up to what *you* need, let
alone anyone else,' he argued. 'You lie to your parents.

What's worse is you lie to yourself. You're so scared of failing you can't take any kind of real risk.'

'And you can?' So hurt, she poured it all back on him. '*You're* the one who constantly has to be the epitome of charm. You're as bad as your parents. You project this perfect façade—all funny and capable and unable to admit to anything being wrong or *needing* anything. *You're* the one who's scared. You're the one who can't take any kind of support.' She paused and saw he'd gone pale.

He drew in a deep breath but she didn't give him the chance to try to argue—because there was no argument. 'We want different things, Brad,' she said sadly.

He didn't answer. And she turned and left.

CHAPTER TWELVE

As DAWN broke on Christmas Day, Gage Simmons pushed his blistered feet and aching back onward. He knocked on the door. She opened it in less than a minute—the woman he wish, wish, *wished* were his mother. The one he'd walked miles and miles to get to. The one he wanted to stay with. The one who'd shown him more love and compassion and simple fun than any of his blood relatives.

'Will it be okay?' His voice wobbled as she pulled him into a super-tight hug.

'I don't know,' she murmured into his hair. 'But we're going to try.' For a moment they watched the sunrise together. 'We have to call them, you know. It's not fair on your parents not knowing where you are.'

Gage closed his eyes and thought none of it was fair. But he nodded.

'Look at the day, Gage.' She kept her arm around him. 'It's going to be a beauty.'

He didn't want the sun to move. It had taken so long to find her and he didn't want to leave. Not yet. He didn't want another second to pass.

'We'll work it out, Gage. I promise.'

* * *

There was a single-sentence mention in the morning news bulletin—that the boy who'd gone missing had been located and was well. Mya desperately wanted to call Brad and ask if everything truly was okay. But it wasn't okay enough between them for her to be able to do that. And there was something else she had to do— urgently.

Utterly sleep-deprived, Mya walked up the overgrown path towards her parents' house. She'd fantasised for so long about turning up there with a property deed in hand tied by a ribbon. Her gift to them—a Christmas gift. Wouldn't that be wonderful? To be able to move them somewhere so much better. And she would do it; one day she would. It just wouldn't be as soon as she'd hoped it might. And she was so sorry she hadn't been able to be everything they'd wanted her to be.

Brad was right, she had lied—to her parents and to herself about what she really wanted. Because she was so scared of letting them down and of being let down herself.

She sat on the sofa and told them—about losing the scholarship, about working two jobs on top of summer school, about what she wanted to do for them more than anything.

Her parents were appalled, but not for the reason she'd feared.

'We wouldn't expect you to do that for us!' her mother cried. 'We're okay here.'

'You're not.' Mya wiped her own tears away. 'I wanted to do this for you so much. I wanted you to be so proud of me and I've let you down.'

'You've never let us down,' her father argued gruffly. 'We let you down. I gave up. I got injured and gave up and put all our hopes on you. That wasn't fair.'

'No wonder you're so thin and tired,' her mother ex-claimed, rubbing Mya's shoulder. 'All we want for you is to be happy.' She put her arms around her. 'What would make you happy?'

So many things—her parents' comfort now certainly helped. There was that other thing too—but she didn't think he was hers to have.

'Can we get rid of all those photos of me winning prizes?' Mya half laughed and pushed her fringe from her eyes, determined to focus on the future and fixing things with her family.

'They bother you?'

Mya nodded. They took down most of them together, leaving a few, finding a few others with the three of them together. The cousins turned up, and the Christmas eat-a-thon began. As the day faded, Mya picked up the dis-carded lid from a soda bottle and started playing with it, twisting it—tempted for the first time in ages to create something silly-but-stylish just for the sake of it.

Brad was almost two hours late getting to his parents' place for the obligatory big Christmas lunch. The calls between Gage and his stepmother and his parents and their lawyers had gone on and on until they'd wrangled a solution for today at least. Gage would stay with his 'stepmother' until this afternoon, when he'd have time with each parent.

Poor kid. But at least now Brad knew what his cli-ent wanted, where he wanted to be and who he wanted to be with. He'd demonstrated it in an extreme way, but Brad was determined they'd work it out. He'd not stop working on it until they did.

He walked into the ridiculously decorated home and spied Lauren looking sulky at the overloaded table. He

wasn't in the least hungry and stared at the twenty perfect platters of food for the four of them. Hell, it was the
last thing he felt like—some fake happy-family thing.
Surely there was a better use for them today?

'Why don't we take all this food down to the local
homeless shelter?' he asked his mother.

She looked appalled.

'We can't eat it all.' Brad shrugged. 'Honestly, Mother,
what's the point? Let's do something decent with it.'

He looked at his mother, who looked at his father,
who said nothing.

'Great idea,' said Lauren, standing up.

'Okay,' said his mother slowly.

'I'm not that hungry anyway,' his father commented.

'Good,' Brad said. 'Why don't you two go down together to deliver it?' He stared at his parents, who both
stared, rather aghast, back at him.

'That's more your mother's scene,' his father eventually said.

'It's Christmas Day,' Brad answered firmly. 'You
should be together.' He moved forward. It'd be a relief
to escape the picture-perfect scene with the empty un-
dercurrents. 'We'll *all* go.'

Open-mouthed, Lauren watched him gather up a couple of platters.

'Come on,' Brad said insistently. 'Let's do it.'

He was surprised that they actually did. They loaded
all the food into his father's car, and Brad and Lauren
followed in Brad's car.

For two hours they stood and served food to the people who'd come to the shelter. Their platters had gone
into the mix, and his parents were now fully engaged
in dishwashing duty.

'This was so much better than a strained dinner with them,' Lauren muttered under her breath.

'I know,' Brad agreed. 'Genius. But are you hungry now?'

'Yeah, but not for any kind of roast.' She looked slightly guilty. 'How bad is that?'

'Why don't we go get Chinese?' he suggested with a half-laugh. 'The restaurant round the corner from me does really good yum char.'

'Shouldn't we have dinner with Mum and Dad?'

'Nah, let's leave them to it. We've done enough family bonding for the day.'

'I actually think they're happy the way they are,' Lauren said as she pulled a chicken dish towards her, half an hour later.

'You think?' Brad asked.

'Yes.' Lauren chewed thoughtfully. 'Surely if they weren't, they'd have done something about it by now?'

'I think they're just used to it.' He sat back and toyed with the food on his plate. 'They're apathetic and simply don't care enough to do anything to change things.'

'It's a waste,' Lauren said.

'It is,' Brad agreed. 'Maybe they'll learn something at the shelter.' He grinned. 'It might be a Christmas miracle.'

Lauren suddenly looked serious. 'Have you seen Mya recently?'

Brad's moment of lightness fled. He shook his head and stuffed rice into his mouth to keep from having to answer.

'She's not really a sister to you, is she?' Lauren said slyly.

The observation caught him by surprise—he half laughed, half choked and shook his head again.

'Is it going to work out?'

He shook his head again—slower that time.

'Have you stuffed things up so badly I'm going to lose my best friend?'

He shook his head more vehemently. 'Be there for her.'

Lauren studied him closely. 'Why can't you be?'

'She doesn't want me to.'

'Really?' Lauren frowned. 'Mya had a thing for you for years. Even when you never saw her.'

Yeah, but the trouble was Mya had got to know him properly now. And though he'd offered her all he could, she'd turned him down. It hurt.

'Don't tell me you're too apathetic to do anything about it, Brad,' Lauren said softly. 'Don't make the same mistake as Mum and Dad.'

Lauren's words haunted him over the next week. The memory of Mya positively tortured him. Night after night he replayed their last conversation in his head and he dreamed of the too few nights they'd been together.

She'd been furious with him for not opening up. She claimed he maintained as much of a false façade as his parents did. He'd not realised he did that. But she was right. He had opened up to her, though—a couple of times he had, and she'd been there for him in a way that had made his heart melt. So why was it that when he'd wanted to support her, she'd pushed him away? Until now he'd been too hurt to try to figure it out, but now he had to *know*.

Lauren was right too: he couldn't be apathetic. He needed courage—Gage's kind of courage. To run to-wards what you needed most—the one person you needed most. The one whose love and laughter meant everything.

He went to the bar and pushed forward to the front of the bar section she was serving. Her eyes widened when she saw him and she asked his order ahead of the people he was standing beside. He refused to get a kick out of that—it was probably because she wanted to serve him so he'd leave asap.

He inhaled the sight of her like a man gulping fresh air after a long, deep dive in the abyss. And as she mixed his deliberately complicated cocktail, he tried for conversation. 'I like your hairclip.' So lame. But true.

She put her hand to her head where her homemade clip resided and smiled self-consciously. 'You do?'

'Absolutely.'

She nodded, looking down to stir some awful collection of liqueurs before speaking quickly. 'I don't have the time right now for entire outfits,' she said. 'But hair accessories I can do. Pretty clips, small statements. Just a little fun and it keeps my fringe out of my eyes.'

'That's great.'

'It's enough,' she said. 'But you were right. I needed it.'

'Good for you.' He wished she needed him too.

For a moment their eyes met, and Brad was too tired to hide anything any more. He was too tired to try to make chit-chat and break the bulletproof wall of ice between them. He just wanted to hold her close—to have her in his arms and by his side and have it all. For ever.

But she moved to serve another person, and it was like having scabs from third-degree body burns ripped off. Coming here was the dumbest thing he'd done. For a guy who was supposed to be smart, he'd picked the world's worst time to try to talk to her. New Year's Eve was the busiest night of the year. Jonny was back—there were five bartenders there and all of them run off their feet. And she couldn't even look him in the eye.

He didn't even touch the cocktail she'd made for him. He just turned round and walked away.

Mya glanced up from making the next customer's cocktail—desperate to make sure he was still there. But he wasn't. She stretched up on tiptoe and just got a glimpse of his back heading towards the exit.

Oh, no. No, no and no. He wasn't turning up for the first time in a week looking all rough-edged and dangerous and for one heart-stopping moment *vulnerable*—and then leaving again. She had things to say to him. Things she'd been rehearsing in her head for days and days and no matter the outcome she was still determined to say.

She pushed her way out from behind the bar and barged through the throngs. 'Brad!' She didn't care who heard her.

But if he did hear her, he didn't stop. She ran out onto the footpath and charged after him. 'Brad!'

This time he stopped.

She looked at him, oblivious to the revellers on the street and the heat in the summer night. And now all those words that she'd been mentally practising just flew out of her head—when he looked at her like *that*?

'Oh, hell, don't cry,' he groaned.

'I'm not *crying*!' she denied. And then sniffed. So what was the point in denial? 'Okay, I'm…crying.'

'Mya.' He sounded strangled. 'Please go back.'

'Mya! Drew is having a fit.' Kirk came puffing up beside them. 'We need you back at the bar.'

'I don't give a damn about the bar,' Mya snapped.

Kirk scuttled away like a dirt bug escaping daylight.

'Mya, you should go back. You don't want to lose your job.'

'I don't, but—'

'And you need to focus on your upcoming exam.'

'I don't give a damn about that exam either!' she shouted.

Brad stared at her, waiting.

'Okay, I do, but...' She broke off to draw a ragged breath. 'I don't care about the bar. But I do. I don't care about the exam. But I do. I don't care about anything that much but *you*,' she admitted softly. 'And I don't want you to walk away from me.' Another fat tear spilt down her cheek.

He sighed and took a step towards her. 'Mya, I've always believed that no one can ever truly put another person first. That ultimately we're all selfish and do what's best for ourselves. But I was wrong about that.' He stopped and breathed out. 'Because I will do whatever *you* need me to do in order for you to be happy. If that means walking out of your life, then that's what I'll do. It's the last thing I want to do. But I want what's best for you.'

She shook her head angrily. 'You might be brilliant but you're not a mind-reader. What makes you think walking out of my life would be best for me?'

'It's what you asked me to do,' he pointed out.

'Well, I was an idiot.'

He stared at her. 'What do you want me to do?'

'I don't know that you can offer me what I really want from you.'

'I know you want to hold onto your independence. I respect that. If you want the big corporate law job, then fantastic. I'll suck up my stupid fears and be right there behind you. If you decide you'd rather make your creations and try selling them, I can afford to support you. You can ask me for anything,' he said.

She shook her head. She didn't want any *thing*. 'I can't

be dependent on you. I just can't.' She couldn't give herself so completely to a guy who didn't feel the same for her as she did for him.

'You want me to give it all away?' he suddenly exploded. 'Okay, I'll give all my money away. I'll give a guy the shirt on my back and stand here naked and with nothing. I just want to support you,' he roared at her. 'And you won't take it from me!'

'It's not your money I want!' she shouted back. 'It's everything else. You have *everything* to give me. Love and *emotional* support, rather than financial. Strength. Humour. Play. Everything that's so wonderful about you. I love you and all I want is for you to love me back.'

He stared at her. Stunned. 'Why didn't you tell me?' He gestured wide. 'You never showed me. You never wanted anyone to know about us. You were embarrassed to want me.'

'I was never embarrassed about wanting you. What was I supposed to do? You're the ultimate playboy. Never with any woman more than a week. I had to protect myself somehow. I had to think of it as just a fantasy. If no one else knew then it wasn't really real.'

He gazed at her, now motionless. 'What do you think I feel for you?'

'Lust.'

'Absolutely. Lust is right up there. Right now so is annoyance.' He walked towards her. 'Also admiration. Frustration. But above all, love.'

She bent her head.

He put his fingers under her chin and lifted her face back up to his. 'Mya, why do you think I want to give you everything I have?' He gazed into her eyes. 'I love you more than I've ever loved anyone. Even myself,' he joked just that little bit.

'Brad,' she choked out.

'Has it not occurred to you that I'm the best person to help you with your studies?'

She laughed, but it was in despair. 'I failed so badly at concentrating that night you found those cases for me. I had the wickedest thoughts going on that night. I can't concentrate with you around.'

'We weren't sleeping together then. We were both frustrated. Wouldn't it be different knowing you can have your way with me when your study goal is met? Won't it be different now you know I love you and that you love me? And that we can be together as much as we want?'

Yeah, she still couldn't quite believe that.

He muttered something unintelligible and then just swept her close, his lips crashing onto hers as if there were no other way to convince her. And she *ached* to be convinced, desperate to feel the security that should only be a breath away. She burrowed closer, opening for him, wanting to give him everything and get it all in return.

'Do I really have to give away my money?' he asked gently. 'If I was a starving student, you'd share everything with me, right?'

'Of course. But you're not a starving student. It feels so unbalanced.' She sighed.

'Only in that one aspect and that's only temporary. In another couple of years you'll be qualified and raking it in, and I'll take early retirement and you can keep me in the manner to which I am accustomed.'

She couldn't help it, laughter bubbled out of her. 'And in what manner is that?'

'Restaurant meals every night,' he said promptly.

'I can do salads from the café down the street.'

'Sex every night of the week.' He waggled his brows.

'And every morning.'

'That too.' He kissed her again. 'You were right, by the way. I do my job because it makes me feel better about myself as a person. I tell myself I'm okay because I help kids. I make a difference, right? So I can't be all bad.' He sighed. 'But I'm not all that great. I chose not to get too close to anyone and never let anyone see behind the façade. That was because, like you, I don't like failure. Growing up in that house with my parents, I saw the falseness of their relationship. Swore I'd never have such a marriage. And that I'd never fail kids like that. That I'd never have them.'

'You don't want to commit. I know that.' She'd never try to fence him in. She'd have him for as long as he was hers to have. No way she could walk away from him now.

He laughed. 'I don't have the choice, darling,' he teased. 'I'm not interested in anyone else. I don't want to be. I want this to work with you. You inspire me to be more.'

'I'm not some perfect creature.' She shook her head.

'No one is. But you kill yourself *trying* to be perfect and you don't have to. You don't have to get the top grade. You don't have to be the best bartender in town. You don't have to excel at everything. You can fail at everything and I'll love you anyway. Do you understand that? I'll love you no matter what.'

Her eyes filled as she felt the intensity of his words, the full emotion behind them. And finally she did understand that.

'You're wonderful and human, and you make mistakes like I do, but you pick yourself up and you fight on,' he said. 'You face your failures and you get it together.'

'I don't fight on,' she cried. 'I gave up on you, on us, before we'd hardly started. I was so scared. I didn't want to change my priorities only to find out what we had wasn't anything more than a bit of fun.'

'It's a whole lot of fun.' He smiled. 'And you don't have to change your priorities. We can have so much more fun together if you'll take a chance on me.'

He stood before her, his expression open, no protective façade in place, just pure honesty and an offer she could never, ever refuse.

Now she saw behind his mask to the genuine, loving man he was. While he could act all cocky, come up with the most outrageous statements as if he fully believed he was God's gift to the female of the species, beneath that bravado was a guy as insecure as any other normal person. Despite that silver spoon, that money, all that success...there was still someone who doubted that another person could love him for just being him. But that was the part of him she loved the most.

'I need nothing but you,' she answered simply.

And he needed someone who didn't give a damn about anything he had, or his image. A person who cared only about him. The *essence* of him. The good-humoured, gorgeous, arrogant guy.

Happily that someone was her.

She wrapped her arms around him and lifted her face for another kiss. Offering her heart. It was a long time before he drew back and sighed. She felt the elation in every inch of him, but also the tension.

'You need to go back and finish your shift,' he groaned. 'New Year's Eve is the biggest night of the year.'

'It is.' She nodded. 'Will you wait for me?'

'Always.'

* * *

'We'll go on a two-hour rotation,' he said firmly the next morning after they'd had breakfast. 'Two hours' solid study, two hours' solid sex.'

'That's finding balance?' she asked incredulously.

'I think so.' He nodded in all seriousness. 'Round the clock.'

She giggled. 'Yeah, that's really achieving balance.'

'No point in trying to fight our natures, now, is there? Might as well roll with it.' He winked. 'Right now I'm on case names and caffeine duty. And then massage services.'

'Massage services?'

'Inside and out.' He lifted his brows lasciviously.

Deep inside her, muscles shifted, ready.

He laughed, reading her thoughts. 'Later, babe. You've got facts to memorise.'

How was she supposed to concentrate when she knew what was coming? She was insanely excited already. 'I think you should feel me up first.'

'No. Work now, reward later.' He put himself on the far side of the desk and refused to look at her.

She sighed and sat up in her seat, pulling her pages of notes closer. 'Better be a good reward,' she grumbled beneath her breath.

'Mya, darling,' he drawled from his desk. 'You know it's going to be out of this world.'

And it was.

TWO YEARS LATER

You know you want this.

Mya smothered a giggle at the photo she'd just been sent on her phone. Brad, buck naked and bold with a party hat magically positioned in a very strategic place.

She quickly closed the message and acted as if she were paying complete attention to the orientation speech for new recruits at the multinational law firm she'd signed with. But her phone vibrated again.

Tonight. Our place. Come as soon as you can.

As soon as the spiels and slideshows were over— as interesting as they were—she escaped. She walked through the city, the warm summer air delightful on her back. Her first week had gone well, long hours, of course, and that competitive component. She relished it. She loved coming home too. Especially to Brad in playboy mode.

'Brad?' She closed the front door and called down the cool empty hallway.

'In the garden,' came his distant shout.

She walked through the house, her footsteps ringing loud. The rest of the house unnaturally silent—until she stepped out onto the back deck.

'SURPRISE!'

There were five hundred people in the backyard.

Mya put out a hand and it was immediately gripped. Lauren laughed as she squeezed her hand to bring her back from the light-headed faint feeling.

'Oh, wow!' Mya couldn't move. Certainly couldn't think of anything to say.

'Breathe, woman, you need some colour back.'

It was already back. Mya felt the blush burning over every bit of her body. OMG, there was a huge surprise party. Here. For her.

Dazed, she glanced around.

Her family were there— her mother beaming, her father standing by the barbecue helping Stella turn the steaks. They were in a new home only about ten minutes away. Brad had insisted he help them as soon as they'd got together that New Year's Eve two years ago. It had made such a difference to her parents.

Jonny and Drew were there from the bar. Some of her cousins were there, also beaming. Many of Lauren's men. Brad's buddies. Some of her law school mates, a whole mishmash of people from her life. And they were all smiling, all celebrating, and they'd managed to keep this whole thing secret from her?

But there was only the one person she really wanted to see this second. And that was the tall hunk coming towards her through the crowd with a glass of champagne.

'You did all this?' she asked as he stepped unnecessarily close to hand the drink to her.

'You know what a good party planner I am.' He bent to whisper in her ear and steal a kiss at the same time. 'But don't be disappointed—we'll have our own private party a little later.'

She giggled. As if she could ever be disappointed! And she knew that they'd have their own time tonight. Everyone else would leave, but Brad would always be there for her.

She sipped her champagne and stepped forward with a smile, Brad alongside her.

She'd dropped the café work and many of the shifts at the bar, working only during the weekends so she saved the weeknights for the two of them. The nights she did work, Brad came down to the bar and kept her company. His gang of mates had been more than happy for it to become their regular. And she'd gone back full-time at university to finish her degree—with a promise to pay Brad back sometime for all the free rent. He didn't bother arguing or answering that one, just rolled his eyes.

She'd had four job offers before her final exams. She

didn't win the gold medal for top law graduate of the year, but she did take out the prize for top family law student. She'd thrown that in with all the contract and company law courses so she could understand what Brad was going on about in the evenings. He'd been right, he was a brilliant coach—firm, but he had a super-fun reward system going.

Yeah, she had the best prize already. She didn't think she could be happier.

She loved the party. There was no catwalk this time, no 'wall of fame' either. It was all friends and family and laughter.

His parents were there too. Mya chatted with them. They all worked the façade to a degree but Brad had become a lot more open about talking with them—quite blunt in some of his views. Mya backed him up. They were his parents, and if he could make that effort, so could she.

'I'm so proud of you.' She leaned back against him several hours later as they stood at the door and watched the last guests leave.

His laugh rumbled in his chest. 'That's my line.'

'I mean it.' She turned to face him, pressing her breasts against his strength. 'You're the most generous man I know.'

He laughed even harder. 'You have rose-tinted glasses.'

Her smile blossomed too. 'You grow the roses for me.'

He brushed his lips against hers and took a step backwards into the hall to close the door.

'I have a graduation present for you.' His breathing quickened.

'I haven't graduated yet.'

'Mere technicality.' He gifted her a teasingly light

kiss. 'I was going to give it to you when they were all here because I figured you couldn't refuse it in front of everyone. But then I thought that wasn't fair.' He put his hand in his jeans pocket and pulled out a box.

Her heart stopped. 'Brad—'

'Two years we've been together,' he interrupted mock crossly. 'Don't you think it's time you made an honest man of me?' He opened the box.

She went hot and cold and hot again in a nanosecond.

His hands gripped her shoulders as if he knew she'd gone light-headed. 'You can't take advantage of me so long. Taking what you want, when you want it. Demanding all those pictures of me and treating me like some kind of sex object.'

'And you're not?'

He shook his head, his eyes dancing. 'No, I need solid commitment from you. I want a public declaration. I want this rock flashing on your finger to show those pups at that law firm that you're taken. And I want a family.'

'Oh, you do?' Her sass answer was totally undermined by her breathless gasp.

'Yes.'

She took a moment to inhale a few times. 'Got anything else to add to this list of demands?'

'Speed,' he snapped. 'I want the big wedding as soon as possible. And one hell of a honeymoon. In fact—' he drew breath '—I've already started planning it.'

'The family?' Her voice rose. She was still getting to grips with that idea. She'd thought he never wanted kids.

'No, that part can wait 'til after you're crowned biggest fee earner at the firm and you've taken me on a round-the-world trip.' His reply was tinged with laughter.

She didn't care about being the biggest fee earner. She

cared about her parents and him and everybody staying well and happy. So happy. 'So it's the honeymoon
you're planning?'

'No, the wedding. I've decided on the flowers already.' He winked.

She giggled. 'Well, we know party planning is your
niche. You should jack in the law practice and just do
parties.'

'Now, that wouldn't be fair on my clients.'

'No.' She sobered and placed her palm on the side
of his face in the gentlest caress. 'They need you.' He'd
worked so hard mediating with Gage's parents and the
stepmother—finally hammering out a solution that had
made that sombre-eyed boy so happy. She leaned closer.
'I need you too. More than I can ever tell you.'

'Same here.' He wrapped his arms around her and
pulled her right into his heat. 'So that's a yes to my proposal, then?'

She rested her head on his chest. Her big, strong playboy loved her no matter what, supported her no matter
what, and together they could build it all. 'Yes.'

'It's going to be one hell of a party, Mya,' he whispered.

Yes. One that would last the rest of their lives.

* * * * *

RESTLESS

BY
TORI CARRINGTON

Multi-award-winning, bestselling husband-and-wife duo Lori and Tony Karayianni are the power behind the pen name **Tori Carrington**. Their more than thirty-five titles include numerous Blaze series, as well as the ongoing Sofie Metropolis comedic mystery series with another publisher. Visit www.toricarrington.net, www.sofiemetro.com, www.myspace.com/toricarrington and www.millsandboon.com for more information on the couple and their titles.

We dedicate this book to everyone who wrote demanding Gauge's story. In this increasingly politically correct world it's nice to know that so many agree that a man as flawed as Patrick Gauge warrants a second look and a happy ending all his own. However unconventional. . .

And to our editor Brenda Chin, for trusting us to push that envelope ever further.

1

THE WEEK-OLD TEXT MESSAGE read: Gone back 2 Jen. Been nice. Sorry.

Lizzie Gilbred sat on her family-room sofa, clicking the cell phone to reread the message from her boyfriend—scratch that, her ex-boyfriend—Jerry, her thumb hovering over the delete button. It had been seven days. Surely the words were burned forever into her brain by now. She saved the message instead, then sighed and tossed the cell to the leather cushion next to her, where she knew she'd just pick it up again in two minutes.

She took a hefty sip from her wineglass, leaned her elbow against the sofa back and stared out the window at the snow swirling in the yellow security light over her driveway. The weatherman was calling for three inches of the white stuff to fall again tonight, casting a festive glow on the two-week countdown to Christmas.

Blizzard Bill the weatherman's words, not hers. As far as Lizzie was concerned, they could cancel Christmas this year and she wouldn't even notice.

She took another sip of her wine, feeling a blink

away from jumping out of her skin. She'd returned late
from the law offices of Jovavich, Williams, and Brent-
wood, Attorneys-at-Law, as was usual for a Wednesday,
and fought to stick to routine even though she'd felt
anything but normal since receiving Jerry's cold text
message goodbye. She'd kicked off her shoes at the
door, removed her suit jacket, cranked up the heat,
poured herself a glass of her favorite Shiraz, started a
fire in the family-room grate, then sat on the rich leather
sofa she and Jerry had picked out together. Usually at
this point she went through her mail or reviewed the
briefs or depositions she'd brought home from the office. Tonight it was a brief she'd had one of the junior
attorneys write up for her. But damn if she could make
it through a single sentence, much less comprehend the
entire ten-page document.

She thought about making herself dinner. She hadn't
had anything since the bagel with jelly she'd half eaten
at the office meeting this morning. But she couldn't
seem to drum up the energy to reach for the television
remote, much less that required to actually rise from the
sofa and go into the kitchen to either heat a frozen dinner or open a can of soup.

So she sat staring out at the snow instead, wondering what her ex-boyfriend, Jerry, and his once-estranged
wife, Jenny, were doing right then.

She groaned and rubbed her forehead.

She hadn't thought of Jenny as Jerry's wife in a long
time. More specifically, for the past six months—ever
since Jerry had left Jenny and appealed for a legal sep-

aration. One that had ended with his surprise text message and virtual disappearance from her life a week ago when she'd come home from work after retrieving the missive to find he'd taken everything he'd had at her house, including the waffle maker he'd bought her for her birthday last month.

What did he want with a freakin' waffle maker? Had he taken it to Jenny and said the equivalent of, *Something for you, honey, to show how serious I am about sharing Sunday-morning waffles for the rest of our lives?* Or, *See, I even took back every gift I ever bought her.*

Well, that wasn't entirely true. Because to take back every gift, he'd have had to go back six years, when he and Lizzie were the established couple on the verge of an engagement and Jenny had been the other woman.

God, she couldn't believe she'd let him do this to her again. Six years ago, it hadn't been a text message; rather, he'd left a quickly scribbled note on her car windshield, secured by the wiper: "It's over. Sorry." With it had been the announcement of Jenny and his engagement from that day's newspaper.

The cell phone chirped. Lizzie scrambled to pick it up, punching a button and answering.

"Hello?"

"Lizzie?"

She sank against the cushions and pulled the chenille throw up to her neck. Not Jerry.

"Hi, Mom. How are you?"

"Okay, considering."

Lizzie made a face. Ever since her parents had announced their impending divorce, the War of the Roses Revisited had begun at the Gilbred house. Both of them, it seemed, were all for the separation. But neither was willing to give up the house. So her father had taken up residence in a downstairs guest room, and her mother went about life as if he wasn't there, up to and including a candlelit dinner with some guy she'd picked up at the country club last month.

Her father had had a fit and nearly clunked the guy in the head with one of his golf clubs, which her mother had tossed into the driveway after he'd taken advantage of an unseasonably warm day and gone out for a few rounds, missing an appointment with their divorce attorneys.

The clubs had gone completely missing the following day and Lizzie had gotten a call from her father asking her to help him find them since he'd had the set specially made. They'd finally hit pay dirt at a Toledo pawnshop, where they found them with an abominably low price tag…until the new owner figured out that they must be worth more and jacked up the price while her father fumed.

But maybe her mother was beginning to come to her senses. Usually she began conversations with whatever outlandish thing her father had done that day. That she was actually quiet and appeared pensive was a positive sign. Wasn't it?

"How about you? How are you doing?" her mother asked.

"I'm just sitting in front of the fire with a glass of wine."

"That's nice, dear. And Jerry? Is he there with you?"

She had yet to tell her mother that she and Jerry were no longer a couple. In all honesty, she had never told her parents that he was still married, even though he was legally separated at the time.

What a tangled web we weave, she thought. "Yes. Yes, he is," she lied.

"Hmm? Oh. Yes. Well, tell him hello for me."

"I will."

Lizzie squinted through the window, making out a shadowy, familiar figure in the falling snow.

Gauge.

She instantly relaxed against the cushions. Her hot tenant of the past four months was walking up her driveway, toward the garage and the apartment above it that he was renting. She craned her neck to see around a large evergreen in order to follow his movements until he disappeared.

The voice at the other end of the line sighed.

"Are you okay?" she asked her mother. "You sound…distracted."

Could it be that Bonnie Gilbred was rethinking her situation? That the reconciliation Lizzie, her sister, Annie, and brother, Jesse, hoped for was just around the corner? Just in time to make Christmas feel somewhat like Christmas again?

"Me? Yes, yes. I'm fine. Why wouldn't I be?"

Lizzie nearly dropped the phone when she heard a male roar on her mother's end. She absently rubbed her forehead and closed her eyes, wanting to hang up yet straining to hear her father's words.

"What in the hell did you put in this, Bonnie? Are you trying to kill me, for God's sake? You are, aren't you? Is it arsenic?"

Her mother's voice sounded much too joyful. "No, it's not arsenic, you old fool. I fixed the meat loaf the same way I always fix it. Your taste buds must not be what they once were."

"Don't hand me that *b.s.!*" There was a clatter of plates and then her father cussed a blue streak.

She heard a door slam.

"Mom?" Lizzie said.

"Hmm?"

Apparently Bonnie still had the phone to her ear, but wasn't much paying attention to the fact that she was having a conversation with her daughter.

"What did you put in the meat loaf?" Lizzie asked.

"Salt. Lots of it."

Lizzie smiled in spite of the exasperation she felt. "You know Dad's watching his sodium intake."

"I know. Why do you think I did it?"

Lizzie rested her head back against the pillow. "So is there a reason you called? I mean, other than wanting someone to witness your evildoing for the night?"

"I'm not doing evil. I cooked him meat loaf."

"Sure, Mom. Is there anything else?"

She could imagine Bonnie thinking for a moment. "Nope. I figure that about covers everything."

"Good. Oh, and next time you want a buffer between

you and Dad, call Annie," she said, referring to her younger sister.

"Will do, dear."

"Good night, Mother."

"Good night, Lizzie."

She punched the button to disconnect the call and checked for any missed messages. None. So she read Jerry's text message before tossing the phone to the sofa again.

God, but she really was a sorry sack, wasn't she?

A sound drew her attention back to the driveway. Gauge had reappeared. He was wearing the same hooded sweatshirt and denim jacket he'd had on minutes earlier. She thought maybe he was leaving again. Only he wasn't carrying his guitar case; he was shoveling her walk.

She found the action incredibly hot.

All thoughts of her mother, Jerry and her missing waffle maker drifted from her mind. Replaced by ones related to the sexy drifter who had taken up residence in her garage apartment in August.

His name wasn't really Gauge. Well, his last name was, but his first name was Patrick. Lizzie folded one arm under her chin and took another sip of wine, the alcohol beginning to work its magic by warming her a bit even as she watched Gauge out in the cold.

She didn't know much about him. Her brother Jesse's ex-girlfriend, Heidi, had recommended him; Gauge was part owner of the BMC bookstore café downtown where Heidi used to work. He was a musician. A guitar player, if the case he carried and the strumming she'd heard coming from his place when it was warmer were any indication.

Their paths rarely crossed. She found his rent—always cash—stuffed into an envelope in her front-door mail slot on the first of the month, and she made sure that any mail that was delivered for him was slid under his door.

That was basically it.

Well, that and the fact that he was exceedingly hot and she liked watching him come and go, with no particular preference for either, because both front and back views were worthy of a long glance and an even longer sigh.

She put her glass back down on the coffee table. Aside from a very brief crush on the drummer that had played at her senior prom, she'd never gone much for the artistic type. Career-oriented, driven guys were more her thing.

Like Jerry.

She groaned.

Of course, that was probably because she was a bit on the ambitious side herself. A bit? She needed to stop lying to herself. In three short years since graduation, she'd made it to junior partner at the law firm with a full partnership whispered to be in the offing in the not-too-distant future.

Of course, Jerry's disappearing act wouldn't help. She'd been counting on taking him to the office party next week to help cement her shot at the partnership slot. With, of course, no mention of his marital status.

Her friend Tabitha had suggested that perhaps she should play at being a lesbian. Lizzie had nearly spewed her iced tea at her over lunch at Georgio's, her favorite restaurant in downtown Toledo.

"What did you say?"

Tabby had shrugged. "Surely you know that being an unmarried woman of childbearing age hurts your chances of success in the workplace."

"And acting like a lesbian helps how?"

"For one thing, there's nothing guys like more than imagining a great-looking chick—such as yourself—getting it on with another woman."

Lizzie had snorted.

"For another, they'd be so preoccupied with the image that they'd forget about your biological clock and the fact that you may get pregnant at any minute."

"But there are no kids in my immediate future. The partners know that."

Tabby had given her an eye roll. "Sure. You think they believe you? They know—or think they do—how fickle a woman is. One minute she'll be spouting off about not wanting children, the next she'll be pregnant with quads."

"Don't be ridiculous," Lizzie told her friend.

But Tabitha's advice had made a twisted kind of sense. While she thought she was being treated as an equal at the office, there were small incidents that sometimes left her wondering. Like the men-only golf outings. Or the times she walked into a room full of male colleagues and everyone would go silent.

Then there was Jerry....

He'd been her first love. She had fully expected to

spend the rest of her life with him when they'd met in college and immediately hit it off. It had been that sense of unfinished business, and his convincing argument that she was his first love, as well, that had compelled her to let him back into her life.

What a mistake that had been.

Lizzie forced herself off the couch and downed the remaining contents of her wineglass. That was it. She wasn't going to think about…him, or work or anything anymore for fear that her head might explode.

She craned her neck, watching as Gauge finished the shoveling and headed up the stairs to his place.

No…she shouldn't. To even consider going over there would be nothing but stupid.

Who was she kidding? At that moment it might very well be the smartest decision she'd made in a very long time.

2

GAUGE BRUSHED the snow from his old cowboy boots and shrugged out of his jacket and sweatshirt, hanging them on the back of a kitchen chair in his small studio apartment. He'd hoped the physical activity of shovelling would help chase away the demons that had been haunting him lately. And it had. But for how long?

He grabbed the bottle of Jack Daniel's on the table and unscrewed the top, taking a long pull from the whiskey, standing still as it warmed his chest and then swirled outward to his cold extremities.

The apartment was small but nice. He guessed it had probably been renovated in the past year or so. All the appliances and fixtures were new, the furniture unworn and scratch free. Unlike most of the places he was used to staying in when he was out on the road playing with whatever band he'd hooked up with. Or all the motels rooms, shabby apartments and run-down houses he'd shared with his traveling musician father when he was growing up.

Not that he paid much attention to his surroundings. As far as he was concerned, they were just details. And he probably wouldn't be staying here except for Nina's involvement. Nina was one of his partners in BMC, a bookstore/music center/café, and she matched him up with Lizzie Gilbred, the sister of Heidi's ex, when Lizzie had listed the studio for rent.

He rubbed his chin and screwed the top back on the whiskey, putting the bottle on the table. It wasn't that he didn't like the place. He supposed it was all right. There was just something odd about living in the good part of town. About parking his beat-up Chevy Camaro at the curb where few cars sat, but those that did were BMWs, Mercedes and Rovers. You'd think that he'd be used to the fluttering of curtains as neighbors watched him come and go, but it bothered him on a fundamental level he was loath to ignore. What did they think—that he was going to break in and rape their women? Kill their children?

He didn't know the names of any of them. And he'd lived there for nearly four months. Surely there was something abnormal about that?

Since the places he was used to staying in were shabby, the neighborhoods where they were located tended to be on the grungy side. Usually downtown, crowded with other people that looked like him, where no curtains fluttered because there were usually no curtains. And while he might not stay long in any one place, he always left knowing the names of most of the people around him, and could count more than a few of them as friends.

Hell, here he'd maybe talked to his landlady a handful of times. And she only lived thirty feet away in the Tudor-style monstrosity she called a house. From what he could tell, she used all of three rooms: the kitchen, the back room with the fireplace and what he guessed was her bedroom on the second floor.

He could only imagine what her monthly heating bill looked like.

That's probably why she or any of the other neighbors weren't home much. They were too busy working to pay the bills that went along with their lifestyle——like astronomical heating bills.

Speaking of heat…

After pushing the arrow and nudging the digital numbers up to sixty-nine degrees on the thermostat, he picked up his acoustic guitar where he'd left it sitting on the edge of the queen-size bed and walked around with it until the baseboard heaters warmed the place. He stopped near the window overlooking the driveway. Already the falling snow was beginning to cover his work. He hit a dissonant chord and automatically adjusted the tension of the wayward string, tuning and testing three times before he was satisfied.

His gaze was drawn to the back of the Tudor where he could see Lizzie Gilbred spilled across the leather sofa in front of the fireplace. He ran his fingers over the guitar strings, playing the distinctive licks of Muddy Waters's "Going Down Slow," the sound making the room feel not so empty. There was a time when he might have brought one of the young women who liked his playing home to warm his bed, but not now. Not since he'd come back to Fantasy, determined to forge a different life for himself.

Not since he'd fallen for a woman he'd had no right falling for. A woman he could never have. A woman who was now married to his best friend.

Gauge closed his eyes and dropped his chin to his chest, his fingers moving as if on their own accord.

There had been times lately when he'd thought maybe returning to Michigan hadn't been such a great idea. But in his lifetime, the three-year span he'd spent here was the longest he'd spent anywhere. And when he'd left, he'd been even more aware of the hollow loneliness of wandering the country in search of his next gig than he'd ever been before. Partly because he'd gotten a taste of what love, real love, might be like. Mostly because his best friends and business partners, Nina Leonard and Kevin Weber, had been the family he'd never had.

Until he went and mucked things up.

He forced all thought from his mind, giving himself over to the music, feeling the blues wash over him, through him.

A knock at the door.

Gauge opened his eyes, convinced he was hearing things, because it was a sound he hadn't heard since moving in.

Another knock.

He leaned the guitar against the bed.

He wasn't sure what he expected when he opened the door. But it sure wasn't what he found.

Lizzie Gilbred.

Hadn't he just seen her in her house? What was she doing out in this weather? What was she doing knocking at his door?

She bounced a couple of times, as if cold, looking smaller somehow in the oversize camel-hair coat she wore.

Gauge had always had a deep appreciation of women. He supposed it came from not having had a constant female presence in his life. But the opposite sex never failed to fascinate him. Even if that weren't the case, Lizzie Gilbred would have made a lasting impression on him. It was more than her golden-blond hair and wide, baby-doll-blue eyes. There was an inherent sexiness to her, and he couldn't help wondering why she covered it up in her strict business suits and pulled-back hairstyles.

He couldn't help thinking that if she hadn't been an attorney, she'd have made a great stripper.

"Can I come in?" she asked, intruding on his thoughts.

Probably a bad idea in a long line of bad ideas. Just as he appreciated women, he knew them better than they sometimes knew themselves. And he knew that for whatever reason, Lizzie had decided to distract herself with him.

Then again, his girl-dar had been off a little lately. She could be there to evict him.

Gauge shrugged and moved away from the door. "Seeing as you own the place, I don't know that I can stop you."

She stepped inside, quickly closing the door after her. She looked around the apartment and then at him. "Am I interrupting something?"

Gauge tucked his thumbs into the front pockets of his jeans. Definitely there to distract herself.

Where once the thought might have mildly amused him, now he was vaguely disappointed. But never let it be said that he ever turned a great-looking woman away from his bed. And Lizzie was absolutely stunning. She'd let her coat hang open and he appreciated the snug black cashmere sweater and clingy black pants she wore.

"Am I late with the rent?" he asked.

She smiled. "No. I just thought I'd come up to thank you for shoveling the snow."

"Mmm."

"May I?" she asked, indicating her coat.

"Be my guest."

She shrugged out of the heavy wool coat and draped it over the back of the same chair that held his jacket. She eyed the bottle on the table.

Gauge watched her closely. He knew she was an attorney and that she worked hard. She drove a convertible Audi that was wasted during Michigan's harsh winters. He guessed that her boyfriend was similarly ambitious with his late-model Porsche and fancy suits.

He'd thought it odd that he hadn't seen the jerk's car for the past week. He'd figured maybe the guy had gone on a business trip. Apparently he'd been wrong.

"You want something to drink?" he asked.

"Sounds good."

"Anything in particular?"

"Whatever you're having is fine."

He wasn't entirely sure that was a good idea, but hell, it had been a while. And though he was able to resist tempting any women home, having one offer herself up on his doorstep…well, he was but a man, after all. And it was obvious that's what Lizzie was counting on.

"Boyfriend away?" he asked as he handed her a glass holding a finger of Jack.

Her eyes grew wide and it appeared to take some effort for her to swallow as she drank. "Something like that." She swiped the back of her hand against her mouth. Her lips, he noticed, seemed bare of lipstick. In fact, she didn't appear to be wearing any makeup at all, which was curious. Whenever he'd seen her, she'd always been well put together.

Then again, one didn't require proper attire when slumming it.

And he guessed that's exactly what one sexy Ms. Lizzie Gilbred, trial attorney, was doing. Slumming it. She'd come knocking on his door in need of a quick ego fix. Probably she'd been dumped by that asshole of a boyfriend and needed reminding that she was still desirable.

Then in the morning she'd regret ever crossing that driveway.

But none of that was his concern. The only question was whether he wanted to take what she was offering.

He watched her cross to sit on the edge of his bed

and he raised both of his eyebrows. Most women weren't quite that obvious with their intentions.

"What?" she asked.

He shook his head. "Nothing. Absolutely nothing at all."

LIZZIE LEANED BACK on the bed, on the mattress she had chosen herself for its durability, if not complete comfort, six months ago when she'd moved into the house and had the apartment furnished so she might rent it out. She was acutely aware of the man picking up his guitar and sitting down on the ottoman in front of the chair across the room. Despite the inclement weather, he wore a T-shirt, a dark brown one bearing the logo of a rock band, the hem not quite tucked into jeans that looked like they'd seen their fair share of wild nights out.

She'd always been a sucker for the tall, dark and handsome type, but Patrick Gauge put a whole new spin on the description with his unruly, longish light brown hair and his lanky, rather than athletic, build.

There was something very enticing about the lost-little-boy look. Even though there was definitely nothing boyish about him.

As he ran his long, callused fingers over the guitar strings, she thought that he was waiting for her to say or do whatever she'd come there for.

Instead she silently sipped her whiskey and took her fill of him while he was otherwise occupied. Watching his biceps flex with his movements. The pull of the denim against his groin. The thickness of his neck above the frayed collar of his T-shirt. God, he was rough.

He kept a neat place, she'd give him that. Not overly so—she couldn't detect the scent of any cleaning products—but there wasn't any dirty underwear lying around. Her gaze went back to his groin. Of course, that might be because he didn't wear underwear.

The idea made her hot.

She leaned back farther on the bed, letting the gold liquid creep through her veins, warming her along with the glass of wine she'd had at her place.

She shouldn't be there. Shouldn't be tempting fate along with her tenant. But when she'd glimpsed the rest of the night gaping before her like a fathomless pit faced with the choice of checking a cell phone that would never ring or coming over here to see what temporary trouble she could get into, well…this was definitely preferable.

"The quickest way to get over the old guy is to take up with a new guy," her friend Tabitha was fond of saying.

Of course, Lizzie didn't really plan to *take up* with Gauge. She merely wanted to indulge in something she never had before. More specifically, she wanted to experience a one-night stand. Find out for herself why they were so popular. Any risks involved would be offset by her psychological need to escape her thoughts, if only for a few precious hours.

"Are you playing at the pub this weekend?" she asked, conscious of the way his fingers stroked the strings with the finesse of a pro.

He nodded and then leveled that intense musician's gaze at her. "I'm surprised."

"By what?"

"I didn't peg you as a pub kind of woman."

She smiled. "I take it women don't surprise you often."

"No. Not often."

She watched the way his thick, long fingers manipulated the strings, noticing that the acoustic guitar was old. Two newer guitars—another acoustic, one electric—sat in stands nearby. Scratches marred the front of the one he held, and there even appeared to have been some patchwork down one side.

He played a few more chords, then switched the CD player on.

"Had that long?" Lizzie asked.

He blinked as if seeing the guitar for the first time. He rested the bottom on the floor and moved it so she could see the back. Dozens of words were engraved in the wood. "This guitar shows all the places I've traveled, cities, towns." He turned it back around. "Wherever my guitar is, my heart is."

He leaned the instrument against the ottoman and rested his elbows on his knees, making no secret of his interest in her where she half lay on his bed.

"Are you sure you want to do this?" he asked, his voice as quiet as his playing.

Direct. She liked that.

"Mmm. I'm absolutely positive."

3

GAUGE HAD LEARNED A long time ago that the touch of a woman could be as intoxicating as any liquor. And while Lizzie Gilbred might emerge more Chivas Gold to his Jack, she was an intoxicant all the same as she slid farther back onto the bed, stretching out like a supple black cat with blond hair

"You don't talk much, do you?" she asked quietly.

His answer was a shake of his head.

"I am. A talker, I mean."

Gauge reached down and took off his right boot, then followed with his left.

He watched her watch him.

"I guess it goes along with the territory. You know, my being a trial attorney. When you come up against opposing counsel, you had better be a pretty good debater."

Gauge took off his T-shirt. He wondered how much debating she'd done before she'd crossed the snow-covered driveway from her large house to his small apartment. Had she considered all the angles? Taken in the possible consequences?

For reasons he couldn't quite name, he had the feeling that she hadn't. Something, some event, had pushed her to come to his place on the spur of the moment. And his silent disrobing across the room from her was his way of giving her a chance to change her mind.

He lowered his hands toward the fly of his jeans and paused. Instead of scooting toward the end of the bed in order to make her exit, sexy Lizzie Gilbred ran her pink tongue along her lips, her gaze riveted to his actions.

Let it not be said that he hadn't given her ample opportunity to hightail it out of there. Realize that what she was about to do was something she couldn't take back or erase.

He crossed the room and sat on the edge of the bed.

"You have a great physique," she said quietly, reaching out to run her fingertips down his right arm. "Must be the guitar playing."

Gauge shifted to face her, taking her hands and bringing her to a sitting position. She appeared ready for him to kiss her. Instead he reached for the hem of her sweater and slowly brought it up, purposely avoiding meeting her lips. This wasn't about intimacy—it was about sex. Pure and simple. An escape as stimulating as spirits. He tugged the soft material over her head, tousling her golden hair and revealing that she was every bit as shapely as he'd suspected. A bloodred satin bra did what his palms were suddenly itching to do, namely curve under the fleshy orbs of her breasts.

He skimmed his fingers over the glossy material and she inhaled deeply.

Gauge looked into her eyes to find a mixture of fascination and curiosity on her beautiful face.

Her tongue made a repeat performance. "Don't you think we should turn out the lights?"

Two lamps filled the room with dim light, and he didn't want to switch off either one of them.

He pretended not to hear her as he slid both of his hands over the satin cups until his hands supported her as much as her bra. He rubbed his calloused thumbs over the firm tips, scratching the delicate material.

He'd never understood a woman's desire for shiny lingerie. To him, there was nothing sexier than a naked woman. Her soft skin, fleshy curves, shadowy crevices. Nothing man-made could ever rival the sight of a woman's trembling stomach, or the cleft between her legs.

He worked his thumbs inside the bra cups until her taut nipples popped out of the top.

Lizzie's breathing quickened, but she didn't move, apparently content to let him take command.

Gauge took one of the nipples into his mouth, reveling in the feel of the stiff, puckered skin against his tongue. She smelled like a mixture of cucumbers and musk. She tasted like heaven. He squeezed the soft flesh with his fingers and took in more of her, sucking deeply. She gasped and grasped his wrist, as if unsure whether to pull him away or urge him closer.

Gauge took the decision away from her by removing his mouth and reaching behind her to undo the clasp of her bra. The flimsy material instantly gapped forward and he helped her the rest of the way out of it, ignoring her attempts to kiss him.

He reached for the catch to her slacks even as she

fumbled with his zipper. Gauge stretched out next to her to make the transition easier. He felt her mouth on his shoulder and neck, hot, hungry, even as he clenched his back teeth and sought the springy curls between her legs with his fingers...only to find... She was completely bare, her flesh as smooth as the satin of her bra.

He groaned in the back of his throat, his erection immediately standing up at attention at the sight of her womanhood looking like a ripe fruit just waiting to be tasted.

And taste it he did....

LIZZIE'S BACK CAME UP off the mattress at the feel of Gauge's hot mouth between her legs.

Oh, dear...

She couldn't remember the last time someone had gone down on her. Keen awareness exploded through her, robbing her breath, making her aware of every swirl of his tongue, every beat of her heart.

Oh, yes. This definitely had been a good idea.

She forced her eyes open and tucked her chin into her chest so she could watch Gauge's dark head as he parted her legs, baring her fully to his gaze. He followed the line of her fissure with his thumbs then opened her fleshy lips, his tongue lapping at her most intimate of intimates.

She was suddenly incapable of swallowing, incapable of thought. She twisted her fists into the downy blanket under her, reaching for something, anything that would relieve the pressure building between her legs...in her veins...filling her stomach. It seemed as if she'd flown too close to the sun in one long catapult, needing to pull away, yet wanting to stay to enjoy the spectacular view.

He slid his index finger inside her throbbing depths and she cried out, coming instantly, the pressure escaping in a series of muscle-deep spasms.

She was just beginning to regain her breath when she realized he was still licking her, apparently lapping her clean.

Lizzie found it difficult to swallow, a convert to lights-on sex. She'd been able to watch every expression on his face, every movement of his tongue. She'd been laid out against the mattress, open to his attentions, vulnerable at her weakest moment.

And she'd experienced one of the best orgasms she'd had in recent memory.

Gauge lifted himself up on his arms, his gaze intense as it flicked over her face. He slid forward until his hips lay between her legs and his chest rasped against the tips of her breasts. Lizzie's hands immediately went to his face, needing to draw him near so she could kiss him.

He buried his face in her neck instead, leaving her little choice but to focus her attention on his shoulder.

He was hard where a man was meant to be hard, no extra ounce of flesh on him anywhere. There was a tattoo on his right arm, but she couldn't make it out as she felt him move between her thighs.

Her throat tightened when she felt him naked and hard against her slick portal.

"Condom?" she choked.

He didn't say anything for a long moment, merely ran his mouth against the column of her neck, creating a wet trail down to her breast and back.

What if he refused to wear one? Sure, she was on the pill, mostly to help regulate her periods, but she'd even made Jerry wear a condom.

"In the drawer to your right," he said quietly.

Relieved, she reached for and found a foil-wrapped packet, freeing the lubricated latex inside and helping to sheath him. When he might have pulled away to enter her, she wrapped her fingers around his thick width instead and measured his length. Her thumbnail barely reached her index fingernail around him, and she guessed that if he got hard in his jeans and his member was positioned upward, you might see the tip there at the waist. Because she'd been right in her earlier supposition that he didn't wear briefs or boxers.

Nice…

He held himself above her, watching her face, his own cast in shadow from his tousled dark hair. His mouth was incredible, his lips generous, almost feminine. She released his erection and licked her lips in preparation for his kiss.

He entered her in one slow stroke instead.

She'd thought his mouth had worked miracles, but that had left her woefully unprepared for the feel of him inside her.

She was almost too tight for him, too small. But as he waited for her slick muscles to adjust to his size, a hungry restlessness built within her. She bent her knees for better traction and tilted her hips upward, taking even more of him in.

She blindly sought his mouth and connected with his jaw instead, kissing him repeatedly as he slowly withdrew and then slid inside her again, filling her almost to overflowing.

"Kiss me!" she whispered, grasping his arms to steady herself for his quickened stroke.

He did. He kissed her cheek nearer her ear. Then he whispered back, "This is fucking, Lizzie. Not lovemaking. It's best that neither of us gets confused."

Then he quickened the pace of his strokes more, giving her little time to protest or to even consider protesting as he shoved her closer and closer to her next climax....

THE FOLLOWING MORNING, Gauge woke to the sound of a ringing phone. Probably one of the neighbors', he thought, rolling onto his back and pulling the pillow over his head. Then he realized that he didn't have any neighbors. At least not ones separated from him by a wall.

He dragged the pillow off his face and stared at the ceiling, guessing it to be around nine or ten. The scent of musk teased his nose and he put the pillow back to his face, glancing at the other side of the bed. Gone.

It was just as well that Lizzie Gilbred had gotten up and left his place at some point during the night.

He reached for the telephone receiver next to the bed, but it stopped mid-ring.

Good.

He reached down and scratched his balls then slid his fingers down his semierect shaft. He'd give Lizzie a lot of credit. Some women might have taken offense at his refusal of intimacy. Not her. If anything, she'd seemed further turned-on by the idea that she was there for sex and sex only. No strings that stretched beyond the perimeter of this bed.

She'd been insatiable. Going from screaming orgasm one moment to frenzied, sex-starved nympho the next. It had been a good long while since he'd enjoyed more than just a ten-minute sack session with a woman.

And months since he'd awakened not thirsting for a swallow from the bottle on the kitchen table across the room.

He tossed off the blankets and rose from the bed, heading for the bathroom and the shower, where he stood for long minutes under the hot spray. He'd promised the band that he'd stop by the pub this morning to practice before they opened for lunch. He shouldn't have a problem making it, seeing as he really didn't have anything else on his agenda.

Hell, he didn't know what he was still doing in Fantasy, Michigan. If he'd known what was good for him, he'd have left right after Nina and Kevin's wedding in August. Would never have unpacked his bag or his guitar and would have hightailed it back out after the reception.

But he hadn't.

For some reason he had yet to fully define, he'd

stayed on, renting the garage apartment from sexy Lizzie Gilbred, sitting in with area bands when they needed him and waiting until either wanderlust or a long-term commitment to a single band saw him hitting the road again.

Then he'd blinked and it was almost Christmas.

He'd hoped to be well out of the northern city before winter hit. While he'd lived through the past three when he'd gone into partnership with Nina and Kevin, he'd been vaguely looking forward to heading someplace south this season, as he had done in the years before the three had become friends.

He pushed his face into the punishing hot spray and ran his hands over the stubble covering his jaw.

Friends. Now there was a word for you.

The ringing started again.

Gauge shut off the water and stood dripping, listening to it. When it appeared the caller wasn't about to give up, he grabbed a towel, rubbing it against his hair as he walked into the other room and picked up the extension.

"Gauge?"

His every muscle tightened as he recognized the female voice on the other end. Nina....

4

LIZZIE CLOSED her notepad and stood up from the conference table. The afternoon strategy meeting to discuss a case going to court the following week was drawing to a close.

"I want to see that deposition, Mark," she said to a junior associate.

"It'll be on your desk by tomorrow morning."

"I'd prefer a half hour." She turned toward another associate. "Mary Pat, how's the witness prep going?"

The pretty brunette smiled. "As well as can be expected. I've got another meeting with the key to go over testimony on Friday. Hopefully this time he won't crack under cross."

Lizzie nodded. "If anyone can handle it, you can."

The room began emptying out as everyone said good-night and hurried off before she could assign them another task or ask another question.

Lizzie was the last one out. Which was usually the case. Her boss, John Stivers, had always said she was one of the hardest workers he'd ever seen. And, of course, the instant he'd said it, she'd determined to work even harder.

It was after six and she understood that many of her associates had families they wanted to get home to. The three senior partners had called it a day an hour or so ago, as had the secretarial pool and most of the paralegals, but she'd requested the late meeting because it was the only time they could fit it in.

She entered her office and put her files on her desktop. Her own paralegal was still on the clock and peeked her head through the door leading to the lobby area.

"Do you need me for anything else?" Amanda asked.

Lizzie glanced at her watch, then through the window. It was dark already. The white landscape looked grim from her third-floor office in the new building built to accommodate the expanding practice.

At least five things sprang to mind, but instead she waved her hand. "Go on home, Amanda. I'll see you in the morning."

"Thanks. Good night."

"Good night."

Lizzie sank down into her coffee-colored leather desk chair and sat for long moments, watching as the offices emptied out.

The partners had conducted a survey that estimated there was a more than thirty percent turnover of new attorneys at high-powered law firms nationwide, while their own partnership was doing slightly better, mostly because of the incentive program she'd helped them devise the year before. While Lizzie and a handful of other associates hungry to climb the partnership ladder put in over a hundred hours a week, most of the others averaged between sixty and eighty. Since much of their time as trial attorneys was spent at the courthouse, the only opportunity to do follow-up and file and prep work was after the regular hours of nine-to-five.

By rights, she should be feeling tired. Instead, she found she was still energized. She smiled as she compiled her notes and put a couple of files in her out-box. Over the past week she'd had to mainline caffeine to keep going. Today...

Her eyes widened. Today, she'd barely thought about Jerry and his leaving her high and dry.

Instead, she found her thoughts trailing to one very hot, very sexy Patrick Gauge.

She squeezed her thighs together, feeling tingly all over again.

Her cell phone chirped. She tilted it on her desk so she could read the display and then answered.

"I need a drink. Meet me at Ciao?" Tabitha asked.

Lizzie smiled. She could always count on her old friend to liven things up. If not for Tabitha this past week, things would have been harder than they had been. She and Lizzie had been close ever since attending University of Toledo Law School together, and they'd seen each other through some difficult times.

Despite their shared interest in the legal system, they'd taken different paths. While Lizzie had chosen trial law, Tabby had gone the bankruptcy route, helping strapped people regain some kind of control over their lives.

Lizzie asked now, "Why do you need a drink?"

"You're right. I probably don't need a drink. But I want one." Tabitha sighed. "A long day, that's all."

"Tell me about it," Lizzie agreed, although she hadn't felt the day had been particularly grueling.

"You're sounding better. Oh, no. Don't tell me. He called."

"Who?" she asked, before thinking. She cringed. Tabby knew her much too well not to read the road signs.

"Hmm. Okay. I suppose the question should be, 'who is he'?"

"Who?" Lizzie asked again.

"Ah, yes. She's taking my advice that the best way to forget about the last guy is to find the next." Tabitha laughed, a throaty sound that never failed to make Lizzie smile. "So you're feeling better then."

"I'm feeling better."

"Good. You've been such a train wreck this past week, I was afraid I might have to drag you to an AA meeting or two. Either that, or you might have to drag me."

"Do you mind if I pass for tonight?"

"Mind? Hell, my credit card will thank you. Unlike you, I don't have access to a bottomless expense account."

"Whatever."

"Call me tomorrow?"

"If you don't call me first."

Lizzie signed off after a few more moments and then sat back in her chair, both glad Tabby hadn't asked again about the man who had taken her mind off Jerry and disappointed. Given the one-night nature of her liaison with

Gauge, a part of her wanted to keep it private. Still, it had been so good, it was nearly impossible not to share.

While she'd never considered herself a good girl, she'd never really been a bad one, either. One-night stands were better left to those who had the time to waste. She'd been so focused first on school, then at the firm, that it was all she could do to stop by her parents' a couple of times a week before dropping into bed at night, exhausted, only to start the cycle over again the next day.

She shifted her watch around on her wrist and looked at the pearly face, even though she knew what time it was. What she was really doing was wondering what Gauge was up to.

She was pretty sure the band played only on the weekends…which meant he should be home.

A warm pool of longing filled her stomach.

God, how long had it been since she'd experienced this heightened awareness? It was too long ago to remember her first time with Jerry. Had she felt the same way? She figured she must have, because she'd fallen in love with him all those years ago. Enough that she hadn't hesitated to take him back six months ago, seeing his return as the fulfillment of what they'd begun all those years ago but never finished.

Or perhaps it had been her own competitive spirit that had made her open that door to him again. After all, stealing him away from his wife was a kind of vindication of their earlier relationship.

She opened her desk drawer and took out her purse. So much for not thinking about Jerry.

But for the first time in days she felt she had a choice in the matter.

THE TENSION at the Weber dining-room table was palpable, with Nina either ignorant of the unspoken words exchanged between the two men…or overly aware of them. Gauge couldn't decide which.

He knew he shouldn't have come. But over the past few months he'd turned down her every invitation to dinner at their place, preferring to meet them in public and avoid what he knew was a need for a showdown of sorts that had been brewing since last February. He'd known he'd have to accept at some point, and now was as good a time as any.

If only Kevin wasn't slanting him looks that said he'd like nothing better than to pummel him to a pulp right there and then.

When Gauge had returned for Nina and Kevin's wedding in August, his long absence had allowed for a lowering of defenses and he'd gladly taken the spot beside Kevin as his best man. But later that day at the reception, Gauge had pushed his luck when he'd asked for a dance with the bride…and found himself right back at square one with his one-time best friend.

Gauge focused on his surroundings now. He was familiar with the house. Kevin had inherited it from his late parents, and Gauge had been there no fewer than a couple of dozen times. Still, it had undergone such intensive renovations he barely recognized it.

"Place looks good," he said, noticing that the wall between the kitchen and dining room had been knocked out, giving an airier feel. "Amazing what a woman's touch will do."

He purposely looked at Kevin, hoping to lighten the atmosphere. But the problem was that Nina had touched them both, in more ways than one.

Nina cleared her throat as she spooned gravy over the thin slices of brisket on his plate. "Actually, Kevin is the one who deserves complete credit."

Gauge narrowed his gaze on her as the couple shared a glance.

"I tore the place up after..." Kevin began, then looked at Gauge pointedly.

Gauge picked up his fork. It seemed everything he said led back to that one night.

"I didn't move in until after we married," Nina said, taking the seat across from him and sliding her hand over Kevin's. He sat at the head of the table between them. "Kevin wanted me to, but I preferred to wait until we got married."

Gauge glanced into the living room, where the gift he'd bought them hung on the wall between the front windows and the door. An authentic dream catcher made by the Ojibwa Indians. It had seemed like a good idea at the time. It would be great if it could really filter out all the bad and leave only the good.

He forked the mashed potatoes and put a bite into his

mouth. He'd been stupid to think he could just come back. That the three of them could take up where they'd left off before that fateful night when Nina had agreed to allow him and Kevin to fix her up with a blind date. More specifically they'd blindfolded her, and she hadn't known which of the two she'd slept with.

The food tasted like sawdust in his mouth. He reached for his water glass to help wash it down.

"So, do you know when you might come back to work at BMC?" Nina asked.

Kevin's fork screeched against his plate and Gauge looked at him. He got the distinct impression that his old friend would like nothing better than for Gauge to just walk out of town and never come back.

Of course, that's not how he'd felt when Gauge had returned at Nina's request for their August wedding. Kevin had hugged him like a long-lost brother. And in that one moment, he'd been glad he'd come back. Been reminded of the deep bond of friendship he'd shared with the other man.

Unfortunately, that's not the only thing they'd shared.

He looked over at Nina.

God, but she was as beautiful as ever. Like a brilliant desert rose whose fragrance he could smell across the table. Her blond hair had grown out a bit from the way she'd once worn it, but it still hung in a shiny curtain around her pretty face. She had on a clingy red, long-sleeved shirt and black pants that hugged her curves in all the right places. It looked like she'd put on a few pounds, and they suited her. Her breasts were a little larger, her bottom high and shapely.

He picked up his knife and started to cut the meat. Only it refused to be cut.

All three of them appeared to be doing the same thing at once. And no one was having any luck.

"Sorry...the beef seems a little on the tough side," Nina murmured.

He watched as Kevin folded a piece onto his fork. "I like big bites anyway."

Gauge grinned, watching him put the food into his mouth and chew. And chew.

He followed suit, folding the slice of meat with the help of his knife and then putting it into his mouth.

It tasted like the belt that held up his jeans. Or what he imagined that must taste like.

The three of them chewed until finally Nina spit the contents of her mouth into her napkin, her cheeks turning an attractive shade of red.

"Mmm," Kevin said. "It's...delicious, honey."

Gauge had to give him credit for swallowing what must have felt like an entire boot in one gulp. Since Kevin had already drained his glass of water, Gauge pushed his own mostly filled glass his way. His friend gave him a look of gratitude as he downed nearly the entire contents.

A sound came from Nina's direction. Gauge and Kevin looked to see her eyes bright with tears. Gauge discreetly spit his own bite into his napkin and followed Kevin's lead.

"It's the best home-cooked meal I've had in a long time."

Only it hadn't been tears of exasperation that sparkled in her bright blue eyes; rather they were inspired by laughter.

Nina grinned. "That's because you probably haven't had a home-cooked meal in so long you've forgotten what it tastes like."

Kevin coughed into his napkin. "Actually, that depends on what home you're talking about. Because in this house, this is what a home-cooked meal tastes like."

Laughter burst from the table and created a happy cloud around the three of them that had been sorely missing.

Gauge was glad for the change.

Nina stopped laughing first. "God, I'm sorry. I followed the recipe to a T. I don't have a clue what happened."

She picked up Kevin's plate and forked the meat back into the serving dish.

"Don't touch my mashed potatoes," he said. "I love your mashed potatoes."

Gauge felt suddenly like an outsider. Which was something he was getting used to when in the presence of his two friends. He could accept them being a married couple. But he still hadn't figured out how to deal with it.

Especially since he couldn't seem to stop himself from wanting what Kevin had. Namely, Nina.

"I should stick to café fare," she said. "Soups and sandwiches I can handle."

"Don't forget baking," Kevin reminded.

"Yeah. So long as you don't mind living on bear

claws, I suppose I'm your dream mate." She rolled her eyes, but her warm smile belied her true feelings as she handed him back his plate. "I'm going to go order pizza. You two clear the table."

An hour and a half later, Gauge picked up the empty pizza boxes while Kevin went to change the CD in the player in the living room. He took the boxes into the kitchen, where Nina was opening another bottle of wine.

"Thanks," she said as he passed behind her on the way to the garbage bin.

"You want some help with that?"

She let out a long sigh. "I swear, I've never been any good at popping corks."

Before he could weigh the wisdom of the move, he curved both of his arms around her, pressing his front against her soft, hot bottom. "It's simple. You just have to remember to keep the corkscrew in perfect line with the bottle."

Damn, but she smelled good. Like warm, summer sunshine. A field full of wildflowers. Like rain against a hot sidewalk.

With his help, she popped the cork.

"Oh!" she said, and he heard her swallow.

It satisfied him on a level he was loath to admit that his close proximity still affected her.

Suddenly she went stiff against him. Gauge looked up to find Kevin standing in the kitchen doorway, his fists looking like meat mallets on either side of his legs.

"Get the hell away from my wife."

5

MERELY DRIVING UP to her parents' house filled Lizzie with memories of the past, and bittersweet thoughts of the present. Her parents had been the family's foundation, their rock. How could they even consider getting divorced now? After thirty years of marriage? It didn't make sense.

Lizzie let herself in through the back door, much as she had for nearly the entire twenty-eight years of her life. The house was one of the first that her father had built after opening his own construction company before she was born. While he'd added on to it over the years to accommodate her mother's wishes for a sunporch and her brother's for a media room, much remained the same. Decor aside, of course. Her mother claimed that she'd been Martha Stewart before Martha even thought about making her first pinecone wreath. The house had undergone a complete makeover nearly every year, with a change in color schemes and throw rugs and artwork.

Now the living room walls were a soft, homey green, which went well with the upholstered furniture, a cream color festooned with tiny flowers of every color. The furniture had remained the same, chosen because it went with almost everything. Photos of the family, especially the three children, dotted the walls and mantel, documenting the various stages of their lives.

"Mom?" Lizzie called out, putting her purse on the kitchen table and shrugging out of her coat, much as she had countless times before. Only this time there was no answer.

She hadn't checked the garage to see if either of their cars was there. It was usually a given at this time of night that her parents would both be home. It was just after dinner and right about now they normally would have been sitting at the kitchen table enjoying coffee and dessert or in the family room watching the news or reading.

The silence seemed to verify with deafening intensity that nothing was normal or usual anymore.

Lizzie sighed and looked around the kitchen. When she was growing up, there had always been something to eat. It was one of the many reasons neighborhood children had liked to hang out there. If there wasn't a pot of something on the stove to sample, there were surely sandwich fixings and a bag of chips somewhere.

The sink was empty, the stove barren and not even the cookie jar held a crumb to lick off the pad of her finger. She opened the refrigerator. Bingo. She smiled as she popped the lid on a container of food and took out a slice of meat loaf.

She sputtered when an overdose of salt assaulted her taste buds.

She moved to the sink and coughed up the meat, running the water to wash it down the drain as she tripped the trash compactor.

"Damn," she muttered under her breath, having forgotten the phone call of the night before.

She dumped the rest of the "poisoned" meat loaf into the garbage can and placed the container in the dishwasher.

She should have known the situation had deteriorated to this degree, but the absence of broken glass littering the floor had convinced her that things were as they always had been.

She opened the freezer and took out a fudge pop, visually verifying that no tampering had taken place. She hesitantly licked it, sighed with relief and then closed the freezer door. Do what you will with the meat loaf, she thought, but leave anything chocolate alone.

Of course, her father didn't like chocolate.

Sucking on the sweet, she left the kitchen, walking through the hall toward the foyer. She immediately spotted her mother's purse on the table near the door.

Huh?

"Dad?"

She stepped down the connecting hall toward the guest room that had once been a den and then a guest room again and rapped lightly on the closed door. No answer. She peeked inside to see the sofa bed open, the sheets and blanket unmade, and then closed the door again.

So her father wasn't there. But her mother?

A sound from the second floor.

Maybe her mother was taking a bath with her headphones on and hadn't heard her.

While the Gilbreds weren't immodest, rare were the times when a bathroom door was locked. Lizzie had spent many a time sitting on the closed commode talking to her mother while Bonnie was immersed in a tub full of bubbles.

Of course, when those same bubbles started to dissipate, she was the first to give her mother privacy…and to spare herself from viewing something that might ruin her for life.

She climbed the stairs, licking her frozen treat as she went. She supposed she could grab a sandwich on the way home. Or see if the Chinese place on Oak Street was still open.

She looked first in the master bedroom to find everything perfectly in its place, the bed made, the connecting bath empty.

Okay…

Had her mother left her purse behind? Was she even now eating out somewhere and reaching for her wallet, only to find she'd left it at home on the foyer table? That was so unlike her mother as to be scary.

Scarier still was the fact that both her parents constantly requested that she act as their attorney. She was grateful she wasn't a family attorney and was only too quick to point that out whenever the topic raised its ugly head. Which was much too often for her liking.

She checked out the main bathroom just to make sure her mother wasn't in there, then shrugged and headed to her old room. Bonnie had kept all the kids' bedrooms decorated the same way as when they'd lived at home, the wallpaper a little harder to change than the color of paint. Lizzie sometimes liked to go into her old room and lie across her white canopy bed, remembering happier times.

Another sound.

Lizzie's footsteps slowed. If she wasn't mistaken, it had come from her old room.

She slowly opened the door and then gasped, standing rooted to the spot. Lying across her old bed was her mother, naked, her hands tied above her head to the canopy posts. Her father was kneeling at the edge, an extra large feather held aloft as he swung his head to look at her.

And the sound? The headboard hitting the wall.

Lizzie screamed and ran from the room. So much for leaving a scene before it ruined her for life. She didn't think she'd ever be able to go into her old bedroom again.

A COUPLE HOURS LATER, Lizzie sat on the leather couch in her family room, flipping through channels on the television, purposely ignoring her vibrating cell phone. Her mother had called no fewer than five times since Lizzie had bolted from the house as if the floor had been covered with burning coals. Much of what had happened since the moment she'd caught her parents playing Pin the Princess on her bed—her childhood bed in her childhood room— had passed in a blur. She couldn't even remember what she'd done with the fudge pop.

And at this point, she didn't care, either. She half hoped she'd dropped the melting chocolate on the white carpet of her old room so her mother would have to clean it up…among other things.

Ugh.

Well, she supposed there was one good thing to come out of the situation. Her parents appeared to have reconciled.

She stuck her chopsticks into the rice container and put both down on the coffee table, pulling the chenille throw across her lap up to her chin.

Her cell vibrated and she turned the display so she could read the caller ID. Her sister, Annie.

She answered.

"Okay, what's up? Mom's going out of her mind with worry because you aren't taking her calls."

Leave it to Annie to cut straight to the chase.

Younger than Lizzie by a year, her sister usually managed to keep up the front that her life was all sunshine and roses. But Lizzie knew it was more like dirty diapers and teething rings. The last time she'd talked to Annie, her sister had been a scant inch removed from running away from her family altogether. Which didn't make any sense to Lizzie, because so far as she could tell, her sister had gotten everything she'd ever wanted out of life. A great husband. A marvelous house. Two beautiful children and another on the way.

Not that little Jasmine and Mason were angels. Far from it. They were loud and smelly and needed constant supervision. And somewhere in there, Annie had to fit in love, as well. Which wasn't always easy.

So Lizzie and Annie had spent a lot of time on the phone lately. The approach suited Lizzie fine. Since she worked such long hours, she wasn't physically able to step in to help her sister out much. The issue of children in her own future still hung like a swaying question mark. Not because she'd had any bad experiences or her sister's situation had turned her off kids. She'd simply been so busy she hadn't had a chance to think about them.

That, and she had yet to meet a man she loved enough to consider sharing another human being with.

Even Jerry.

So Lizzie paid back her sister's brevity with a concise rundown of the evening's events.

A silent pause stretched after she finished. Then, finally, Annie's laughter filled her ear.

Lizzie scooted down farther into the sofa. "I'm glad to be a source of comic relief."

In truth, her sister's response irritated her.

"Tied to your bed…a feather? Oh my God, Liz, this is classic Mom and Dad."

"Yeah, maybe. But not when they were in the middle of a divorce."

"Maybe."

Another silence as both considered a future in which their parents weren't married. Fractured holidays spent running from one parent's house to the other, never satisfying either of them, always hearing a litany of the ex-spouse's flaws.

They'd both seen it happen to friends. And it was a way of life they'd counted themselves lucky not to have to confront.

There was a brief cry at the other end of the line. Lizzie realized her sister must have been holding Mason, her youngest.

"Shh," Annie said soothingly.

Surprisingly, the sound served to make Lizzie feel better.

"Remember the time we caught them going at it in the garage in the middle of the day?" Annie asked.

Lizzie groaned. "Did you have to remind me of that occasion? I mean, my God, we were like, what? All of ten and eleven? And we had friends with us."

"I forgot about that. But what I can see clearly is Mom with her tennis skirt hiked up around her hips sitting on the washing machine, Dad's shorts down around his ankles, the two of them going at it during the spin cycle."

Lizzie rubbed her forehead. "Or how about the time they took us to the drive-in when we were even younger than that?"

"Oh, God! And they started going at it right there in the front seat, thinking the three of us were asleep in the back."

"Yes, well, if we had been, the squeaking of the car springs would have woken us."

"If Mom's shouts hadn't."

They shared a laugh. "Well, you can't say that it hasn't been an interesting run."

"No, that you can't. But what I don't understand is

why, after all these years, the two would even contemplate divorce."

Lizzie worried her bottom lip. "Maybe they ran out of places to do it?"

"There's that."

"Have you really talked to either of them about it?" Lizzie asked.

"Me? Are you kidding? I'm almost afraid to ask, what with all I've got going on." Mason made a few cooing sounds. "How about you?"

"No. I mean, I tried a couple of times. But the two of them seem so caught up in the act of divorcing that my questions hit a wall."

"What about Jesse? Do you think he's talked to them?"

Lizzie didn't even bother answering. Jesse was going through an interesting time of his own, what with dumping the girl he'd been engaged to practically since junior year of high school for a pole dancer from Boston.

"Maybe it's time we called a family meeting," Lizzie suggested instead.

"A what?"

"You know, make an appointment for all of us to come together so we can talk this out."

"I don't know if that's such a good idea. Think about it, Liz. You can't handle the idea of them still having an active sex life—"

"I can handle the idea of them having sex…I just don't want to view it."

"Anyway, do you really want to hear what's driven them apart? All the gritty details?"

"Somebody's got to."

Annie sighed. "Yeah, well, after today, let's hope there's nothing more to worry about. Let's hope they've worked out their differences and that life goes back to normal again so Christmas can go ahead as scheduled."

Lizzie dropped her head back against the couch and closed her eyes. "I forgot all about Christmas."

"I finished my shopping yesterday."

"Shocker. I haven't started."

"Shocker. What are you going to get Mom and Dad?"

"How about an appointment with a shrink?"

"Ha-ha. No, really."

"I have no idea, Annie," she said quietly, considering all that had happened that night. Hell, over the course of the past week.

She didn't ask her sister what she'd gotten them. Annie always had a great handle on the perfect gift for everyone.

"Okay, I'd better put Mason down. Do you want me to call Mom? Or will you?"

"I'll call her in the morning."

"Fine, I'll call her now."

"Do what you will."

"Good night, Lizzie."

"What's good about it, Annie?"

Her sister laughed and signed off.

Lizzie pressed the disconnect button and tossed the cell phone to the other side of the sofa. She nearly jumped out of her skin when she heard a light tap on the patio windows behind her.

She jerked around to find Gauge standing outside holding up what looked like a mug of something. Hmm…

6

"GET THE HELL AWAY from my wife."

The words seemed burned into Gauge's mind, the three hours since he'd heard them doing nothing to diminish their effect.

There he'd been, standing in Kevin and Nina's kitchen, his arms around Nina from behind, helping her to open a fresh bottle of wine. Yes, he had maybe stood a little too close. Yes, he'd sniffed her hair as if he'd like nothing more than to bury his nose there. Yes, he'd felt her bottom, hot and hard against his promising arousal. But he would never have pushed things any further.

As he stood on Lizzie's back steps waiting for her to open the kitchen door, he called himself the liar he knew himself to be.

Nina had been the one to hold up her hands. "Please, Kevin, let's not ruin what's turning out to be a perfectly nice evening."

Gauge had moved away from her, but not quickly enough, it appeared, because Kevin looked a scant breath removed from delivering the pummeling his expression promised.

In a fair fight, Gauge might have been able to take him. But there was nothing fair about a man in love, afraid his best friend was making a move on his woman. Gauge got that.

What Gauge didn't get was why he had done what he had. Beyond it seeming like a purely innocent act at the time.

There had, however, been absolutely nothing innocent in his reaction. Or in the hitch in Nina's breathing. And he knew that if he could have taken it further, he would have.

The door opened suddenly in front of him and he grimaced, forgetting for a moment where he was. What he was doing.

Until Lizzie's provocative face filled his line of vision. He found himself grinning. A natural grin, despite the night's awkward events.

Nina had tried to force an air of normalcy on the last hour of his visit, but there had been nothing normal about eating dessert in the living room of a man who would just as soon Gauge disappeared from the face of the earth.

As Nina had uncomfortably kissed him goodnight—a peck on the cheek that he wished would have lingered a little longer—she'd smiled and said, "I think it's a good first step."

First step toward what? He'd wondered. A first step toward resurrecting a friendship among the three of them that was better left to wither away?

He'd heard it said over the years that platonic friendship between a man and a woman was impossible. That sex always managed to get in the way. And he'd believed it. Until he'd met Kevin and Nina. For three years they'd been friends, as well as business partners. For three years they'd enjoyed a nonsexual, if flirtatious, relationship.

Then he'd found a way to screw even that up.

"Gauge?"

He focused again on the woman in front of him.

Lizzie.

She pulled her sweater a little closer.

"Do you want to come in?" she asked.

He stepped through the open doorway, allowing her to close the door after him.

"Hi," she said, coming to stand back in front of him.

There was a lot in her expression he couldn't read.

He lifted the empty coffee cup he held. "I was hoping to borrow some sugar."

She laughed, a happy sound that made him feel slightly better. "Do people really do that? Borrow sugar, I mean? I thought that was just something that happened in the movies."

"Or back when there wasn't a corner market open twenty-four/seven."

She didn't make a move to take the cup, merely stood looking at him as if curious about more than the questions she'd asked.

"Are you okay?" she asked quietly.

Gauge squinted at her. Was there something in his appearance that indicated that he wasn't all right? That spoke of what he was going through?

Something that Lizzie had picked up on?

He wasn't sure how he felt about that. Because it meant either she was extraordinarily observant. Or she possessed those insights only when it came to him.

He put the cup down on a nearby counter, a prop in the game that had become his life.

Hell, he wasn't even sure what he was doing here. Just that he couldn't stand the thought of being anywhere else at that moment. His apartment was quiet. Too quiet. The bar too noisy. His bottle of Jack Daniel's unappealing.

He felt a bit like Goldilocks in the story of the Three Bears. And right now Lizzie was his just right bowl of porridge…not to mention her bed.

"Do you want to come in?" she asked.

"If I'm not interrupting."

"To the contrary. You're probably saving me from an hour wasted watching a television show that doesn't interest me." She turned. "Would you like some coffee or something to drink? Bourbon or whiskey?"

He shook his head, following as she led him into the family room.

He'd viewed the room from the outside in, but it looked different from this vantage point, the recessed lighting and knickknacks and bookshelves giving it a cozy feel. Lizzie picked up the remote and shut off the television.

"Please, sit down."

He did. And if she found it intriguing that he chose the spot he usually saw her sitting in, pushing the lap blanket to the side, she didn't say anything. Instead she sat on the other side of the same couch, tucking one of her legs under her as she faced him.

"Do you want to talk about it?" she asked.

He found himself peering at her closely again. "Talk about what?"

"About what put that crease between your brows."

He gave a halfhearted grin. Maybe this hadn't been such a good idea. He'd come here to forget what had happened, not dwell on it.

"I'd just as soon not talk about it."

She looked at him for a long moment and then nodded. "That's fine." She settled in a little more comfortably against the cushions. "We can just sit here and say nothing if you want. I've had a bit of a...trying day myself. And right now, with you here, I feel quiet."

He raised a brow. "Quiet?"

"Mmm. It's a good thing. About a half hour ago I was ready to jump out of my skin."

He couldn't imagine what could have shaken what he guessed were nerves of steel. But he didn't ask, either. Normally, he didn't have to. He found that others talked about what they wanted to regardless of whether you wanted to hear it or not.

Which made Lizzie's silence all the more resounding.

"Do you mind?" he asked, gesturing toward her stereo system.

"Go ahead."

He got up and crossed to crouch in front of the expensive system. It took a moment to find the power button, and instantly the room was filled with the sound of Nina Simone. Her choice of music surprised him.

In the months that he'd lived there, he'd formed his own opinions about her and her likes and dislikes. He would have guessed her more the classical type. Bach. Or maybe Schumann. But not the blues.

He glanced over at her DVD collection, finding some interesting action films, and then got up to walk to her bookshelf. She had Jules Verne, Asimov and Wells. There was even a section on what looked like contemporary romantic novels.

Definitely not what he'd expected.

Which meant there was far more to the driven attorney than he'd thought.

He picked up a five-by-seven frame of her with a guy and a girl who had the same blond hair and similar features. Her siblings?

"So?" she said softly.

He turned to see her watching him as he put the frame back. "So what?"

"So what do you make of me?"

He gave her a lopsided smile. "That you're more complex than I thought."

"Is that good or bad?"

"Neither. It just is."

She smiled and tilted her chin into her chest, causing her golden blond hair to fall over her face. The flames in the grate seemed to light it on fire and gave her an almost ethereally sexy look. "Good answer."

He moved to stand next to her side of the couch. "I

get the impression that you like to classify everything neatly into either the good or bad column."

She looked up at him.

"Where do I fall?" he asked.

She languidly reached out and hooked her index finger into one of the belt loops on his jeans. "Both."

"Oh?"

He watched the pupils enlarge in her blue eyes. "Mmm."

Her hum was husky, vibrating.

"Bad because I shouldn't have done…shouldn't be doing what I'm doing."

Her long, manicured fingers slid from the waist of his jeans to cup his arousal beneath his closed fly. "And good because?"

She licked her lips. "Good because it seems to be just what I need right now."

He caught her hand against his fly, pressing it more insistently against him, absorbing the warmth of her that seeped through his veins as effectively as any whiskey.

"Tell me, Lizzie," he murmured, tipping her chin up with his other hand. "Is there any room for gray in your life?"

She blinked, staring at him from under the fringe of her dark lashes. "None."

She shifted her hand so that her fingertips dipped inside the waist of his jeans, wedging between the heavy material and his skin. The movement, combined with her boldness, made him rock hard.

He'd known many women in his life. Some shy and

submissive. Others brash and forceful. The ones he chose to spend time with depended more on his mood at the time he met them rather than the qualities of the women themselves. But Lizzie… Beyond her confident, icy exterior, he glimpsed something soft and vulnerable, and the contrast drew him in.

She began undoing the buttons on his jeans. He let her.

Within moments, she weighed his length in her hot palm. She shifted on the couch until she sat on the edge. The movement caught his attention in the glass of the balcony doors behind her. The recessed lights shone like a spotlight on her so that her hair glowed, while he stood in shadow.

It was surreal to be standing on this side of the window, watching their reflection, rather than on the outside looking in.

She slid her mouth over the head of his erection. He closed his eyes and clenched his teeth together, sweet sensation pooling in his balls.

Lizzie curved her fingers around the base of him and held him straight as she took more of him in, swirling her tongue around his shaft then backing away before going down on him again.

Gauge slowly touched her hair, fingering the soft strands. There were few things more beautiful than a hot woman who knew how to please a man. Knew how to please *him*.

He reached behind her, tugging on her sweater until she broke contact and allowed him to strip it from her. Her back was long and graceful, appearing ghostly white in the glass. He smoothed his palms down her shoulders and unhooked her bra, watching as she shook it off, the orbs of her breasts swaying tantalizingly.

Gauge groaned as she once again took him into her mouth and increased suction, his hips bucking involuntarily.

He pushed her hair back from her face so he could view her attentions directly, mesmerized by the fit of her lips, the flicks of her tongue, the grip of her hand…a hand that squeezed him and then curved down to cup his balls.

He stiffened in preparation for orgasm, hoping she wouldn't pull away too soon. Instead, she sucked until he was sure he'd filled her mouth, and then moved his shaft to her breasts, squeezing the full mounds of flesh together to sandwich him there, prolonging his climax until he was afraid he'd emptied himself….

7

LIZZIE RAN her tongue along the head of Gauge's erection, finding that he was surprisingly still hard. His fingers were entwined in her hair, not quite pulling, not quite caressing. They shifted from her head to her shoulders, where he coaxed her to rise from the couch.

She stood quietly facing him, the taste of him still ripe in her mouth. He seemed to be inordinately interested in her lips, his gaze lingering there even as he unfastened the catch on her slacks and pushed the fabric down over her hips along with her panties, skimming his fingers across her bare bottom, where they dipped into the shallow crevice before moving up her back. She shivered. Not from the cold but from the intensity of his expression, combined with his knowing touch.

Then he did something she would never have expected, given his words of the previous evening: he kissed her.

Lizzie caught her breath at the first feathery pass of his lips against hers. She was a little more prepared when he returned, kissing him back.

There was an art to kissing. A finesse that she found most men either chose to ignore or didn't take the time to master, but if done right, was almost enough to bring a woman to climax without touching her anywhere else.

Gauge's kiss was a masterpiece.

She made quick work of stripping him of the rest of his clothes and then melted into his embrace, satisfied to be making out with him. Enjoying the tangling of his tongue with hers. His mint-fresh breath mingling with hers. He slid his right hand from her back to her front, gently cupping her breast. He caught her nipple between his thumb and index finger, rolling the tight, sensitive tip. She moaned, curving her own hands down over his backside, reveling in the muscled length of him as she pressed her stomach against his thick erection…aching to feel him somewhere else.

Lizzie realized she had closed her eyes and slightly opened them again, wanting to verify that she was, indeed, standing completely naked in her family room, curtains wide-open, kissing an equally nude Gauge. He seemed to sense that she was watching him and his eyes opened slightly, as well. She read vague surprise in their green depths.

He switched his attention from her mouth to her neck and shoulder.

Lizzie couldn't help thinking that his movement wasn't generated by a sudden desire to taste her skin, and she felt a moment of loss. She tried to guide his mouth back to hers, but he resisted, distracting her instantly by plunging his fingers into her damp channel from behind, parting her to the cool air.

He grasped her hips and turned her. It was only then that she became aware that they were fully reflected in the balcony doors. She readily bent over, arching her back so her bottom thrust up toward him in open invitation. He gamely responded by sheathing himself with a condom he took from the back pocket of his jeans where they lay on the floor.

Lizzie placed her hands on the couch back, bracing herself for his breach. Instead, he used his hand to caress her with his hard-on, moving the head along her damp opening and back again, then sandwiching himself between the folds of her swollen flesh and pressing the head against her clit.

She gasped, pure, wanton need pulsing through her veins. She hungered for him to fill her, and the longer he delayed the more she wanted him.

She reached between her legs and took his thick, heavy length in her palm, restlessly positioning him against her portal and bearing down on him even as he continued to stand still. Inch by inch, she slid back, her breasts seeming to throb along with the rest of her.

Lizzie caught his gaze in the glass as he watched their coupling as openly as she did. She restlessly licked her lips. He finally grasped her hips, his fingers imprinting her skin as he thrust into her.

She moaned, filled beyond expectation with hard, hot man and sweet, erotic desire.

He thrust again as she clutched the couch and braced

herself for his deep strokes. She watched her breasts shudder as flesh slapped against flesh. Felt his balls sway against her with each meeting. She'd never witnessed herself in such a carnal state and was mesmerized by their reflection. By the fullness of her breasts, the pertness of her ass, the provocative bowing of her mouth. The intense expression on Gauge's face, the rippling of his abs, the easy way he held himself as if taking her from behind in her family room was what he was born to do.

She reached between her legs again, finding the sensitive sac and fondling it. Gauge made a sound deep in his throat, the intensity of his thrusts increasing. When he stiffened in climax, deep within her, she tumbled happily and wantonly right after him....

"So who he is?" Tabby asked her the following day.

Lizzie stared at her friend across the cafeteria-style table. They were supposed to meet at a restaurant for lunch, but Tabby had talked her into going to the mall instead, where they could combine two tasks in one: Christmas shopping and a quick meal. So they sat in the food court, purchases propped on the chairs on either side of them, trays on the table. Lizzie had gone with a calzone, while Tabby opted for a garden salad.

"Who's who?" she asked, taking a sip of her diet soda and watching a couple pass by arm in arm.

Tabby waved her hand and stabbed at her salad with her plastic fork. "You're eating a calzone."

Lizzie raised her brows. "I'm not following you."

"We both eat salads at lunch…unless one of us has had some hot, sweaty sex the night before."

Lizzie threw her head back and laughed. "Maybe I just felt like a calzone."

"Yeah, and I'm Mother Teresa."

Lizzie concentrated on eating as she looked at her watch. She was already running late. She wanted to get in at least a half hour of note reading before this afternoon's meeting.

But that's not really where her mind was. Instead, Tabby's question had made her remember last night and her sexy time with Gauge.

He'd kissed her. Just the once. And he'd gone out of his way to keep from kissing her again. But she hadn't minded because she'd been too occupied with other things to notice much.

Tabitha was right. She'd chosen the calzone because she could.

"So what gives?"

Lizzie gave an exaggerated sigh. "Nothing," she insisted.

And, all things considered, she was being honest, wasn't she? There was nothing going on. Nothing fit to mention, anyway. While she and Gauge had had great sex—twice—there was nothing beyond that, and there was absolutely no guarantee that it would happen again, so why introduce the subject? Especially since she was sure to hear "So how's that sexy musician you're screwing?" for weeks afterward.

"Anyway," she said, wiping a smear of tomato from

the heel of her hand. "Don't even mention the word *sex* to me. Not after what I saw in my old bedroom at my parents' place."

Now that episode she had no problem telling Tabby about. Her friend had already heard the majority of the Gilbred kids' stories of their parents' shenanigans while they were growing up. This made a nice little addition to the collection.

"Do you think they're reconciling?" Tabby asked.

Lizzie knew that her friend's own parents had divorced long ago and that they didn't even acknowledge the other's existence, much less show any signs of possible reconciliation. Tabitha had told her she'd never been so happy as on her graduation day when she wouldn't have to rely on her mother or father financially again. She'd felt liberated from their lingering bitterness. She now joked that her only future worries were the day of her wedding—if she married—and any possible events surrounding children she might have. Otherwise, she was as free as a bird, planning out holidays way in advance just so everyone knew what she was doing when. She'd long since become a pro at dodging leading questions like "What did your father give you?" or "Does your mother have her talons into any new men?"

That was precisely the reason Lizzie was worried about her own parents' marriage. If their acrimonious separation was any indication, then life for the Gilbred offspring would be hell on earth from here on out.

"I don't know," she replied honestly. "I haven't

talked to my mother yet." And, boy, she was dreading the moment.

"I hope they are. I wouldn't wish that part of my life on anybody." Tabby chewed on a bite of salad. "One of the reasons I made friends with you in college was because I wanted to adopt your family."

"More like my family adopted you."

Tabby's smile of gratitude warmed Lizzie.

When Lizzie looked at her watch this time, she did so with genuine concern. "God, I'm so late."

"Yes, but just think what Christmas shopping you got done."

"Considering that I don't even know if there will be a Christmas," Lizzie said, "I'm not so sure how smart that was."

What she *was* sure about was that thinking of Gauge and wondering what he might like for Christmas was a dumb idea.

8

GAUGE SAT on the bandstand, tuning his guitar without the aid of the amp. He was early. The rest of the band wasn't due to arrive for another hour.

But he wasn't there because he wanted to win any brownie points. He'd come because Kevin had called and asked him to.

He ran his fingers along the frets, practicing one of the songs in the first set of the night—Bob Seger's "Night Moves," which was always a hit with the Michigan natives. There were a few people in the pub, mostly lingering over dinner, and no one save for a woman in the far booth and one of the waitresses was paying any attention to him.

He put the guitar pick between his teeth and ran his hand through his hair, the strands still damp from the snow that had been falling as he walked from his parked car to the pub. It was going to be a cold, nasty night. The type of night that should keep people indoors until the storm passed. But it was also Friday, and no matter the weather, most people were determined to get out and celebrate the end of another workweek.

Yes, he knew what that was like. Although his first attempt at an ordinary life had happened so long ago it was now little more than a bad memory. And seeing as it had lasted only six months, well, it was easy to understand why he didn't think about it often.

What he did remember was the girl responsible for the one-eighty he'd tried to make.

He took the pick out of his mouth and played a song from those days. A song he refused to play for entertainment purposes, although it was probably the one he played best.

Over the years he'd learned that he had at least two half brothers and a half sister out there somewhere. Love children created by his father with different women during one- or two-night stands. Gauge had never considered trying to bond with any of his half siblings. He figured one reason might be that they were spread out across the country, conceived during travel gigs that had taken him and his father as far north as British Columbia and as far south as Key West. But the truth was, he had never felt a desire to get to know any of them. And apparently none of them had any desire to meet him, either. Maybe because he was his father's first illegitimate son, he'd gotten the attention that none of them would.

It was difficult to ignore one child. Easier to ignore four.

He recalled a time when one of his half brothers had confronted them at a bar they were playing in Santa Fe. Gauge had been maybe fifteen at the time, old enough to play at the bar, but not old enough to drink at it. The kid, Gorge, had been about twelve, thirteen, and was a good-looking kid of obviously mixed heritage. At first, Gauge thought Gorge might sucker punch Thomas Gauge. And he'd been fully prepared to let him do it. He figured the kid deserved at least that. If not more.

But his father had walked off with the troubled teen and the pair had talked in the gravel parking lot for about a half hour. Gauge had stood right outside the door during the unexpected break from playing and smoked a cigarette, watching the two men from a distance. Then his father had taken some money from his back pocket, pressed it into the kid's hand and given him an awkward hug.

Gauge had waited for his father to explain. If not then, at some point. But he never did. He'd merely slapped Gauge on the shoulder as he passed him on his way back inside the bar—alone—and said, "Come on. We've got to do what we were paid to do."

"Gauge."

He hadn't realized he'd closed his eyes until he heard the waitress's voice.

He automatically twirled the guitar and positioned it in its stand, pretending that her interruption had not mattered. But it had. He didn't know what was responsible for his visit to the long-ago past, but he was positive that it was something he didn't want to think about.

"Kevin's at the bar asking for you," Debbie said, poking a thumb over her shoulder.

Gauge leaned over to see around her. Sure enough, Kevin sat on one of the stools with his back to Gauge, pretending to be relaxed even though it was obvious he was anything but.

Sorry sap.

Gauge rose from his playing chair and slid the pick into his jeans pocket, then stepped from the slightly raised stage.

He headed over to the bar, slanting his old friend a glance while he placed his order. "Hey, Charlie, slide one of those cold drafts my way."

"Sure thing, Gauge."

If he'd thought Kevin was rigid before, he now figured his friend's spine might snap in two. He couldn't help but be amused, even though there wasn't anything remotely funny about their situation.

Charlie put a glass in front of him and he gestured toward Kevin. "You sure you don't want something stronger than beer? Looks like you could use it."

His friend's expression told him he needed something else that had nothing to do with alcohol and everything to do with evening the score.

Kevin reached into his brown suede jacket and took out an envelope. Gauge frowned as Kevin put it on the bar and slid it toward him. "Your monthly take."

The money owed him for his third share of BMC. He folded the envelope three times and slid it into his back pocket without looking at it.

"Don't you want to see how much it is?" Kevin asked.

"No."

"We had a good month what with Christmas shopping and everything. You should be pleased."

He wasn't.

In fact, he had yet to cash a single one of the monthly checks that Kevin and Nina had given him. They sat in a kitchen drawer at his apartment, all but the first envelope unopened.

Kevin stared straight ahead and sipped his beer. Which reminded Gauge of the reason the bar was the favorite place of loners. You could sit all night and drink and not have to look at or talk to anyone if you didn't want to.

"That's why you asked me to meet you here? To give me the check?"

A pause, and then, "Among other things."

Gauge rested his forearms on the counter. "Plan on getting to the point anytime soon?"

That got an irritated rise out of Kevin.

"Look, we could pretend for forever and a day that what happened ten months ago didn't happen, man," Gauge said, surprised to find he was growing agitated. Damn it, if you had a problem, you put it out there. It was as simple as that. He didn't like the hemming and hawing that so many people indulged in.

He didn't like the beating around the bush that Kevin was known for.

He laughed without humor. "You know, it's that silent brooding of yours that got us all into trouble in the first place."

Kevin swiveled toward him so fast Gauge nearly put his arm out to ward off an impending blow. He knew that he deserved whatever was coming his way and almost hoped that his friend would finally unleash his anger on him the way he apparently wanted to.

But, as usual, Kevin kept a tight rein on his emotions. "Are you saying I'm to blame for your sleeping with my wife?"

"She wasn't your wife then."

"No, but you knew how I felt about her, damn it. And you still slept with her."

He'd heard the words before. And nothing had changed. And nothing would unless he forced it. He looked carefully, purposely at his friend and said, "Actually, I don't think you can call what Nina and I did in the back of the music center as sleeping. What do you think?"

Kevin clenched his jaw so tightly, Gauge swore he could almost hear his friend's teeth grinding. "I think I rue the day you ever came to this town."

They stared at each other for a long moment, then Gauge sighed and faced the front of the bar again, resting his boot heel against the brass footrest.

He recalled a time when that hadn't been the case. When he'd been welcome in this town, not only as the owner of the music center, but as Kevin's friend. His best friend.

And as much as it pained him to say it, it bothered him that he no longer held that title.

In fact, it was the sole reason he'd come back to town. To try to repair burned bridges. And while it was taking far longer than he would have expected, he didn't think it was a lost cause. Not yet.

Truth was, he was searching for something more meaningful than this ceaseless wandering from place to place, bed to bed.

And he'd gotten a glimpse of it during his three-year friendship with Kevin and Nina.

He looked to find his friend staring straight ahead, as well. If only Gauge didn't suspect that any forward progress depended on repairing things between them.

He cleared his throat. "It's probably not a very good idea to marry someone you don't trust. They say trust is the bedrock of any good relationship." He shook his head. "If you don't trust Nina now…"

Gauge purposely left his words hanging. He knew he was essentially egging on a grizzly bear by taunting Kevin. But beyond offering himself up as bait, he didn't know how else the two of them were going to move beyond this bar counter, much less beyond what had happened between the three of them ten months ago.

Kevin stared at him. "I trust my wife with my life."

"But do you trust her beyond your bed?"

Finally, Kevin reacted in a way that went beyond words. He got up from the stool so fast he nearly knocked it over and grabbed the front of Gauge's shirt, hauling him up. "Goddamn it, Gauge, you're not going to be happy until I offer to fight you, are you?"

Gauge looked down to emphasize their positions. "If that's the case, it looks like I'm about to get what I want."

Kevin's breathing was hard as he considered his options.

Finally, he released Gauge and gave him a bit of a

shove. "No. No matter how much I'd love to bury my fist in your smug face, I'm not going to do it. I'm not going to let myself be manipulated into communicating in the only way you apparently know how, through sarcasm and physical force." He picked up his coat from a neighboring stool and shrugged into it, keeping his gaze locked on Gauge's. He pointed a finger at Gauge, nearly poking his chest. "I wouldn't even be here if not for Nina. She has some romanticized idea about the three of us becoming friends again. Says you need us." He shook his head. "And before you can make another smart-ass remark, let me tell you this—I'd do anything for my wife. Anything. But if we're going to get through this, we're going to do it my way, not yours. I will not be badgered into a physical fight."

He peeled off a few bills and laid them on the bar.

"Oh, and one more thing," he said, turning toward Gauge. "It's not my wife I don't trust—it's you. And until—if—I can, then we have nothing to say to each other."

Gauge sat back on the stool and watched his friend go.

There had been few men in his life that had made him proud. And, he realized, Kevin was one of them.

While he teased him for his quiet ways, Gauge had always known that underneath his polite exterior lay cold steel. Kevin was more than bookishly smart, he was wise.

And no matter how angry he was, he'd never give himself over to the dark side that Gauge had known for so much of his life.

He absently sipped his beer, still staring at the closed door.

"What was that about?" Charlie asked, taking Kevin's abandoned mug and wiping the bar.

Gauge shook his head. "Nothing."

But that wasn't true, was it? Because it was about everything. At least everything that had once been important to him.

And still was.

The question was, how did you regain trust once you lost it? And was it even possible to do?

He didn't know.

What he did know was that he wasn't leaving town until he figured it out.

9

LIZZIE PUT the delicate angel on top of the small tree she'd set up next to the fireplace in the family room and then sat back on her heels, considering her handiwork. She hadn't planned to decorate her place for Christmas beyond having a professional hang the plain white lights on the front of the house along with a large wreath, as was the tradition in the neighborhood. But she'd knocked off from the firm early and found herself stopping to pick out a tree from a lot that had been temporarily rented for the season and stocked with all sorts of different varieties of evergreens. She'd purposely chosen a small, potted pine that she would replant in the backyard after New Year's.

She glanced toward the window at the snow falling, lightening the darkness. Spring seemed so far off just then.

She got up and plugged the lights in, standing back and smiling as the multicolored string began dancing and blinking.

She'd always loved the holidays. Her parents had made sure to make the days between Thanksgiving and New Year's as magical as possible for their three kids. She remembered hunting through a tree farm in the snow with their father, animatedly trying to decide which tree would grace their home that year. Sleigh rides through the snow-covered fields. Heaping mugs of hot chocolate piled with marshmallows. And always, always, there were Christmas carols playing in the background. Whether they were decorating cookies with their mother in the kitchen, or wrapping presents or getting ready to head out to church in their new clothes on Sunday, the carols seemed to set the mood.

Lizzie smiled now, listening to the Ella Fitzgerald Christmas CD she'd put on as she positioned one of the five poinsettias she'd bought around the fireplace. Of course, her memory was probably distorting things a bit. It was impossible that the holidays had been all that perfect. There had been bruised knees during ice skating mishaps, tears after sledding accidents, and on more than one occasion, the three Gilbred siblings had happened upon their parents demonstrating their own kind of Christmas cheer by getting it on wherever and whenever they could. It seemed that Bonnie and Clyde never failed in their ability to shock their three children.

And now wasn't any different. Only the shocks they were delivering went well beyond passionate little quickies.

Lizzie moved to the couch and considered the Christmas cards she'd bought and laid out, along with a pad and her laptop, which held her electronic address book. Like the decorating, she hadn't planned on sending out cards, but as soon as she'd given in to one thing, she'd found herself going the whole nine yards.

Well, she'd also been spurred on by her sister Annie's frantic call to go to a specialty store near the law firm to pick up a particular type of boxed cards because she'd run out. Annie always sent everyone the same card because, as she explained, what if someone thought that somebody else's card was better?

Besides, it kept things simpler that way and basically guaranteed that the same cards wouldn't be sent out the following year.

There was a certain logic to her sister's way of doing things, Lizzie thought, however boring.

While she was at the store she'd chosen individual cards for herself, some with music, some sentimental, others with a racy humor that would make Santa drop his jaw in shock.

"So what do you think?" her sister had asked her when she'd dropped the requested cards off at what Lizzie called the House of Chaos. "Do you think we're going to have Christmas at the parents' this year? Or should we maybe do it here?"

Lizzie had looked down at a cookie-crumb-covered Mason in her arms, drooling on her two-hundred-dollar sweater, then eyed three-year-old Jasmine's race through the living room on her tricycle. Any direct route in the house was impeded by scattered toys and a stray pet or two.

"Absolutely not," she said.

Lizzie was going to insist that they all gather at the

Gilbred family home and make the holidays happen, come hell or high water. She didn't care if her mother poisoned the turkey or if her father locked himself up in his study. Come Christmas morning, that's where she planned to be and she told Annie that she and their brother, Jesse, should have the same plan.

While Annie had looked dubious, Lizzie could see the wheels begin to turn in her head. Probably she was already thinking about going over to decorate the house like her mother used to and was planning the menu for Christmas dinner. So be it. As long as she did it in the house where they'd all grown up, Lizzie could eat her sister's idea of a holiday dinner, which would likely be a recipe out of one of her hundred cookbooks with *l'orange* something or other.

In the midst of her thoughts she realized she'd relaxed into her sofa with a cup of hot chocolate that was more lukewarm and was staring out the window.

It didn't take a rocket scientist to know what she was looking for. Or, more specifically, who.

But Gauge wasn't in his apartment. It was Friday night and he was playing down at the pub.

The image of him strumming his guitar on a bandstand made her hot.

But even if he had been home, there was no guarantee that they would be spending the night together. As he'd so refreshingly pointed out during their first night together, their relationship was all about sex. Nothing more. Nothing less.

And if her mind kept wandering back to their long,

leisurely kiss from the night before…well, that was because it had been so good. Nothing more. Nothing less.

At any rate, that morning while checking her cell-phone messages, she'd come across Jerry's text good-bye. And had taken great pleasure in pressing the delete button.

Jerry…

Was it a bad thing that she hadn't really thought about him the past couple of days? After all, she'd thought the guy was the one. Not just now, but six years ago. Was it natural for her to have moved on so quickly after his departure? Or was she practicing some sort of avoidance therapy by not dealing with whatever deeper emotions were connected to him and their breakup?

She sipped her drink and rolled the thought around in her head as Ella sung a swinging version of "Joy to the World." But the more she tried to concentrate, the clearer the memory of last night with Gauge became.

She checked her watch. After ten. Surely it wasn't too late to drive down to the pub and catch him playing with the band. She looked out the window at the accumulating snow. Three additional inches must have fallen since she got home from work.

Lizzie chewed on her bottom lip. If she did see him tonight, it would be three times in a row.

Was she replacing one obsession with another?

Not that she thought there could ever be anything serious between her and the sexy musician. They were too different for that.

Then again, she and Jerry had shared almost a scary

number of things in common, and they hadn't been able
to make it work.

"God, what are you thinking about?" she said under
her breath, getting up from the couch and carrying her
nearly empty cup into the kitchen. She rinsed it out and
placed it in the dishwasher then stood for long minutes
at the sink, listening to the silence of the house around
her, which was even more pronounced because of the
softly falling show outside.

Funny, she'd never really realized how quiet it was
until that moment. Considering she'd lived there for
half a year, that was saying something.

And here she'd thought Jerry's leaving wasn't bothering her in the least.

She sat back down in the family room, picked up the
remote to lower the volume on the CD and then
switched on the television to see what she could find to
distract her for one blasted night. *It's a Wonderful Life*
popped on.

She immediately turned the channel until she found
an action flick. *Die Hard.* Yes. That should do the
trick….

THE FOLLOWING DAY at lunch, Lizzie sat across from her
mother, trying not to notice how…happy she looked.

When she'd finally spoken to her mother, it was only
to arrange the Saturday-morning meeting. She hadn't
mentioned the other night at the house. And neither had
her mother. And that was fine with Lizzie. She'd rather try
to forget the scene than further entrench it in her memory.

And now that her mother sat opposite her at a booth in the Greek restaurant Dimitri's in Sylvania, not too far from the law firm, where Lizzie had put in a morning of work, she wondered if it had been a good idea to meet so soon after their last encounter.

"Mmm, everything looks so good," Bonnie said, reading the menu. "You've been here before?"

"What? Oh, yes. I come often enough."

She squinted at her mother, trying to pinpoint a reason for the improvement in her appearance. A reason that didn't have anything to do with her indulging in kinky sex with her father in Lizzie's childhood bed.

"Are you going to have time to fit in a bit of shopping after lunch?" her mother asked, once they'd placed their drink orders with the friendly waitress who was one of the owner's two daughters.

"Depends."

"On what?"

On whether or not the meal goes well, Lizzie thought. "On whether I get a return call from one of the clients I was supposed to meet this morning. Why?"

Bonnie shrugged. "I don't know. I figured if we were going to do a fair amount of walking at the mall today, then I could indulge a little now. But if we're not going to, then I should keep it light."

That was it. The difference. Her mother had lost weight.

Not that she'd needed to. While Bonnie Gilbred had always been a little on the round side, she'd never really been overweight. But now that she seemed to have shed at least ten pounds, she looked almost Lizzie's age.

Lizzie frowned. Okay, maybe not her age. But certainly younger than she had looked before, which was about five years older than she was.

Lizzie rubbed her forehead, her thoughts making no sense even to herself.

"I'll just keep it light anyway," her mother said.

"Have you changed your hairstyle?" Lizzie asked.

Bonnie's hand went to her hair. "Why yes. I decided to get some of those fancy highlights put in, you know, like all you kids get nowadays." She made a face. "Your father always liked my hair dark, but now that we're not going to be married anymore, I figure it's *my* hair and I can do anything I damn well please with it." She gave a secret smile. "But between you and me, I think he liked it."

Lizzie held up her hand. "You can stop right there, thank you very much."

"Why? What's wrong?" Lizzie didn't say anything and her mother gazed down at the table. "Oh. This is about the S and M bit you walked in on the other night. I'm sorry, honey. I would have preferred you not to have seen that."

S and M? What did her mother know about S and M?

Stupid question.

"It's not that, really," Lizzie said. "Well, yes it is." She leveled a stare at her mother. If they were going to talk about this, then she might as well be honest. "It was my bed."

She didn't know what she expected. A guilty expression. An apology. Instead, the elder Gilbred said, "It was the only bed in the house with four posts."

Lizzie's mouth gaped open. "Mother!"

"What? It's true."

"The bed is...was...mine."

Finally, it seemed to dawn on Bonnie why her daughter was so upset. And rather than being compassionate, she gave an eye roll to rival all eye rolls. "Oh, for god's sake, Lizzie, it's just a bed. A frame with two mattresses on it."

"It was my bed. My initials are carved in one of the bedposts."

"Yes, I was meaning to ask you when you did that. It's going to affect resale value, you know."

Lizzie's mouth worked around a response...only it refused to come. "What?" she fairly croaked.

"Well, you didn't think we were going to keep it forever, did you? Especially the way things stand. With your father and me getting a divorce, we're going to have to sell everything, divide up the money and move on with our lives..." She trailed off. "Although Clyde's saying he'd rather work out a different arrangement. Something like he buys out my half of the house and I pay him rent."

"Rent?" Lizzie repeated. How could her mother talk about these matters with such ease, as if they were as unimportant as the shape of the water glasses on the table? "You haven't worked for years. How are you going to pay rent?"

"There will be the money I get in the settlement," she said. "And then there's the job interview I have in January."

"What job interview?"

"With a fancy airline." She shifted and grinned. "I want to be a flight attendant."

Lizzie nearly spit out the water she'd just put in her mouth. "A what?"

Bonnie waved her hand. "Don't look so shocked. I was a great waitress in my day. And one of my old high school friends just got a job doing the same thing in California. The airlines are looking for us older girls with more life experience."

"And probably less pension requirements."

"Okay, fine. They don't pay as much as they used to, but seeing I've wanted to do this since I was a kid, well, I'd pay them for the experience."

Her mother. The flight attendant.

Someone wake her up from this nightmare.

Bonnie opened her mouth again and Lizzie held up her hand. "Please. That's enough for one day. What's say we just order and enjoy our meal, all right?" She rearranged the salt and pepper shakers, something, anything so she wouldn't have to look at her mother's crestfallen expression. "Have you talked to Annie today?"

Thankfully, Bonnie was just as happy to talk about her pregnant daughter as she was about the other areas of her life. Lizzie encouraged her as she reached for a bottle of extra-strength pain reliever in her purse.

10

SATURDAY NIGHT, Lizzie met Tabby for a late dinner. But rather than heading to a movie they were both ambivalent about seeing, Lizzie suggested they go somewhere else.

"A bar?" Tabitha said to her as she held aloft the last nacho oozing with cheese. She put it down and reached for a napkin. "Are you suggesting we, gasp, go to a meat market?"

Lizzie slowly sipped her coffee, hiding her smile. "It's not anything as nefarious as that. The place I'm thinking about is a pub, not a full-out bar."

"Meaning that they serve frozen chicken nuggets with the beer."

"Or nachos," she said, indicating the congealed mixture on the plate that had been on their table since their appetizers were served. Tabby had refused to allow the waiter to take it because she intended to eat every last one if it killed her.

"Ha-ha. You're a real hoot, Liz." Tabby sat back in the booth. "God, I wish you had said something before I ordered. I feel like I've put on five pounds in the past hour."

"That's because you probably have."

Tabby grimaced. "That's what Mondays are for. To fast to make up for Saturdays."

"You mean, Mondays, Tuesdays and Wednesdays."

"Yeah, what is it with that, anyway? Is it just me, or are the days gone when you could cut back one day and lose five pounds?"

"Definitely not just you. Which is why I ordered the black-bean soup."

Tabby waggled her finger at Lizzie. "No, you ordered the black-bean soup because you knew you were going to suggest going out. Only, you don't have to worry about any temporary tummy bulges showing on that sleek physique of yours."

"We don't have to go if you don't want to."

"Aha!"

"Aha what?"

"You knew I wouldn't be able to resist going to a bar with you. Now you'll have room for drinks, and I—" She sat back in the booth and groaned again. "God, I feel like a stuffed turkey."

"Yeah, well, you look great."

Tabby raised a skeptical brow. "Here I was planning on going light at the movies, you know, choosing a box of Raisinets over the Goobers and popcorn with extra butter, and all along you were saving room for apple martinis."

"I already said that we don't have to go."

"Of course we have to go. What, and pass up the opportunity for me to see this guy you've been sleeping with?" She raised her hand, ignoring Lizzie's gasp. "Check, please. Oh, and bring one of those take-out cartons, will you?"

Gauge wasn't sure how he knew the moment Lizzie entered, but he did. He rarely if ever watched the door, but tonight his gaze had gone to it the minute it opened and she walked inside with a dark-haired girlfriend. Just seeing her shrug out of her coat as the two took a table that had emptied in the middle of the room made it seem suddenly hot inside the bar. Not that she was wearing anything overtly sexy. That wasn't Lizzie's style. But knowing how very hot she was under that conservative clothing filled his mind with all sorts of erotic, welcome images.

The song ended and the group of young women who were already half in the bag near the front of the stage whistled and hooted and hollered. They'd just started the set or else he'd have asked the lead singer to break. As it was, he had to get through another hour of playing before he could think about making his way to Lizzie's table.

He only hoped she stayed long enough.

Last night, the echo from the amplifiers ringing in his head, he'd lain awake wondering if four in the morning was too late to go knocking on Lizzie's door. Of course, it had been. Her house had been dark when he'd returned home.

So he lay for a long time going over everything in his head. His conversation with Kevin. The night at the bar. Lizzie sleeping alone in her bed across the driveway. The fact that with anyone else, he wouldn't have thought twice before knocking on her door.

So why hadn't he gone over to Lizzie's?

He looked at her now as she took a long sip from a Guinness, returning his gaze as she did so. Damn, the woman was beautiful. But so were at least five other females in the joint that night. Why, then, did he feel like the air was being forced from his body when he looked at her?

His father had told him once that a man was lucky if he found love, real love, at least once in his life. And given his own experiences, Gauge was beginning to fear that was true. Oh, there was the temporary thrill of the hunt. The rush of sex with a stranger. But both were almost always followed by the desire to chase the same person from your bed the next morning with absolutely no interest in finding out what they liked for breakfast.

Then there was the fact that he *had* found love. With a woman who was married to his best friend.

Was it greedy to want another go at it? Was it even possible that he could be given the chance? Or would what he was feeling for Lizzie pass when he awakened one morning to find that she wasn't beautiful at all, but painfully normal? And that it wasn't enough for him anymore?

The lead singer acknowledged his playing along with the other band members and the patrons ignited in applause and cheers. He gave a thank-you run, but the only person that mattered was Lizzie. And she was standing and giving a wolf whistle.

"WELL, OKAY THEN. Mystery solved," Tabby said after Lizzie sat back down.

Lizzie slanted her friend a look, only to find her grinning.

Tabby held up her hands. "Hey, he's the hottest guy in the bar and he's a musician. What's not to like about that?"

She took a long pull of her Guinness.

"What?"

Lizzie shook her head. "I'm waiting for the rest."

"Rest? There is no rest." Tabby stuck her finger into her apple martini and sucked on the tip.

The band segued into the next song and Lizzie felt the incredible urge to dance. An urge she battled back because she knew her friend wasn't done. Tabby was never done. And Lizzie felt she needed to hear whatever she had to say.

"Just tell me the sex is great."

"The sex is mind blowing."

"Great. Great would have covered it. Mind blowing?" Tabby sat back and made a face. "It's official. I hate you."

Lizzie smiled. She'd never been officially hated before.

She began to rise and pull her friend up to go dance on the narrow floor in front of the band. Tabby caught her arm.

Uh-oh. She was afraid this was the "real rest" she'd been waiting for.

"You do know that it's temporary, though, right? I mean, I don't know anyone who goes on to marry one of these guys."

Lizzie laughed and yanked on her hand. "Of course I know it's temporary," she said. "Let's dance."

"Dance? We don't dance. Oh!" She stumbled to her feet and had to fight to keep balanced. "Okay, so we're dancing...."

THREE HOURS LATER, Gauge left the pub and made his way home. Lizzie and her friend had left some time before. Which had surprised him. He had hoped she would stay. Or at least made arrangements to meet up with him either at his place or hers.

Instead, she'd given him a brief wave from across the room and she and her friend had left.

He'd been disappointed, but not entirely surprised. When she'd introduced him to her friend, Tabitha, she hadn't said anything about his renting the apartment above her garage. So probably she'd left to make it look like they weren't returning to the same place.

He parked his car at the curb and walked through the snow that had accumulated on the driveway toward the back of the house, the tire tracks left by her car when she'd come home almost covered. He stopped short of the garage and turned toward Lizzie's place. Not a single window was lit.

He squinted against the light snowflakes that blew into his eyes. A sign that she wasn't looking for company tonight?

If so, then he'd misread her every signal at the pub. Because every time he'd looked at her, she'd worn the sly, suggestive expression that was timeless when it came to the mating dance.

Still, it appeared she'd come home and gone to bed. Alone.

If she'd wanted him to interrupt, at the very least she might have left a candle in the window.

He absently rubbed his chin, hunkered down further into his denim jacket, and continued on toward the garage. He climbed the stairs, shaking off the snow and cold before stepping inside. It was warmer than he expected. Hadn't he lowered the thermostat before leaving? He was pretty sure he had. But maybe he was remembering yesterday.

He shrugged out of his coat and went to the refrigerator, the inside light the only thing brightening the rest of the apartment. He took out the bottle of cold water there, drank a good portion of it, then walked toward the bed. He sat down and began taking off his boots.

"I thought you'd never get home," a familiar voice whispered. "One of the perks of being the landlord—I have my own key."

He grinned as a warm hand reached from between the sheets and touched his back, tunneling under his T-shirt to make contact with his skin.

He had never been happier that his ability to read women was target on.

LIZZIE HADN'T KNOWN what Gauge might make of her waiting for him, naked in his own bed, but she'd been unable to help herself when the idea occurred to her at the pub. She supposed it was the combination of the beer she'd drunk and the heightened sense of awareness that had grown all night.

She'd wanted Gauge, and she'd wanted him now.

But now that she had him, she was in no hurry. They had all night long to satisfy the hunger that roared inside her.

"On the surprise scale, I'd say this one rates a ten," he said, kicking off his boots and pulling off his T-shirt. He stretched to lie on top of the bedding while she was underneath. He rolled her closer to him, burying his hand in her hair.

"A good surprise?"

"Mmm. A very good surprise." He folded his other hand to support his head. "It was nice to see you at the pub tonight."

Lizzie splayed her fingers against his chest and the soft, light hair there. He was cold from having been outside, but was warming quickly. He smelled of freshly fallen snow and one hundred percent hot male. "Are you sure? There seemed to be about five other girls there vying for your attention."

"Mmm." He rested his chin on top of her head when she laid her cheek against his chest. "No, they were vying for the lead guitar player. You were the only one genuinely there for me." He turned her face to look at him.

"How can you be so sure it was you I was there to see?" She smiled. "Maybe I go to the pub all the time. Maybe it was a coincidence that you play there. Maybe Tabby's a frequent visitor."

He chuckled softly. "Right."

"God, I hate that I'm so predictable."

"Honey, your being there tonight was as unpredictable as they come."

She pressed her cheek against his shoulder, enjoying being this close to him. "Tabby liked you."

"Mmm. Your friend."

"She liked you a lot."

He didn't respond immediately, then said, "Well, I suppose I should be glad I came home to find you in my bed instead of her then, shouldn't I?"

She laughed and rolled on top of him, straddling him so that her naked womanhood rested against the front of his jeans.

"Would you have been that disappointed?"

He reached up, curving his hand around her neck and urging her closer to him. He paused when she was a breath away from kissing him. "I would have been very disappointed, indeed."

11

"I WANT TO SEE YOU…"

Gauge listened to the message on his machine that must have been there since before he returned home last night. He glanced across the room at his bed, where Lizzie still lay sleeping. The white sheets were tangled and, halfway down her back, her hair spilled across his pillow like liquid sunshine.

He knew a pang of regret. He'd gotten up to use the bathroom with every intention of returning to the warm bed with Lizzie in it. But he'd seen the message button flashing and checked it just in case one of the band members had called with a change of plans.

Instead it had been Nina.

He went into the bathroom and took a quick shower and then stayed in the kitchen, which gave him privacy from the sleeping area, and went about making coffee. It was after nine on a Sunday, but he knew that Nina would be at the bookstore café already.

Nina…

He stood, waiting for the coffee to brew, his mind filling with images of another time, another woman… and the other man who loved her.

"I would never have figured you for a morning person," Lizzie's sleepy voice said from behind him.

Gauge frowned, jerked from his thoughts. "I'm not."

There was a long silence. He turned to see her leaning against the counter, a sheet wrapped around her body. Her expression was pensive.

"Are you okay?" she asked.

Damn.

He still hadn't completely figured Lizzie out. But for reasons he had yet to fully explore, she seemed tuned into him on a level he couldn't ignore.

"Yeah, I'm all right. Just got a call from an old friend, is all."

She apparently noted the honesty of the answer and came up behind him, holding him for a long moment, her soft warmth encompassing him so that he longed to turn into her and carry her back to the bed.

But he couldn't. Not now. He needed to take care of some unfinished business.

Lizzie immediately seemed to sense his withdrawal and released her embrace.

"I've got to go," he said quietly.

She nodded, glancing at the floor before blinking back up to look into his eyes. Exploring. Seeking. But nowhere did he see judgment.

He went to put on his boots and then picked up his jacket and shrugged into it.

"And the coffee?" Lizzie asked, not having moved from the kitchen area.

"I made that for you."

How LONG had it been since he'd visited the store? Ten months, he realized, just before he'd left town. He sat outside in his car, taking in the exterior of the place and watching a plow make quick work of the snow in the lot that served several businesses.

It seemed strange being there now. Although he'd been back in town for some time, he'd made a point of avoiding the area. Avoiding any thought connected with it.

For three years this place and his partners, Nina and Kevin, had been an everyday part of his life. Begun when they decided one day over lunch at Nina's café to combine their three separate businesses into one mammoth one. All it had entailed was signing a few papers and breaking down a few walls.

Gauge rubbed the back of his neck, realizing that the physical walls weren't the only ones that had come down. For the first time in a long time, he'd let down a few of his emotional barriers. Allowed Nina and Kevin past defenses that had taken a lifetime of disappointment to build up and fortify. And for a short time he'd gotten a taste of what a family, a real family, was like.

At least until the day he'd proposed a night of anonymous sex to Nina…and encouraged Kevin, who'd always secretly been in love with her, to be the man to meet her.

He shook his head to clear the memory and climbed out of the car, the biting December air penetrating his clothes.

Signs of Christmas were everywhere. White lights blinking. Red bows blowing in the wind. Bells both big and small ringing. As a kid, Christmas Day had loomed much like any other to him. Usually he and his father would hang around the motel room, waiting for the hours to pass, watching TV. Maybe they'd go out for a turkey dinner at a nearby diner in whatever town they happened to be in.

If he was lucky, his father would give him a gift. One year, it had been a leather coat. Another a pair of boots. Mostly practical items that wouldn't take up too much room in the car and didn't cost too much, because there wasn't much money to spend.

He'd never really bought anyone a gift until the first Christmas Eve that he and Nina and Kevin had spent together. He'd found a rare edition of a Mark Twain novel for Kevin, and had bought Nina a gold necklace with cooking utensil charms on it.

What they had given him in return had been more than anything anyone could have bought: They'd given him inclusion and unconditional love.

Until he'd broken their trust by taking advantage of a vulnerable and confused Nina, who'd seemed to think he was her anonymous lover, not Kevin.

He stopped in front of the store and stared at the closed sign. They didn't officially open until eleven on Sundays, but he knew Nina would be there. He looked at the windows above the store where she used to have her apartment. Now it was seeing her car parked in the lot that told him she was there, since she had moved into Kevin's house after they married. He tried the door to find it locked and then knocked.

Almost immediately he saw Nina emerge from the

entryway to the music center, probably coming from the café beyond, and he was swept into the past, when he'd watched her make the journey several times a day. She paused for a moment on the other side of the glass, holding his gaze, then looked behind her before stepping forward to unlock the doors.

"I got your message," he said simply.

"Sure. Yes." She closed the door and locked it again, visually sweeping the parking lot. "Why didn't you use your key?"

It honestly hadn't occurred to him. "You alone?"

"Um, yes. Kevin should be in soon. I had to come in to get the normal morning baking out of the way." She passed him. "Come on. I have some sticky buns in the oven."

He followed, watching her own personal set of nicely rounded buns, even though he told himself he shouldn't. Hey, he was only human. And a man at that. Surely looking never hurt anybody.

They started walking through the music center and he paused, taking in the many changes that had been made. Where he had favored darker, more intimate lighting, fluorescent bulbs had been installed, brightening the area. His posters of classic blues and rock icons had been exchanged for life-size stand-up cardboard cutouts of current pop sensations. He stopped in front of one of Britney Spears and frowned.

"The new manager had his own ideas."

He nodded. Hey, while he might still own a third of the shop, he'd forfeited his right to say how the place should be run when he'd left town ten months ago. It wasn't his space anymore.

"Making more money?"

Nina stood in the doorway to the café, watching him. "Profits of the music center are up fifteen percent."

He raised his eyebrows and then nodded. Nothing like being told that someone else was doing a better job than he had.

"Come on," she said, turning again.

Gauge followed, the hollow feeling in his stomach beginning to grow.

Nina disappeared into the kitchen and he opened the door, watching her take the buns out of the oven, big, red oven mitts on her hands. She donned a snowy-white apron over her standard uniform of black stretchy pants and white, short-sleeved shirt, everything hugging her slender body to sleek perfection. She took the mitts off and then slathered the sticky glaze on top of the fresh buns.

How many mornings and evenings had the three of them hung around in this kitchen in the café or the large, stone fireplace in the bookstore, just chatting and enjoying one another's company? It seemed to have been just yesterday, yet at the same time years ago.

"Want one?" Nina asked, breaking off one of the buns and putting it on a plate. She placed it on the stainless-steel prep island close to where he stood.

Gauge released the door so that it could close and stepped fully inside the kitchen. "Thanks."

She shot a brief smile at him, appearing to be going out of her way not to meet his gaze as she put in another batch of baking and took out a finished tray. She frowned, testing for doneness. "Damn oven. It's been acting up for a couple of days now."

"Would it be better if I came back later?" he asked.

"What?" His question had apparently caught her up short. Finally, she ceased her nonstop activity. She grasped the edge of the counter, took a deep breath and then smiled, meeting his gaze. "Sorry. Things have been hectic around here, what with the Christmas rush and losing Heidi to her catering company. I didn't expect you so soon, that's all. I guess maybe I was hoping you'd call so we could meet when…"

"When Kevin's around?"

She caught her bottom lip between her teeth then nodded. "Yeah."

She fidgeted with her left hand. Gauge realized she was moving her wedding ring back and forth.

"How about some coffee to go with that roll?" she asked.

She started past him to go back out into the café area. Gauge caught her arm.

He took in the catch of her breath, her hard swallow and the widening of her pupils as she stared at the door rather than at him.

He knew in that one moment that if he wanted to, he could pull her into his arms and she'd come.

The realization hit him with the force of a bulldozer.

Could she really still be attracted to him? Drawn to him the way he was to her? Why? She'd taken vows with another man. A man he knew she loved. Kevin. A best friend to both of them.

No matter how much he might have liked to test the possibility, he instead picked up her left hand and admired the wedding band there, along with a rock the size of Gibraltar. She deserved the largest diamond ever mined.

He released her hand. "It suits you."

She blinked at him curiously. "What?"

"The ring…being married. It suits you."

Her chin dipped as she smiled. "Thanks."

He reached out and held the door open for her, and could hear her sigh of relief as she passed him.

Moments later both of them sat safely at the counter, near enough to touch but purposely not touching.

Gauge felt he'd passed some sort of test. Not of Nina's making, but of his own. When he'd refused to act on the rush of testosterone in the kitchen, he'd broken through a threshold he hadn't known had been waiting for him.

"So," Nina said, smiling into her coffee mug. "I hear that Kevin came to see you the other day."

Gauge had hoped Kevin wouldn't have entered their conversation so early. The problem was, Kevin was the main issue between them.

Or was he?

No. Nina was trying to make it Kevin, but the truth was he and Nina had their own business to attend to. And until they did, no one was going to move forward.

"Yeah," Gauge said. "He came to see me. Came close to finally hitting me."

She looked alarmed.

"Don't worry. He kept his ever-present cool."

She didn't say anything for a long moment. Merely held on to her coffee cup until her knuckles whitened. "And you?"

Now there was a question. "I tried like hell to taunt him into knocking my lights out."

"Of course."

Gauge went silent, looking around at everything that was familiar, and those things that weren't.

Then he asked the question that he'd come there to ask. "That night…"

Nina went instantly stiff.

"Don't you think it's time that we both stopped pretending? You knew as much as I did that Kevin was the mystery man. So why did you sleep with me?"

12

GAUGE WASN'T one for scrounging around in the past for an answer he needed today. He'd come to learn that the past was best left where it was.

At least that's what he used to believe.

Now…

Well, now, he wanted…no, needed, to continue rebuilding that bridge he'd started three years ago.

Nina didn't respond to his question. At least not verbally. Physically, her every movement gave away her uneasiness.

"I don't know that I'm following you," she finally said, looking everywhere but at him.

Gauge felt defeat settle in around him. If he couldn't convince her to confront what had really happened between the three of them ten months ago, he held out little hope of repairing their relationship.

"Come on, Nina," he said quietly. "You can't tell me that in your heart of hearts, you didn't know that Kevin was the man you'd slept with. And that when you came to me—"

She quickly held up her hand. "No. Please. Stop."

He turned toward her. "No. I can't. Whatever's said here stays here. Between us. Between you and me. But we need to talk about this. You need to understand the role you played in what happened that night."

"A mistake happened."

Gauge winced, feeling as if she'd just sucker punched him.

And she had. Not physically, of course. But she'd landed an emotional wallop that was even more effective.

And the frustrating and saddening thing of it was, she knew it.

He started to get up. "Then I guess we have nothing to talk about. Don't call me. I won't call you."

"Gauge, wait." She reached out, grasping his coat sleeve. It was a light touch, but could have been a handcuff for all the control Gauge had over his own response.

He stopped, waiting.

"I don't know. Obviously you've been thinking a lot about that night."

"And you haven't?"

She looked down and nodded.

"And what conclusion have you come to, Nina? Beyond recognizing it as the mistake we all know it was."

She blinked up at him. "I…I…" She took a deep breath and let it out slowly, then laughed without humor. "You're really not going to back down from this, are you?"

He shook his head.

She appeared a blink away from tears.

Gauge reached out and cupped her face in his hand.

"Look, Nina. I'm not trying to hurt you. I came back to Fantasy to try to fix things. Make my way back to where we were."

She narrowed her gaze.

"Not that night. No, before then. Before you and I slept together."

She appeared relieved but only marginally.

"And if we stand a chance of doing that—and I think even you're coming to realize it's a long shot—then we have to understand why we did what we did."

She grasped her coffee mug again. "You're right."

Gauge sat back down and pretended an interest in his own coffee.

"So...where do we start?"

"Probably at the beginning."

SOMETIME LATER, Gauge felt better than he had in a long time. And he recognized that it wasn't only understanding that needed to happen, but acceptance. He felt that he and Nina had made great strides toward that end.

The problem was they'd forgotten about one other person: Kevin.

They heard the footsteps before either of them had a chance to react. Gauge had just said something in response to Nina and she had leaned into him much as she once had, laughing.

Nina looked over her shoulder at her husband and Gauge followed her gaze. Kevin's face was drawn tight as he gave them a once-over and then turned to walk back toward the bookstore without saying anything.

Thankfully, Nina didn't get up to run after him. She didn't even seem that concerned about his being upset.

Gauge would like to think it was because of the inroads they'd made that morning.

Nina's soft sigh spoke of her frustration when it came to her husband. "Do you think you two will ever be able to work this out?"

Gauge tilted his cup to find it empty. "I don't know, Nina. I don't know."

She touched his upper arm and squeezed. "Yes, well, I want you to make it right. I miss you. I miss us as a threesome."

He grinned at her.

Rather than blushing or acting coy, she smacked his arm and laughed in a teasing manner that told him that the two of them had definitely turned a corner for good.

"Get your mind out of the gutter, Patrick Gauge."

"Never."

LIZZIE SPENT the better part of the morning back at her house feeling…odd. As if something important was left hanging in the air, just out of her reach. But it was going to take Gauge's cooperation in order to reach it.

She glanced away from the Christmas cards she was hand addressing toward the garage and the apartment above it for the fifth time in so many minutes.

"Oh, just stop it," she ordered herself, putting double the energy into her card-writing efforts.

Her brother, Jesse, had called, asking if she had some coffee to spare. She'd readily invited him over. Anything to keep from wondering where Gauge had gone. And if he was going to help her reach that something important. Or leave it hanging there forever.

Of course, it only stood to reason that Jesse would arrive and Gauge would return at the same time.

She watched as her brother drove his pickup down the driveway, stopping just short of the garage so he could come in the back, as all of them had been taught to do at their parents'. Just as he was getting out, Gauge was walking to his place. The two men shook hands, and Gauge glanced toward the window and gave a wave before disappearing up the stairs.

Damn.

Damn, damn, damn.

Jesse and his bad timing. Would things ever change?

She opened the back door before he reached it and directed him to wipe his boots on the rug there. She looked to see if Gauge was still in view. He wasn't. She closed the door.

"He's still here, huh?" Jesse asked.

Since it had been Jesse's ex-girlfriend Heidi who had recommended Gauge for the place, her brother was familiar with him. That, and the fact Jesse seemed to have spent the better part of his adult years in the pub where Gauge occasionally played, though she understood he still partially owned the BMC.

Lizzie stretched up on tiptoe to kiss her younger brother. "How's it going, kiddo?"

Even though only a few years separated them, it seemed like more to her. Her mother had told her it had something to do with emotional intelligence. That men didn't age as quickly as their female counterparts. But Lizzie was beginning to wonder if it was just the way they were made.

"Hey, yourself." He gave her a once-over as he shrugged out of his sheepskin coat and hung it on a hook near the door. "You look good. Did you go to church or something?"

"Mmm. Or something."

She wasn't dressed especially nice. Liar. Okay, so she had put on a nice pair of slacks and a black cashmere sweater that kept slipping down over either one or the other of her shoulders.

"Coffee?"

"I'd prefer a beer if you got one."

"I thought you came for coffee." She looked to find it after noon and took a beer from the fridge. She kept his favorite brand especially for him.

"I was talking figuratively."

"Right. Well, you don't mind if I have coffee since I made it already."

"Not at all."

He walked into the family room as she fixed herself a fresh cup of coffee and then switched off the maker. She'd already had two cups and should probably pass on another, but seeing as she hadn't gotten a whole hell of a lot of sleep the night before, she figured it couldn't hurt.

She took a seat on the couch next to Jesse, who was going through her cards.

"Why are you sending one to the Wilsons? Doesn't Mom say they're the rudest couple on earth?"

"Yes, but she also sends them a card every year, too."

He gave her a "whatever" nod and then settled back on his side of the couch. "So I hear you and the parents had an interesting run-in the other day."

"Annie has a big mouth."

"And that's news how?"

Lizzie laughed. "Got me there. I just hope she waited until the kids were out of the room before she said something."

"Right. No point damaging their lives like our parents did ours."

Lizzie took a sip of her coffee and then put it down on the table. "So what brings you around my way? Has something happened with Mom and Dad?"

"You mean, beyond their continued World War Three battle plans?" He shook his head. "No. Nothing on that front."

Lizzie grimaced. She should have stopped hoping something would have happened by now. That some sort of lightbulb would go off above their heads and make them realize they were still in love and should remain a couple.

This from the most unromantic woman in existence, if you listened to her friend Tabby.

"No, I came to ask your advice on something."

Lizzie curled her right leg under her and faced him better. "Shoot."

"It's about Mona."

She pretended neutrality at the mention of her brother's new girlfriend but must have missed the mark.

Jesse tsked. "What is it with you guys and Mona? Why don't you like her?"

"I never said I don't like her." She'd just liked Heidi, his ex-fiancé, better.

"You don't have to. It's written all over your face whenever I bring up her name."

Lizzie sighed. "I'm sorry, Jesse. I guess maybe we just need a little time. You know, to get to know her."

"She's been around far more often than Heidi ever was."

"Maybe that's the problem."

Jesse squinted at her, looking so much like the handsome kid she remembered growing up. "How so?"

"I'm just saying that I'm surprised you didn't bring her along with you here today, that's all. Everywhere you go, she goes."

"She's my girlfriend."

"So she is."

"So why isn't she here today?"

Jesse looked down at his clasped hands. "She's mad at me because I forgot our three-year anniversary."

"Three-year anniversary? You guys have only been a couple for the past few months."

"Yeah, I know. She's counting from the time we met in Boston."

Lizzie forced herself not to say anything. Mona was including, of course, the time Jesse had officially been engaged to Heidi.

"Anyway, that's not why I'm here. I don't give a flying fig if any of you like her. I love her. And you're just going to have to deal with it."

Lizzie nodded, praying that Mona finally delivered on her frequent threats to head back to Boston…alone.

"I want you to help me come up with a really unique way to propose to her on Christmas Eve…."

Lizzie looked around for something to hit him with but came up short. "Don't you think it's a little too soon?"

He glared at her.

"Oh, right," she said. "It's been three years." She drummed her fingers against the sofa back and tried to pretend that she was concentrating. "I'd have to say that if you want to be unique, you shouldn't propose on Christmas Eve then."

"God, I should have known you'd say something like that. You're all just hell-bent on trying to get us to break up, aren't you?"

Lizzie leaned forward, affronted. "Jesse, it wasn't that long ago that you were engaged to be married to someone else."

"Someone else who's now marrying my best friend."

"Oh. Yes. Right." She waved her hand. "Anyway, that's not what we're talking about." She sat back and sighed. "Look, you just said you wanted it to be unique, didn't you?"

"Really unique."

"Right. Really unique." She turned her hands palms up. "Then that means not proposing on any of the days that other holidays are celebrated. You know, like Valentine's Day, birthdays, Halloween, Christmas…" She counted them off on her fingers.

Jesse blinked at her. "Mona told me that if she doesn't get an engagement ring on Christmas, she's going back to Boston."

The words *let her,* followed by a loud hooray, weren't going to get her anywhere, so she bit her tongue.

"So what's keeping you from doing it today?"

He appeared spellbound. "What?"

She shrugged and reached for her coffee cup, unable to believe she was helping her brother propose to a woman who had to be the biggest slut, the most manipulative shrew Lizzie had ever met. No matter how sexy she was. "Sure. It's your third anniversary, right? So propose to her today. Now. Go out and buy her a great ring—"

"The biggest."

She gave an eye roll. "Right. The biggest ring you can afford," she said, putting emphasis on the last word. "Go back and tell her to get ready, and then take her out somewhere so you can propose."

"Where?"

"I don't know! God, do you want me to cinch the deal by sleeping with her, too?"

Jesse flashed a grin. The same grin that had nearly every woman he met swooning for the chance to go out with him. And here he'd brought a slut back from Boston.

"I've got it!" he said.

"Great," Lizzie muttered.

"I'll take her sledding."

"Sledding as in 'trudging up a hill and getting all covered with snow' sledding?"

"Yeah. She won't expect anything then."

"And she'll probably shove your face in the snow." Lizzie tapped her finger against her lips. "Take her sleigh riding."

It seemed to take him a moment to lock on to what she was saying.

"Yes," she said, leaning forward and warming to her own idea. "Go to Mom and Dad's and get the thickest, softest, nicest blanket you can find, pick up a bottle of champagne and a couple of glasses, and tell her it's to celebrate your anniversary…only the gift you'll give her is a proposal."

Jesse catapulted from the couch. "Perfect!"

He pulled her up from the couch and gave her a big hug, swinging her around in a circle. "Thanks, sis." He kissed her loudly on the cheek. "I knew you'd come through for me."

"Yes, well…whatever."

He chuckled as he grabbed his coat in the kitchen and opened the door.

"Good luck!" she called after him.

She wasn't sure if he heard, since he practically ran for his car, nearly slipping on the ice as he went.

Lizzie pulled her sweater up where it had slid down her shoulder again, watching as Jesse backed out. Then she switched her gaze to the apartment over the garage, wondering if she should trek out and see Gauge.

Instead she slowly closed the door and decided she'd wait and let him come to see her.

13

MUCH LATER that afternoon, Lizzie lay back in her bed watching dusk begin to darken the eastern sky, the top sheet sliding from her naked right breast…a breast that Gauge instantly took into his mouth and suckled, reigniting the fire that seemed to forever be in her belly whenever he was nearby.

Oh, Gauge had come over to the house, all right. A scant five minutes after Jesse had left. And the two of them had been in bed in the hours since.

"Mmm." Lizzie arched her back, stretching her sore muscles and reaching for a piece of blue cheese from a tray she'd prepared during a break earlier and put on the side table. "You can't possibly be ready to go again."

Gauge leisurely licked her nipple, then pulled the sheet from her left breast and gave that nipple equal time. Lizzie wriggled as the pressure built between her legs.

Gauge plopped back down onto the pillow next to hers and they both lay staring at the ceiling. "You're right. It's going to take another minute or two."

Lizzie laughed and tossed a grape his way. It landed

on his stomach, where he trapped it with his hand. Picking it up, he sucked on it briefly, and then tunneled his hand under the sheet. Lizzie gasped when she felt the cold fruit make contact with her overheated genitals. Then she spread her thighs to give him better access.

He rolled the grape around her clit and then down and back up again.

Then he took his hand out and ate the grape.

"You naughty, naughty boy, you," she murmured, now ready for another round herself as she rolled to her side and kissed him.

He returned her kiss while chewing on the grape until she ended up with a portion of it in her mouth.

Then she collapsed next to him and groaned. "I don't think there's a single part of me that doesn't hurt or pulse or both."

"That's a good thing."

Lizzie smiled from ear to ear. "That's definitely a good thing."

"So, I didn't get a chance to ask you earlier. What did your brother want?"

"Mmm. He was soliciting advice on how to propose to his whore of a girlfriend."

Gauge's laugh was so unexpected it made Lizzie grin, though she kept her eyes closed and nestled her head deeper into her pillow.

"Mona's not a whore," he said. "She's a woman who knows her sexual power and isn't afraid to use it."

"That's right. I forgot that you already know her. You know, her being the bar slut that she is."

He chuckled again. "And here I thought you were the nonjudgmental type."

"Me? The successful trial attorney?"

"Mmm. Stupid of me."

"Blame my parents. Only a couple named Bonnie and Clyde would have a Lizzie, Annie and Jesse as children. Seems I've been trying to buck expectations since the day I was born."

She opened her eyes and stared at the ceiling and the three pools of light for long moments. Gauge had decided he'd had enough of the dark last night and had turned on the lamps, wanting to watch her face when she came.

"Gauge?"

"Hmm?"

"Are you sleeping?"

"Not yet."

She heard the sheets rustle.

"What is it?"

"Nothing. It's just that, do you ever wonder if love is just something we convince ourselves to feel?"

She realized she'd just introduced the ultimate four-letter word into a bed that had been reserved solely for sex.

"Not us," she said quickly. "I'm thinking about my brother...my parents...."

She forced herself to look over at him, to make sure he hadn't taken her words wrong. She found him staring contemplatively at the ceiling, his hand against hers, absently rubbing it.

"I don't know," he said. "It could be."

His response made her feel better. She relaxed again and entwined her fingers with his. "I mean, just look at my parents. They're supposed to be in the middle of a divorce…scratch that, they *are* in the middle of a divorce after thirty years of marriage, and yet every time my sister or brother or I turn around, they're having sex somewhere or other in the house."

She moved her head toward Gauge at the same time he looked at her.

She burst out laughing. "I know. TMI. Welcome to my life. I can't remember a time when one of us didn't stumble upon them. The other day I caught them in my old bedroom with leather and feather."

He rolled to his side and propped his head up on his hand. "Sounds like an idea to me."

Lizzie made a face. "I don't think I could get the picture of the two of them out of my head long enough to enjoy myself."

Gauge trailed his fingertips over her shoulder blades, into the valley between her breasts, around her nipples, and then down to circle her navel. She shivered. "Oh, I don't know," he said quietly, leaning over to blow in her ear. "I think I could make you forget."

She smiled at him. "You know what I mean."

"Yes. I think I do. The same thing used to happen with me when it came to my father."

His expression seemed faraway.

"Oh?"

"Mmm. Since we were on the road so much, and my dad didn't make much money as bass player in whatever band he'd temporarily hooked up with, we always shared a motel room." He focused on her and grinned. "You can't imagine how many times I walked in on him. Or woke up in the middle of the night to sounds of sex from the next bed. Or went into the bathroom to find a strange woman in the shower or on the commode."

"You're kidding?"

"Nope. Lost my virginity to one of those women when I was thirteen. She had some fantasy of being a virgin's first. And I…well, I was thirteen."

Yikes.

Lizzie was transfixed, listening to him tell the story as if he were a visitor from another planet and was casually talking about the weather.

"And here I've been used to being the odd one out with horny parents. Never mind that they're named Bonnie and Clyde and named their kids after notorious outlaws."

"Did they ever have sex somewhere where they knew you'd find them?"

"What, like exhibitionists? No. They just liked to have sex, I guess. And when you have three kids running around the place, you're bound to get caught."

Gauge reached for another grape. She gasped when he pressed it against her right nipple.

"But enough about me. You apparently have me beat hands down on childhood horror stories."

He rolled the grape over to her other nipple, following the cold trail with the warmth of his tongue. Not with any destination in particular, merely appearing to enjoy the journey. "I don't see them as horror stories. My life was what it was. And I knew I was lucky to have it."

"Lucky?" She watched him move the grape down to her navel, where he left it and reached for another one.

"Mmm."

"If you guys traveled so much, did you go to school?"

"When I could."

Lizzie raised her brows. She had almost nineteen years of school, all told, what with getting her bachelor's and then her law degree. "Did you graduate?"

"I passed the GED." He grinned at her. "I also have a few semesters of college. Music mostly. Some literature. Not enough credits in either for a degree, but not too far off."

She couldn't remember seeing any books in his apartment. He told her one of the first places he checked out in a new town was the local library.

"Where's your father now?"

He fell silent.

And Lizzie wished she could take the words back...

WHERE WAS HIS FATHER NOW, indeed...

Everyone had parents. It was a fact of life that it took a man's sperm to fertilize a woman's egg. Yes, he had parents. Biologically speaking. And he supposed his father had done the best he could. Most times Gauge was satisfied with leaving it at that.

Then there were times when he wondered what if.

What if his parents had been a couple rather than a one-night stand that had resulted in a pregnancy and pretty much an unwanted child? What if his mother hadn't dumped him on his father's doorstep when he was six? What if he'd had a normal upbringing in a normal neighborhood and gone to a normal school, rather than living the vagabond lifestyle he'd come to know, if not love?

"There's a lot to be said for the way I was raised," he found himself saying quietly. "I've traveled to a lot of places. Learned firsthand what might take others years to understand about music. Met some incredible people. Jimmy Witherspoon, Bo Diddley, John Lee Hooker, Stevie Ray Vaughan…I mean, man. What talent. I'd listen to any one of those guys and spend the next month trying to emulate them on my secondhand acoustic guitar…."

He paused, snapshots from different bars, different blues players, smiles and laughter coalescing into a musical collage.

"When I was a teen, I didn't have a curfew or rules. I could do pretty much what I wanted when I wanted. Every teenager's dream, I'm told."

At the time, he hadn't known any better. Sure, through television shows he watched, and some of the other kids he came in contact with, he understood that the way he and his father lived wasn't the way everyone lived. But it had been his reality. It was completely normal for him to sit at a beat-up table in the back of a bar during the day going over his math homework with a waitress while his father practiced with the band.

Meals were grabbed when he or his father thought about it, often bar fare serving to tide him over. He'd once gone five days with nothing more than peanuts and pretzels as nutrition, and orange juice that was meant to be mixed with alcohol.

When he was too young to play in the band, he'd swept floors and cleaned out toilets and was once awakened at one in the morning in a motel to go clean up vomit in the men's room of the bar because the waitress refused to do it.

He'd been nine and hadn't thought anything unusual about the request. He'd merely done the job and pocketed the two bucks the owner gave him.

"My father was a good man," he said aloud. "'I ain't never hit a woman, or hurt a child,' he used to say. Of course, later on, he'd added the word *intentionally* to the latter part of the statement because he'd fathered at least three other children with three other women that he knew about. All of them in different parts of the country."

He glanced at Lizzie to find her shocked or fascinated or a combination of both.

"Do you... I mean, have you fathered any children?" she whispered.

"Me?" He smiled. "No. As soon as my father figured out I was sexually active, he threw a box of condoms at me. Told me not to make the same mistakes he did."

Lizzie cringed. "Ouch."

"Tell me about it." He rubbed a small, narrow scar

just above his right eyebrow. "This is where the corner of the box hit me."

He fell silent for a minute, marveling at all he'd told her. At how easy it was to let the memories flow out like water from a rusty can.

She curled closer to his side and he slid his arm under her head and rubbed her arm. So soft.

"So you haven't said where he is now. Your father, I mean."

Gauge's throat tightened. "He's in Saint Louis."

"Is he still playing?"

He gave a lopsided smile as he imagined his old man playing bass guitar in heaven. "Maybe." He turned his head to look down at her. "He's buried in a small church graveyard just outside East Saint Louis."

"Oh, God. I'm sorry. I didn't know… I mean, I assumed…"

"Don't be sorry. You didn't kill him. Booze did."

He'd had no idea his father was ill. There was nothing to suggest there was anything wrong with him. If he moved a little slow, Gauge had guessed it was because he was getting older. If he clutched his side every now and again, he'd say it must have been something he ate. Or maybe it was those damn kidney stones his own father used to have.

Then came the day Gauge had come back from trying to charm one of the town girls outside a private school a couple of miles away. He needed to get his father up so he could go pick up his pay from the bar…but his dad wouldn't wake up.

He'd been sixteen. No other family that he knew of outside the kid in Arizona. And no idea where he went from there.

"His old beat-up truck and his guitar and a half-empty bottle of Jack is about all he left me."

He heard Lizzie's thick swallow and looked down to find her eyes bright with tears.

"Shh," he said, wiping her cheek with his thumb. "That was a long time ago. And I'm here now. And okay."

"I know," she said haltingly, as if doubting her ability to speak. "It's just… God, that must have been so hard for you."

"It wasn't easy. But like I said, it was what it was." He continued stroking the soft skin of her back. "I stepped in to play for my father that night. Everyone chipped in to help bury him. And two days later, I stood over his grave with the waitress that had been his stop-over lover."

"What did you do after that?"

"What we did together before. I went from town to town, gig to gig. Turning down any offers of a permanent spot in a band in exchange for a change of scenery and a different bed and different woman every other week or so."

Lizzie curved her arm around him and squeezed, kissing his neck. "Was there never anyone special?"

"Once." He squinted at the ceiling. "Maybe twice." If you counted Nina, he silently added. And he did.

Then there was the woman in his arms. It was still too soon to say whether anything would come of his and

Lizzie's affair. But the mere fact that he'd shared what he had, that she'd found a way to coax it out of him, spoke volumes.

And when it came to sex, she definitely ranked right up there with the best. Inventive. Wanton. And thoroughly insatiable.

"How did you end up here in Fantasy?"

He chuckled softly and kissed her. "Let's just say that there was something tempting about fulfilling all my fantasies in Fantasy."

She smiled as she shifted her left leg over his and then slid on top of him, straddling him even as she kissed him.

"Let's see what I can do to help…."

LIZZIE GASPED when Gauge turned her back over, wedging his hips between her thighs. She felt his hard, thick erection pulsing against the tender folds of her womanhood, unprotected and hot.

She stared up into his face. Taking in the scar above his brow. Noting the other scars that he hadn't shared the origins of. Compassion for this man crashed over her, flowed through her, until all she knew was this one moment in time. This one instant when nothing else mattered.

She'd never known anyone with a past so different from hers. And that he had shared as much as he had touched a part of her deep inside. She combed his thick hair back from his forehead with her fingers, hotter for him than she could remember ever being for another man. And connected in a way she didn't want to explore.

He reached for the bedside table and plucked a grape from the plate. He placed it between her lips. She bit into the fleshy fruit and then welcomed his kiss. He pulled away and she swallowed, watching as he took another grape and placed it on her breastbone. She fought to regulate her breathing, transfixed as he used his nose to nudge the fruit down between her breasts, licking her skin as he went.

THE RINGING OF THE FRONT DOORBELL roused Lizzie from a state that teetered between wakefulness and sleep. Gauge's arm was around her waist, pulling her backside to his front.

"Expecting company?" he murmured.

She glanced at the clock. Just after seven. Gauge would have to be leaving soon.

She ignored the doorbell and snuggled closer to him, wiggling her bottom against his semiaroused member. "I don't want to get up."

"So don't."

The shrill ring of the doorbell sounded again, as if in response to his comment.

Lizzie groaned. "Whoever it is knows I'm home. Probably they saw the lights on up here. And my car's in the garage."

"So?"

She closed her eyes and smiled. Was life really so simple?

Yes, she realized. It could be if she wanted it to.

Then the different options of who the visitor might be ran through her mind. She'd set the home phone to privacy so all calls went directly to voice mail. And her cell phone was down in the family room on vibrate. The only sure way anyone could get in contact with her in case of emergency was if they came to her house.

She thought of her brother, who might have taken his girlfriend on that sleigh ride to propose. Could the horse have bolted and Mona broken her neck? One could only hope. Then again, it could have been Jesse who'd been hurt.

Then there was the whole situation with her parents.

She groaned again and wriggled out of Gauge's arms, grabbing her robe from the post at the foot of the bed where she'd left it earlier to get the cheese plate. He rolled to his back and folded his arms behind his head, looking like a Greek god as he watched her. A scraggly, battle-scarred Greek god with tattoos and, she was learning, a heart of gold.

"Sorry. I've got to get this."

"By all means," he said with a grin. "Mind if I use your shower?"

"Go ahead."

She put her slippers on and tied her belt as she went. The humongous one-size-fits-all Turkish terry-cloth robe was the one she'd bought from a hotel in Chicago and big enough to cover everything.

Well, everything but the stubble burn she felt on her chin and neck. But that was okay. She could always

claim she wasn't feeling well. That would justify a day
in bed as easily as the reality.

Although the reality was much better than any fantasy she could have concocted.

She hurried down the stairs and pulled open the door
in the middle of the next ring.

And stood staring at the last person she'd expected
to find there.

"Jerry!"

14

LIZZIE COULDN'T HAVE BEEN more surprised had the pope been standing on her doorstep. It took a full minute for the reality of the situation to sink in. Her ex-boyfriend, who'd dumped her via text message two weeks ago, was there…and her new boyfriend was upstairs in her bedroom.

The facts were dizzying.

She expected him to look at her and know instantly what she'd been up to. Instead, Jerry brushed right by her into the house, something in a brown paper bag tucked under his arm.

"What took you so long? It's freezing out there."

He turned to face her and Lizzie closed the door after him, trying to decide what her options were. But she was slow to come up with any answers.

Jerry grinned and held out his right hand. "I'm free, baby. I've left her for good this time."

Lizzie made herself blink.

Had he just said what she thought he had?

He put the bag down on the foyer table. "I just couldn't be there anymore. Not after I realized that this is where I want to be. That you're the one I love. Not her."

Lizzie stared at him, as if incapable of bringing him or his words into focus. Worse, she completely failed to relate what he was saying to her current predicament.

And he couldn't have been more oblivious to her condition had he worn a blindfold.

She watched as he took out the item from the bag. Her waffle maker.

"Jerry," she said quietly.

He appeared not to hear her as he looked around. "I never realized how much this place feels like home."

"Jerry," she repeated, more loudly.

"These past two weeks have been hell." He started shrugging out of his London Fog overcoat. A coat she'd helped him pick out. "I've missed you."

"Jerry!" she almost shouted.

He blinked at her as if she'd punched him in the stomach.

Lizzie could now see the man she'd spent so much of her life convincing herself that she loved in a new light. He was handsome enough with his light brown hair and pale green eyes. Working out at the gym guaranteed he had a nice body. An expensive dentist had given him an expensive smile.

But somehow she'd never recognized the…useless air that clung to him like his expensive cologne. A clueless bearing that made him seem to work on autopilot. He hadn't looked directly at her once since she'd opened the door. Probably because he was concerned about what she might say if given half the chance.

Then again, no. That would be giving him too much credit. Instead, his shallowness rendered him immune to any and everyone around him as he went about his own business, expecting the world to expand and contract to accommodate him.

"What are you doing here?" she asked, now that she finally had his attention.

He glanced over at her then looked at his watch. "What are you doing in a robe at seven o'clock on a Sunday night?"

No, *Are you feeling all right? Is everything okay?* Instead, he'd chosen to couch his remark in a way that might have made her feel underdressed two weeks ago.

Now it made her mad.

"Answer my question, Jerry."

"What question?" He folded his coat over his arm. Probably because he'd have to get by her in order to hang it up in the closet.

"What are you doing here?"

"I told you, baby." He stepped toward her, putting on his best grin. "I've come back to you."

Movement in the upstairs hall caught Lizzie's attention. She gasped at the sight of Gauge, still completely nude at the stop of the stairs, leaning against the wall, his arms crossed.

Before she could recover enough to distract Jerry, her usually clueless ex turned to follow her gaze.

Gauge crossed his feet at the ankles, his semierect

penis curving down his right thigh for God and everyone to see.

Lizzie wished the robe would swallow her whole.

Jerry narrowed his eyes, as if unable to believe what he was seeing. Much the way Lizzie had looked at him as he'd brushed his way inside her house.

Gauge gave a little wave.

Lizzie was instantly furious with two men rather than one.

A LITTLE WHILE LATER, Lizzie paced back and forth in her bedroom, trying to get a handle on her emotions. Jerry had left—shocker—taking his waffle maker with him. Gauge had gone on to take his shower—double shocker—and she was left to sort through things on her own as she listened to Jerry's BMW peel rubber out of her shoveled driveway and the sound of the shower in the master bedroom where Gauge stood under the spray naked.

Had the world gone insane? It was difficult to believe that her life could take a complete one-eighty in such a short period of time. One minute she'd been connecting to Gauge in a way she hadn't known it was possible to with another human being…the next she was looking for the exit to a ride that she would never have boarded had she known how dangerous the dips and turns were.

Finally, she plopped down on her bed. She stared at the twisted sheets under her feet and pulled at them almost violently. She nearly spilled onto the floor as she tugged until she could throw them back over the bed she'd spent the afternoon with Gauge in.

She knew a moment of pause as she rested her hand against the mattress.

Gauge headed back into the bedroom, rubbing a towel against his hair, completely dressed. She snapped her hand back from the bed as if burned.

She stared at him and he stopped his approach and leaned against the bathroom doorjamb.

"What were you thinking?" she asked in a half whisper.

He didn't say anything for a long moment. Then he tossed the towel to the counter behind him and walked over to sit in an armchair near the cold fireplace. He moved his boots toward him.

"Are you going to answer me?" she repeated, wondering if perhaps she only thought she was speaking aloud. Perhaps the one-sided conversation was taking place solely in her head.

"I wasn't thinking anything," he said, pulling one of his boots on and adjusting the bottom of his jeans over it. "I heard voices. It sounded like you were stressed. And I went to see what the trouble was."

"Then stood leaning against the wall wearing nothing but your dirty grin, looking like a feral wolf staking its territory."

His movements slowed as he put the other boot on. He finished and then planted his feet evenly on the floor. He looked directly at her. "I don't hide from anyone."

"Who asked you to hide? I'm not asking you to hide. But discretion would have been the better part of valor here."

"Sounds like hiding to me."

He rested his forearms on his knees and continued looking at her as she sat on the bed.

"You're angry."

Lizzie moved her mouth a couple of times but nothing came out. Then she sighed and ran her hand through her tousled hair. "I'm upset, yes."

"Upset that I'm here? Or upset that he left?"

"Neither. Both." She pushed off the bed and started pacing again, her bare feet moving from thick flokati rug to polished wood and back again. "I don't know."

Gauge watched her quietly. Then he got up, grabbed his jacket and stood looking at her. "Don't worry, Lizzie. He'll be back. Men always want what they can't have."

He turned to leave.

Lizzie was on him so quickly she surprised herself with her actions. She grasped his arm to stop him and then rounded to face him. "What?" The word was barely a whisper.

"Trust me. He'll be back."

"I don't want him back. That's not the point here."

He raised a brow in mocking question.

"The point is…" She dug in her heels, refusing to give in to the restless energy that packed her veins. "The point is, you took a decision away from me that was mine to make."

He remained silent. Doubtful.

"Don't you get it? It wasn't your job to chase Jerry away. It was mine to tell him why he couldn't stay. Why I didn't want him to stay."

"And if I hadn't been here?"

She mulled over that one.

"If you and I had never slept together? What would have happened then, Lizzie?"

As a trial attorney, she was used to giving good cross-examination. But not when it came to close personal re lationships. That might even be the reason she'd chosen the branch of law she had, since her personal life was rife with things unsaid.

But apparently not now. No. Gauge wanted to engage her in a conversation she wasn't so sure she wanted to have just then.

He leaned in and kissed her. Slowly. Leisurely. Curving the fingers of his free hand along her jaw and staring deeply into her eyes.

"We both agreed from the beginning that this was just about sex, Lizzie. There's no changing the rules now."

She felt as if he'd taken one of the jagged icicles hanging from her eaves and stabbed it straight through her heart, even though there was a ring of truth in his words. It had been about sex. Hadn't both of them made that completely clear in the beginning?

But that had been then. This was now. Somewhere down the line, it had evolved into much, much more. Through the sex they'd knocked down barriers they hadn't known they'd erected and made inroads into virgin territory, surrendering parts of themselves no one had laid ownership to before. They were tied together.

Her lungs refused air. No. She was the one who had surrendered parts of herself to Gauge.

Apparently it had been entirely one-sided.

He stepped toward the door as she wrapped her arms around herself, watching him go.

He never looked back once.

15

DON'T WORRY. He'll be back. Men always want what they can't have.

The words, his words, resonated through Gauge's brain as he navigated his way through the next couple of days. Sunday night, he'd played with the band. Monday and tonight, he'd made sure to be out of his apartment by six, before Lizzie returned home from work, commandeering the stool at the end of the bar where others left him alone for the most part.

And he'd been right about men wanting what they couldn't have. Judging by his own tortured hell when it came to Nina…well, he couldn't compare what he felt now for Lizzie to Nina. Rather, he'd come to accept that what had gone down was basic human survival instincts at their worst.

For three years, he and Nina and Kevin had been friends. While they enjoyed flirting, it had been harmless and purposely platonic.

Then the dynamic had changed when Gauge had arranged for the one night of anonymous sex between Nina and Kevin.

In that one instant, Nina graduated from friend to a woman in play. She had been something for which to compete. Someone to woo and seduce. And Kevin had become his nemesis.

Gauge had long since learned that hormones could get men into all kinds of trouble. That the fundamental urge to spread their seed meant that they often intruded in others' territory, putting their very life at risk in the quest for a woman's affection.

Except he hadn't expected to have to vie for Lizzie's attention.

"One last one?" Charlie asked, holding a bottle of Jack up.

Gauge pushed his shot glass toward him. "Sure. Hit me."

He'd lost count of how many he'd downed. Not enough to quiet the voices in his head. Enough to blur the edges of the man opposite him.

"Why don't I drop you off on my way home?"

Gauge shook his head. He'd driven in far worse condition than this. And it was late. There would barely be a soul on the road for him to threaten.

"I'll take him."

Gauge glanced at the waitress who had slid up to sit on the stool next to him. She'd taken off her apron, revealing that the deep vee that had been visible even with it on was made by unbuttoning a cotton top, complementing the generous curve of her breasts. She was a brunette and pretty and nice.

And just what the bartender ordered.

LIZZIE SAT in front of the fireplace watching the last embers burn out, the chenille throw doing little to warm her from the cooling room. She couldn't sleep. Had gotten precious little of that essential commodity since Sunday and Jerry's unannounced visit and Gauge's territorial display.

She scratched her head and looked through the window at the garage again. It was dark. Just as it had been for the past two nights. She suspected that Gauge was avoiding her. Which was just as well, because she hadn't much wanted to see him.

Until now.

"Talk to him." Tabby's words from earlier in the evening haunted her.

"I can't. I don't know how. I mean, what do I say?"

"Tell him that you acted like an ass and that you're sorry."

This advice from a friend who had reminded her earlier on that this thing with Gauge was only a temporary fling. Pointing out that nothing serious could come from a relationship with a musician.

"But he's part owner of the store downtown," Lizzie had said.

"Oh, well, that changes everything. Propose marriage then."

She'd known her friend was being facetious. She also understood that if Tabby had her way, Lizzie would dump Gauge and move on, take the experience with him as it was, a run of great, short-term sex.

But Tabby didn't know what Lizzie did. Hadn't felt the connection that she had. Couldn't possibly understand.

"Maybe not. But what I do understand is that you have a bad habit of clinging to every man you date, no matter how bad he is for you."

Lizzie had winced at that one, and winced again at the memory.

"Jerry was always a jerk," Tabitha had gone on. "From day one. Yet you kept on seeing him, convinced yourself that he was The One. I was actually happy when he ran off and married that other idiot. But then last summer you started talking about how he'd left the idiot and was back in your life. And I couldn't help thinking, *Oh, no, here we go again.*"

"How come you didn't say anything?"

"Because you never asked me."

"And now?"

Tabitha had fallen silent, as if unprepared to give her opinion of the moment.

"You know, there's a saying that applies to people like you," Lizzie had told her. "Hindsight is always twenty-twenty."

"Maybe." To her surprise, her friend had sounded contrite. "I don't know. Let me ask you this. What would you have done had you not been seeing Gauge? Had he not come out, grabbed his Johnson and pissed all over Jerry's thousand-dollar shoes? Would you have taken Jerry back?"

Lizzie honestly couldn't say one way or another what she might have done. She only knew that she wouldn't take Jerry back now if he held a divorce decree in one hand and the biggest diamond on earth in the other.

But it seemed that Gauge had been right about Jerry coming back. Later that night, Jerry had called her.

She hadn't picked up, of course. He hadn't left a message on her home phone, but she had another text message from him on her cell.

I miss you, it read. Call me.

Right. First thing in the morning. Right after her bagel.

"Look, Lizzie, I'm not going to tell you what to do. You're right. I wasn't there. I'm not you, and you're not me. I just want to make sure you're not trying to hold on to this guy because of some mistaken sense of wanting to succeed at everything you try your hand at."

That was a new one.

Okay, so she was driven in her career. But was Tabby right in suggesting she applied that same ambition to her personal life?

Then again, Gauge was so unlike the men she usually dated as to be an aberration.

Which made her double think her options all the more.

Where did she hope a relationship with him might take her?

Well, for one thing, she was entertaining the thought of children.

She drew her knees up to her chest, wondering if she should turn on a light or restart the CD player or turn on the television. Instead she considered that last thought.

Yes, she admitted, for the first time in a long time she could see herself in the role of mother. Could envision lazy Sundays spent around the house, Gauge teaching them music, her fixing breakfast, all of them lounging on her and Gauge's bed reading the Sunday comics.

She'd really never fantasized about anything like that before. Her future with Jerry, when she'd thought about it, had been filled with investments and European vacations, boat purchases and expensive cars and clothes and nights at the opera. Children, when the subject presented itself, had included images of the nannies she'd need to look after them as she pursued her career and Jerry pursued his.

Strange that she'd never really viewed that as selfish before. So different from her own upbringing.

She grimaced. Speaking of her own upbringing, she really needed to get updated on what the family intended to do next Thursday for Christmas.

Did she love Gauge?

Now there was a question.

And, strangely enough, it was one she'd asked herself countless times over the past few days in the wake of Sunday's events. At first, she'd answered with an angry, unqualified no. But as time ticked ever ahead, she was coming to doubt her own quick judgment. She'd experienced a connection with him that she'd never felt before with another human being, much less a man. Had spent a full day of doing nothing but making love and had not felt one iota of guilt for wasting the time. She had not only listened to him talk about his past, but wanted to take away the pain so evident in his voice and absorb it into herself.

She'd once heard that true love meant putting the other person before yourself. And that the only way you could do that was if you loved yourself first.

Did she love herself?

And if she did love Gauge, what happened from there? Would he accept her love? Could he accept it? Could he let her in and let her love him even if he couldn't admit that he loved her, too?

So many ifs.

Which was part of the reason that she was growing more convinced that she did love him. Or was falling in love with him. Since she was beginning to think that she'd never really experienced the emotions before—except on the shallowest of levels—she couldn't begin to say. But the uncertainty of it felt like a thousand butterflies fluttering in her stomach, trying to get out.

She'd never felt so miserable in her life.

She'd never felt so euphoric.

Wasn't that how love was described?

She stared at the embers in the fireplace grate. She couldn't say for sure if she was in love with Gauge. But she did know that she wanted to love him.

She turned to look out the window again and saw the lights on in his apartment. Her heart skipped a beat.

He was home.

She tossed the throw to the other side of the couch and got up, determined to find out if he wanted to love her in return.

GAUGE STOOD at the window, staring out at Lizzie's house, much as he had over the past two nights. The place was dark. Not that he was surprised. He did find, however, that he was disappointed.

Hadn't he been the one to plan it that way? To avoid Lizzie at all costs? To be away when she returned from work? To come back after she had gone to bed?

Why, then, was he wishing she had left a light on?

"Gauge?"

He turned toward the female voice, so lost in his thoughts that he was almost startled by the appearance of Debbie, the waitress from the pub, sitting on the side of his bed.

Damn it all to hell, but he couldn't help remembering when Lizzie had sat the same way a scant week earlier.

Is that all it had been? A week? It felt like he'd known her a lifetime.

Debbie patted the mattress next to her. He grimaced, rubbing the back of his neck.

Inviting her back to his place had seemed like a good idea at the time. A decision made by his old friend Jack rather than him.

But that was a cop-out, wasn't it? In truth, he'd brought Debbie back here for one purpose, and one purpose only: to exorcise Lizzie from his mind and his life. And he knew that nothing would do that quicker than a roll in the hay with another woman.

Coward, a voice in the back of his mind whispered.

Who did he think he was kidding? All he was doing

was beating Lizzie to the punch. There wasn't a snow angel's chance in hell of anything between them working out. She was garden parties and career driven. He was bar crowds and happy if he had enough to see him through the next day.

Still, he couldn't help wishing that wasn't the case.

None of that changed the fact that Debbie was here and Lizzie was not.

"Gauge?" Debbie's voice held a thread of uncertainty.

Do it, he told himself. Go over there and take what she's offering. Forget about Lizzie. She deserves better than you.

He began walking in her direction. Debbie immediately relaxed and slid back on the bed, prepared to welcome him.

There was a brief knock on the door and then it opened inward.

"Thank God, I thought you'd never get home…"

Gauge froze, staring at Lizzie, who had just walked in, her words trailing off as she realized he wasn't alone.

She looked from him to Debbie then back again. Her sensual mouth worked around some sort of response, but nothing came out.

Then she turned and ran.

16

LIZZIE FELT as if her heart might beat straight out of her rib cage as she hurried from the apartment. She took the stairs two at a time, nearly slipping on the icy driveway, practically tripping over her own feet in her hurry to get out of there, to get away from Gauge, to banish the image of him leaning over the bed to kiss another woman.

She felt sick to her stomach, and was dreadfully afraid that the sob gathering at the back of her throat might erupt as she ran.

"Lizzie!"

She knew a moment of terror at the sound of Gauge calling for her, lending wings to her feet as she navigated the snowy path back to her house. She grabbed the back door handle and tugged, only to realize that she'd locked it when she'd left a few minutes earlier. She reached into her sweater pocket for her keys, desperate to lock herself inside where nothing and no one could ever hurt her again.

She finally worked the right key inside and ducked into the kitchen. She gasped when Gauge grabbed the door, preventing her from pulling it closed.

She turned and resumed running. She could find a room, lock herself inside. Somewhere, anywhere to hide herself away. To hide from him. To keep from showing him how very much he'd just hurt her.

She'd made it to the hall when he caught her around the waist.

She twisted to face him. "Don't you touch me! You've lost all rights to ever lay a hand on me again."

He ignored her pleas, holding her tight.

Lizzie pressed her open palms against his chest at the same time he released her. She stumbled backward, realized she was free and turned to run. Gauge reached out to steady her and she slapped at his arms, trading her balance for pure, angry need. She fell to the floor and he followed after her, his weight trapping her against the lush Oriental hall rug.

"Let...me...go!"

Lizzie twisted and turned, horrified that her cheeks were wet with tears. She couldn't believe she was doing what she was. Even in her darkest times with Jerry, she had never lost control of herself. Never demonstrated such raw, feral emotion.

Because she had never felt it.

"Shh," Gauge said, placing his hands on either side of her head as he fought to still her.

"Don't you tell me to be quiet! Damn you!"

She lashed out with her legs, trying to make him get off her. This couldn't be happening. Not to her. She was the one who always knew what she was doing, what she was getting into. And this...this was more than casual sex

with just anybody. Somewhere down the line she had
fallen in love with Gauge. Fully. Completely. Irrevocably.

And now he knew that.

Humiliation landed squarely on top of the maelstrom
of emotions rushing through her body.

As hard as she fought, he calmly held her in place,
not physically hurting her, but not letting her go, either.

Finally, the rage slowly seeped from her body, leaving her a heaving mass of pain and regret.

"I can't believe I let you do this to me. I can't believe
I did this to myself."

Gauge pressed the side of his head against hers. She
could feel his breath against her ear. "What did you do,
Lizzie?" he whispered, his own voice rough with emotion.

She wriggled until he was forced to look into her
face. "Why?" she asked. "Why did you do that? Why
when…"

He searched her eyes. In his, she saw the same grab
bag of emotions roiling inside her.

But that couldn't be. He didn't care about her. If he
did, he would never have taken another woman back to
his place. Another woman he'd planned to sleep with
in the same spot he'd seduced her a week ago.

Only he hadn't seduced her, had he? She'd seduced
him. She'd been dumb enough to think that a wild night
of sex with the guitar-playing tenant would help distract
her from her breakup with Jerry.

Stupid her.

"Why won't you let me love you?" she whispered.

GAUGE FELT as though she'd jabbed her fingers through his chest and ripped his heart clean out at her softly spoken words. Her eyes glistened like blue diamonds. Her cheeks were red and damp. And even though she'd settled down some, her body still heaved, bursting with pain and hatred and anger.

It seemed odd that the word *love* could fit into the equation anywhere. But in that instant, he knew that it was true. Lizzie did love him.

And, shocking as it was to admit, he knew that he was falling for her.

"Why?" she said again.

Gauge winced as if she'd shouted instead of whispered. He closed his eyes and smoothed her soft hair back from her face over and over again, his hands trembling, his stomach feeling like the years of whiskey he'd fed it had just rotted it.

He realized they were still on the floor, that he held her trapped against a rug. But he couldn't seem to force himself off her. He knew a need so strong to keep her there, a fear that if he let her up, she might never be in his arms again.

"This is so crazy," she said, sniffing harshly, as if equal parts sad and determined to regain control over herself. "I didn't believe it, either. Not completely. Not until this instant." She drew in a deep breath. "God, I never knew I could hurt this much."

Gauge rubbed his thumb against her bottom lip "Shh," he said, not wanting to put words to the moment, to the feelings.

"I mean, I barely know you. How could I have fallen for you in such a short time? How can seeing you with another woman make me feel like I want to die?"

Gauge opened his eyes, viewing the truth in her face. A face made more beautiful in that one moment than it had ever been.

Had he ever been loved in this way? Had he ever loved in this way? Was this even love, this obsessive, possessive need that pressed on him, inside and out?

"I thought I knew love," she said, shaking her head. "But I didn't. Not really."

Gauge didn't want to hear any more. Couldn't bear to. So he did the only thing he knew would stop her.

He kissed her.

LIZZIE FOUGHT the gesture. She turned her head from side to side, not wanting to feel anything for him. She fought with everything that she had against the tidal wave of emotion threatening to undo her. Gauge merely kissed her harder, demanding access to her mouth, pressing his body insistently against hers. He worked a knee between hers and forced her thighs open, settled himself against her even as he sought access to her mouth.

No! her mind cried.

Yes! her heart responded.

She finally gave in and opened her mouth to him, bittersweet emotion filtering over her. How could she go from pain to pleasure within a heartbeat?

Gauge kissed her hard, his breathing coming in rapid gasps as he reached for the front of her blouse. Lizzie could taste the whiskey on his tongue. Could feel the persistent hardness of his erection between her legs. She helped him open her blouse and he nuzzled her breasts through the fabric of her bra before half-tearing it off so he could pull a nipple deep into his mouth.

She gasped, her back coming up off the rug as she tore at the catch of his jeans. He followed suit, stripping her of her pants. Within moments they were joined. Nothing between them. No condom. No inhibitions. Only wild, needy, bittersweet sex.

Lizzie moaned, grabbing his backside roughly as he thrust into her. She hooked her feet around his calves and kissed him hungrily, wet, openmouthed kisses that bruised her lips. He sank into her and she met him thrust for thrust until the world exploded into vivid shades of red.

Gauge rolled off her. They both lay out of breath, staring at the chandelier hanging from the foyer ceiling above them.

Lizzie felt strangely numb.

Gauge slid his fingers under hers and held her hand. She held his back.

This was it, she thought. This was the point where they decided what happened. Either they went on from here, tried to heal the wounds of the night and build on what they had. Or this was where they parted ways.

She didn't know which she wanted. Couldn't say. Half of her wanted him so desperately to stay, it scared her.

The other…well, the other half was scared of the power of that emotion.

So she lay there and allowed Gauge to make the decision.

When, long minutes later, he sat up, fixed his jeans and then got to his feet, she knew what his decision would be. And she was helpless to stop him.

She lay there, prone, as his boots sounded against the marble tile, then the tile of the kitchen, and he let himself out of the back door.

17

GAUGE SHOVED his things into his duffel. His apartment had been empty when he returned, saving him the trouble of telling the waitress to go home. All he knew was a need, a burning desire to get the hell out of there as fast as he could.

"The Gauge men are known for itchy feet," his father had once told him during a three-day bender. "They can't stay in one place for too long before the need to roam sends them on to the next place."

Gauge had never believed him. Had always thought that his father had left a town behind in exchange for the next one because it was the easy thing to do.

But his own decision to leave had to be the most difficult thing he'd ever done. Harder still than leaving last February after his friendship with Nina and Kevin had disintegrated.

"Why won't you let me love you?"

Lizzie's tearful words just minutes ago tore at his soul. He fell back against the wall, causing a small shelf to slant, dumping a potted plant onto the floor.

Not that he noticed. His heart was beating a million

miles a minute, his mouth was dry, and he wanted nothing more than to go across the yard and spend the next fifty years in that bed with Lizzie Gilbred.

Which was exactly the reason he couldn't.

He was damaged goods. He knew that. Had always known that. He had too much of his father in him not to be. Give him a good thing, and he would surely turn it bad sooner or later. This time it had just happened sooner rather than later.

No. He had to leave. For Lizzie's sake.

Liar.

The word echoed through his brain.

What was he supposed to do? He couldn't stand to remember the heart-wrenching pain on her face earlier when she'd spotted the waitress sitting on his bed, the same spot she'd been just a short time ago. He'd hurt her. Perhaps beyond repair.

But even if he could repair things, would he?

To what end?

He'd never been one to subscribe to or aspire to the Great American Dream. He'd taken over the music shop on a whim when he started spending copious amounts of time there while passing through Fantasy. The old man who'd owned it turned out to be a kindred spirit. Albeit one who had changed his own life. After ten years out on the road traveling from gig to gig when he was younger, he'd met the woman who would become his wife in Fantasy and they'd gone on to have three kids.

At first, Gauge hadn't understood his fascination

with the man. Sure, he was a talented artist. And he'd never been much for judging others on their decisions, probably because he didn't want to be judged on his. But Colin Murphy…well, he'd intrigued Gauge.

Was it possible to change?

Then the old man had died and deeded his shop to Gauge. A surprise considering his wife and three children were still alive. But the family—who happened to be well-off because Murphy's wife was a physician and the children had careers and families of their own—had been pleased, understanding that Gauge had come to mean a lot to Murphy.

Not even Gauge had realized how fond Murphy had been of him until he'd been given the shop.

He liked to tell himself that the reason he'd accepted the incredible gift was to honor Colin Murphy. But while that was true to a certain extent, it wasn't the whole truth. He'd accepted it because somewhere deep down, he'd wondered if he himself could change. Forge a different path than the one his father had shown him.

That decision had snowballed into a series of others he might never have made if not for Colin's gift, further fueling his desire for change. He'd joined forces with Nina and Kevin to create BMC and…well, after what had happened with Lizzie, he now knew that his father's blood ran deeper than he'd acknowledged before.

If there was one thing he was coming to understand, it was that you couldn't change blood. It would always tell.

The telephone began ringing again. He ignored it as he snapped out of his reverie and continued packing.

Minutes later he heard footfalls on the steps outside his apartment. They seemed to hesitate a moment, then there was a brief knock on his door and it opened inward.

Lizzie stood there, coatless, her face pale, her eyes still smeared with pain, her arms wrapped around her body.

He turned and put the last of his things in his bag. He walked to the table, avoiding her gaze, and stared at an envelope on the table. He picked it up and put it in the bag.

"There's been a fire," she said quietly. "It's BMC."

FLASHING LIGHTS BRIGHTENED the night sky, but they were no match for the flames that licked out of the upper windows of the building that housed BMC. Fire trucks were positioned at different angles in the parking lot, one from a bordering city, another a volunteer engine, all working to knock down the fire that looked to be consuming the bookstore/music center/café whole.

Gauge brought his car to a squealing stop just inside the parking lot and climbed out, barely remembering to shut off the engine and take the keys from the ignition. He rushed toward the building, his heart thundering in his chest.

A firefighter caught him before he could cross the line created by the trucks. "Sir, you need to keep back and let us work."

"I've got to get inside!" he shouted.

Please let Nina and Kevin be safe, he silently prayed. Let them have been at home.

"Gauge!"

He turned toward the familiar male voice. Kevin. He stood across the parking lot, a crying Nina in his arms.

Thank God.

Gauge hurried toward them.

"Was anyone hurt?" was his first question as he eyed his friends, looking for apparent injuries.

"No. Everyone's safe. The place was securely locked down for the night."

Nina looked pale. "It was the oven, I know it was." She squeezed her eyes shut. "The replacement is…was due to be delivered tomorrow."

Assured that everyone was all right, Gauge turned back toward the store. The firefighters appeared to be concentrating on keeping the fire from spreading to neighboring establishments. The absence of wind helped, but the cold temperatures did not.

"Nina, I want you to let Heidi take you home," Kevin said. And for the first time Gauge noticed Nina's friend and former employee standing a few feet away.

"But I don't want to go home by myself. Not with our lives going up in smoke."

Gauge watched as Kevin gently touched his wife's pretty face. "Not our lives, baby. Our business. That can be rebuilt."

"But—"

"Come on," Heidi agreed, apparently sensing the same thing Gauge did: that Kevin had something to say to him. And he didn't want to do it with Nina present.

Finally, Nina went with Heidi, looking over her

shoulder as she did. Kevin waited until the two women were out of sight before he lit into Gauge.

"What in the hell did you do?" he demanded.

LIZZIE SAT on the floor of the apartment that had been Gauge's. Only it really hadn't been his beyond his name on the lease, had it? He'd never made it his home. Not if he could clear out of there in five minutes flat and not leave a single thing behind beyond the bottle of Jack Daniel's on the table.

She leaned her back against the wall, making out shapes in the dark. The chairs. The kitchen counter. The bed.

She swallowed hard, crowding her fingers through her hair, surprised she still had tears to cry.

What was that saying? You never knew what you had until it was gone?

Or, rather, after you'd chased it away?

She gave a humorless laugh. First she'd chased Gauge away after what he'd done with Jerry the other day. Then today he'd chased her away.

And that's what he'd done, wasn't it? Just as she'd desperately been looking for a way to ease the pain of her breakup with Jerry and found it in Gauge's bed, he'd been looking for a final break from her by inviting a woman back to his place, where he'd known she'd be sure to see her. If not tonight, then in the morning when the woman left.

Or, maybe not. Maybe she was giving herself far too much credit. Maybe Gauge didn't feel for her what she felt for him, and tonight had just been another night to him.

She remembered the trembling way he'd held her at her place just a short time ago, refusing to let her go, his face mirroring her anguish, and couldn't bring herself to believe it.

Why, then, the betrayal?

It was almost funny, really. It wasn't so long ago that she'd thought Jerry was the man for her. Had been devastated when he'd dumped her...not once, but twice. But now...

Well, now she recognized her feelings in the wake of Jerry's betrayal as pride. The first time, she'd been unable to see beyond what looked good on paper. Jerry and her, a successful marriage to go with their successful independent careers. She had known there was no love between them. At least not true love.

But she wasn't completely to blame. If only because she'd had no idea what true love entailed. What it demanded.

She hurt in ways that surpassed the physical. Her entire body seemed to throb. Her heart seemed to shiver, trying to hide from the pain that ricocheted through her. Tomorrow loomed bleak and meaningless, a gaping black hole to fill with...with what?

If told two weeks ago that it would be sexy musician Patrick Gauge who would steal her soul, show her what love truly was, she'd have laughed at the messenger.

But there you had it. No matter what arguments she

tried to use against it, how hard she battled against it, there was no ignoring or denying the truth. And the truth was that she loved Patrick Gauge. Despite his flaws. Despite his betrayal. Merely being with him made her feel whole and no longer alone in the world.

She only wished she had figured that out before it was too late.

GAUGE STUMBLED back a couple of steps, losing his balance when Kevin pushed him.

"What in the hell did you do?" Kevin demanded, advancing on him like a man gone mad.

"What are you talking about?"

He blinked at his partner and one-time best friend, trying to figure out the way his mind was working.

"The fire!" Kevin shouted. "Did you want out of our partnership that badly?"

"What?" Gauge's response was quiet as he digested his words.

Was Kevin accusing him of having set the fire? Of being responsible for the chaos being played out behind him?

Both his friend's anger and physical shove had knocked him off-kilter earlier, but now he found his footing and stared him down.

"Well, now, that's a new one," he said darkly. "Now you're accusing me of arson?"

Kevin advanced on him. Gauge held his ground, daring him to hit him. Not so Kevin could unleash his emotions at Gauge for having slept with Nina, but so

Gauge would be justified in hitting him back. Of giving outlet to his own unresolved emotions for Lizzie that were crowding his chest, leaving him little more than a walking bag of hormones and confusion.

"Tell me you didn't do it," Kevin demanded. "Tell me you didn't destroy BMC so that you could leave here once and for all."

Gauge leaned forward, putting them almost nose-to-nose. "I didn't set that damn fire, Kevin. So you'd better back off or else I won't be held responsible for my actions."

"What, are you going to hit me, Gauge? Go ahead. Because this time I won't be the one who holds back."

"I'd love nothing better than to sock you in the mouth just now, you smug bastard. But I won't. No. Not this time. Not so you can come out smelling like the rose you always do."

He was surprised by the caustic words but couldn't stop them.

"I did not set that fire," he repeated. "I can't believe you would even think that."

"What do you want me to think? You don't want to be involved in the running of the business. You don't cash the checks. Then overnight the place goes up in smoke? It's all a little too neat for me. The place burns down, you get a substantial little check to add to your pile, and you're free of BMC, of us and this town. Isn't that what you came back for, Gauge? To find a way to finally cut the ties you have here?"

He didn't know what to say, so he didn't say anything. There was a logic to Kevin's thinking that was a little eerie, because it was plausible.

"Admit it, Gauge, you're a liar and a cheat. You excuse yourself for doing things that someone else wouldn't do. Maybe you have good reasons for it. Maybe you don't. I can't say as I care anymore. Because now you'll be judged solely on your actions."

"Actions I didn't take."

Kevin held up his hand. "I said I don't care." He exhaled a long breath, looking a little more under control but no less dangerous. "Why do you think every other person in this town does the right thing, Gauge? You think it's because it's the way they were raised, or because it's easy? No. Making the right decision sometimes is the hardest thing you can do. But in the end it's up to you, as an individual, to make that decision. To weather that hardship.

"What, did you think that you could come here and have everything just drop into your lap? This perfect life? Well, I'm sorry to tell you, pal, you don't get it just because you open yourself up for it. You have to earn it. That's right, I said earn it. Not because you were dealt a crappy hand in life. Poor you. Get over yourself. Because that's just not going to fly anymore. Not with me. Not with my wife. Not with my family—the one you've tried to destroy."

"I didn't set the goddamn fire."

"I'm not talking about that."

No, he was talking about everything. And that "everything" explained why Kevin would think he was behind the fire. It stretched back to when he'd chosen to sleep with Nina. To put selfish need above the greater good. To do what was wrong instead of right.

He'd told himself that it had been hard to do what he had. But in truth, it had been easy.

It would have been much harder to have done the right thing.

The thought of what might have happened had he pushed Nina away that night, where he might be, where they as friends might be, knocked him back on his feet more forcibly than any shove Kevin could give him.

And he knew that he'd finally screwed this up beyond recovery.

He stalked to his car, grabbed something from his duffel and then went to stand before Kevin again. He held out the white envelope that had been on his table, the last thing he'd taken from his apartment.

"Go ahead. Take it."

Kevin did, holding it out as if he didn't know what to make of it.

"Those are papers signing over my third of BMC to you and Nina for one dollar."

He'd had the legal documents drawn up two days ago, after things had gone south with Lizzie. He figured it would give them all a clean slate to start over.

"And I know you don't believe this but..."

The end of the sentence seemed helplessly lodged in his throat. Maybe because it included a word he'd never said before, much less felt.

"I'm sorry."

He turned to leave. Not just the conversation or the parking lot or Lizzie…but Fantasy. For good.

18

SECONDS MELTED into minutes, minutes into hours, until two days later, without knowing that's where he was heading, or that his destination actually lay there, Gauge ended his journey in a dusty town in Arizona. A place familiar to him because he'd passed through years ago with his father.

He'd seen many towns in his travels. Some changed over the years, others seemed to be frozen in perpetuity, as if they were some sort of time capsule of what life might have looked like in the nineteen-fifties. Dirt roads on which modern cars kicked up red dirt; storefronts that still bore the same tin signs from that era, hanging from metal hooks, swaying in the dry, light wind

Gauge had parked his car in a lot he remembered from long ago. The old roadhouse was set back from the two-lane road, the Closed sign turned, no indication of life when just a few short hours before it would have been teeming with people who might have driven over thirty miles for a night out, pickup trucks choking the gravel he now stood on.

He stared at the brightening eastern horizon, a haze

of purple. He wore only his T-shirt and jeans and boots, having shed layers of clothing the farther south he drove. He'd slept when he'd had little choice but to sleep, eaten when his body forced him, and driven the rest of the time, the car's worn tires taking him farther and farther away from Fantasy, Michigan.

Now he felt as if he'd stepped off the edge of the earth, having gone from winter snow to summer warm.

He wondered what Lizzie was doing. Considering the time difference, she was probably at work, striving to return to normalcy. Hiding her pain away.

He opened his car door and climbed back inside, within minutes pulling up to a nearby motel he'd stayed at with his father. He paid the man at the front desk and took the key, letting himself into a small bungalow at the end of a ramshackle row. The room smelled of cigarette smoke and booze and old carpeting. He dropped the key onto the small table inside the door and then went out to get his things. It didn't take him more than a few minutes to make the room home for however long he needed it.

He glanced at the bed, but even though his eyelids scraped against his eyes like sandpaper every time he blinked, he knew he wouldn't be able to go to sleep.

Instead, he grabbed his guitar and stepped through the back door that opened onto a makeshift patio of old bricks, desert weeds poking through the cracks. He sat down on the rusted metal chair there and pulled his guitar onto his knee. He closed his eyes and took in a deep breath of the dry, desert air, feeling the sun against his face rather than seeing it rise as the fingers of his left hand ran over the strings, strumming with the thumb and index finger of his right hand, even though he always carried a pick in his pocket.

He remembered the first time he could play a song on his own without looking at his hands. He'd been about nine and had been left in a random motel room by himself for the night, trusting that his father would be back at some point the next morning. He'd sat on the edge of the walk outside the room, his feet on the parking-lot asphalt, feeling his away around the song without the benefit of sight, trusting that his hands knew the way. They had. And from then on, he and his guitar had become best friends, conversing in a way that he'd never really learned how to with others.

As he played, images filled his mind. Of his father sitting across the room from him on a chair, smiling his grizzled grin as he smoked a cigarette, listening to Gauge play. Of the face of the woman who'd turned him into a man, and nearly every woman he'd found pleasure with since. Of Nina and Kevin and him laughing around the fireplace at BMC.

Of Lizzie's golden blond hair spread across his chest as she curved against his side like a sexy she-cat, smiling up at him in provocative invitation and, yes, love.

He also saw the hurt shine in her beautiful blue eyes as he'd held her down.

"Why won't you let me love you?"

Her words had been spoken so softly he nearly hadn't heard them.

Nina's smile followed on the heels of the memory, the morning they'd talked things out at the café, the last time he'd ever visit the place that had been a fixture in his life for three years.

"Admit it, Nina," he'd said. "In your heart of hearts, you knew that Kevin was the mystery man. Yet you slept with me anyway...."

He'd feared she would run away from the question. As a married woman, deny that she'd harbored feelings for another man not her husband. A husband who had at one time been Gauge's best friend, too.

But she hadn't. She'd looked down at her coffee cup, taking her time.

"I've thought about that night often," she'd finally said. "And, yes, I have come to admit to myself that when I came to you, I did so knowing full well that you might not be the man I'd been with before." She'd bitten her bottom lip. "But I had to know, Gauge. I had to know if there was a chance between us. Had to know if it would be as good between us as it was between Kevin and me."

"And was it?"

She'd swallowed hard but steadfastly held his gaze. "It was."

Gauge had known a satisfaction then that he'd felt instantly guilty about.

"But something was missing."

Love.

He'd known that's what she was going to say before she even said it. Because by then he was already falling in love with Lizzie. And it was only then that he'd recognized what he felt for Nina hadn't been the type of emotion that built relationships strong enough to weather whatever storm came their way. Not like the bond between Nina and Kevin, who had not only survived Gauge's ultimate act of betrayal, but had blossomed in spite—and, yes, perhaps even because—of it.

That's when Gauge had to confront the fact that he'd slept with Nina, claimed her physically, because of some desire of his own to win a competition that had started the instant the three of them quit being friends, and Nina and Kevin had become lovers. A battle of wills on a primitive level he wasn't entirely sure he understood, although he now recognized the drive to do so only too well.

Kevin's final words echoed through his mind: "Making the right decision sometimes is the hardest thing you can do. But in the end it's up to you to make that decision… What, did you think that you could come here and have everything just drop into your lap? This perfect life? Well, I'm sorry to tell you, pal, you don't get it just because you open yourself up for it. You have to earn it…."

Gauge hadn't realized that his hands had increased the pace, moving from a soothing piece to a hard, quick tempo, his fingers flying over the frets, his thumb strumming like there was no tomorrow. And there wasn't, was there? At least not a tomorrow with which he was familiar.

He finished the song with a final, almost violent strum and rested his hands against the body of the still vibrating instrument, his heart beating heavily in his chest, his breathing labored, the throbbing in his temples growing into a full-blown ache.

But nothing that matched the ache in his heart....

"So are you going to buy it, or are you just going to stand there looking at it all day?" Annie asked.

Lizzie blinked her younger sister into focus, her hand still grasping the black cotton T-shirt that read, Got Blues? and featured a drawing of an electric guitar. She and her sister had been passing the store in the mall and she'd wandered in without saying anything, leaving her sister to walk past two more stores before she figured out that Lizzie was no longer with her.

Now Annie stood with her arms crossed, staring at her sister, the bags hanging from her hands making it hard to see her as much of a threat.

Lizzie forced herself to release the T-shirt. But rather than follow her sister outside the store, she instead headed over to the store counter, looking at jewelry made of musical instruments, as well as plaques.

"God, that's so tacky," Annie said, eyeing a pair of earrings made out of amber-colored guitar picks.

Lizzie figured it was a good thing that her sister didn't know anything about her brief tryst with Gauge or else she'd probably find that highly tacky, as well.

"What's going on with you?" Annie asked, looking at her a little too closely. "Beyond a CD here and there, you've never showed an interest in music."

Lizzie picked up an acoustic guitar from a stand,

running her hand over the lacquered front. "Yes, well, maybe I'm thinking about taking it up."

"Well, at least choose something worthwhile. Like piano. Or if you're set on a stringed instrument, a harp."

Lizzie ignored her.

She couldn't say exactly what it was, but she felt somehow...more at ease in the store. She felt better than she had in the past five days since Gauge left. She kept waiting for the ache to lessen, for her heart to go back to beating normally, her eyes to close at night. Instead, the opposite seemed to be happening. The more time that passed, the more she seemed to think about him. About what could have been and how well they'd suited each other.

For the first time in her life, she'd met a man and didn't care whether or not he had a stock portfolio, or if he wore the right clothes or drove the right car. And while she'd convinced herself at the time that it had only been about sex, somewhere down the line she'd come to care about Gauge in a way that seemed insane.

He made her feel...like a woman.

Since the night she'd climbed into Gauge's bed, she'd become aware of herself in ways she hadn't imagined before. She'd always known she was as capable as a man in the business world, but in life...well, she found that she wanted to make Gauge breakfast in bed. Wanted to lick syrup off his body. Wanted to look sexy for him.

Of course, now that she'd realized the impact he'd had on her, she wouldn't be able to take full advantage of the changes he'd wrought in her. At least not in the sexual sense. But given the way she felt more in touch with herself as a woman, she craved more of a connection with everyone around her, an almost nurturing need for closeness. Perhaps not all was lost, she thought.

"Come on," Annie prodded her. "We're going to be late."

It was the Sunday night before Christmas and they were going to help their mother make holiday cookies.

She put the guitar down and allowed her sister to lead her out of the shop.

BEFORE LIZZIE KNEW IT, she was sitting at the kitchen table at her parents' house, her shirtsleeves rolled up, wearing her father's Kiss The Cook apron and stirring a fresh batch of frosting. Her sister had gone into the other room to take a call from her husband, and Lizzie and her mother were working in companionable silence. Her father was around somewhere, popping up every now and again to stick his finger in the icing.

Lizzie couldn't help thinking that it looked as if her parents had returned to normal. But at this point, she'd given up hoping.

"You're awfully quiet," her mother said as she sprinkled red sugar glitter onto a batch of freshly baked chocolate-mint cookies.

"Hmm?" Lizzie looked up. "Oh. Yes." She smiled as she pushed her hair back from her face. "I could say the same of you."

"Yes. I suppose you could."

They fell silent again. Every now and again they heard Annie raise her voice from the next room.

"I give her five minutes before she's out the door to go home to take care of whatever emergency popped up," her mother said.

"I give her three."

They were both wrong. Within a minute, Annie slammed the cordless back into the wall holder and sighed as she took off her apron. Hers read, If You Want Breakfast In Bed, Sleep In The Kitchen.

"Kid crisis. He can't find Jasmine, and Mason's having a conniption. I've got to go."

"Sounds like normal kid stuff to me," Bonnie said.

"Yes, well, my darling husband insists he's about to go insane and is begging me to come home now."

Lizzie shared a glance with her mother.

"We're almost done, anyway, right?" Annie said, giving her mother a kiss on the cheek and crossing to hug Lizzie. "I won't be missed."

"No, but you'll miss this," Bonnie said. "Don't forget to take a plate with you. If anything's guaranteed to make Jaz come out of hiding, and Mason to stop crying, it's a batch of the Gilbreds' annual Christmas cookies."

Annie smiled as she prepared a plate and then waved at them on her way out the door.

"And she actually wants another one?" Lizzie asked.

Her mother shrugged. "She's a better mother than I ever was."

"How can you say that? Don't get me wrong, I adore

my niece and nephew, but sometimes I want to check the back of their heads for a six-six-six tattoo."

Bonnie laughed. "God, I was an awful mother."

"You were not."

"Sure I was. I can't remember a time when I didn't stay awake nights terrified I was scarring you kids for life."

"I thought that came with parenthood."

"Yes, I suppose it does. To a certain extent, but…"

She seemed lost in her thoughts and Lizzie concentrated on frosting the rest of the cookies in front of her.

"Do you think you're a good wife?" Lizzie surprised herself by asking.

Bonnie stared at her.

"What? It's a fair question."

If she had her own personal agenda for asking, she wasn't going to say. While a part of her wished that she'd told her family about Gauge, another was glad she hadn't. For all they knew, she was still dating Jerry.

"I was the absolute worst wife imaginable," Bonnie said quietly, stressing the word *was*. She went to remove a tray of cookies from the oven. "What does that mean, anyway? What is a wife's job? To make her husband happy? And what is a husband's job? To make his wife happy?" She snorted indelicately.

Lizzie watched her father sneak up behind her mother and snatch one of the cookies just out of the oven, putting his finger to his lips to tell Lizzie not to say anything. He tossed the hot cookie from hand to hand, trying to cool it, and then ducked out of the room again to go back to whatever he was doing.

Lizzie shook her head. "I don't know. I suppose it once meant that a husband was supposed to take care of the family financially. And the wife was supposed to keep the house running."

Her mother dropped her arms to her sides. "Roles. I've always hated prescribed roles."

"But you've always been a great wife and mother."

"Whatever." She fell silent for a few moments. Lizzie stepped to the kitchen island to transfer the warm cookies to cooling racks and peeked inside the oven to make sure everything was progressing as it should.

"You know, the only reason I ever married your father was because I was pregnant with you."

Lizzie experienced a moment of shock. "No. No, I, um, didn't know."

"That's not to say that I don't love your father. Or that we haven't had a good life together."

Lizzie returned to her side of the table, resisting the urge to guide the conversation.

"I've never been a traditional kind of girl." Bonnie frowned as she looked around her. "Holidays and my children aside."

"Define traditional?"

Bonnie blinked up at her. "For one, I never wanted to be married. Never thought a piece of paper mattered when it comes to emotional unions." She placed her hands on the table and leaned forward. "It's like ownership papers. And it wreaks terrible havoc on a relationship."

"Mom…why do you love Dad?"

That seemed to catch her up short. "Why? Well, that's simple. He balances me. Completes me."

Bonnie smiled, as if to herself.

"Now your dad…he's the traditional one. If I'd fallen in love with anyone else, I could very easily be making these cookies with you in a tent somewhere."

"Tent?"

"Sure. Why not? It's your father who wants all the traditional trappings. The house. The cottage at the lake." She gave Lizzie a sidelong gaze. "The marriage."

She walked two trays of cookies into the dining room and then came back, wiping her hands on her apron, which read, Some Like It Spicy.

"Expectations and assumptions can sink a relationship faster than you can burn cookies," her mother said, then glanced over her shoulder. "Speaking of which…"

"They're fine. I just checked."

Bonnie looked thoughtful.

"So," Lizzie said. "You're really going to go through with this divorce thing then…?"

Bonnie looked surprised. "Of course I am. There's no question of that."

Lizzie felt suddenly sad.

"Don't look so down in the mouth. As far as you kids are concerned, nothing's going to change."

"What? How can they not change? Our mother is divorcing our father."

Bonnie smiled mischievously. "Yes, but your mother and father are not splitting up."

To Lizzie, that made absolutely no sense at all.

She braced herself for her mother's explanation.

19

MUCH LATER that night, Lizzie sat in her own kitchen, sipping an Irish coffee and thinking about the Bonnie Gilbred take on divorce.

"Labels, roles, expectations…what a bunch of malarkey. I'm tired of making joint decisions, of worrying I'm not living up to a standard others set. In this case, your father. And he's not the only one to blame. I do the same thing. Before you know it, you're taking each other for granted. Or falling short of the mark so often your self-esteem doesn't just take a hit, you wake up one morning and it's gone altogether."

So her mother's solution to the problem was that they should get a divorce. No longer would she be beholden to some archaic way of thinking, but a woman free to make decisions as she saw fit. A woman who wasn't part of a pair, but an individual who could walk away with no ties if she wanted.

As a result, she explained, her father would appreciate her more. And she would appreciate him. Enjoy him.

"Our sex life hasn't been this good since you guys were kids."

Lizzie hadn't wanted to travel any further on that particular train of thought, although she had to admit that her mother's take on marriage had its own kind of twisted logic.

Which, of course, brought her thoughts back to Gauge.

She looked through the kitchen window at the garage apartment, dark and cold. Everything remained exactly the way Gauge had left it, down to the sleep-rumpled bedding. Of course, he'd been gone less than a week, and his lease didn't end until the end of February, but she knew that he wouldn't be returning.

She sipped her coffee, the Irish cream warming her.

Given how she felt about Gauge now, why hadn't she seen him as a threat to her freedom, to her heart, when she originally crossed the driveway and climbed the steps to his apartment? Was it because he was a transient musician and didn't fit any of her previous qualifications for the type of man she thought she'd spend the rest of her life with?

"He balances me," were her mother's words.

Lizzie recognized that to be true. Where her mother was flighty and fiercely independent, her father had always been the rock. Every aspect of their lives reflected that. Her father was a builder, using solid materials to make long-lasting structures that could weather the worst storms.

Her mother was going to be a flight attendant.

She shook her head, still having trouble wrapping her brain around that one.

She supposed that was because she was so much

like her father. Or, rather, his type. Driven. Career oriented. Ambitious.

Could it be that opposites attracted for a reason? Could Gauge be the yin to her yang? The other side of the seesaw? Could he be the home to her house?

And on the flip side, could she be the rock he clung to in a storm? The one who took care of the financial end, not because she had to, but because she wanted to, so he could be a guitar player, free to choose which gigs he took.

Of course, all this was speculation. What remained was that the physical pain she'd experienced upon his departure felt like a lingering wound that she feared might never heal.

So if that was the case, and she was in love with him, did any of the other stuff really matter? Should she, like her mother, do something strictly because it felt good?

She recalled the day she and Gauge spent in bed. Without qualification, it remained the single most sublime time of her life. And he, and only he, had given that to her.

She glanced around her house. Stuff. Stuff she liked, but in the end, just stuff. She could do without it if she had to.

Gauge…

She caught her breath, her heart hurting all over again at the thought that odds were she was going to have to live without him.

Although it was after eleven on a Sunday night, Lizzie picked up the phone and dialed a number.

"Hello?" Her ex-almost-sister-in-law Heidi answered her cell on the fifth ring.

"I need you to tell me where Gauge might have gone…"

WHEN GAUGE WASN'T THINKING about Lizzie, he was dreaming about her. When he wasn't dreaming about her, he was thinking about her. Every moment of every day.

He'd never known any woman to take a hold of his soul and his sanity like this. All he wanted to do was touch her. To make love to her. To make her smile, make her laugh. Everything else came a distant second. And time and distance was doing nothing to change that.

He crossed his arms as he leaned against his dusty old car, squinting against the setting winter sun on the desert horizon. He'd spent his life playing the blues. While he understood the concept of existential blues, he really hadn't gotten the ones about love. Oh, he'd thought he had. But it wasn't until he'd surrendered his heart to Lizzie, and betrayed her love, that he truly understood the meaning of singing the blues.

A rusty pickup kicked up dust on the road in the distance. He cupped his hand over his eyes to watch it approach. It was just after five, the time the man he wanted to see would return home from work. He glanced at the old two-bedroom trailer some hundred yards away, noticing the way the curtains fluttered at the window. It wasn't much, but it was obvious the family that lived there took pride in what they did have. The area around it was clean, everything well tended.

The truck slowed and pulled off the road onto the dirt area that served as the trailer's driveway. Gauge had parked there and stood waiting as the driver pulled to a stop and eyed him warily.

There wasn't much to connect the man before him with the boy he'd been when Gauge had last seen him. But there was enough of their father in him to recognize him as Gorge, his half brother.

"I don't know if you remember me, but I thought we might talk," Gauge said, squinting into the sunset and then back again.

"I know who you are." Gorge glanced at the trailer. The honey-skinned young woman Gauge had spoken to earlier appeared holding a toddler on her hip, her belly round with another child on the way.

Gauge thought for a minute that his half brother might tell him to come back some other time and continue on to his family. Instead, he waved at the woman, shut off his engine and climbed from the truck.

"Hey, man," he said, offering his hand. "How long you been out my way?"

Gauge welcomed the physical contact, patting the back of Gorge's hand with his other one and holding it still for a long moment as he searched his face.

He'd never tried to make any sort of contact with his father's other children. His brothers and sister. But he'd come to realize over the past couple of days that it was that need that had brought him here, to the one brother he had met.

What remained was whether Gorge would want anything to do with him now.

"I just got into town the night before last," he said, finally releasing his hand.

Gorge nodded. "Got a gig in town?"

"No. Just decided to drive down."

"Down? So you were up north then. Winters can get pretty bad up that way."

Gauge smiled at the congenial way Gorge spoke to him, automatically trying to put him at ease. "Yes. Yes, that they can." He gestured toward Gorge's soot-covered jeans and denim shirt. "You working the copper plant in Hayden?"

"Yeah." Gorge made to brush himself off. "Ever since we moved off San Carlos."

Gauge recognized the name of the Indian Reservation nearby. He had known Gorge was of mixed heritage, but hadn't known the origins of his mother. Was she Apache? Or was Gorge's wife?

"Good work?" he asked.

"Good enough."

Gauge nodded.

Since he wasn't all that clear on what he wanted beyond a chance to see the younger man, and know that he was doing well, he didn't quite know what to say.

And Gorge also appeared to have run out of small talk. He shifted his stance, scratching his head as he looked at his young wife again. "Look, I hope you're not here looking for money or anything—"

"No, no," Gauge said quickly, holding up his hands. "That's not it at all. I…"

He, what?

He'd thought about what he might say. About what they might talk about. But all of it seemed insignificant in the dimming light.

"I just wanted, you know, to come by to see that you were okay."

Gorge considered the dirt under his boots and then cocked his brow. "To give me money like the old man used to do when he came through town?"

Gauge grimaced. "No. I was looking for something more, maybe…"

To his surprise, Gorge merely nodded.

"You wanna come in for a beer or something, man? Meet the wife and the son?" He looked suddenly surprised. "Wow. I just realized that he's your nephew."

His nephew.

Gauge tried the word out as he looked toward the trailer and the woman and child that still waited.

Gorge must have taken his slow response as reluctance. "Hey, you know, you don't have to or anything."

"No, no." Gauge smiled. "I'd like to come meet your family…my nephew and sister-in-law. I'd like that a lot."

20

"YOU'RE GOING into the office on Christmas Eve?"

Annie's voice sounded incredulous over the phone.

"Yes. Along with nearly every other working citizen," Lizzie said. "At least until noon."

"That's sacrilegious."

Lizzie resisted giving an eye roll even though her sister couldn't see her.

"Isn't Roger going in?"

"Yes, but he's different."

"Different how? Because he's a man?"

It was hard to believe that her sister used to be one of the most in-demand ad execs in Toledo. Four years out of the professional workplace, four years locked in a house with toddlers would do that to a woman, she guessed.

"Never mind." Annie sighed, and Lizzie heard Mason crying. "Anyway, what time are you going to be at Mom and Dad's tonight?"

"I don't know. The usual time, I guess. Around eight or nine?"

"So late?"

"Why? What time were you planning on going over?"

"Around six or seven."

"That makes for a long night."

"That makes for a good time to get the kids to sleep in my old room so I can have a little bit of fun. You know, the adult kind that doesn't include sticky fingers and cranky demands."

Lizzie sighed as she rinsed out her coffee cup in the kitchen sink and then put it in the dishwasher. "I'm meeting Tabitha for a late lunch, then running a couple of errands. I suppose I can try to speed everything up so I can get there at around…seven." She opted for the later time rather than the earlier one.

"Great! On your way up, can you stop by Brieschkes and pick me up a bear claw?"

Lizzie's jaw dropped. "What about all the Christmas cookies?"

"I'm craving a bear claw."

Pregnant women and their cravings. Sometimes she thought her sister enjoyed being pregnant a little too much.

Well, at least she wasn't asking for her to stop at Krispy Kreme, which was a couple of miles in the opposite direction.

"Fine." She gave in.

"Buy three."

"You can only eat one."

"Yes, but I might want another one in the morning. And the other…is for backup."

"Fine," Lizzie said again. "Anything else?"

She'd meant the question to be sarcastic, but her sister appeared to be thinking about it. She was glad when Annie finally said, "No, that should about cover it."

"Great."

Lizzie looked at her watch. Almost eight-thirty. She was already running later than she intended.

"Look, sis, I've really got to go. Kiss the kids for me."

The doorbell rang. Lizzie craned her neck to stare into the hall as if she could tell who was outside just by looking at the door.

"Okay. Call me when you get off."

"Sure."

Lizzie pressed the disconnect button and put the phone down on the counter. The doorbell rang again.

"I'm coming, I'm coming."

Not an auspicious beginning to the holiday. She was already feeling rushed and harried.

She looked through the peephole to find one of those fantastic-looking UPS guys grinning at her, his teeth looking a little threatening given the fish-eye lens.

She hadn't ordered anything. Had she?

"Merry Christmas," he said as she opened the door.

"Same to you."

"If I can have you sign here."

Lizzie accepted the digital signing device as she looked at the three-by-two foot box he'd placed next to his feet. "Does it say where it's from?"

"It appears to be a personal delivery. From Arizona."

She didn't know anyone in Arizona.

She thought about investigating further before accepting, but curiosity got the better of her. If it ended up being intended for one of her neighbors, she'd simply deliver it herself.

"Thank you. Have a great holiday."

Lizzie accepted the package and distractedly wished him the same, closing the door again.

For long moments she stood in the foyer staring at the box, her heart beating a steady rhythm in her chest.

She really should be getting to work.

She really needed to open this box, a little voice argued.

For reasons she couldn't define, her palms felt damp and her throat thick. She opened the drawer in the hall table and withdrew the letter opener there, using it to slit open the tape on the top and sides of the box. She carefully laid it on the floor and then pulled open the flaps. Packing material. Lots of it. She reached in, hauling out Bubble Wrap and crumpled paper. A few moments later she stared at the item nestled inside, feeling as if her breath had been stolen from her.

She backed up until her heels met the bottom stair and then she sank down to sit on the steps, unable to believe what she was seeing.

It wasn't possible, was it? Of all the things she could have imagined receiving, this would have been the last.

Through misty eyes, she clicked open the protective case and took out an item she thought she'd never see again. Something so person specific, so magnificently unique. She handled it with the awe and respect and gratitude a curator might give a priceless work of art, carefully turning it over, tracing the scratches on the back with her fingertips.

Gauge's acoustic guitar.

"Wherever my guitar is, my heart is."

She remembered his words, spoken softly on the first night they spent together, before they'd begun their sexual journey.

She sat for long minutes holding it. Placing her hands where she imagined his might have lain, her touch warming the wood, feeling connected to him.

Reluctantly, she put the guitar back in the case and searched the box for a note. There was nothing. But she did know something important. It had come from Arizona.

Which meant that's where Gauge was.

Mixed emotions swirled through her. She was touched beyond description at the gift. Hurt that he wasn't there to give it to her himself.

Beyond all that, she was soul-stirringly aware that she hadn't seen the last of Patrick Gauge and that their love affair might not yet have reached its end.

THE NIGHT WAS QUIET. As it should be on Christmas Eve, he thought.

Gauge stood on the doorstep, tentative. A lot had happened over the past week. Much that he couldn't name. A good deal that he could.

He'd gotten to know his brother, had been accepted by his wife and embraced by his nephew, who didn't care what had gone before, or what existed between his father and this man, but judged him solely by his ability to give a belly tickle. It was something Gauge found he was quite proficient at, even though he had no prior experience. The sound of the boy's laughter had touched him in places he hadn't known existed. Places that he might not have been able to reach a short time before...before Lizzie opened them, made them accessible. Before she had made him take a new look at life and love and the future.

So in a roundabout way he had her to thank that he was now Uncle G to little Thomas, a honey-skinned boy Gorge had given their father's name.

"Looks like you're doing well for yourself," he'd said to Gorge a couple days into his visit when the two had been enjoying a beer outside after dinner, poking at a fire Gorge had started to chase off the desert chill of the early evening.

Gorge had shrugged, looking toward the trailer that was home, and probably thinking about the woman inside doing the dinner dishes, his son asleep in his crib in their bedroom, the baby due in a month.

"Not bad, considering. I'm saving to get us into a real home hopefully sometime next year. But until then, we're okay."

More than okay, they were a cohesive family unit. Happy. Loving. Affectionate. Gauge could see it in the way they touched, smiled and spoke. It was evident in their every move. And he envied them for how easy it seemed.

"Your mother...does she live nearby?"

"Yeah." Gorge pointed the bottle northeast. "On the rez."

"You're Apache, then."

"Half." Gorge grinned at him, likely realizing that Gauge would be one of the few people who would know that.

"I'm glad you've had solid family support. A home."

His brother leaned forward and looked at him. "Not so much as you would think. My mom married when I was three and went on to have three more children. I was always the odd man out." He looked into the fire, his thoughts far away, then glanced back at Gauge. "No. My home, my family is that woman in there. My wife. The mother of my children." He shook his head. "I know so long as we're together, so long as she loves me, then I'll have all I'll ever want in this world."

Gauge blinked now, slowly coming back to the present and the door he stood outside. He had more than a few regrets. Gorge was a wonderful man, strong and honest and hardworking. He wished he had made the effort to know before. But he supposed it was good enough that he was coming to know him now. And both men had vowed to seek out the other children their father had sired in the coming year—together.

The door suddenly opened. Had he knocked? He didn't think he had.

"Gauge! I thought that was you." Nina threw her arms around him, crowding him close. She felt good. But not in the way she might have a couple weeks ago. Now she was as dear to him as a sister. Or the best friend she'd once been. And was again.

"Merry Christmas," he said quietly.

She looked happy. "Kevin said he'd heard someone on the porch. I couldn't believe my eyes when I looked out the peephole." She took his hand and led him inside. "Just having you here makes it a merry Christmas, indeed." She closed the door against the cold. "Babe? Guess what the storm blew in?"

Gauge braced himself. He and Kevin hadn't exactly parted on good terms. In fact, his friend would probably not be happy to see him again, turning up like a bad penny on this, his first holiday with his wife.

But Gauge had come to understand that his friend's final words rang with truth: If he wanted something good in his life, then he had to work at it. And he was now ready to put in that work. So whatever the other man hit him with, he was determined to weather his way through it. Because this time, he wasn't going anywhere.

Kevin rounded the corner from the living room and stopped before entering the hall, a box of matches in his hands.

Gauge tried to read his expression. He didn't see anger. Surprise, yes. Exasperation? No.

"Hey," he said awkwardly.

"Hey, yourself." He allowed Nina to help him shrug out of his jacket, taking the bag of gifts he'd brought along. Just a couple of items he'd picked up during his trip that he thought they might like. Things for the house.

Gauge stepped closer to Kevin, overriding his awkwardness, and hugged his friend. "Merry Christmas."

Kevin stood rigidly. But Gauge couldn't judge him on that. Kevin had always been ill at ease with displays of affection.

Gauge merely held fast.

Finally, Kevin put his arms around him, too, and they hugged. Really hugged, for the first time in a very long time.

Kevin chuckled and pulled back. "I didn't think I'd ever say this, but it's damn good to see you, Gauge."

"Same here," he said. "Same here."

GAUGE WASN'T SURE what he'd expected, but it certainly wasn't what transpired. He hadn't even dared hope the evening would go as well as it had.

Was it possible that once you committed to a plan, things only got easier?

Or was it the holiday that cast a sentimental glow on the threesome as the evening progressed?

After a casual dinner, they sat in the living room, Nina and Kevin on the couch, Kevin with his arm around his wife, Nina's hand resting on his knee. Gauge sat in front of the fireplace on an ottoman, the three of them talking like the past ten months had never transpired.

"Oh, this has been so nice," Nina said, as if reading his thoughts, smiling first at Kevin and then Gauge. "Just what I needed to shore me up for tomorrow's visit to my parents'." She patted Kevin's leg. "Thank God I no longer have to go to these things alone."

Gauge poked at the fire. "I thought your grandmother made the gatherings livelier."

Nina grimaced. "She's the reason things are going to be especially tense. She's bringing her 'boy toy,' as she insists on calling her movie-usher paramour."

Gauge laughed. "Paramour. Now there's a word you don't hear enough in songs."

Kevin rubbed his wife's back. "Or in general. I vote that we make a conscious effort to bring it back."

Nina smiled. "I think it's best if we just leave it where it lies."

The three laughed, enjoying the moment.

"Speaking of paramours…" Nina said, leaning forward and pouring more wine into their glasses on the coffee table. She handed Gauge's to him. "Anything to report on the romance front, Gauge?"

He turned back to the fire and took a sip of his wine, pretending to ignore her question. He caught their shared glance out of the corner of his eye.

"On that note," he said, getting up from the ottoman, "I think it's time we called it a night."

They protested, but didn't put much heart into it. It was obvious the couple wanted to be alone.

Besides, there was someone else he wanted to see so much he ached with the need of it.

Nina got up first, coming to hug him.

God, she felt good. Like a fresh spring shower.

"I'm so glad you're back home, Gauge."

"Me, too."

She kissed him on the lips. A brief, friendly peck.

"Hey!" Kevin said.

Gauge released her and they both saw that he was

smiling. If there was any wariness lurking in Kevin's eyes, Gauge couldn't spot it.

And for the first time in a long time, he relaxed completely.

"I'm just going to clean up and leave you two to say goodbye." She kissed Gauge again and gave him a quick hug. "Merry Christmas, big guy."

She collected the plate of cheese and crackers they'd all but demolished and disappeared into the kitchen.

Gauge led the way to the foyer, Kevin clapping him on the shoulder.

"It was good to see you, buddy," Gauge said. "Felt like old times, didn't it?"

"Yeah. Yeah, that it did." Kevin reached to take something out of his back pocket. "Here. Nina and I wanted to return this to you."

Gauge recognized the return address of the law office he'd had draw up the ownership transfer papers. He opened the flap and saw the contract torn into small pieces.

"Don't say anything," Kevin said. "You're our partner and best friend. We'd like you to stay that way as we rebuild."

Gauge shook his head and then gave him a man hug. "I love you, man. And I love that wife of yours, too."

Kevin chuckled. "Yeah, well, just so you remember that she is my wife, then we're all good."

Gauge grinned as he shrugged into his coat and opened the door.

"Hey?"

He looked back at Kevin.

"You got somewhere to go?"

Gauge braced himself against the cold night air. "Yeah. Yeah, I think I do...."

21

LIZZIE RETURNED home late from her parents' house, having taken in far more holiday cheer than she could possibly handle in one night.

Not that her family was to blame. They'd all been one-hundred percent their dear, unique selves—divorce papers, teething babies and god-awful Christmas gifts aside—as they honored the longstanding Gilbred traditions of trimming the family tree, singing dirty Christmas carols, and enjoying a late meal that served as a prelude to the one that would come the following day.

All in all, everything had been much more enjoyable than Lizzie would have thought. So much so that a couple of times she nearly forgot about the gift waiting for her at home.

Nearly.

Truth was, her mind repeatedly returned to the box throughout the evening, wondering what it meant. Why would Gauge send her his guitar?

Slipping her boots off just inside the door, she put on her slippers, grabbed a glass of club soda from the refrigerator to settle her stomach, then went into the family room and started a fire.

Long minutes later, Ella's voice flowing over her, she sat down on the sofa and pulled the guitar into her lap.

As her sister, Annie, had taken joy in pointing out, she'd never been musically inclined. Growing up, she'd rather have a book in her hands than a musical instrument. But merely holding the guitar made her feel as if she were somehow closer to Gauge. Connected.

She pressed her fingers against the neck and strummed her thumbnail over the strings. She made a face and tried again.

Hands appeared from behind her. She stilled, the scent of fresh winter air filling her senses. Her breath exited in a soft rush as Gauge slid his fingers down her arms and then over her hands, placing his face next to hers.

Lizzie felt so overwhelmed with emotion that it took every ounce of restraint she had not to let go of the guitar and turn and pull him over the back of the couch on top of her, making up for the time lost.

Instead, she allowed him to play it out his way. She closed her eyes, rubbing her cheek against his, feeling whole for the first time since he'd left Fantasy. Left her.

"Your back door's unlocked," he said quietly.

She licked her dry lips. "I know."

He positioned her fingers on the neck, pressing them down with his, then guided her other hand farther down the strings. The chord they struck sent tremors of need quaking through her.

"I missed you," she whispered.

She thought he might not respond. Then he said, "Funny. I felt you with me the entire time I was gone."

Warmth spread across her chest like an ink stain, just as pervasive, just as permanent.

Gauge slowly lifted the guitar and placed it on the floor next to the couch and then drew her up to face him, her kneeling on the cushions, him still standing. She stared into his eyes as his gaze raked her face and neck and breasts.

"God, you're so beautiful," he murmured, cupping her face in his hands and rubbing his thumbs over her cheeks, his focus moving from her eyes to her mouth and then back again as if he couldn't look his fill. "There wasn't a moment that went by that I didn't ache for you, Lizzie. Ache for this."

He kissed her softly, lingeringly.

"And this."

He kissed her again.

Lizzie's eyes fluttered closed as she curled her fingers around his wrists, where he gently held her head still.

He rested his forehead against hers. "I've thought about this moment. What I might say. What apologies I should make—"

She pulled back and pressed her finger against his lips. "Shh. There are no apologies. Not anymore."

He stared deep into her eyes. "Yes. Yes, there are. I don't ever want to hurt you like that again."

The image of them on the hall floor, Lizzie fighting him, Gauge holding her still...the two of them having desperate sex, emerged in her mind.

She looked down at his T-shirt, leaning her forehead against his chin. "It took you hurting me to understand how very much I've come to care about you."

He tipped her head back with a finger under her chin and kissed her. And kissed her again. Languidly, thoroughly, sensuously.

"I think I'm falling in love with you, Lizzie."

The back of her eyelids burned and he became a handsome blur.

He smiled slightly. "Those aren't words I'm used to saying. But I promise that it won't take what we went through for me to say them again."

Lizzie did what she'd been longing to do and pulled him over the side of the couch until he lay on top of her, pressing her into the cushions with his welcome weight.

She swallowed thickly, surprised by the rush of emotion that had nothing to do with the holiday and everything to do with the man she cradled between her legs. "It seems crazy, doesn't it? I mean, I don't think either one of us was looking for love, but…" She trailed off. "We've found it, haven't we? You and me? When we weren't looking, it crept up on us and grabbed us—"

"By the balls?"

She smiled, thrusting her hands under the back of his T-shirt, reveling in the hot, silken feel of him against her palms as she pressed her sensitive breasts against the hard wall of his chest, wanting, needing to be closer still. "I was going to say unawares, but, hey, balls works."

He smiled and framed her face with his hands again,

as if he couldn't believe he was there, that they were there, looking at each other.

"I don't know what tomorrow will bring, Lizzie." The dark shadow she'd grown used to seeing eclipsed his eyes and she knew a moment of fear. "I can't make promises I don't know I can keep." He kissed her, pulling her bottom lip into his mouth, the shadow moving on, affection taking its place. "I'm going through a lot of changes. Changes I think your loving me has set off…"

Lizzie took in his every word, desperately wanting to believe him, wanting to give herself over to him fully, completely. Not just with her body, but with her mind and soul.

"And I probably have no right to ask you this, but…"

She suddenly found it impossible to breathe, her heart pounding against her rib cage.

"Will you consider being my woman?"

She searched his face and then his eyes. His tortured, dark, fathomless eyes. Exploring the planes of his face with her fingertips. "On one condition."

He waited.

"That you promise to be my man."

Epilogue

June, six months later…

IF ASKED A YEAR AGO where he would be now, Gauge never would have said in the backyard of Lizzie's parents' house with her siblings, their significant others and children, celebrating the official signing of her parents' divorce papers with a blowout family barbeque. Lizzie tried explaining the situation to him since Bonnie and Clyde Gilbred appeared to be a couple in every way, and apparently had no plans to part ways except on paper, but he didn't get it. More importantly, he felt no need to get it. So long as they and their family were okay with the situation…well, he was coming to accept that was all that mattered.

With the officially unofficial toasts out of the way, everyone had drifted to different areas of the yard. Gauge sat holding his guitar on a stretch of thick grass under an old maple tree complete with requisite tire swing. Lizzie's niece, Jasmine, lay on her belly in front of him, her arms propped under her chin, her eyes huge and adoring. Her younger brother Mason tried out his new walking legs, his understanding of sibling rivalry growing as he untied Jaz's shoes and generally poked at her for reaction's sake only. Their three-month-old brother snoozed in his stroller nearby, quiet for the first time since the festivities had begun a couple of hours earlier. Lizzie's brother, Jesse, and his new wife, Mona, were sitting on a bench nearby. Lizzie's parents and her sister, Annie, and her husband, Roger, were still gathered around the table on the deck where they'd all eaten.

Lizzie's family made him think of his own expanding role in the Gauge family. His nephew, Thomas, had received a little sister in March, and Lizzie had driven down to Arizona with him to help welcome the chubby bundle of joy into the world. Gorge had been genuinely happy to see him, and Gauge intended to make sure that no Gauge born in his lifetime went without love and the solid foundation that could only be built by family.

Lizzie turned her head where it rested against his thigh, reminding him of the biggest change in his life.

Funny, but he had the feeling that if he'd taken a logical approach to their relationship from the beginning, he probably never would have moved into her mammoth house, would have believed the contrasts between their lives too great. Insurmountable. Instead, he'd followed his heart. And found himself watching her blossom from an uptight trial attorney who favored designer-label black turtlenecks and slacks to a more relaxed woman whose clothing choices ran more to colorful sundresses and all things soft and sexy. They were still designer labels, but the fact she was lying in the grass without concern for stains was proof she was willing not only to meet him in the middle but also enjoy the journey every step of the way.

Or should he say every orgasm?

He grew hard just thinking of their hot sex life. He'd never wanted a woman so much. And with each passing day, it seemed incredible to him that he should want her more, not less. And knowing she returned the sentiment blew his mind.

Then there was Nina and Kevin. He'd felt like a man on death row being given a reprieve when they'd allowed him back into their lives. That alone was enough to be thankful for. But to have Lizzie bond with them, as well…it was more than he could have dared hope for. They met up with the other couple at least once a week, enjoying good food, good conversation and, more importantly, one another.

With the help of insurance monies and the close-knit Fantasy community, BMC had celebrated its grand reopening last month, bigger and better than ever. Although, at Gauge's insistence, the music store was now on the other side of the bookstore, putting Kevin between him and Nina's café…just in case.

Human nature was a funny thing. He understood now that it wasn't enough to resist temptation, but it was necessary to ensure that temptation, period, was made less available. Which meant going home directly after sitting in for a night with local bands. Passing on accepting pretty, flirty music students. And allowing the part-timers at the store to attend to customers who might have at one time turned his head.

It was bad enough that once or twice he'd entertained the possibility of him and Lizzie sharing more than friendship with Nina and Kevin….

He caught the dangerous thought and forced it out.

He didn't deserve what he had. He knew that. But he intended to make sure that at some point he would be worthy of what fate had brought to him.

He finished playing "Puff the Magic Dragon" with a flourish, eliciting wild applause from Jaz and even her brother, who appeared not to know why he was clapping but happy to do it just the same.

Lizzie shifted her head to look up at Gauge. He reached down to cup her beautiful face, grazing the pad of his thumb against her plump bottom lip. Instantly her pupils dilated and her breath exited in a soft sigh.

Damn, but he didn't deserve her. He tangled his fingers in her hair. But so long as he had her, he was going to take complete advantage.

"More, Gauge, more!" Jaz cried.

He didn't take his gaze from Lizzie's sexy face. Mmm. Yes. More, indeed….

* * * * *

*Runaway bride Payton Harwell thinks she's hit rock
bottom when she ends up in jail – in Australia!
But then sexy rebel Brody Quinn bails her out and lets
her into his home, his bed, his life. Only Payton's
past isn't as far away as she thinks it is...*

Turn the page for a sneak preview of

The Mighty Quinns: Brody
by Kate Hoffmann

The Mighty Quinns: Brody
by
Kate Hoffmann

Queensland, Australia—June, 2009

HIS BODY ACHED, from the throbbing in his head to the deep, dull pain in his knee. The various twinges in between—his back, his right elbow, the fingers of his left hand—felt worse than usual. Brody Quinn wondered if he'd always wake up with a reminder of the motorcycle accident that had ruined his future or, if someday, all the pain would magically be gone.

Hell, he'd just turned twenty-six and he felt like an old man. Reaching up, he rubbed his forehead, certain of only one thing—he'd spent the previous night sitting on his arse at the Spotted Dog getting himself drunk.

The sound of an Elvis Presley tune drifted through the air and Brody knew exactly where he'd slept it off— the Bilbarra jail. The town's police chief, Angus Embley, was a huge fan of Presley, willing to debate the King's singular place in the world of music with any bloke who dared to argue the point. Right now, Elvis was only exacerbating Brody's headache.

"Angus!" he shouted. "Can you turn down the music?" Since he'd returned home to his family's cattle station in Queensland, he'd grown rather fond of the accommodations at the local jail. Though he usually ended up behind bars for some silly reason, it saved him the long drive home or sleeping it off in his SUV. "Angus!"

"He's not here. He went out to get some breakfast."

Brody rolled over to look into the adjoining cell, startled to hear a female voice. As he rubbed his bleary eyes, he focused on a slender woman standing just a few feet away, dressed in a pretty, flowered blouse and blue jeans. Her delicate fingers were wrapped around the bars that separated them, her dark eyes intently fixed on his.

"Christ," he muttered, flopping back onto the bed. Now he'd really hit bottom, Brody mused, throwing his arm over his eyes. Getting royally pissed was one thing, but hallucinating a female prisoner was another. He was still drunk.

He closed his eyes, but the image of her swirled in his brain. Odd that he'd conjured up this particular apparition. She didn't really fit his standard of beauty. He usually preferred blue-eyed blondes with large breasts and shapely backsides and long, long legs.

This woman was slim, with deep mahogany hair that fell in a riot of curls around her face and shoulders. By his calculations, she might come up to his chin at best. And her features were…odd. Her lips were almost too lush and her cheekbones too high. And her skin was so pale and perfect that he had to wonder if she ever spent a day in the sun.

"You don't have to be embarrassed. A lot of people talk in their sleep."

Brody sat up. She had an American accent. His fantasy women never had American accents. "What?"

She stared at him from across the cell. "It was mostly just mumbling. And some snoring. And you did mention someone named Nessa."

"Vanessa," he murmured, scanning her features again. She wasn't wearing a bit of makeup, yet she looked as if she'd just stepped out of the pages of one of those fashion magazines Vanessa always had on hand. She had that fresh-scrubbed, innocent, girl-next-door look about her. Natural. Clean. He wondered if she smelled as good as she looked.

Since returning home, there hadn't been a single woman who'd piqued his interest—until now. Though she could be anywhere between sixteen and thirty, Brody reckoned if she was younger than eighteen, she wouldn't be sitting in a jail cell. It was probably safe to lust after her.

"You definitely said Nessa," she insisted. "I remember. I thought it was an odd name."

"It's short for Vanessa. She's a model and that's what they call her." Nessa was so famous, she didn't need a last name, kind of like Madonna or Sting.

"She's your girlfriend?"

"Yes." He drew a sharp breath, then cleared his throat. "No. Ex-girlfriend."

"Sorry," she said with an apologetic shrug. "I didn't mean to stir up bad memories."

"No bad memories," Brody replied, noting the hint of defensiveness in his voice. What the hell did he care what this woman thought of him—or the girls he'd dated? He swung his legs off the edge of the bed, then raked his hands through his hair. "I know why *I'm* here. What are *you* doing in a cell?"

"Just a small misunderstanding," she said, forcing a smile.

"Angus doesn't lock people up for small misunder-standings," Brody countered, pushing to his feet. "Es-pecially not women." He crossed to stand in front of her, wrapping his fingers around the bars just above hers. "What did you do?"

"Dine and dash," she said.

"What?"

Her eyes dropped and a pretty blush stained her cheeks. "I—I skipped out on my bill at the diner down the street. And a few other meals in a few other towns. I guess my life of crime finally caught up with me. The owner called the cops and I'm in here until I find a way to work it off."

He pressed his forehead into the bars, hoping the cool iron would soothe the ache in his head. "Why don't you just pay for what you ate?"

"I would have, but I didn't have any cash. I left an IOU. And I said I'd come back and pay as soon as I found work. I guess that wasn't good enough."

Brody let his hands slide down until he was touching her, if only to prove that she was real and that he wasn't dreaming. "What happened to all your money?" he asked, fixing his attention on her face as he ran his fingers over hers. It seemed natural to touch her, even though she was a complete stranger. Oddly, she didn't seem to mind.

Her breath caught and then she sighed. "It's all gone. Desperate times call for desperate measures. I'm not a dishonest person. I was just really, really hungry."

She had the most beautiful mouth he'd ever seen, her

lips soft and full…perfect for— He fought the urge to pull her closer and take a quick taste, just to see if she'd be…different. "What's your name?"

"Payton," she murmured.

"Payton," he repeated, leaning back to take in details of her body. "Is that your last name or your first?"

"Payton Harwell," she said.

"And you're American?"

"I am."

"And you're in jail," he said, stating the obvious.

She laughed softly and nodded as she glanced around. "It appears I am. At least for a while. Angus told me as soon as he finds a way for me to work off my debt, he'll let me out. I told him I could wash dishes at the diner, but the owner doesn't want me back there. I guess jobs are in short supply around here."

Brody's gaze drifted back to her face—he was oddly fascinated by her features. Had he seen her at a party or in a nightclub in Fremantle, he probably wouldn't have given her a second glance. But given time to appreciate her attributes, he couldn't seem to find a single flaw worth mentioning.

"Quinn!"

Brody glanced over his shoulder and watched as Angus strolled in, his freshly pressed uniform already rumpled after just a few hours of work. "Are you sober yet?"

"You didn't have to lock me up," Brody said, letting go of the bars.

"Brody Quinn, you started a brawl, you broke a mirror and you threw a bleedin' drink in my face, after insulting my taste in music. You didn't give me a

choice." Angus braced his hands on his hips. "There'll
be a fine. I figure a couple hundred should do it. And
you're gonna have to pay for Buddy's mirror." Angus
scratched his chin. "And I want a promise you're gonna
behave yourself from now on and respect the law. Your
brother's here, so pay the fine and you can go."

"Teague is here?" Brody asked.

"No, Callum is waiting. He's not so chuffed he had
to make a trip into town."

"I could have driven myself home," Brody said.

"Your buddy Billy tried to take your keys last night.
That's what started the fight. He flushed the keys, so
Callum brought your spare." Angus reached down and
unlocked the cell. "Next time you kick up a stink, I'm
holding you for a week. That's a promise."

Brody turned back and looked at Payton. "You can
let her out. I'll pay her fine, too."

"First you have to settle up with Miss Shelly over at
the coffeeshop and then you have to find this young lady
a job. Then, I'll let you pay her fine. Until you do all
that, she's gonna be a guest for a bit longer."

"It's all right," Payton said in a cheerful voice. "I'm
okay here. I've got a nice place to sleep and regular meals."

Brody frowned as he shook his head. It just didn't
feel right leaving her locked up, even if she did want to
stay. "Suit yourself," he said, rubbing at the ache in his
head.

Payton gave him a little wave, but it didn't ease his
qualms. Who was she? And what had brought her to
Bilbarra? There were a lot of questions running through
his mind without any reasonable answers.